THE LION AND THE SWAN

Michele James

www.BOROUGHSPUBLISHINGGROUP.com

THE LION AND THE SWAN
Copyright © 2020 Michele James

ISBN 978-1-951055-50-9

For Jim Forrest and Caitlin

ACKNOWLEDGMENTS

To Elizabeth Archer and Stephanee Ryle, my fellow MNMer's. To Kathleen Canney Lopez, my IT guru. And to the members of RWA San Diego – my tribe.

THE LION AND THE SWAN

CHAPTER 1

Summer's Eve

Summer's Eve had a full moon rising, the weight of its portent and import hung from Asad's shoulders with the heft of an anvil stone, cinching the richly embroidered hems of his robe tight as a noose around his neck. He tugged at the constricting garment and surveyed the torch-lit courtyard filled with the royalty of the Seven Tribes, marking a path through the tables that would get him to the inner wall. A wall he could scale with one leap. But it may as well have been a thousand-foot cliff of sheer rock for all the escape it would offer.

"What ails you, Black Mane?" his brother, the Cheetah, asked as Asad pulled harder at his robe.

"My betrothal nears," Asad said with a low growl, "and I can see no way free of it." He glanced back over his shoulder at the women's table and eyed the Fox, his intended, who wore a gown of russet weave that pushed her fleshy breasts up to almost spilling out of the tight, low-cut bodice. The last time he had seen her, she had been a girl of ten and five who had liked her sweets as much as she disliked the word no, and by the way she had indulged in the honeyed dates that were the last of the seven-course feast, she had not changed much in the three years since.

Her father, the Jackal, King of the City of Walls, host of this meeting, had not sought a marriage bargain for his daughter during their last meeting, though she had been of age. No, the Jackal had held his eldest daughter close and waited until Asad came of age. She would be Asad's first wife, and her marriage to the Black Mane, eldest son of the Panther, King of the Great Valley, would mean that she would one day be queen, the idea of which had set a frown between the brows of his mother, the current queen, for many moons now.

"Duty and honor to family and kingdom," Asad said as much to himself as to his brother, "all require that I sit here like a sacrificial goat and let myself be bound and caged."

"At least the Fox will be your first wife of seven," the Cheetah offered with his cursed calm.

Asad fixed his brother, second eldest and second in line for the throne, with a baleful glare. Though they had different mothers, they were the Panther's sons, and their father would choose their wives for his own purposes, without any consideration for their wishes. It was how it was done. How it had always been done. It was the tradition of the Seven Tribes. And it had ensured his parents as miserable a marriage as Asad expected to have with the Fox.

"How do you see six more wives chosen by our father as any recompense?" he grumbled, for as long as his father was king, he would choose his sons' brides, and the Panther was still hale and hearty at forty and five years of age.

The Cheetah looked out over the courtyard at the royal blooded women of the Seven Tribes, the only women they, as princes, could marry.

"Surely," he said, "there is at least one woman here whom you would be satisfied to marry?"

Asad huffed and then cocked his head. There was a rustling beyond the path that led from the stage of polished sandstone into the dark shadows of the garden. The still air moved, and he caught the sweet scent of night-blooming jasmine. He sat forward on his haunches as the Jackal, a thin, balding man with a nervous twitch of a smile, stood from his stool at the king's table and held his cup high. The Jackal had threatened his household with beatings if the secret of his dowry gift was revealed to the Panther before this evening, but Asad's manservant, the Crab, knew every servant in every palace of the Seven Tribes, and had the entire story before sunset, though they had only arrived that noon.

The gift, the first and most valuable of seven to be given, were two sisters from the far north called the Swan and the Dove, whose pale, otherworldly beauty left the menservants speechless, the maids jealous, and the women of the household sour with envy, especially the Fox of the Swan.

The sisters had tried to escape twice already, and had made it as far as the city's third wall the first time, and the stables the second, after which they had both been thrown into hot holes. They had been sentenced to three days in the deep pits dug into the ground and covered with tightly slatted palm fronds that could sweat the water out of a full-grown man in five days, but the Swan had become ill in two and the Jackal had been forced to pull her out or lose her. Tonight, she would sing and dance for the gathering, and her sister, the Dove, would play the harp and sing. Then they would be given by the Jackal to the Panther as dowry for the Fox's betrothal to the Black Mane: eldest son to eldest daughter, as was tradition.

"Welcome, friends," the Jackal said, his tongue darting out and sweeping across his thin lips. "Welcome to my home on this Summer's Eve." Claps and loud murmurs broke out all around the courtyard and the Jackal raised his cup higher. "I am honored to host this, the hundredth gathering of the tribes. For the next twenty and one days my home is yours." His lips twitched up and he licked them again before nodding to the Panther. "And now, my honored guests, I bring to you the Swan and the Dove."

A bare foot, as white as milk, arched out of the garden's shadows and stepped onto the torch-lit path, the trim ankle turned just so, the calf long and leanly muscled, the knee as well turned as the ankle. Asad sucked in his breath as shimmering panels of white weave parted from a thigh as long and lean as an alabaster column. He let his breath out slow and measured, watching the graceful sway of shapely hips that nipped up to a slim waist draped with a finely wrought gold chain. A sheer bodice gathered beneath breasts as round and firm as pomegranates, and collarbones of chiseled ivory winged out from the one-shouldered gown to arms as long and lean as the legs they swung in time with.

A veil of hair as pale as moonlight framed high, angular cheeks, and finely drawn brows, a darker shade of pale, arched over eyes as big and round as mossy river rocks. Eyes that met his and held, and studied him as keenly as he studied her.

Oona had seen a lion once before in the marketplace at the slave port where she and her sister, Lyrra, had been tied to a stake no more than ten paces from the caged beast, all of them for sale to the highest bidder. For three days Oona had observed the lion pacing the confines of his hated cage, his powerful muscles coiled and bunched beneath his taut hide, his ears upright and tail twitching. His golden eyes aware, alert and wary, the threat of unleashed power unmistakable in their amber depths. The eyes she stared into now were equally alert and wary, and watched her as intently as the lion's had. These eyes could only belong to the Black Mane, the Panther's eldest son, and the Fox's intended.

Even if his eyes had not given him away, his mane of black hair surely would have. Neither oiled or curled, it hung in thick waves as black as pitch down to his shoulders, his short beard and thick brows the same ebon hue against his tawny skin. His forehead was high, his nose broad, and his mouth full, and he wore a finely woven robe of black linen, its hems embroidered with worm weave threads of black, red, and gold that tapered down from wide shoulders to his belted waist. His only ornamentation: a gold wrist cuff on his left arm. But his eyes called to her, and Oona's gaze returned to them as she stopped and stood no more than five paces from him on legs as sturdy as wet sea grass. *Eyes that burned.*

Those amber eyes never left hers as servants brought out Lyrra's harp and a stool, setting them in the middle of the sandstone stage. Eyes that neither censured or shamed her as any other man's in this desert land would have done, for here she was a woman and a slave, unworthy of holding a man's gaze, much less a prince's.

Lyrra sat on the stool and pulled her harp close whilst Oona stood with her hands clasped before her, a hundred pair of dark, curious eyes crawling over her.

"Sing." The Jackal clapped his hands loudly twice, and Oona jumped back half a step. "Dance."

Oona dipped a knee to the Jackal, her current master. Taking a deep breath in and blowing it out, she gave in to the inevitable and looked to the Jackal's right at the man she knew would be the Panther, who was soon to be her new master. She met his hooded gaze for no more than a breath before dropping hers, but it was enough.

If, as their grandfather had often said, Lyrra's gift was the ability to listen to a person, to hear if they spoke the truth or lied, if they were crying behind their laughter, or laughing behind their tears, then Oona's was the gift of sight. She could look a person in the eye and know if they were true or false, cruel or kind, and the Panther was a hard man who kept his intentions hidden behind hooded lids.

He was a man large in height and girth and importance among the Seven Tribes, and his import, and the wealth of his city, were why the Jackal wanted his daughter to marry the Black Mane, and why Oona the Swan, and Lyrra the Dove, were to impress the Panther this night, or be thrown back into the hole.

Oona shuddered at the thought of spending another moment in the close, fetid air of the hot hole, its earthen walls etched in dried blood where others had tried to claw their way out. A fine sheen of sweat beaded on her nose. She swiped it off with her fingers, straightened her spine, blew out her breath, and lifted her chin to face the crowd, only to find the Black Mane's keen eyes still watching hers.

"We sing 'Sailor's Tale.'" She spoke in the desert tongue to the lion's eyes, and he dipped his head once, almost imperceptibly, but Oona saw.

Lyrra began to pluck Nightingale, the harp their grandfather had made for her tenth birthday, to play their father's favorite song to a desert people who held his daughters captive a thousand leagues from their home. She and Oona sang in a mix of desert and highland tongues, telling the tale of the sailor who left his wife and young sons to sail for faraway lands, searching for great wealth and adventures.

They sang of the sea's vastness, of its changing hues and moods, and Oona began to sway her body as if to the surging movement of a ship's deck. They sang of the kings the sailor met, the storms he braved, the monsters he fought, and Oona glanced at the Fox, her own personal monster in this cursed desert city, wishing she could fight her without the threat of the infernal hot hole.

As if feeling Oona's gaze on her, the Fox stopped yapping into another young woman's ear and turned her pointy nose up and at Oona, who quickly dropped her eyes and lost her place in the song. When she looked up again, it was to the Black Mane's cocked head and steady gaze. Lyrra had slowed the rhythm of her strumming and her singing, giving Oona a chance to rejoin her, and as they sang of the sailor finding his treasure, she took in the young man sitting beside the Black Mane, who would be the Cheetah, the Panther's second son. Built straight up and down with long, light brown hair, quick brown eyes, and an even quicker smile, he was tapping his foot along to the song, his dreamy gaze fixed on Lyrra.

Lifting her eyes to the North Star, Oona sang of the sailor turning his ship back toward his home at last, of him sighting his home shore, his homecoming with his wife, gray-haired and wizened with twenty years of watching and waiting for him: ever hopeful, ever faithful. Oona silently vowed for the hundredth time since they had been captured that she would get Lyrra home again, safe in the fold of their family.

She sang this vow to Lyrra in their highland tongue as her sister played the last lingering notes, and Lyrra gave a faint smile, her forehead pressed into Nightingale's carved frame as the music faded into the night.

The gathering of dark-eyed, dark-haired desert people burst into applause, and Oona stepped over to Lyrra and took her by the hand and pulled her to her feet. They bent their knees to the king's table.

"A reel," the Jackal called out, and Oona groaned as she and Lyrra took their places.

She had tried to explain to the Jackal time and again that a reel was to be worked up to. That Lyrra's fingers, nimble as they were, needed to warm up to playing such a fast-paced tune, that Oona's legs needed to work up to such a vigorous dance, but the Jackal never listened. They were women, slaves, chattel, he did not care about their fingers or legs, other than that they do what he wanted, when he wanted, and he wanted a reel. He always wanted a reel.

Lyrra plucked Nightingale's strings to the tune of the "Cat's Cradle," a simple reel they had learned as children, faster and faster as Oona tapped and kicked and jumped and twirled, the gathering clapping their hands and bobbing their heads in time to the music much as their own clansmen had done at many a feast when the sisters had played and danced for them. And as with their clansmen, most of the men and many of the women had their gazes fixed on Oona's bouncing breasts and kicking legs, but not the Black Mane. His amber eyes were on hers every time she looked his way, which was more often than she should have done, and not half as often as she wanted. Lyrra plucked the last warning notes and Oona slammed a foot down, arms akimbo and chest heaving as the music stopped and the clapping grew louder.

"A wedding song," a woman's voice called out.

The Raven, the Jackal's first wife and mother of the Fox, whose daughter was much like her in looks and temper. Oona dipped her head to the Raven and flashed a sympathetic smile at the Black Mane, who sat back slightly, his shoulders stiff and the line of his full mouth grim.

"*Rithill Aill,*" she said to Lyrra.

"*Welcome, gentlemen,*" they sang in the desert tongue.

"*Welcome, and here's a health to you,*
Tonight, there will be a wedding,
Tonight, she will be a maidservant,
The soldier is my darling."

They sang it again in their highland tongue, and then again, Oona jumping in two lines behind Lyrra. They sang it three more times, one behind the other, and ended it together on the last verse. The crowd clapped, the Fox preened, and the Black Mane sat still as stone.

"Have you a request, Prince Black Mane?" the Fox asked, and Oona swore he grimaced before he grinned, showing straight, white teeth.

"A love song," he said. He spoke directly to Oona, and his voice, deep and low in timbre, resonated in her bones.

"'Somebody,'" Oona said without conscious thought, her voice more husky even than usual. "I will sing 'Somebody.'"

It was a song Oona had sung skipping across the open fields of her homeland, dreaming girlish dreams of beautiful maids and handsome heroes. A song she had never before sung to any man other than her father and grandfather. Why she chose to sing it now to the Black Mane, a man she had never seen before this day or spoken a word to before this night, she could not have said. But sing to him she did.

"*My heart is sore,*" she sang in his desert tongue.

"*I dare not tell,*
My heart is sore for Somebody,
I would walk a winter's night
All for a sight of Somebody.

If Somebody were come again
Then one day he must cross the main,
And everyone will get his own
And I will see my Somebody.

Ohh, hey, for Somebody
Oh, ooh, hey, for Somebody,
Oh, I would do, would I do not
All for the sake of Somebody.

Why need I comb my tresses bright,
Oh, why should fire or candlelight
Shine in my bower day or night
Since gone is my dear Somebody.

Oh, I have wept many a day
For one that's banished far away,
I cannot sing and must not say
How sore I grieve for Somebody.

Ohh, hey, for Somebody,
Oh, ooh, hey, for Somebody
I would do, would I do not
All for the sake of Somebody."

The last strains of the harp's melancholy tune floated through the air as Oona fought to keep from tumbling forward into the pull of the Black Mane's eyes, and then the sound of clapping filled the courtyard and Oona blinked.

"Sing a telling song," the Cheetah said.

Oona tore her eyes from the Black Mane's smoldering gaze and smoothed her skirt. She dipped her knee to the Cheetah, who was watching Lyrra.

"The Spring Maid, the Sun God, and the Lord of Winter," she said in the desert tongue.

She stepped back and the Cheetah sat forward as Lyrra set Nightingale to the side and took center stage, kneeling down and tucking into a ball. Lyrra began to sing, her voice thin and reedy at first, growing stronger as she slowly unfolded and stood, a crocus pushing up through the snow of late winter.

She unfurled one arm and then the other as her voice rose, her gaze, her arms reaching up to the sky, which was Oona's cue. She set one foot onto the stage and then jutted her head out over it, looking this way and that, and then shuffled her other foot forward, hunching her back and singing in a low, guttural growl. She stopped as she spied Lyrra, the Spring Maid, singing to the sky, the birds, the first brave sprouts to seek life above the frozen ground, and she held her arms out with clawed fingers as she clomped over to the Spring Maid and enveloped her in the Lord of Winter's icy hold.

The Cheetah sat on his hands as the Lord of Winter blew and moaned over the frozen Spring Maid, and Lyrra curled back into her frozen ball as Oona swirled off the stage. Unfurling her clawed fists and straightening her hunched back, Oona strode back on, one sure, regal foot at a time, her spine upright, her shoulders squared, her voice full and strong. The Sun God striding onto the snow-covered meadow and singing life back into the earth with his warming breath. The Sun God spied the frozen body of the Spring Maid and went to her and stood over her, reveling in her frail beauty and singing to the heavens of light and warmth, and rebirth.

The Spring Maid slowly thawed, stirred, and began to arise, her smile reflecting the sun's light, her voice the new life stirring within her, and Oona glanced at the Cheetah, whose smile was as bright as Lyrra's. The Sun God held his arm out to the Spring Maid, who stepped into its fold, and they stood together facing the rapt audience and held their arms out to them, singing of the fruitful bounty of their union.

"A reel," the Panther demanded before the clapping even slowed, his voice low and gruff. Beside Oona, Lyrra flinched. "And make it a fast one."

Oona tapped toe to heel to the quickening beat of the harp, and the sea of brown heads began to bob along. She kicked her legs up and out and down, and the heads followed and hands began to clap. The Black Mane was not watching Oona for the first time since she had stepped out of the garden's shadows. He was watching the Panther and the Jackal, who were grinning and slapping each other on the back, the sign of a bargain sealed. His betrothal to the Fox was about to be announced, and she and Lyrra to be gifted to the Panther.

The music quickened and Oona leapt and whirled to the dizzying beat, her head spinning even faster than her body. All she could see in her mind's eye was the Panther on top of Lyrra as Oona had seen Beorne, a neighboring chieftain, on top of Igrid the night of the Rowan Feast, the same night he had offered for Oona's hand in marriage. It had not seemed to Oona a pleasurable experience for Igrid, Beorne's bare, hairy backside thrusting away at her, her hands gripping his sides as he grunted and panted, not even his tunic between her backside and the cold, barren ground, her eyes pinched as tight as her fingers.

Because Oona had refused Beorne, because she would not be ploughed like a field at her husband's command, she and Lyrra had sailed away with their father across the Mid Earth Sea to trade for spices and worm weave in lands far east, and it had been wonderful out on the open sea, until the pirates attacked. The last time Oona and Lyrra had seen their father, he was lashed to the mast of what had been his ship alongside three of his crew, his head hanging slack-jawed, his face and body beaten black and blue and bloody. Oona and Lyrra had been taken prisoners and held in the belly of the pirate's ship for four days before being tied to the post next to the lion in the portside market, where they had been sold to the Jackal. It was Oona's fault they were in this mess. It was because she would not marry and do her duty to the clan that she and Lyrra were now slaves, about to be given from one man to yet another. It would be up to her to get them out of it.

She glanced at Lyrra, her forehead pressed into Nightingale's frame. She looked at the Cheetah, who sat smiling content as a cat basking near a fire on a winter's night as he watched Lyrra's fingers fly over the harp's strings, and a thought flew into Oona's spinning head, half formed and fully mad. The last note of the reel played out and she set her heel to ground and sucked in air as much to steady her resolve as her body. Claps and whistles filled the courtyard as she took Lyrra by the hand and pulled her up to stand.

"Come with me," she whispered to Lyrra, "and say nothing, do nothing but smile at the Cheetah."

"Who is the Cheetah?"

Oona dipped her chin. "There, the brown-haired son sitting beside his black-maned brother." *With the amber lion's eyes.*

Clasping Lyrra's hand, Oona took in a deep breath and slowly blew it out.

She looked directly at the Black Mane, and she spoke directly to him. "I, Swan, be Oona, daughter to Aaron, granddaughter to Olwain, *chieftain*, king of *clan* Macleod." Oona dipped her knee to the Cheetah, and spoke to the Cheetah. "She, Dove, be Lyrra." She glanced from brother to brother as they both listened intently. "In my land we be princess. I eldest daughter, Dove be second daughter." The Black Mane cocked his head to one side and the Cheetah to the other.

Oona closed her eyes and took in one long, steadying breath. She opened her eyes and met and held the Black Mane's keen gaze. "I propose marriage. Marriage between Black Mane and Swan, Cheetah and Dove, eldest to eldest, second to second."

CHAPTER 2

Proposals

Only a lifetime of princely training kept Asad from dropping his jaw to the ground. All around him outraged shouts and hissing whispers turned into a stunned, waiting silence, yet none looked more stunned than the Swan herself. She was no fool. One look into her big, round eyes that seemed to look right through a man had told him as much. And she had learned the desert tongue in three moons and spoke it surprisingly well in that enchanting voice of smoked honey. Surely, she had learned of the tribe's traditions too, traditions that forbade a prince of the Seven Tribes from marrying any but a princess of the tribes, traditions that could leave her back flayed open for speaking to him unasked, much less for proposing marriage to him. *So why had she?*

Her gaze flicked over to the kings' table and she wrapped a protective arm around the Dove's waist and pulled her closer. She glanced at the Cheetah, who sat forward on his stool, his intent gaze fixed on the Dove, who had buried her face into her sister's shoulder. *Ah.*

Asad stood and a collective gasp filled the courtyard. The Swan's chin lifted and her gaze never wavered from his.

"You tell the truth?" he asked. He knew it was impossible, what she had proposed, but still it intrigued him. She intrigued him. "You are who you say?"

"Aye, I speak truth to you, only truth to you, Prince Black Mane," she said with a solemn dip of her head. "Always, this I vow."

As prince of the Great Valley, lies both large and small were a part of Asad's daily life, and her simple vow lodged somewhere deep in his chest. He growled, silently cursing the gods, the tribes, his father, for truth be told, given the choice he would gladly accept the Swan's bold proposal, and not only to escape marrying the Fox. But the choice was not his.

He held her watching waiting gaze a long moment, letting his own tell her what his next words would not. Her chest rose and fell, as did the corners of her rose hued lips.

"Father." The Fox's screech rent the night, rousing the stunned crowd to grumbling whispers. "Do something."

"You insolent whore of a slave." The Jackal jumped up and jabbed his finger toward the Swan. "How dare you speak so to a prince of the Seven Tribes. It is an insult for which you will pay."

The Swan stood her ground, hugging the Dove even tighter. "My prince?" she entreated Asad, her voice quaking. *Desperate.*

"Your prince?" The Panther shot up, snarling at Oona. "My son and heir, my prince, will not answer you, slave." He bristled to his full height and breadth, facing Asad. "Duty, tradition, your father, all demand it."

Asad swallowed a roar. "I know full well my duties as a prince of the tribes, Father," he ground out. "They have been ingrained into me since birth."

The Panther huffed. "See you hold to them then."

Asad leveled his gaze. "When have I not." He turned away from the Panther, neither waiting nor expecting an answer. Turning his back on his king in such a public manner was not considered good, princely manners, but slamming his fist into his father's face would be so much worse. Clenching his balled hands at his sides, Asad met the Swan's wide-eyed gaze.

"As you have vowed to me, I vow to you, Oona the Swan, to speak only the truth," he said loudly and clearly enough for all to hear. "And though your proposal does intrigue me, it is true that duty, honor, tradition, all forbid such a marriage."

"You two are lucky the Panther lashed you only with his words," the Sparrow, the woman tasked with teaching Oona and Lyrra the ways and language of the Jackal's tribe, chided them back in their chambers. "Else I'd be peeling the bloody strips of your gowns from your flayed backs right now."

Oona said nothing as she slipped out of her gown of worm weave and held it out to the Sparrow, her hand shaking.

"And here I was bragging to the Black Mane's manservant what quick students you two are," the Sparrow continued her scolding, folding the gown over her arm. "How you had learned our language with such ease in three moons' time." She beaded her gaze on Oona's. "Whatever made you propose such a thing?"

Burning eyes of amber came to Oona, the Cheetah's easy smile. "I think," she said, "better wives to princes than slaves to king."

"Did you truly think you could marry a prince of the Seven Tribes?" the Sparrow tsked. "Did I not teach you better?

"Yes, Sparrow, you did. The fault is no yours, is mine." Oona glanced at Lyrra, who sat rocking and humming to herself on her sofa, a long, reclining chair that was stuffed and covered with fabric on which a person could sleep or lounge, or entertain on. "I be afraid, Sparrow," she whispered, "afraid for Dove. She can no be pleasure woman to Panther. It will kill her. He will kill her. I can no do nothing."

"Well." The Sparrow dug her hand into the pocket of her skirt and pulled out a vial of brown oil. "If you had waited."

Oona gasped. "Is Dream Flower?"

The Sparrow grinned. "It is."

"How you get?" The oil of the Dream Flower was costly, and not easy to come by.

"I am not without some standing and connections in this family, though I be but a second widow to a second son." The Sparrow tucked the vial back into her pocket. "Now get ready, you two, while I give the guard his midnight libation."

Asad crouched on a branch of the ancient cedar that stood sentinel in the middle of the women's courtyard. He had climbed this tree before with the Cheetah, the summer his brother was ten and Asad ten and four. They had spent entire nights prowling the courtyards of every palace they had stayed in since, and had never once been caught. The Panther had never spoken to them of it, and he would have had he known or even suspected it, for their father was not a subtle man.

Their mothers, on the other hand, knew how to keep a secret. It was understood amongst them that as long as certain lines were not crossed, then they would keep their sons' nocturnal prowlings secret. As would the Crab, who had informed Asad that the Swan's window was the fifth one in on the southern wing of the women's quarters while trying to talk him out of anything and everything that was going through his head regarding the beautiful, otherworldly Swan.

Everything the Crab said to warn Asad off was true, but so was the fire in his belly and the hole in his cheek from chewing on it. He intended to see the Swan again, to talk with her alone and away from prying eyes and ears even though he was beyond certain it would be crossing that unspoken line.

That was why he had neither told the Cheetah of his plan tonight nor asked him along, despite knowing his brother would have leapt at the chance to speak with the Dove. He had been waxing poetic about her melodious voice and hummingbird fingers all the way to the chambers they were sharing, and had fallen into his bed mumbling of the sweet-faced Dove. Once assured that the Cheetah was fast asleep, Asad had donned a short tunic and sandals and jumped over his balcony into the night's shadows.

The shutters of the sisters' window were open and the yellow glow of a candle shone low. A guard sat beneath the window, a sword by one side and a horn by the other. The guard lifted a cup to his mouth and drained it, burped, and slumped onto his side, cup still in hand. It was unlikely the guard had been drinking in excess, for the penalty, should he be found out, would be severe. Someone had drugged his drink, and that someone was most likely the Sparrow, who had been the Crab's source of information regarding the sisters.

Asad settled in to wait. One thing his father had taught him was never to wager against a certainty. And he would wager coin that the sisters would be climbing out of that window some time tonight.

Not more than ten breaths later the light in the window went out and a head covered with a dark scarf poked out of the window, yet even from his perch Asad could discern the pale oval of the Swan's face. He sat back on his heels as she looked up into the tree. She stared long enough that Asad thought she might have actually seen him with those mossy green eyes that gazed right through a man and into his soul.

But then she ducked back in, and as Asad lifted onto the balls of his feet, a sandaled foot snaked out over the windowsill, followed by a long, lean leg, and then a hip, a shoulder, a covered head. The Swan pushed up off the sill and danced backward on her foot as it hit ground and then swung her other leg out the window and over the slumbering guard's head. Slim arms handed a pack out to the Swan, and then another, and then the Dove swung out over the guard with both feet and landed next to her sister. They shouldered their packs and looked up into the sky, pointing and whispering before turning north.

Asad jumped down from the tree and the Dove whirled around, followed by the Swan. He held his hand up, palm out, and the Swan's head tilted. A door slammed, the sisters jumped, the guard snorted, and a light flickered and shone from the open window.

"Swan? Dove?" The Fox's shrill yap sounded from their chambers, and then a high-pitched giggle. "Oh, they are in soooo much trouble."

Asad closed the distance between them in an easy lope and stopped at the Swan's side. She stood her ground, clutching her sister's hand, her eyes as big as an owl's. He leaned in closer to the Swan and breathed in the sweet perfume of jasmine. He whispered in her ear. "Do you trust me?"

She blinked once. "I do."

Asad took her free hand in his. Her fingers were cool, almost cold, and he rubbed his thumb across them. She did not pull away, and he twined his fingers through hers. He had large hands, even for a man, yet her long, slender fingers slid through his and curled up and around them with the ease of a perfect fit. Asad growled low in his chest. The Crab had been more right than he knew, for the Swan was beyond dangerous for Asad.

"Just wait until I tell my father." The Fox was talking to herself, enjoying herself. "That stork and her sister the crow will be thrown back into the hot holes. Let the Black Mane see her then when she comes out of the pits half dead and smelling of days-old sweat, he will not be so smitten with the whore then."

The Swan sucked her breath in and let it out in a slow hiss. Asad was not sure if the Dove had even taken a single breath since he dropped out of the cedar tree. He squeezed the Swan's hand.

"Come with me Swan, Dove," he said in a low voice. "Have no fear of the Fox."

He stepped up to the window, the Swan in hand, the Dove clutching onto her sister's sleeve. He coughed loudly, twice.

The Fox's pointy nose thrust out the window. "Black Mane? What are you doing out there, in the middle of the night, with the Swan and the Dove?"

"That is my affair."

"Affair?" The Fox looked down her pinched nose at the sisters. "Once we are married, Black Mane, you will have no need of affairs with the likes of them."

"Us, married?" Asad cocked his head as if surprised. The Swan's proposal had caused such an uproar that the Jackal and the Panther had never gotten to the betrothal, postponing Asad's life sentence, for a day or two anyway. "Are you announcing our marriage for our fathers, before our fathers?" He shook his head at the Fox. "They will be interested to hear this."

The Fox opened her mouth and squeaked wordlessly.

"But they will not hear it from me," Asad told her, "nor from you. You will not tell a single soul, or I will tell all how you presumed to know a king's will."

The Fox's face pinched and her body actually twitched as she looked from Asad to the Swan, who stood so still he would have thought her an ethereal vision, but for the cool tenacity of her fingers clasping his.

"I will not tell," the Fox said at last, dropping her eyes, her face, from his, acting the meek and obedient tribeswoman.

"Good," Asad said. "Then we have a bargain, which is all our marriage will ever be." The Fox dropped her head lower and nodded, and the Swan glanced from the Fox's bowed head to Asad, her mouth slightly open. "Now hasten back to your own rooms," Asad told the Fox. "And keep to our bargain."

He waited until he heard the chamber door shut.

"You are safe now, Swan," Asad assured her. "The Fox will not break our bargain."

"Fox want marry you so much?"

"She does not care two figs about me. She cares about what I can make her, first wife to a prince, queen to a future king of the Seven Tribes."

"She is fool."

"Yes," Asad agreed, inordinately pleased at the vehemence in the Swan's tone, "she is." He stared into the Swan's big, round, serious eyes, eyes that shone like moonlight over deep water. "But you, my jewel, are not."

Oona could not speak, think, or breathe, for the man standing with her in the dark of night, holding her hand in his with his lion eyes staring intently into hers, the Black Mane, had called her his jewel. Not a jewel, his jewel. She sucked in air at last, but still could not speak a single word. The Black Mane chuckled low, and Oona laughed, soft and happy, which she had not done for too many moons.

"Oona." Lyrra plucked at Oona's sleeve. "We go back in now."

Lyrra was right, they should return to their room, but Oona truly did not want to. She did not want to walk away from the Black Mane. She wanted to stay and speak with him once her mind and her tongue found the desert words, to laugh with him more. But Lyrra was right.

She nodded to her sister. "We go, Dove," she spoke in the desert tongue. "We go," she told the Black Mane. "We be no more trouble." She lifted their intertwined hands and laid her other over his. "Thank you, my prince."

Oona made to pull her hands from his, but he held tighter.

"Will you stay with me, Oona the Swan?" he said. "Will you walk with me and talk with me awhile?"

No man or woman other than Lyrra had called her Oona since the day they had been taken by the pirates, the day they became chattel, property to be bartered and ordered about, until tonight, until the Black Mane.

Lyrra tugged at her sleeve and hissed in her ear in their highland tongue. "Oona, we must go. You canna, sister, you shouldna."

But Lyrra's entreaties fell on ears deafened to anything other than the sound of Oona's name on the Black Mane's lips.

"Aye, Prince Black Mane," Oona said. "I walk with you."

Lyrra gave Oona one last narrow look over her shoulder before climbing back through their window, and Oona half expected her sister to pull the shutters tight and lock them. But Lyrra did not. Nor did she light a candle to disturb the drugged guard's sleep or the night's welcoming shadows.

The Black Mane wore a short, one-shouldered tunic of dark linen, and his hair was tied back with a leather strip, emphasizing the line of his high-boned cheeks and square-cut jaw. He wore no adornment, and his waist belt and knife sheath were of plain, dark leather. He was dressed for the dark of night, as was Oona in her plain brown work tunic and scarf. He gripped Oona's hand tighter and grinned like a lad given the afternoon off from chores to run wild in the fields. "Come, Oona," he said, tugging gently.

He led her to the huge cedar in the middle of the courtyard.

"You be in tree," she said.

"I was, and we," he let go of her hand and jumped up and grabbed a low branch with both hands, then climbed his feet up and swung them over the branch, "will soon be."

He reached down and held his hand out to Oona. She wrapped both her hands around his wrist, as strong and corded as an anchor rope, and ran her feet up the cedar's trunk as he pulled her up, lifting her high enough to get her legs up under her onto the branch. She steadied herself with one hand braced against the trunk and the other still gripping the Black Mane's. She was breathing hard, and not only from the climb.

"There is a higher branch that would give us a better, more hidden seat," he said, his breathing as rapid as hers.

Oona followed his gaze to the next branch up, as wide and long as a ship's plank.

"Do you want a pull or a push?" he asked.

Oona let go of his wrist and stood and eyed the branch. "Push."

He cupped his hands and Oona stepped into them and up as he lifted. She swung a leg up onto the branch and rolled onto her belly and then got her hands and knees under her and looked down at the Black Mane, who was grinning from ear to ear.

"Where I sit?" she asked.

"With your back against the trunk, though I do not think I need worry about you falling off."

Oona scooted back and tucked her knees tight to her chest to give him room to climb up, and tried to keep her mouth from gaping open as he placed both hands flat on the branch and swung both legs up, landing with his knees bent on the branch. He sat with his legs dangling, and Oona did the same, so that they sat knee to knee, face to face, the only sound in the hush of the tree's canopy their racing breaths. Oona slowed hers with deep, purposeful breaths and eyed the man sitting across from her in a tree in the middle of the night a thousand leagues from her home.

His shoulders were straight and broad and his bare arms thickly muscled. Oona followed the corded veins of his forearms down to his hands, the broad palms spread out on thighs as thick as oak branches, his long, square-tipped fingers splayed out on his knees. She flexed the fingers of her left hand, the hand he had held, missing the feel of his big, warm, cat's paw. He was grinning again, his teeth shining even and white against the black of his close-cropped beard, and his eyes glowed like burnt embers.

Oona looked up into the cedar's canopy before those eyes seared her to the bone. "How many times you climb tree before?" she asked.

"Three or four, though always before with my brother, the Cheetah."

"Never with girl?" Oona could have bit her tongue as soon as she said it, but he laughed, low and deep.

"No," he said. "Never before with a girl, though I have climbed other trees with my sister."

"You have sister?"

"I have one full sister, six half-sisters, and ten half-brothers."

Oona's jaw dropped. "I have only one sister, Ly— the Dove," she said. "But people of my tribe, they have one wife, one husband, at a time."

"And do they get to choose their one wife or husband themselves?"

"Some do."

"Could you?"

"No," Oona said, her cheeks flaming with her shame. "I be like you, my marriage was to be for *clan*, for tribe. But no like you, I would no marry where I should. I would no stay and do my duty, and now Lyrra, Dove, and I be slaves, our father be…" Oona hung her head and squeezed her eyes tight against the instant welling of hot tears. She had not spilled a single tear since the day her father's ship had been taken almost four moons ago. She would not cry now.

The Black Mane laid a hand over hers. "You do not have to speak of it, Oona," he said, the sound of her name, the kindness in his low, resonant voice threatening to break down the dam she had erected against her unshed tears, "if you do not wish to."

Oona looked up into eyes she had sworn to never lie to, eyes she did not think she could lie to even if she tried.

"I want tell you," she said, not really understanding why it was important that he hear her story, only knowing that it was.

He scooted closer until their knees touched, and Oona sucked in her breath. He laid his hands over hers, tucking them into his, and Oona let her breath out in a slow, steadying stream.

"I would no stay to marry man I should have," she told him, "*chieftain*, king to tribe who trade with ours. All elders want this marriage, all but my grandfather, who would no see me, ahh…" She searched for the word.

"Trapped?" he said, and Oona nodded. They both knew what it was to feel a trap closing in on them. Yet he would stay and face his. Oona had fled from hers.

"My *mathair*, my mother die last autumn," she said, her heart tripping over the words she spoke. "My *athair*, my father say he can no stay where she, her memory, be everywhere, he sail east after winter storms. I beg him take me, no make me marry, and my *piuthar*, my sister, Dove, she go where we go. If I had stay, marry Beorne, my father would no sail." Oona closed her eyes to the vision of her father tied to his mast and took a ragged breath. "He be sing at my wedding, no be dead."

"It is not your fault," the Black Mane said. "People will do what they will, what they must. Your father sailed away from his grief, and you flew away from your trap."

"And now I must save sister."

"From my father?"

Oona held his keen, probing gaze and nodded. The tension between king and prince this night had been obvious, even before her desperate proposal, but the Panther was still the Black Mane's father.

"My sister," she tried to explain, "she change, she afraid, not so strong as she was. You father, Panther, he kill her, here." She pulled a hand from his to touch her forehead and her chest over her heart. "Here."

"That is why you proposed our marriages?"

"Better wives to princes," she said, choosing the cold, hard truth of her impulsive decision over reasons she could not explain, even to herself, "than slaves to king."

The Black Mane removed his remaining hand from hers.

"Eldest to eldest, second to second," he said.

Oona touched tentative fingers to his.

"I see in Cheetah's eyes, his smile when he watch Dove. He be kind. I know he no hurt Dove."

"And when you looked into my eyes?"

Oona stared into burning embers and swallowed her heart. "I see you, Black Mane."

"Asad," the Black Mane said, his voice a low, resonate growl. "My name is Asad."

Asking the Swan, Oona, to stay with him was not the smartest thing Asad had ever done, but asking her to call him by his given name surely was. Sitting with her in the close quiet of the cedar, breathing in the tantalizing sweet perfume of her, was like dangling a piece of choice meat before a caged lion. Yet the self-inflicted torture was more than worth the trial as she smiled and spoke his name with her voice of smoked honey.

He asked her of her homeland, the Green Isles, and learned she had lived in the far northeast of them, a land of mountains and rivers and forests and lakes, that she lived in a manor house, a palace of wood and stone, with her parents and her grandparents, her mother an only child, Lyrra and Oona the only grandchildren. Her father was a Northman trader from the east who had sailed into their port one summer day, taken one look at their mother, and never left.

"He was spellbound, your father," Asad said, feeling a kinship with this man he had never met or even heard of before this night.

Oona tilted her head and lifted her brows, and her eyes glistened in the moonlight filtering through the cedar's canopy. Asad took a slow, deep breath and sat back a little from her. It was either that or fall into those eyes and off the tree.

"You said your father was a king? That you were princesses?"

"I lie, a little." She gave him a sheepish grin that Asad could have forgiven anything. "My father is no king, but my grandfather, he *chieftain*, king, our mother princess, so we be princess, yes?"

"Well, as you say, a little lie," Asad teased. "And it was before you swore to tell me the truth, only the truth, always."

Asad had knowingly told his first lie at the age of ten, after his father had struck him in a fit of rage. Asad had been trying to protect his mother from his father, and he lied to everyone else afterward for the same reason, blaming his own clumsiness for his blackened eye.

He had lied often to his father since as a matter of survival, and he had learned the necessity of lies both large and small in navigating the public and private worlds of palace life, and he hated the lies. To have this woman who was innocent of all the deceit and lies he had lived with for so long swear to speak the truth to him left him longing for a world free of lies, a world where Asad and Oona could speak to each other openly and freely, where they could be friends or lovers or even man and wife if they so chose.

But that world was a dream world, and they lived in a world where Asad's wives would be chosen for him, at least until he became king, and Oona could be whipped to death for sitting in this tree with him, staring at him with eyes as deep and reflective as a fathomless pool, the apples of her cheeks rounding under his heated gaze. Raking a hand back through his hair before he did something foolish like reach out and rub the backs of his fingers across her cheek, Asad asked her of the journey she had taken from her world to his.

Her eyes lit up as she told him of sailing through a strait where a mountain of rock jutted out from the north, and a shore of desert sand could be seen to the south and into the Mid Earth Sea.

"I have only been to trading ports on the sea's shores," he said. "I have never sailed. What was it like?"

She closed her eyes and took in a deep breath and held it, and then she let it out with a slow smile. "The air smell of salt, sun, and wind. Wind blow warm and clean, and fill sails." Her eyes opened and her arms spread wide. "It feel…" she began to rock from side to side on the branch, to roll her shoulders and wave her arms in big swooping dips "…like dance."

"You liked it, the sailing."

"Oh, aye. My father say I have his sea legs, Lyrra, not so much. She have much sickness at first."

"What was the most amazing thing you saw?"

"Sea creatures big as goat, sleek as fish, gray as storm cloud, with hole on top of head that blow air. They swim with ship, leap out of sea and dive down." She arced her hand up and then down, undulating her arm up and down, up and down. "They rise up on tail fins, swim backward." She lifted her hand and moved her arm backward. "Truth." She held her arm still, palm forward. "I swear it."

"I believe you," he said with a laugh that brought a quick grin to her face, and a knot to his gut. She was, without exception, the most enchanting creature he had ever encountered. "So, you were having the time of your life on that ship?"

"Aye," she said with that mesmerizing lilt of her tongue that he could listen to for eternity. "I mean, yes." She smiled, and then her smile turned sad. "Until pirates. They attack ship, kill many men, take others, take Lyrra and me aboard their ship, throw us in hold, sail four days to port to slave market."

"How long were you in the slave market?" Asad had been there twice in his life, with his father as buyers. He ground his teeth at the thought of her there, being touched by other men, poked and prodded at like some herd animal.

"Three days."

Asad gave a low whistle. An exotic pair of beautiful women the likes of the Swan and the Dove who could sing and dance should have been bought up the first day before noon.

"Those pirates," he said. "They must have been asking a high price."

"Highest ever, Jackal say." She gave a wry arch of her fine brows. "He tell us we better be worth it." Her brows knitted. "You marriage to Fox, it be much wanted by more than Fox."

"It will keep the tradition of the Seven Tribes, as well as the trade road open between our cities, protected between our tribes."

"And we be Fox dowry. To be made pleasure women for Panther." Her voice was flat, her shining eyes dulled.

"A pleasure woman is a slave of some standing in this world, Oona," he told her. Yet even as he said it, he clenched his hands into fists, fists he would gladly ply into the face of his father, or any other man who dared touch her.

Her eyes flashed crystalline. "Pleasure woman is still slave. In my land pleasure woman be lowest of women, is better to be dead."

She meant what she said. Asad knew this as he had known she would try to escape her cage again tonight. A cage her sister the Dove waited in. A cage the Dove would not fight. She would submit and her spirit would give, as would her body to the Panther. But the Swan, she would not give in so easily. She would fight until her wings beat bloody against the confines of her cage, or until her back was stripped and bloody from his father's whip and her incandescent spirit dulled and broken.

Asad unclenched his fist and held his hand out to her. He would do for her what he could not for himself.

"Do you trust me, Oona?" he asked her for the second time that night.

She smiled and set her hand in his and answered him without hesitation. "I do."

"Then I have a proposal for you," he said and her head tilted. "Do not try to escape from here again."

"I...we must." She pulled her hand from his. "I must keep Dove safe."

"My father will never have the Dove or you. I promise you this." Her head stilled and her big, round eyes widened. "There are traditions he must follow, training for you. It would be three moons at least until you would be ready for him, and he will not touch you until then, for he is, above all else, a staunch keeper of traditions."

"You want we wait? Three moons?"

"No, not three moons, but twenty and three days. From here it would be too dangerous, with an entire city to get out of, an entire guard to chase you down. But once we are out in the desert there will be only my father's men, and time for me to plan your escape."

"You would do this? You would help us escape you father?"

He took her hand in his and sang to her in his low, coarse voice, *"I would do, would I do not, all for the sake of Somebody."*

CHAPTER 3

The Betrothal

Oona woke to a rapping at the door and opened it with a yawn. The Sparrow stood on the other side, wide-eyed and gape-jawed.

"What happened?" The Sparrow pushed her way past Oona into the room. She stared hard at Lyrra, who sat up in her bed, pushing loose hair from her face. "Why are you two still here?"

"Fox come to our room, find us gone," Oona told the Sparrow, who clapped her hand over her mouth. "We be fine. Black Mane, he save us. Make Fox swear she no tell."

"The Black Mane?"

"He was in tree."

"What? Why?"

Oona shrugged, but her traitorous cheeks flushed hot.

The Sparrow held both hands out from her sides, as if trying to find her balance. "So, what exactly happened?"

"We outside window, Fox come into room, start yelling, Black Mane drop out of tree, walk us to window, tell Fox she no tell or he no marry her."

"That is all?"

Oona pressed her lips together and nodded.

"Except for Black Mane ask Swan to walk with him after Fox leave," Lyrra chirped as she got up out of her bed.

"He what?" the Sparrow squawked.

"And she go with him." Lyrra sauntered past a glaring Oona.

The Sparrow shook a bony finger at Oona. "You had better hope the Fox keeps her silence. The Panther is already angry enough after what you did at the feast. If he found out about you two going off into the night together…"

"He will not," Oona assured her, glowering at Lyrra, "if Dove learn to keep mouth shut."

"You never tell me not tell Sparrow."

"It is not me you need to be worrying about," the Sparrow warned as she flitted about the room. "I was sent to tell you to bathe and prepare yourselves to serve at supper tonight. There is to be a feast to celebrate the betrothal announcement of the Black Mane and the Fox."

Despite Asad's assurances that he was to marry the Fox no matter what, Oona still felt badly for her part in it, and more than a little jealous of the Fox. He was a man any woman would be proud to have as a husband. But he would never be Oona's. However, he seemed to be her friend, and he would help her and Lyrra escape the lives of pleasure women.

"You, Swan," the Sparrow said. "You are to wear your green linen and the Dove her gray. There will be no worm weave for you two tonight, they cannot have you outshining the star of the night. Neither she nor her mother will put up with that. No kohl or cheek stain either."

"Oh no." Oona clapped her cheeks with mock disappointment. The stain on her cheeks and lips made her look like a painted doll, and the sheer worm weave made her feel naked, especially when her nipples were stained.

"Oh yes." The Sparrow narrowed her eyes on Oona. "You are to be plain and quiet tonight, to keep your eyes down and your mouths closed."

As she sat on the stool beside him at the center of the main table, Asad looked long and hard into the Fox's face. She was a pretty enough girl, with a soft, generously fleshed body, long black-brown hair, and dark brown eyes lined black with kohl. Yet all Asad saw, all he had ever seen in their brown shallows, was a sharp-nosed, shifty-eyed vixen.

"How are you this evening, Black Mane?"

"I am well, Fox."

As prince, it was his right to call her by her birth name if he chose. But that was more familiar than Asad cared to be with his soon-to-be betrothed, and may all the gods help him, his first wife and future queen. He smiled grimly, envisioning his mother attempting to teach the Fox her queenly duties. He would wager gold on the Fox driving the Snow Leopard to show her claws within the first day.

"And you, Fox," he said, remembering his manners as their fathers took their seats flanking them. "Are you well this evening?"

"Yes, Prince Black Mane, quite well."

"I am heartened to hear it. A woman should be happy at her feast of betrothment."

"And a man, Prince Black Mane?"

"A man is content to know he has kept his word and done his duty." That was all their marriage would ever be as far as Asad was concerned. A bargain struck and honored for the sake of duty: duty to his family, his city, and the tribes. "So should a woman be," he added, tacitly reminding her of their bargain struck last night at the Swan's window.

"A woman's contentment is nothing to a man's," she answered as she was taught, to always defer to the man. "Her only happiness is his."

As a man and a prince, Asad had been raised to expect a woman's subservience, but last night with the Swan, with Oona, he had liked that she had a will and a mind of her own. As queen, his mother deferred to her husband the king, but as the Snow Leopard she knew her own mind and spoke it as plainly as any man, and made more sense than most, certainly more than the Panther, who was ruled by tradition and temper, and who now watched Asad from beneath hooded lids and listened openly to every word spoken between him and the Fox.

Oona shifted the pitcher of beer in her hands. As a slave she was not allowed to partake of the drink, brewed by women priestesses and served only at feasts, but she had snuck a few sips of the foamy, yeasty drink, and did not really care for the taste of it. Lowering her gaze from the pitcher to the floor, she entered the salon. A grassfire of whispers swept through the room, but Oona kept her eyes ahead of her feet until she came upon a row of sandaled feet beneath the long table. She recognized the Black Mane's instantly, the length of his lightly furred toes, the broad pad, high arch, and rounded heel that he strode silent as a cat on, the scar on the top of his left foot. He had strong, perfectly formed feet, a strange thing to say or notice about a man, but Oona had become familiar with looking at the feet of these desert people, more familiar than looking them in the eye, for she was a slave here, not worthy enough to meet their direct gaze, except for Asad's when others were not looking.

She stopped a few steps from the table in front of the Panther's thicker, flatter, hairier feet, and stood, gaze down and waiting as Lyrra stepped up beside her.

"Fill our cups, slaves," the Jackal demanded, "that we may toast the betrothal of the Panther's eldest son, the Black Mane, to my eldest daughter, the Fox."

The Panther thrust his cup forward toward Oona, his thick fingers covered in rings of gold set with rubies, amber, and onyx. She filled the cup without spilling a drop despite the Panther snatching it and pulling it away quickly. Oona pressed her lips together to keep from smiling. She had learned to pour slowly and to pay close attention, for this was an old game that the Fox and her brother, the Falcon, often played with her, and that they lost more often than not.

She stepped over to stand before the Black Mane, who wore his wrist cuff of hammered gold, which had a roaring lion's head etched into it with eyes of polished amber. Oona poured the beer into his cup, and almost spilled some when the tip of his sandaled foot touched hers. Catching her breath, she steadied her hands and slowly let her breath out as the Black Mane pulled his foot back beneath the table.

The Fox played her usual game with her cup, but Oona was ready for her, and for the Falcon, who, if he behaved this night as he normally did, would be well into his cups before the feast was over, and then Oona would be dodging his hands.

The Jackal had never done anything but ignore his son's wandering hands, and Oona hoped that the presence of the other kings would keep him on his best behavior. And it did, for his first three cups of beer, but by his fourth, he was leaning over and grabbing and patting her backside every time she walked past him, and as he was sitting at the end of the table where she was to stand and serve from, it was impossible for her to avoid him or his hands as the feast wore on. At least it was her backside and not Lyrra's.

"Sho, Black Mane," the Falcon said, raising his sloshing cup high and grinning lopsided after Oona filled it for the sixth time. "How many shons do you expect to get from my fine shister?"

"As many as the gods see fit," the Black Mane, who had drunk no more than two cups of beer, answered. The Fox blushed and giggled, and Oona considered letting her win the next game and accidentally spilling an entire pitcher of beer down the low-cut bodice of her tight-fitting gown.

"Pray give her at least one daughter too," the Raven, who sat between her husband and son, said. She smiled adoringly at the preening Fox. "For though a son gives his mother pride, a daughter gives her ease."

Oona could not imagine the Fox giving anyone ease, but wisely held her tongue as the Black Mane raised his cup and took a long draught.

"And a son gives his father progeny to carry on the family line, the tribe's traditions," the Panther said, lifting his cup to his son.

"And a daughter?" The Black Mane lowered his. "What does she give her father?"

"A true daughter gives him her heart."

"And if she gives him her heart, a heart pure and innocent of any blame, and that heart is cast back at her through no fault of her own, bruised and squeezed dry by the father?"

The Panther glared across the room at the Oryx, the youngest king of the tribes and newly come to his throne, and who started and went still, but for the narrowing of his eyes. "Then she is no true daughter," the Panther hissed.

"Or her true father is blinded by his own blackened heart." The Black Mane spoke coldly, but there was fire in his glare.

The Panther, the Black Mane, and the Oryx all took long draughts from their cups, glowering at one another over the rims. The Falcon, too drunk to give them any heed, his bladder likely in need of relief, stood on unsteady legs and grabbed Oona's shoulder with one hand and patted her on the backside with the other whilst she concentrated on keeping the pitcher in her hands level. He lurched around the table and then yelped as his feet flew up into the air and he landed flat on his back. The salon went quiet for a moment, and then erupted into loud guffaws and more than a few claps. Slowly, and with much swaying, the Falcon stood and glared at the Black Mane.

"You tripped me," he screeched.

"You need to learn to stay on your feet," the Black Mane said, his voice deathly calm, "and to keep your hands to yourself."

Being slaves of great cost and import, Oona and Lyrra were in the strange position of living in the women's quarters of the Jackal's palace, elevated above most servants, but beneath every other woman they lived their daily life amongst, women who considered them dirt and treated them as such, but for the Sparrow, who had no love for her dead husband's brother, and was their only friend in the Jackal's household.

This morning she had excused Oona and Lyrra from their lessons while the palace slept off the last two nights of feasting. Lyrra chose to stay in their room and sleep the heat of the afternoon away, but Oona made for the quiet and peace of the garden in the women's quarters, as far away as she could get from the Fox's incessant yapping about her betrothal to the Black Mane.

The Fox had bragged on it at least a hundred times since she woke at noon, and for the hundredth time that day Oona's thoughts went to the words spoken between the Black Mane and the Panther about daughters. They had been short in number, but as long in meaning as the looks passed between father and son. And they had captured the Oryx's attention and caused his soft brown eyes to harden and his smiling mouth to set in a grim line.

Swirling her hand in the fishpond's cool water, Oona watched the ripples seek out the lily pads and the reeds, making them sway to and fro. She closed her eyes and tried to remember the feel of a bracing wind, the taste of a cold, wet rain, but all she felt was stillness and heat, and all she tasted was sand and dry air.

"Where did you go?" a low voice, resonant and instantly familiar, murmured above her.

Oona opened her eyes to golden orbs flecked with bronze and umber smiling down into hers, eyes she had never seen in daylight until now, eyes that burned with the heat of the sun.

"Home," she whispered.

The Black Mane gave the garden, a place neither he nor any other men were allowed in, a quick look over before he sat on the bench beside her. He was dressed in a green, one-sleeved short tunic, and Oona tried hard not to stare at the tawny breadth of his lightly furred chest, or how it tapered to a waist ridged with muscles. His brawny thighs rested casually against hers, causing her cheeks to heat and her pulse to quicken.

"Home is where you will be soon enough."

He ran the knuckles of his closed hand up the length of her bare arm, the amber eyes of the lion on his gold wrist cuff reflecting the sun's light. He trailed his knuckles back down her arm and Oona shivered at his touch. He smiled as he took her hand in his and gently pried her fingers open and placed a vial of dark brown liquid in them.

"Have the Sparrow put all of this into your guard's drink tonight," he told her, folding her fingers back over the vial. "Be at your window after dark. Dress to move and cover your head and arms."

Oona nodded, unable to find her voice. He gave her hand a gentle squeeze and then he stood and peered down the garden's path.

"Dove come too?" she managed to squeak.

"It would be safer if only you came."

Lyrra would worry while Oona was away, but she could ask the Sparrow to sit with her, to send anyone looking for the Swan on a wild-goose chase.

"Only I come." She stood and offered him her hand, as she would have done to any man in her homeland, and he took it, as no man in this land would have. She clasped his hand and shook it, and he clasped hers back and shook it in kind. "In my land," she explained, "handshake is person's oath."

"I like it," he said, still clasping her hand.

"I glad."

Oona was grinning like the village idiot at him, but she could not help it, nor did she even try when he grinned back at her, his teeth showing straight and white against the black of his beard and the tawny warmth of his skin. But then he stiffened and cocked his head toward the gate, and soon enough Oona heard the voices.

"Tonight then," he said, and disappeared past the hedge of lush foliage.

Oona stuffed the vial into her bodice and prayed it wouldn't bulge out and show, for as the voices drew nearer, she recognized the Fox's shrill yap and the Raven's crowing. It would do her no good to run, they were too close and she would be seen, so she stood where she was with her head hanging low and waited for the Fox and her mother to pass. She was a slave, not worth their notice.

But, of course, the Fox did notice her, and would not let her be.

"Here she is, Mother." The Fox circled Oona. "The slave who thought she could marry a prince, my prince. As if any prince of the desert would want such a skinny, milk-faced stick of a whore."

"Now, now, Fatima," her mother said as Oona kept her gaze on her feet. "It is you the Black Mane will marry, you who will be his queen, who will share his bed and bear his children. Do not trouble your pretty little head over such as she. She is dog meat, not fit for a lion."

Asad pulled the drugged guard from under the window and set him back against the wall a few feet farther down. He had barely straightened when a long white leg swanned out the window and he managed to close his mouth as a shapely backside followed. Oona slid her other leg up and over the sill, and Asad's whole head followed the arc of her sandaled foot as it found the ground next to its twin without so much as a wobble of its finely turned ankle.

"Damn."

"What?" she whispered.

"I said good." He nodded at the scarf pulled up over her head. "Your head, your arms, they are covered. That is good."

She smiled. "We go?"

Blinded by her smile, Asad blinked and swallowed, and then took Oona by the hand, thrilling to the feel of her fingers twining through his. "We go."

They moved fast and quiet, Oona's long dancer's legs keeping stride with Asad's, their fingers clasped together as he led them through the courtyard and along the inner wall of the palace grounds, keeping to the night's shadows. They followed the wall to the Jackal's stables and then hugged a line of fences out to the kraals. Asad stopped at a gate bearing the red and black flag of his tribe and gave a low whistle, holding tight to Oona's hand as she started to back away at the thundering of hooves.

"Do not be afraid," he said as several horses pulled up at the fence, blowing and snorting. Still holding Oona's hand, he reached out his other and patted the biggest, blackest horse on the neck. "This is Storm Chaser, my stallion. And this," he patted the roan mare beside the stallion, "this is Star. This is who I brought you to meet." He lifted Oona's hand and placed it gently on the mare's cheek, smiling as the mare gave a soft whinny. "She will take you home."

"Take me home?"

"You will ride Star from our camp in the desert and your sister will ride my brother's mare, Wind Song, here." He scratched the forelock of the smaller mare and then pulled a scroll from the inside pocket of his tunic. "We came up with a plan, my brother and I."

He and the Cheetah had spent the better part of the afternoon planning and drawing the map on the sheepskin he rolled out along the kraals' top pole, the markings visible under the moon's light. "Here is where you will leave from, three nights out from the Jackal's." He pointed to the bottom of the map and then slowly ran his finger up the road he had drawn, marking safe camps and water holes. "Ride north and west, keeping the North Star to your right and the Scorpion to your back. You should make this seaport in four days, five at the most."

She looked up into the sky and followed the line of the Bear down to the North Star. The sailor's daughter knew her stars.

"You must ride hard and long to keep ahead of the men my father will send after you." He swallowed his gall at what would happen to them if they were caught, but she would try to escape whether he helped or not. Better he helped. "Ride at night by the stars and all morning and afternoon, and rest during the heat of the day, taking turns sleeping and keeping guard. Once you reach port, you can sell Star and Wind Song for passage on a ship. They are good brood mares, any man with a sense of horses will see it, so do not take any less than your full price of passage for them."

She nodded and then traced the map's line north with her finger, slim and pale in the moon's glow. Her finger stopped and held at the woman's face that Asad had drawn for the North Star, long and angular with high cheek bones and big round eyes, her face.

"How we escape Panther's camp?" Those big round eyes met his. "We no be under guard?"

"I know the Jackal's apothecary, and he has already sold me enough Dream Flower to drug the entire camp. They will be sleeping sound as babes all night and half the morning through."

"But, Panther, he no suspect?"

"He might, but he will not speak of it. He would never speak publicly of his sons going against him in such a way."

Her eyes held and studied his. "The Panther," she said at last, "he no speak of sons, but he speak to them, yes?"

Asad shrugged. "Let him." Let the Panther do or say anything he wanted to Asad and the Cheetah, as long as Oona and the Dove were safely away from his father. On this, Asad and his brother were agreed.

Oona laid her hand on his along the fence. "Thank you, you and you brother. My sister and I, we owe you our life."

Asad rolled her hand into his. "It is our honor." He lifted their hands and pressed his lips to the backs of her fingers, breathing in jasmine and tasting honey. He heard the sharp intake of her breath as her hand, her whole body stilled, and his went rigid.

He, Asad, the Black Mane, Prince of the Great Valley, who had had carnal knowledge of his father's pleasure women since he was ten and four, was half hard simply kissing this virginal maid's hand. "Come." He let go of her hand, and temptation. "Let us ride."

"Ride?"

"It will go better in the desert if you ride Star now. Get used to her and her to you. You have ridden a horse before?"

"Yes," she said. "Horse for plow fields, bigger, slower. Lyrra too."

Asad nodded and held his hand out to the mare named for the white star on her forehead. "Star here is sweet tempered and a comfortable seat, so is Wind Song. They are both favorites of my sisters to ride."

"You sister who you climb trees with?"

"Yes," he said, "my sister Rasha, the Gazelle. Our mother is Noor, the Snow Leopard, the Panther's first wife, Queen of the Great Valley."

She was grinning from ear to ear, a bright, incandescent smile that lit her from within.

"Why do you smile, Oona?"

"You, you tell me their names, you call me Oona."

"I like saying your name. Oooonnaaa. Saying it is like watching you move, like a cool breeze rippling over green summer grass."

"You are poet, Prince Black Mane," she said with a teasing lilt that lifted the corners of her smiling eyes. *Eyes he could lose his soul in.*

"I am a man spellbound," he confessed, and was saved by Storm Chaser rudely nosing his arm. "We had better ride."

Oona held tight to Star's mane and hugged her back with her knees as they raced across the paddock. They were flying, and still they pulled up to the fence a good two strides behind the stallion Asad rode

"You are a natural," Asad said, and Oona, breathing as hard as if she had done the running, laughed.

"Plow horse at home no run like this. I like."

"Why am I not surprised?" His low, easy chuckle vibrated from Oona's ears to her toes.

"Asad?"

"Oona?"

"We ride longer?" she asked, though the waning moon was already descending westward.

"A little longer," he said. "But before we go back, there is something I want to show you."

"Race you back?"

She wheeled Star around and urged the mare into a full gallop before he could even answer, but soon enough he was laughing behind her and his stallion's hooves were pounding earth as they overtook her and Star. She made a face at Asad as he grinned in passing and another as she pulled up to the fence, where he sat waiting.

"You always win race?" She slid off of the mare and gave her neck a pat.

"If it is a horse race, yes, but if it is a foot race, then the Cheetah, he will win."

"You won last race?" she asked, even though she knew he had. It was one of the many things about him that the Fox yapped ceaselessly of.

"The last two, this next will make three." He puffed his chest out and posed on the fence rail.

"You no lack pride," she teased.

"Ouch." He grabbed at his chest. "You are a poor loser. Who would have thought?"

Oona laughed. "Only anyone, everyone, of my *clan*, my tribe."

"Come then, my poor little loser." He jumped off the fence and took her by the hand, which fit into his as easily and naturally as breathing. "Let me show you the prize I have picked for my winnings."

"Oh, Asad," Oona exclaimed as she watched the white and gray dappled filly prancing around the yearling kraal. "She be beautiful."

"She is a long-legged, high-stepping filly. But then I have always found the lankiest yearlings turn into the sleekest, fleetest mares."

He said this to Oona as if he knew what a gangly, awkward girl she had been. And his words did much to ease the old pain of being called bean pole and stick for as long back as she could remember, although it had stopped the autumn she turned ten and six, when the rest of her had caught up with her legs and her breasts had finally filled out.

"What you name her?"

"Cloud Dancer."

"It fit her, Poet Prince."

"Yes, well." He gave Oona a quick grin. "I was inspired."

Oona flushed from head to toe and turned her face from Asad's even though it was still the dark of night.

"Falcon, he plan on win race," she told him as the filly pranced off. "Win Storm Chaser."

"He and every other man racing, including my father. Let them try. Storm Chaser and I have never been beaten."

"In fair race," she said, and he cocked his head. "I hear Fox say Falcon plan to win, by hook or by crook she say."

"Did she?"

"The Fox, she have no…" Oona searched for the right word.

"Intelligence, grace, humor, discretion?"

Oona burst out laughing. "You poor man," she said, and she meant it. He was too good a man to deserve the Fox as a wife, even if he was allowed many, the idea of which turned her insides as bilious as Lyrra's skin when she had the seasickness. "You will have to spend much time with her after you marry?"

"No. Not really."

"Good, I glad, for you sake."

"Thank you."

"When will marriage be?"

"Summer's Eve next, so that our firstborn may come in the spring."

"You born in spring?"

"No. I was born in the heat of late summer, when the Lion shone bright."

Oona's jaw dropped, though it should not have surprised her. One look at the man had told her who he was. "You be lion four times through," she said, "by birth, by name, by mane, by eyes."

He stared at her long and hard with those piercing lion eyes, and Oona could do nothing but stare back.

"You give me praise where my father finds fault."

Even she could hear the hurt in his voice. "I no understand." How could anybody find fault with him? His face, his body, had surely been carved and molded of bone and muscle and sinew by the hands of the gods themselves. His mind was quick and clear thinking, his spirit strong, and his heart honorable.

"I should have been born in the spring, or early summer at the latest," he said. "That it took my mother six moons to conceive me was quite a blow to my father's pride."

"But surely, when you do come, firstborn son, Lion, you," Oona waved her hand from his magnificent black mane to his perfectly proportioned sandaled feet, "you father, he be proud?"

The Black Mane shook his head and stared out over the kraal. "It was too late. I was too late."

Oona laid a hand on his forearm and corded muscle twitched beneath her fingers. "He not have pride in man you be now?"

"He has pride enough when I win a race or best a challenger in a fight. But he does not know what manner of man I am, nor does he really care to. All he cares about is that I do what he wants, what is expected of me. He does not know me, and so he does not know what I will do in any given situation."

"Such as help slaves escape?"

He laid his hand over hers and gave her a wry smile. "That makes me dangerous in his mind, a son he cannot control."

"And Cheetah?"

"Is the peacemaker between our father and me."

"His birth, it no harm you father's pride?"

"He was born under the Bull, ten moons to the day after our father married his mother, a good and obedient son from the start, unlike me."

"I know how is, to be trouble child," she told him. "I be that to my family. Dove be like Cheetah. She be quiet and good, she sing and sew. I run across field, climb tree."

"I would have liked to see the young Oona running across a field on those long legs," Asad said with a grin that made her blush again. "What stars were you born under, Oona?"

Oona smiled at the sound of her name. She could not help it, nor did she try to hide it. Not from him. "I born under Scales, under full harvest moon at midnight," she told him. A sailor's daughter, she had learned of the stars at a young age, their names, their lore, and their great import in navigating the world's seas. As a slave she had been taught their desert names and lore, their import in how the desert tribes navigated their world. "Dove born under Water Bearer."

Asad straightened and stared hard at Oona, his eyes burning into hers with a blistering heat she could not look away from, even if she had wanted to.

"We are Fire and Air, you and I," he said. "And they are Earth and Water, the Cheetah and the Dove. Fire cannot live without air, and the earth will die without water."

"Oh." It was all she could think, all she could say, all she could do to keep from being drawn in to him, her breath consumed by the fire in his eyes.

A horse whinnied sharply, and Oona and Asad both jumped back from the kraals' rail as if it were ablaze.

"We had better go," he said.

They stood under the cedar they had climbed together two nights ago. The night they had each of them vowed to tell the truth to the other, only the truth. And it was true what Asad had told Oona: fire could not live without air, and he had never felt more alive than when he was with her, which made what he had to tell her even harder.

"Oona," he said, and her eyes smiled at him, as they did every time he spoke her name. He reached out and ran his fingers down a lock of her hair, as pale as moonlight and smooth as worm weave. "Last night, when you served and we supped..." He tucked her hair back behind her ear. He wanted to make her understand, not hurt her feelings or her pride.

"I know. I see. I see Panther watch you. Jackal, Fox, Falcon, I see all watch you like hawks. Watch me."

"And they will continue to watch me, to watch us, until their suspicions have lessened." He growled low at how the Falcon had fondled her. He was not the least bit sorry that he had tripped the drunken sod and caused him to fall so publicly. He hoped the Falcon would heed his not-so-subtle warning, for Asad would not be so easy on the fool the next time he tried to lay so much as a finger on Oona.

Asad laid his palm on Oona's face, the callus of his thumb tracing the high, pale arc of her cheekbone, which rose and rounded as she smiled. "Ahh, Oona." He traced the full softness of her lips with his thumb, felt the warmth of her breath wash over his skin. Since the age of ten and four, all Asad had to do was crook his finger at one of his father's pleasure women and she was his for the night, or however long she held his interest. He had never had to woo a woman before. In truth, he had never cared to, until now. Until Oona. "I am going to miss that smile."

"Miss?"

Asad touched his forehead to hers, their eyes and mouths no more than a breath apart. He breathed in jasmine and the cool night air and her. "The race," he said, fighting the caged beast inside him, the urge to close the chasm between them and claim her lips, to see if they tasted as sweet and soft as they felt. "It is in eight days and I need to be training with Storm every day and resting up every night." He lifted his head and cupped her chin so that her gaze met his. "Do you understand what I am telling you?"

Oona's gaze held his, but the smile had left her eyes.

"We not meet again as Oona and Asad." Her voice dropped, and so did her eyes. "We must only be Black Mane and Swan."

CHAPTER 4

The Race

The next night the Black Mane came to the supper table late, freshly bathed, and he drank one cup of wine, and no beer. He ate a plate of roasted meat and greens, but few grains, and had figs, not honeyed dates, as a last course. He left the table as soon as he finished his meal, and the Cheetah followed soon after.

Oona could not have said if he even glanced her way once during the meal, but the Panther's black eyes were on her constantly, the Fox's too. Every time Oona looked up, the vixen was glaring daggers at her. For the first time since she had been a slave in this household, Oona was glad to keep her head down and eyes averted.

The next day and night passed much the same, except that every man at the prince's table came late and freshly bathed, ate and drank sparingly, and left early. By the third night the kings were eating less and retiring earlier, and by the fourth night every man entered in the race was doing the same.

"The stables and kraals are never empty of men and horses these days," the Sparrow told Oona and Lyrra. She was teaching them the song of the desert hero, Gilgamesh, to sing at the feast after the race. "And the pleasure house has been empty of all men but for those too old or too lazy to race. The contestants seem to be adopting the Black Mane's training habits, hoping to beat him and deny him his third straight win."

"Is usual," Oona asked, taking a seat at the small, three-legged table in their room, "for Black Mane no go to pleasure house before race?"

"No." The Sparrow shook her head and perched on a stool across from Oona. "It is not. In fact, it is said the Black Mane has not so much as stepped foot inside the pleasure house yet this meeting of the tribes, which is more than unusual."

"How so?" Oona asked casually, though there were butterflies as big as bats fluttering and flapping in her belly.

"Before, the Black Mane had always been a frequent visitor of the houses, a visitor the pleasure women were always glad to welcome," the Sparrow said, and Oona's butterflies turned to stones in the pit of her belly. "It is said that they are angered by the Black Mane's absence, and the absence of those emulating him, that they are taking it all as a personal insult."

"Perhaps is his way to train, to save his strength," Oona posited as the stones in her belly took wing once more.

"Perhaps," the Sparrow said, her eyes beading in on Oona's.

"What Fox say about Black Mane training?"

"She has been yapping about nothing else but the Black Mane training and winning, that and her new gown of red worm weave for the feast."

That was not what Oona meant, but she let it go. The desert tribes had a different view of relations between men and women than the clans of the Green Isles. Here the women acted proud of their men going to pleasure women. They even bragged about it, about their men's needs and virility, whispering to each other about some new trick their man had learned from a pleasure woman and brought back to their bed.

In Oona's homeland, if a clanswoman learned her husband had been with a "loose woman," that man would likely never share his wife's bed again, and consider himself lucky she did not geld him. Of course, the Black Mane would never be the Swan's husband, despite her desperate proposal, but somewhere in the deepest corner of her caged heart there beat the faintest hope that Asad could be Oona's man. And like a true clanswoman, Oona did not like the idea of sharing her man one bit, even if he was only her man in her dreams.

And yet, when he held her hand, or ran his thumb over her lips…

"…and you will wear your green."

"What?" Oona said.

"I said," the Sparrow repeated as Lyrra took a seat beside Oona, "that the Dove will wear her blue worm weave to play and sing at the feast, and you, Swan, will wear your green. Now, let us get back to your lesson. There are three more verses to learn of the 'Song of Gilgamesh' and only four days left before the race and the feast to follow."

"My eldest son wins this race three times straight," the Panther ranted at the Cheetah, though Asad stood not five paces from them, "and what prize does he pick? The Jackal's stallion, a proven brood mare?" He laughed, short and harsh. "Oh no, he picks some leggy, unproven yearling filly."

"A leggy filly she may be." Asad pulled off Storm's saddle and handed it to the stable boy, a stout lad with a good sense of horses. "But she will prove out." He had raced across seven leagues of hard desert and he was hungry, thirsty, and tired of his father's tirades. "I will stake my word on it."

"Stake that stallion of yours and we will have a bargain," his father said.

Asad shook his head. "The only time I wager on Storm is when I race him, and I will retire from the race before I lose him." He unwound his headscarf and ran his hand back through his hair, slick with sweat and gritty with sand. "I am tired and covered in dirt and satisfied with my choice," he said. "I am going to go soak in a hot bath and sleep before the feast tonight, the feast celebrating your eldest son's victory."

"Do not go showing your claws to me, boy." His father bristled, ready for a fight. A fight Asad did not want. Not here, not now.

"Forgive me, Father. As I said, I am tired and hungry." He shrugged apologetically and his father's hackles lowered. "I tell you what, I will wager my mare Star on the filly proving out. She is a proven brood mare, and I did bring her to trade." The Panther said nothing, but he was listening. "This filly, she is fast on those legs," Asad said, stoking the Panther's interest. This would give him the perfect excuse not to trade Star, to take her back across the desert, where the Swan would ride off on her. "Imagine her speed and Storm's size and strength." The Panther stroked his beard. "Who will you wager on?" Asad lured him in. "Which of the mares you brought to trade are you willing to lose to me?"

"Honey," his father said. "That dun steppe mare of mine."

Asad went through the motions of thinking on it, and then nodded to his father.

"Deal," he said.

"Deal." His father slapped Asad on the back. "See you at the festivities tonight, my son."

The Panther headed off for the bath and bed Asad had spoken of and would eventually get to, but not yet.

"Hold up," he told the Cheetah, who had turned to follow their father.

"Brother?"

"Wait awhile," Asad said. "Then come with me if you like."

"Where? To do what?"

"To speak with the Swan and the Dove."

"Let us go." The Cheetah was already off his heels and starting for the stable's door.

Asad held a hand up. He and the Crab had spent last night in the stables, taking turns sleeping and keeping watch over Storm, and had caught the Falcon's man trying to feed the stallion a fig full of Dream Flower. How the Falcon thought drugging Storm would help him win, Asad did not know, for the pollution of a drunken sod had finished twentieth out of a field of twenty and one. "First I have a ring to collect from the Falcon."

"He is lucky that is all you are claiming from him for his attempt on Storm. Luckier still you kept it quiet."

"He is lucky I wanted the ring more."

"He won, he won, he won." The Fox's screeching could be heard clear out to the garden pool where Oona and Lyrra sat. "The Black Mane won for the third race in a row. My betrothed won."

"Apparently, the Black Mane won," Lyrra said with an impish grin that Oona was happy to see on her sister's face again. But then

Lyrra's grin disappeared as she stared over Oona's shoulder. "And he is here with the Cheetah."

Oona turned and stood as Asad stepped up to her, his teeth a slash of white in his dirt-streaked face.

"You do it," she said, and he dipped his head to her, his amber eyes holding hers, smiling into hers. "You win."

"I told you we would."

Oona did not know if it was she who swayed or him. All she knew was that he was suddenly close to her and that the scent of sweat and leather, horse and man, was more enticing than she could have imagined. A cough brought them both up short.

"I am Nasim," the Cheetah said to Lyrra.

"Lyrra," her sister answered, her voice barely above a whisper. "I am Lyrra."

The Cheetah dipped his head to her. "It is an honor to meet you, Lyrra, who sings sweet and mournful as the dove she is named for."

"You honor me, Cheetah."

"Nasim."

Lyrra's cheeks turned red as a ripe pomegranate, the most color Oona had seen in her sister's face these four moons past. "Nasim," she said.

Asad took Oona's hand, turned it palm up, and placed a ring in it. A ring of gold set with a ruby the size of a robin's egg. A ring Oona recognized.

"Is Falcon's?" She held her open palm out to him, the ruby shining blood red in the sun's light. "I can no take."

"Yes, you can. It was your warning that made me put a guard on Storm. We caught the Falcon's man trying to drug Storm last night, and this ring is the Falcon's payment for my silence. It will buy you many things on your journey."

Oona stared at the ring gleaming in the palm of her hand. Such a ring could buy them food, lodging, their very lives.

"Take it." Asad pressed his hands over hers, curling her fingers up and over the ring. "Say you will."

"I will." Oona's grin was as shaky as her legs.

"I am glad." He lifted her hand with the ring clasped inside and pressed his lips to the back of it, the warmth of the too-brief touch spreading from Oona's knuckles to her hairline.

"Not my green, you stupid bitch." Oona jumped back and made to pull her hand from Asad's as the Fox's shrill voice rent the garden's peace, but he held tight. "I will never wear green again. Bring me my new red. The Black Mane likes me in red."

Oona raised her brows to Asad, who narrowed his on hers.

"There is not a shade of red in this natural world," he said in an exaggerated whisper that made Oona giggle. He took both her hands in his, and his eyes were sunlit amber. "We should go," he said, and Oona meant to nod her head but shook it instead. His hands moved up her arms, big, warm, and strong, stopping before gently holding her shoulders as the Fox's incessant yap grew louder. "Sing to me at the feast tonight, Oona?"

This time Oona nodded.

Asad sucked in a deep breath at the first sight of Oona's legs, long, lean, and pale as moonbeams, flashing in and out of the panels of a skirt of pale green worm weave that bared a waist as lean, pale, and supple as her legs. The garment had a low-cut bodice of the same light green that cupped her taut, round breasts, and he let his breath out in a guttural groan as his gaze traveled up from her breasts to the ivory column of her throat to her mouth, whose full, rose petal-pink lips he had come close—too close—to kissing in the garden this afternoon.

He'd had kept himself away from her for the past eight days and nights while training for his sake as well as hers, making do with fleeting glimpses as she had served at meals, as ethereal and silent as a passing ghost.

Meeting her in the gardens today, basking in the warmth of her smile, smelling the sweet perfume of her skin, so cool to the eye and warm to his touch, had almost proved too much for his fraying control. And he needed to keep control to free her and her sister, not seduce her.

The sisters stopped at the stage and Oona's emerald eyes found his. The light in them lit a fire in his belly that had been simmering since he first saw her stepping out of the night's shadows on Summer's Eve.

He sat front and center to the stage, in the seat of honor, with his father to his right and his brother to his left, and he felt more than saw the Panther watching him. Forcing his gaze from Oona's, Asad turned to his father and held his victor's cup high.

"To the horsemen of the Great Valley," he toasted. "May their steeds carry them swift and sure to their journey's end."

"To the horsemen and their steeds," his father seconded.

"Swift and sure." The Cheetah held his cup up to Asad's with a wink. "To their journey's end."

This seemed to satisfy their father, who sat back and ogled the sisters with a hungry leer. Asad growled low in his throat, and even the Cheetah glared at the Panther. The Dove shifted on her stool and the Cheetah's head swiveled. He gave the Dove one of his quicksilver smiles that had charmed women from the age of two to two and sixty, and the Dove smiled in return, quick and shy and fleeting. The Panther's head shot up.

"Our father watches," Asad whispered into his brother's ear, his back to the Panther as he made a show of turning around and facing the women's table. Catching the Fox's eye, he dipped his head and grit his teeth as her high-pitched twitter clawed its way up his spine. He turned back around and nodded to the Panther, giving him something else to chew on besides the Cheetah and the Dove.

As victor of the race, it was Asad who would choose the songs to be sung tonight, all but the "Song of Gilgamesh," which was traditionally the last song of the night celebrating the race.

"'The Sailor's Tale,'" he told the Swan.

It was the first song he had ever heard her sing, and he had felt the vastness of the sea echoing in her voice that night, and had seen the fear in her eyes, as deep and dark as the waters she had sailed. But tonight, as she sang of sailing home in her enchanting desert tongue, her voice was strong and steady, and her eyes were shining, though her voice did catch at the end as she sang of the sailor's homecoming, and her eyes welled as she sang of him sitting at his home fire, his ever-faithful wife by his side.

Asad looked to the Cheetah as the applause died down. "Your choice, brother," he said.

"A song of fare-thee-wells," the Cheetah said with a solemn nod to the sisters.

The Swan stood silent and looked to the Dove.

"'Deep Peace,'" the Dove said.

The Swan tapped her foot, one, two, three times, and they began to sing together in a lilting desert tongue.

"Deep peace of the running wave to you,
Deep peace of the flowing air to you,
Deep peace of the quiet earth to you,
Deep peace of the warming hearth fire to you,
Deep peace of the shining stars to you,
Moon and stars pour their healing light on you,
Deep peace of everlasting love to you."

They sang it once more together, and then the Swan swayed gently to the music as the Dove sang it alone, her voice rising mournfully sweet over the still and silent courtyard.

The Cheetah sat staring gape-jawed at the Dove, whose cheeks grew round and red as applause broke out all around. The Panther was staring at the Dove as well, licking his lips and rubbing his hands together.

"The next song shall be your choice, Father," Asad said to the Panther, who puffed his chest out and gave his son an approving nod.

"A reel," the Panther called out.

The Dove plucked the harp's strings, and the Swan skipped, jumped, kicked, and twirled, her skirts swirling high around her long, lean dancer's legs as the Panther's and the Jackal's heads bobbed in time with her breasts.

While Asad appreciated the sight of her legs and breasts as much as any man, it galled him that other men, any other men, sat there watching and gawking. He had never before cared what man appreciated which woman, even if she had been one of his favorites for a time. But Oona the Swan was not any woman, not to Asad. She was a rare beauty true, any man could see that, but what Asad saw was that her mind was as sharp and fleet as her flying hands and feet, and her heart as sure and strong as the legs she twirled and leapt about on. He sat with his arms crossed tight against his chest as the Swan stomped her foot down and the Dove stilled her flying fingers.

Shouts and whistles filled the air.

"'The Wedding Song,'" the Raven called out without invitation from Asad.

He nodded his consent to the Swan.

"*Rithill Aill*," she said and dipped a knee to the Raven. Oona whispered something to the Dove that caused her to giggle, and then the Dove began to play and they began to sing.

"Welcome, gentlemen,
Welcome, and here's a health to you,
Tonight, there will be a wedding,
Tonight, she will be a maidservant,
The soldier is my darling."

They sang it together twice, and then the Swan sang it alone, her eyes never leaving Asad's.

"Welcome, gentlemen,
Welcome and here's health to you,
Tonight, there will be a wedding,
Tonight, she will be kind to him,
The prince is my darling."

Asad went as still and silent as stone as applause broke out from the women's table, the Swan's song, her words, flying round his head.

"Brother." His shoulder was jostled. "Black Mane, Asad." Dazed, he looked to the Cheetah. "It is your choice, brother. What song will you have?"

"'Somebody,'" he said, his gaze returning to Oona's as fire sought air to light, to flame, to burn. "I will have 'Somebody.'"

"My prince," she bowed to him, and he sat as if smote, and it wasn't until she drew in breath to sing that he let his out.

"My heart is sore, I dare not tell,
My heart is sore for Somebody."

Asad closed his eyes and let her voice fill him.

"I would walk a winter's night
All for a sight of Somebody."

Opening his eyes, Asad met and held her emerald gaze, blazing bright with the same longing that twisted his gut and tightened his cock. He swallowed a groan and shifted in his seat, glad of his loose robe.

"Oh, I have wept many a day
For one that's banished far away,

I cannot sing and must not say
How sore I grieve for Somebody."

Her voice was as rich and smooth as aged wine, her words, her song a soothing balm to his red-hot anger at his father, and at the traditions of the tribes he was bound to uphold, traditions that would saddle him with the vixen Fox and separate him from Oona the Swan for the rest of his natural life.

"Oh, hey, for Somebody,
Oh, ooh, hey, for Somebody,
I would do, would I do not
All for the sake of Somebody."

Asad took a slow, deep breath in and then blew it out as he joined in on the applause. He dipped his chin to the Swan, which was all he dared do with the Panther's eyes boring a hole into the side of his head. But it was enough, the Swan's eyes smiled into his as she dipped a knee and then stepped back and stood with her head low and her hands folded, the good slave awaiting her master's command.

"To the Jackal." Asad raised his cup, his voice surprisingly steady. "Our gracious host, I give you the last song of the night, the 'Song of Gilgamesh.'"

Oona roused from sleep to a sharp rapping as the door to her chambers pushed open and the Sparrow poked her head inside.

"What time is?" Oona yawned and glanced at the closed shutters to the window where specks of sunlight peeked through the cracks.

"Daytime," the Sparrow said. "High noon to be exact, and high time to get out of your beds and into the bathing pool."

"The bathing pool?" Oona sat up in her sofa bed, stretching her arms over her head. The bathing pool was one of the few things she enjoyed about this dry, hot, desert city, but it was unusual to be sent there so early in the day. "Now?"

"You are to be bathed and oiled and serving supper before the sun sets. The Fox's dowry is to be announced tonight."

And Oona and Lyrra would be the first gifted.

The bathing pool in the women's quarters was as big as the entire bedchamber Oona and Lyrra shared. It had been dug out of the earth and bricked with tiles of white and blue that also made up the floor. There were stacks of drying linens in one corner beside a table covered with vials of tinctures and oils, and a slab of onyx sanded and polished and propped on the table beside a candle so that a person could see their own reflection in it.

There were pots full of the candle wax that the women here heated and smeared onto their legs and then let cool and pull off along with their leg hairs. Oona had watched them do this many times, and they would scream and curse every time they did it, a thing she could not understand at all, but then her legs and arms were covered with a down so fine and pale as to be naked to the eye, another thing that added to her strangeness here.

Floating on her back, Oona stared up at the ceiling of mosaic tile worked into the image of a pond with fish of white and gold swimming among green padded water lilies with flowers of white, yellow, and purple in full bloom. She floated there in a city a moon's sailing from her home, soon to be slave to a man who intended to take her even farther away, and all she could think of was his son, who vowed to get her free and smiled at her with amber eyes that melted her insides.

She rolled onto her belly and let her legs sink to her knees, keeping her arms out and floating chin deep.

"I canna believe I called him my prince, my darling," she told Lyrra, who stood lathering her hair.

"I canna believe it either, and in front of the Panther like you did. You are lucky he didna hear you."

"Oh, the Panther heard me." Oona shivered at how the Panther's black leer had been fixed on her legs and her breasts. "But he didna listen."

"The Black Mane listened keenly enough," Lyrra said. "I swear I could hear his breath leave him." She lowered herself into the water and dipped her head under, and then she stood and shook the water from her hair, spraying Oona and grinning. "Like yours has left you."

Oona opened her mouth to belie her sister's words, but she spoke the truth. The thought of Asad the Black Mane took Oona's breath.

"Oh, *piuthar*." Lyrra eyed Oona. "I've ne'er seen you like this."

Oona shrugged and shook her head with a grin the village idiot would have been proud of when the Fox's shrill voice rang out in the tiled chamber.

"What is that I hear, Mother?" she yapped. "Is that a slave speaking in a forbidden tongue?"

Oona and Lyrra both froze, Oona chin deep, her pale angular body that was so disgusting to these women hidden beneath the water, but poor Lyrra stood only waist deep.

"What were you saying, slave?" the Fox demanded, her sharp eyes beading on Lyrra.

"Answer my daughter, Dove." The Raven's gaze raked her.

Oona stood, hoping the Raven would not take offense to her answering for Lyrra. "We say, mistress, what great dowry you daughter bring to her marriage. How honored we be part of it."

Oona dipped her knee and her head, and Lyrra quickly did the same, which looked to smooth the Raven's ruffled feathers as she eyed them down the length of her haughty beak. She plunked herself down at the table of oils, sniffing at one as the Fox plopped down beside her. Oona looked to Lyrra. They were under orders to be oiled for the night, but she did not think the Raven would respond kindly to any request to vacate the table.

Walking past the Fox soaking wet and naked was not a thing Oona wanted to do either, but she could see no other way. They made it as far as the table of drying linens when the Fox drew in her breath and puffed out her considerable chest.

"My brother tells me the men went to Father's pleasure house last night to continue their celebration of the Black Mane's victory," she said loudly, her voice echoing in the chamber, and in Oona's head. "He said my future husband picked the Shell for the night, a soft, round, curvaceous woman, and that the Shell was looking pleased with herself this morning after the Black Mane left."

Oona's drying linen hung midair and her belly dropped to her feet.

"This bodes well for you, my pet." The Raven patted her daughter's plump arm. "A man who can please a woman, well, that is always a good thing. And if that man is your husband, then so much the better."

Oona held the linen to her flaming cheeks. How could the Fox and her mother be pleased that the Black Mane had gone to another woman, had lain with another woman, when it knocked the breath from her?

"What are you looking so flushed for, Swan?" The Fox grinned slyly as she stood and sidled over to Oona, who hung her head and said nothing. "Perhaps you are thinking of how the Black Mane pleasures you when you sneak off to meet him."

Oona snapped her head up. "I, no…he never."

The Fox whipped her hand up and out and Oona could have easily stepped back and avoided the swipe, but she knew enough to stand firm and take the slap full on her cheek. She heard the crack before she felt the sting, and her eyes filled with hot tears.

"Get out of my sight, you pasty stick of a whore."

Oona grabbed her short brown work tunic and thrust it over her head and yanked it down over her hips. Keeping her head down, she turned and strode away from the only woman she had ever truly despised, and walked out of the bathing chambers, Lyrra running to catch up to her.

"Swan?" Lyrra cried, stopping at the corridor to their room.

"Go on," Oona said over her shoulder, barely breaking stride. "I be fine."

The garden gate slammed shut and Oona the Swan strode up to the lily pond, her knee-length work tunic soaked to the waist by her dripping wet hair and plastered to her lithe curves. Her fists clenched and unclenched at her sides, and her jaw jutted forward, yet even angry as she clearly was, she moved with an innate grace that pulled at Asad's loins. She stood glaring down into the pond's still waters and then threw her head back, thrust her chest out, and flung her arms wide.

"Do not fly away, Swan," Asad said, stepping out from the bushes. Her eyes flew open. "Not yet."

She turned her face from his as he stood before her, and would not meet his gaze.

"Oona?" He cupped her chin and turned her face to his, growling deep in his throat at the red welt covering her right cheek. "Who did this to you?"

"Fox."

Asad growled louder. "That sinister-handed bitch."

"I...I think she know about us." Her eyes were wide and her voice hushed.

"Tell me what happened."

"Fox and Raven, they come into bathing chamber when Dove and I there. The Fox, she talk of how men go to Jackal's pleasure house last night, she say..." Oona hesitated, and then she took a deep breath and her words spilled out. "Say you take pleasure woman named Shell, that Shell look well pleased this morning. Then Raven say a man who can please a woman is good, and tell Fox if that man is husband, even better. That when Fox look at me, see my cheeks like this." She flicked her fingers at her cheeks, the right now only slightly redder than the left. "She say to me, why you flush, Swan, perhaps you think of Black Mane, of how he please you when you sneak off to meet him. I tell her you...we...never."

Asad let out a slow breath. The Fox knew nothing other than her own jealous nature.

"That when she slap me," Oona said.

Asad ground his teeth.

"I can explain about the Shell, Oona."

She turned her head away from him with one breath and then back toward him with the next, her chin high.

"I be in Jackal's household three moons now," she said. "I know how is with men and pleasure women. You no need explain."

"But I want to explain," he told her. And it was true. He did not have to. He was a man, a prince, yet he wanted to, to her.

Oona blinked and sniffed and crossed her arms across her chest. "I listen."

"It is true that I went with the other men to the pleasure house after the feast last night. It was expected, what I would have done any other time, but you know that." Oona bit her lower lip and nodded. "But last night I went and I chose the Shell, an older woman of the Jackal's pleasure house with no great love for him who gives a good rubdown and knows how to keep a secret and always has a wagering debt." He reached into the pocket of his tunic. "She had this ring I remembered. A ring I had always thought beautiful." He pulled out an oval of swirling blues and greens and silvers set on a silver band and twirled it in his fingers. "Do you like it?"

"It is, as you say, beautiful. It is colors of sea. Colors that move like sea."

"It came here from the sea, like you. It is called abalone." He held the ring out to her. "When you are safe away from the Jackal and the Panther, will you wear this ring for me, Oona, to remember me by?"

Eyes as big and round and wet as mossy river rocks smiled into his.

"I will," she said.

He took her hand in his and slid the ring onto her marriage finger, surprising her no less than himself. Surprised at how right it felt, and fit.

"You will hear and see many things of me in the next days," he told her. "Things meant to throw my father and the Fox and the rest of the cursed pack of seven off my scent." He lifted her hand with the ring shining in the sunlight and pressed his lips to her knuckles, breathing in the clean scent of soap. "But I am here now, and I, Asad, am telling you, Oona, that I want you as a man wants a woman, though I am honor bound to keep you a maid."

Oona's hand trembled in his as she lifted it and laid her good cheek to his knuckles.

"You my prince." She turned her cheek and pressed her full, soft lips to his hand. "You my somebody," she whispered fiercely. "This I, Oona, tell you, Asad."

His mouth followed her whisper, taking her breath from her lips. She tasted of cool, fresh air and then warm, wet heat as her full, lush lips parted slightly. He twined one hand through her wet hair and ran the other down her leanly muscled back to the soft swell of her hips. Cupping the firm roundness of her backside, he pressed her to him from forehead to knees, his manhood hardening against the taut warmth of her belly.

He felt her breath catch, her belly suck in, and he pressed her closer, nipping his teeth along the smooth skin of her jawline, plying feather kisses across her lips, gently probing the wet, welcoming heat of her mouth with his tongue. She tasted as sweet as honey, and as earthy as woman, and when she moaned deep in her throat, the tip of her tongue shyly touching his, he groaned down to his molten core.

Asad had kissed and been kissed by pleasure women in all seven kingdoms of the tribes, yet none of them, trained and skilled as they were in the carnal arts, inflamed his passions as hotly as Oona's tentative, guileless kiss. Perhaps it was because she was unschooled, because it was she, Oona, responding to him, and her body could no more lie to his than she could to him.

His own body responded with a heat and an urgency that had his manhood throbbing against the stays of his loincloth and his heart hammering in his chest. He took hold of her upper arms and stepped back from her, his cock growing to fill the space between them even as she leaned in to close it.

"Oona." He pressed his forehead to hers, caging his beast, his breath racing. He would go no further. Not with her. Duty forbade it. Honor forbade him. If the Panther even suspected they had kissed he would flay the skin from her back, and if she were found to be no longer a maid before Asad could get her away, the Panther would whip her to death. "As much as I wish otherwise, I cannot. We cannot."

"I know." She was breathing as fast as he as she pressed the tip of her nose to his, and then she turned and walked away from him, leaving him holding air.

CHAPTER 5

The Desert

Oona kept her gaze down and her good cheek to both the Jackal and the Panther while serving their supper that night, the tender swelling on her other cheek hidden beneath a layer of white powder courtesy of the Sparrow. Oona never thought she would be grateful that some men seldom looked above her chest, but it kept her cheek unnoticed as she continued to fill their cups, and tried not to look the Black Mane's way too often.

Oona had been kissed once before, by Beorne when he had been sure she would be made to marry him, but it had been nothing like Asad's kiss. Beorne's had been coarse and sloppy, and his embrace rough, a man demanding his due without a care for the woman. Asad's kiss had been a give and take of breath, warm, wet lips and deliciously tantalizing tongues, a coursing of blood through her veins, a surging of heat everywhere his big, strong hands had touched her, roiling her woman's core until she actually ached. And by the stiff staff of manly heat that had been pressing into her belly, she knew that Asad had ached as well.

Where that ache, that kiss would have led to had Asad not broken it off, Oona was not exactly sure, and though every part of her wanted to find out, to ease that ache with him, she understood why it would not be wise to do so. Even discounting what would happen to her should the Panther find out, she would be a fool to attempt fleeing into the desert and back across the sea with a growing babe in her belly. And if she and Lyrra did make it home, what man would marry her if she were no longer a maid, much less carrying another man's child?

What other man could make her melt as Asad did?

His words, the tensile memory of his hands, his kiss, his fire, put her in such a dream-like state that she had to remember to react at the feast later that night, to let her fear show when it was announced that the Swan and the Dove were the first of the Fox's dowry gifts, else the Panther become suspicious.

The next morning Oona woke with her moon flow and was excused from serving until her flow stopped, not for her comfort, but for her masters, who considered a woman bleeding to be unclean. That night after supper the Sparrow was at her chamber door.

"I told the Black Mane it was naught but your moon flow," she told a red-faced Oona. In her land a woman was not considered unclean, but neither was it talked about outside of the women in a house. "But he insisted I make sure you are well. I think he was worried the Fox had marked your other cheek."

"Tell him I be fine," Oona said, pressing her palms to her flaming cheeks. It was actually quite good timing, for her moon flow would be over by the time they left the Jackal's for the Panther's. Lyrra's had not come since the day the pirates had taken them prisoner, though she was still a maid. It was as if her body had withered and dried with fear.

"Tell him yourself, tomorrow, high noon in the garden."

Oona beamed. "Tell him I be there."

"Tell him this, tell him that," the Sparrow squawked. "Do I look like your own personal messenger?"

Oona threw her arms around the Sparrow's bird-thin shoulders and hugged her tight.

"You look like best and truest of friends, Sparrow."

Oona walked up the garden path in her plain work tunic of brown linen, her white-blonde hair falling like a veil of worm weave down to the middle of her back, her big, round eyes shining bright in the oval of her face. Mesmerized by the lithe length of her legs and the natural grace of her stride, Asad shook himself and reached out and pulled her to him her first step around the hedge, burying his nose into her hair and breathing her in.

"I am glad you were able to come." He nuzzled her ear and she shivered. Stepping back, he studied the slight puffiness beneath her eye. "You are well? The Fox has left you alone?"

"I am well. Fox only slap me with her words."

"What words?"

She shrugged and looked away from him.

"Oona, what words?"

"Fox brag of you nights with pleasure women, and complain of you days with horses."

"Does she now?"

Oona sniffed and nodded and still would not look at him.

"And what do you think?"

Oona toed the ground with her sandal. "I think she have it backwards."

"Which is why I am here with you and not her," he said, smiling slowly as she finally met his gaze. Asad leaned closer, swimming in a sea of mossy green, and then he shook himself and stepped back. "I want you and the Dove to each tear an arm's length of hem from your work tunics and to wear these strips close to your body for a day, then give them to the Sparrow. The Cheetah and I will braid them into Star's and Song's bridles."

"So they smell us, know us?"

"Exactly."

She was as quick-witted as she was swift-footed, as rare and beautiful a jewel as her emerald eyes. Asad pulled her to him and held her tight. Her body melted into his, her head tucked under his chin, her arms encircling his waist, a perfect fit. He buried his nose into her hair to keep his mouth from seeking hers, though he wanted nothing more than to kiss her again, to taste her honeyed lips and feel her body meld with his.

Her kiss, the feel of her in his arms, had haunted his every waking moment, and he hadn't fared much better asleep, waking with an iron rod between his legs as the sun rose this morning.

"We should not meet again as Oona and Asad." He spoke into her hair and her body stiffened. "My father has been nosing around again, asking my manservant about my comings and goings." She lifted worried eyes to his, and Asad gave her a reassuring smile. "Do not worry, my jewel. My manservant, the Crab, tells the Panther that the Black Mane carouses all night with the Jackal's pleasure women, sleeps all morning, and spends all afternoon at the stables."

"Panther believe this?"

"So far, but still he watches me, and you. I will not chance my father finding us out. He would mark you, or worse. Do you understand?"

Oona nodded. "Sparrow tell us, if Panther catch us, he whip us."

"He would try."

Her head tilted at the low growl in his voice.

"You would stop him," she said and shook her head. "I no be reason father and son, king and prince, come to blows." She ran her hand along the length of his jaw, her fingers curling through his beard, and Asad half groaned, half purred. "I will miss you, Asad, Black Mane, poet prince of Great Valley, freer of Swans and Doves. Lion four times through."

"And I will miss you, Oona the Swan, my green-eyed jewel." He pressed his hand over hers, rubbing his cheek into her palm and placing a chaste kiss there. "You will sing to me, at the Leaving Feast, one last time?"

"I sing 'Somebody' to you, my lion. Only to you."

Asad tore a strip of dried meat with his teeth and chewed it over and over, getting sustenance and salt, and the chance to gnaw on something, anything, other than his father and his future wife.

"I be forbidden."

Those had been the last words spoken by the Swan to the Black Mane, her answer to his request to sing "Somebody" two nights ago at the Leaving Feast.

Asad had barely spoken to anybody but the Cheetah or the Crab since, and then only to answer with nods, shrugs, or curt, one-word answers as they rode east into the desert. The Panther left his son alone, and the Fox was easy enough to stay away from. He rode with his back to her and spread his bedroll as far as he could get from hers, and she, showing uncommon sense for once, left him alone as well.

"The Panther warned the Fox to keep her distance," the Cheetah told Asad when he finally unclenched his jaw and spoke of it to his brother on the third day of their journey home. Tonight, he and the Cheetah would drug the camp and set the Swan and the Dove free. Glad as he was that he could do this for the sisters, for Oona, he could not help but worry for their safety, two women alone and on the run in the desert. And he could not be accountable for his temper once she was gone. "Fortunately for you, the Fox has taken his advice."

"That is the least our father could do for saddling me with the twit," Asad growled. "Can you imagine how it will grieve my mother, knowing a woman such as the Fox will be queen to her city one day?"

"She will not be happy," Nasim agreed.

"No, she will not." Asad ran a hand through his beard, a poor substitute for the Swan's slender fingers. He rubbed his jaw, sore from being clamped tight the past two days. "Yet she will do as she should, she will welcome her daughter into her home and try to teach her to be queen, may the gods help her. She will need each and every one on her side."

Four tribes had set out together from the Jackal's home city, but this morning the Cobra and his company had taken the road leading south and west, and the Bull's would be turning south after they reached the oasis two days east. The Heron's company was to travel with them another two days before turning northeast, and tonight the Swan and the Dove would ride north and west.

"How far to the oasis?" he asked the Cheetah, though he knew as well as his brother.

"We should reach it after high noon," the Cheetah answered him anyway.

Asad glanced up at the sun reaching its noon zenith and fought the urge to turn around in his saddle and gaze back along the line of horses to seek out the Swan's pale head. He would have to wait until they made the oasis to see her, and to speak with the Crab, who he had charged to keep an eye on her this journey.

"Oona?"

Oona lifted her throbbing head and turned toward her sister's voice, which sounded thin and reedy and far away.

"Are you ill?"

"I am fine.

"You dunna look fine."

Oona forced the slits of her eyes to widen and focus on Lyrra's face, but it swam before her in the blinding light of the relentless sun. She raised a shaky arm up to shade her aching head and shuddered as goose bumps prickled from the top of her head down to her toes.

"'Tis this cursed desert sun." She licked her cracked lips with her dry tongue. "Once we make the oasis, water, I will feel better."

Lyrra's face bobbed toward her, and Oona swayed back on her horse.

"I will feel better when you can sit your horse without falling off," Lyrra said.

Oona grit her teeth. She felt as if she was back in the cursed inferno of the hot hole, but she would not give in to it. She could not. "We are three days out in the desert, one night from freedom, and I am still on my horse."

"You are sick."

"I can still ride, and I am not throwing up like you were with the seasickness."

"And you and Father didna miss a meal," Lyrra said. "Whilst I couldna so much as look at food."

Oona's belly lurched at the mere mention of food, but she gritted her teeth tighter.

"I will be fine," she said with the big sister voice Lyrra hated. "Now let me dream of cool shade and quenching water."

"Fine."

Oona closed her eyes and took a slow breath of dry, hot air that left her chest aching for a cool, brisk breeze. She let her head hang forward, moaning at the pull along the back of her neck, and tugged her scarf low over her brows as the desert people did, and while it kept the sun's glare from her eyes, it did nothing to lessen the heat. Rivulets of sweat trickled down her chest and pooled at her waist, where a dark, damp stain grew. She concentrated on her breathing, keeping it slow and steady, using her dancer's breath.

Her mind wandered from the relentless heat to the summer day ten years ago when she had jumped out of the old oak and landed wrong and broken her arm. Of how her father had held her shoulder and her grandfather had held her hand, telling her to breathe and blow like she was dancing a reel while they pulled and twisted until the bones had snapped back into place.

The breathing had helped, giving her something to think on besides her arm, keeping her from crying out with the pain, but the pain then had been nothing compared to the pain she felt every time she thought of her father and her grandfather now, of the last time she had seen either of them. At least her grandfather had been alive, waving farewell from the dock. Her father had been beaten bloody and senseless and tied to his ship's mast, more dead than alive.

Lifting her gaze beneath throbbing brows, Oona peered up the line of horses, past the seven men-at-arms the Panther traveled with, past the Fox and her trio of maidservants, to the Panther and his sons. As slaves of some value, she and Lyrra were above the horses in importance, which were above the cook and house servants, who were last in line. The Black Mane's manservant, the Crab, rode there. A moon-faced man of middle years with a balding pate, he had a habit of walking by Oona and Lyrra every time they dismounted or made camp, his quick brown eyes assessing hers before he made his way over to the Black Mane.

Oona's mount, though an easy-tempered gelding, felt hard as stone after two and a half days of constant riding. Her backside was either aching or numb, and a groan wracked her as she tried to straighten her back and lift her head high enough to see the back of Asad's red headscarf. Giving up the effort as the muscles and tendons around her spine tightened and clenched, she relaxed her jaw and slowly let her head hang and her shoulders slump, the fire of the sun scorching the back of her neck. She raised her hand to pull her scarf down, but her arm floated away from her and she tried to follow it with her blearing eyes.

"Oona?"

"Ly?"

She tried to lift her gaze to her sister's voice, but her body was already following her wayward arm.

"SWAN!"

Strange, Oona thought, Lyrra calling her Swan, and then she was floating through air for what seemed a long way. She hit something hard but giving, and a strange voice spoke in her ear.

"I have you, my lady Swan," the man said as Oona tried to focus on the voice's face.

She opened her mouth to ask who it was that had her, but her voice cracked like caked mud and her words were about as clear.

"My master will not be pleased about this," the somehow familiar voice said from far away, and then the air buzzed with a thousand bees and the sky went black.

"Sshhh, Swan." Asad pushed a damp lock of fine white-blonde hair from Oona's cheek and tipped a cup of cooled mint tea to her chapped lips. "Drink now, Swan." He dribbled the tea into her mouth and watched her swallow. "There you go, drink up."

He let her take three more swallows and then he exchanged the mint tea for a cup of salted water and tucked her tighter into his hold before putting the cup to her pursed lips, which puckered at the taste. She thrashed her head against his shoulder and he only managed to get about half of a swallow down her throat before having to reposition her for the next.

"Please, Oona," he whispered into her ear, though everyone but the guards were fast asleep. "You need to drink this. You need the salt."

She turned her head away from the cup and muttered words he did not understand into his tunic, and he sighed and changed the salted water for the mint tea.

"You are as stubborn as you are beautiful," he said as her nose twitched at the minty scent. He tipped the cup to her lips and shook his head as she drank greedily. "Well," he amended, cupping her firm backside in his hand and shifting her in his lap, her long legs dangling over his. "Almost as stubborn."

She murmured something and turned her head from the cup and settled into him, one hand tucked between them and the other resting on his chest, her head nestled beneath his chin, her breath tickling his skin. Asad swallowed hard and tasted his own gall as he glared over at his father, who slept soundly and without a care that he had kept this woman from him and given him the vixen Fox instead.

Asad rumbled deep and low in his chest and Oona stirred and pressed closer. Her brow furrowed and the hand resting on his chest clutched a handful of his tunic. He let his breath out slow and steady and ran his hand back through her hair, pushing it from her face and neck, a habit newly formed this night that he found he could not get enough of.

"Do not fret, Oona," he whispered into her hair. "I am here."

"Asad?"

Her voice was a cracked whisper and her hand fell from his tunic. He cupped her chin and lifted her head and gazed down into heavy-lidded eyes

"Aye, my jewel," he said, using her highland word, "it is I, Asad."

Her eyelids fluttered open, her gaze slowly focusing on his. She licked her lips.

"What happen?"

"You have the heat sickness," he told her. "You fell off your horse, but my man, the Crab, caught you before you hit ground."

She stared up at him with glazed eyes for a long moment and then her lids fluttered and closed.

"I remember," she said, slowly opening her eyes again. They focused much quicker on him this time. "The heat, the sun."

She shivered, and goose bumps rippled on her arms, though it was a warm summer night. Asad closed his arms around her, and her legs tucked in tighter.

"The sun is gone for now." He pushed an errant strand of hair from her cheek. "Our friend the moon is out and all the camp sleeps."

She turned her gaze to the night sky, slowly and with obvious effort, and took in her first full deep breath since she had fallen.

"Night good," she sighed. "Air good. Cool. Can breathe."

She coughed and Asad held the cup of mint tea to her lips.

"Drink this," he said.

She took a sip, and then she wrapped both hands around his and gulped the rest of the tea down.

"Is good," she said when she had drained the cup. "I like."

"I know." Asad set the empty cup down and lifted the cup of salted water. "This you do not like so much," he told her. "But I need you to drink it, all of it.

"What is?"

"Salted water."

Her nose crinkled up and Asad laughed softly as he put the cup into her hands.

"Drink it fast. It will not taste so bad that way."

She drank it down quickly and handed the empty cup back to him with a grimace.

"You lie," she said with a shudder. "It still taste so bad."

"I am sorry about that, but it will help your body heal, and keep you from breaking into the heat sweats."

"I will need drink more?"

"Not until tomorrow morning now that you have finally gotten a full cup down you."

"Tomorrow." She closed her eyes with a sigh, and then opened them wide. "But tonight is night we leave, yes?"

Asad shook his head. "No, not tonight. You are too sick to go anywhere tonight."

"Tomorrow night?"

"No. Not tomorrow night, or the night after, or any night until we get back to my home."

"But...you promise."

Asad hated the look of disappointment in her eyes, but he would have hated sending her out into the desert with the heat sickness even more. Once a person was stricken, it took less to strike them each time, and this was her second attack. The next could kill her.

"I promised to get you free of my father and on your way home," he told her. "And I will. But I will not send you off into the desert, sick and alone but for your sister."

"But—"

"Do not ask it of me, Oona." He was resolute. "I would be sending you to almost certain death."

She turned her head away from him, tears wetting her cheeks. Asad cupped her chin and turned her face to his.

"I will get you free of the Panther, you and the Dove. I swear it. But it will take longer than we planned."

Her eyes pooled, but she nodded. "Does Dove know?"

"She knows, and she understands. She saw what the heat sickness did to you, what it would do to you again, only worse."

"Worse?" Her voice cracked.

"I will explain more," Asad said as he slipped his arms under her legs and lifted her up from his lap and set her down on his bedroll. "But first, you need more tea."

"Tea." Oona dropped her arms from around his neck, unaware, he was sure, that she had even placed them there as he had moved her, or that the hairs at the back of his neck still stood on end where she had touched them. "Tea good."

"Yes," he said as he sat back on his knees and she lay down on his bedroll, her hair fanning out like moonlight. "Tea good."

Oona's head pounded and her neck kinked into her shoulders with a slicing pain that even slow, purposeful breaths could not ease. She rolled over onto her side and curled into air, missing the hard warmth that had been Asad even as it came to her how he had been holding her, cradled in his lap, her head resting on his shoulder. She followed her nose down into the blanket and burrowed into it, breathing in a newly familiar masculine musk that calmed her mind even as it made her heart beat faster.

The air around her stirred and she rolled her head and opened her eyes. Asad was crouching no more than three feet away, pouring steaming, minty tea from a cooking pot into a cup and then setting the pot back onto the glowing embers of a small fire. He caught her watching him and the corners of his mouth lifted and his eyes shone amber over the fire's coals.

He straightened and took one step toward her and then folded his legs up underneath him and sat down beside her in one cat-like motion without making a sound or spilling a drop.

"Your tea." He held the cup out to her.

Oona sat up and took the cup in both her hands, wrapping her fingers around its heat as she smiled over the cup's rim.

"What?" Asad cocked his head at her.

"Is you, prince, serving me, slave." She took a sip and felt its wet heat slake her dry throat and slide down to her belly and spread its calming warmth. "This can no be tradition."

"No." He reached out a hand and pushed a stray lock of her hair back behind her ear, and Oona leaned into his touch. "It is not tradition, prince serving slave, but I am also the only healer in our company, which is why my father had no choice but to let me tend you or lose you."

"Lose me?"

"People die from the heat sickness, Oona."

Oona had been much sicker this time than last. Even she knew that. She had thrown up what fluids she had not sweat out in the hot hole, but the world had not gone black for a day, nor had she been this weak.

"Which is why," Asad said, "if you do a bit of acting and pretend to still be sick for another day or two, I will still be able to tend to you."

"We can still talk like this?"

"We can sit and talk like this at night," Asad said, his teeth showing white in the dark. "And we can ride alongside each other during the day as well."

Coughing and touching the back of her limp hand to her forehead, Oona fluttered her eyelids and Asad chuckled.

"Well done, my beautiful actress."

Oona crossed her legs with slow deliberation, her hips popping and her knees creaking. She straightened her back, lifted her arms, and filled her chest with air, and then she leaned forward and let her breath out as she lowered her hands to the ground in front of her, her shoulders to her knees, her head hanging down between them, taking in slow, steady breaths as the tendons and sinews in her neck and shoulders and back eased their grip. She rolled her head first one way and then the other and startled as big, warm hands splayed across her back between her shoulders. Strong fingers kneaded the knot that was the fulcrum of pain radiating up and down her spine and across her shoulders.

Oona sighed. "Aahh."

He kneeled behind her and took the knot between his thumbs and pressed deep. "What was that, Swan?"

"Ooohhh." Oona's head lolled and Asad chuckled. He fanned his hands out over her shoulders, and his thumbs pushed in and kneaded their way down her spine as his fingers moved with a tensile heat down her back

"Uuuunnnn." Oona stretched forward and licked her lips to keep from drooling. His hands slid down and cupped her buttocks. His big, warm, cat's paws began to knead and Oona purred. "Mmmmmmmm."

The kneading stopped, and where Oona had felt Asad's heat she felt only night air.

Asad sat back on his heels, his hands on his thighs, fighting the urge to lie along Oona's back and tuck her into him, to taste the skin of her neck and feel her move against him as he rubbed his engorging cock up and down her backside.

"I ah, I need to ah…" He stood and turned his back to the sight of hers, because looking only made the hardness he was trying to hide from her worse. "I will be back," he said over his shoulder. "Finish your tea."

He strode over to the horses and checked the tie lines.

"If I stay away long enough, perhaps she will fall back asleep," he muttered to Storm, who snorted and blew into Asad's face. "But then I will not be able to talk with your new mistress," he told Star. "And our time is limited." He moved to Cloud Dancer and ran his hand along the arch of her dappled neck. "Trouble is," he confided to the filly, "as much as my head enjoys the talking, my body seems to have ideas of its own."

When he had finally talked himself down, he returned to find her curled up on her side, her knees tucked up to her chest, forehead to her knees, eyes closed, her chest rising and falling, slow and steady. He stood staring down at her, torn between relief and disappointment, when her eyes fluttered open. Craning her head, she reached out and touched the scar on the top of his sandaled foot.

"Lion hurt paw?" Her fingers traced the rough contours of his scar, sending a shiver of torturous delight up his leg to his eager cock.

"Aye," he said, and saw her smile at her word.

"How?" She pushed herself up so that she sat on one hip and unfolded her long legs. "Tell me, please, Asad. Sit and talk with me while night last."

Asad nodded, not trusting his voice quite yet, and as he began to lower himself down onto the ground beside her, she scooted over on the bedroll and made room for him. Asad hesitated, and then berated himself. What she needed now was a healer, a friend, an honorable man, not some rutting beast.

"You heal fast," he told her, shifting onto the bedroll beside her. "Most people struck as hard as you remain ill for days."

"I have good healer," she said, and though she smiled, her voice was hoarse and her eyes were bleary.

"And your healer is telling you not to push yourself. In fact, your healer is telling you to lie back down, rest your head, and close your eyes. Sleep."

"I will lie." She stretched out on her side facing him. "But I no sleep. We will talk?" Her voice cracked and she coughed and held her belly with one hand and her head with the other.

"I will talk." Asad stretched out on his side facing her, his head propped on his hand. "You will rest."

"I rest. I listen," she said with a weary smile. "I like listen to you voice in the night."

Asad went instantly still but for the tug at his chest and the twist of his gut.

"You have pain, Asad?"

"A little." He took a deep breath and blew it out with a shake of his head and a half laugh, half growl. "Now then, my jewel, what would you like to hear me talk to you of?"

"You scar. You promise tell me."

"So I did."

Oona lay her head down with a sigh and Asad laid his down so that they were eye to eye, and tried to concentrate on his tale rather than her nearness.

"The summer of my eighth year, the Cheetah and I went on a hunting trip with our father. We were camped at a mountain lake, a beautiful place of clear water and green grass with snow still on the mountain peak. One morning we started racing and wrestling around and I stepped into the fire pit and a coal that was still burning fell into my boot."

Oona cringed.

"My father washed and wrapped my foot and we continued our hunting and by the time we returned home my foot was infected and so swollen I could barely walk. My mother was furious at my father, which was nothing new. The palace physician healed my foot over the course of a moon, and began my lessons in the healing arts, which have lasted to this day."

"Prince, poet, and healer," Oona said. "I impressed."

"My father was not. He thought it below my station as prince to practice such skills, until he got his head split open in battle two summers ago and I sewed it back up."

"You sew his head?"

"I did. The Cheetah says I sewed it too tight though because the Panther has been even more short-tempered since."

Oona giggled, sweet and melodious as water trickling over river rock.

"I like hearing you laugh," Asad said.

"I glad."

"What of you?" He reached out a hand and pushed back a lock of her hair, trailing his thumb over the soft, round apple of her cheek. "What childhood injuries did you incur running across fields and climbing trees?"

"I break arm," she told him, lifting her left arm. "The autumn I have ten years, I jump out of tree and land wrong. My father hold my shoulder, my grandfather hold my wrist, and they pull and set bones right again. My arm be in sling for three moons."

"A swan with a broken wing." Asad ran his hand down the slender length of her arm.

"Lion with burn paw." Oona twined her fingers through his.

"We are a quite a pair, are we not?"

"Aye," she said with a sad smile. "We a pair."

Asad pressed her hand to his lips, drinking in the bittersweet tonic of her smile.

"Tell me of you family," she said. "You mother, you sister."

"My mother," he said, rubbing the pad of his thumb over the backs of her knuckles. "My mother was the eldest daughter of the Lynx, King of the Northern Steppes, and she was married off to the Panther, eldest son of the Tiger, when she was ten and seven and he was twenty and one."

"She was glad to marry Panther?"

"No." He stilled his thumb. "She was in love with another, and he with her, but her father was more interested in strengthening his ties with the Tiger's tribe than he was with his daughter's feelings."

"And she would do her duty," Oona said softly. "As will you."

"As will I." He lifted their hands in a bitter toast. "And my marriage to the Fox will no doubt be as happy as my parents' has been."

"What happen to other man you mother love?"

"He did his duty and married another as well. He died last summer, and their eldest son, the Oryx, sat at the king's table for the first time at the Feast of Summer's Eve."

"I see him. He be youngest at king's table. I see Panther talk to all but him."

"You saw that?

"Aye."

"You see much then."

"Is my gift, so my grandfather say."

"You have the eyes for it." He smiled into those eyes, deep and reflective as a mossy pool.

"Tell me of you sister, Rasha, the Gazelle, who be ten and three," she said, and he chuckled.

"You remember as well as you see."

"I remember every word spoken between us," she said, her simple declaration striking Asad dumb. "I never forget."

"Nor will I," Asad said when he could speak again. "Not the sound of your voice, the look of your eyes, or the feel of your skin." He trailed his fingertips up her wrist, her arm, along the finely winged ridge of her collarbone. "You are a rare jewel, Oona the Swan. A jewel I burn to claim."

"You sister?" she squeaked.

Asad dropped his hand.

"My sister the Gazelle is the seventh daughter of the Panther and my only full sibling. She was born under the Twins to a mother and brother who love her dearly and a father who does not."

"Why he not?"

"He does not believe she is his." Oona's eyes widened and her mouth formed a delectable "oh." Asad blew out his breath and willed his cock to behave. "She is, of course," he said, his voice straining with the effort, "but he will not hear it. He does not want to hear it. He would rather believe our mother was unfaithful."

"With Oryx father?"

Asad nodded.

"Was…" she hesitated, "was it Gazelle heart Panther squeeze dry?"

"You truly do not miss much, do you." It was more statement than question. And truth be told it was one of many things Asad admired about Oona, how she watched and saw and remembered things about others, how she paid attention to their ways, and wants and needs, not simply her own. As she surely realized, he had not answered her question, nor did she push him for an answer.

"You say she like to ride Star, you sister?" she asked instead.

"She does. I gave her Star's last foal for her own, but the filly is barely two and still needs to be broken. I will be training her and Cloud Dancer this summer."

"She be good rider, like you?"

"She is."

"She be lucky to have brother such as you."

"A brother does not make up for a father. Or from being seventh daughter and worth only what marriage can bring to her tribe."

"But she only ten and three. Surely she no marry so soon?"

"She will be ten and six before the next meeting of the tribes," he explained. "She will be of age then, as will the Cheetah."

"How old you are?"

"I will be twenty and four come the Lion's moon," he told her. "That is how I escaped marriage the last meeting of the tribes. I was two moons too young, which angered my father no end. But the Jackal was so kind as to keep his daughter unbound until I was of age."

"Be there another you wish marry last meeting?"

"No," Asad assured her. "There was not. There never has been." *Until now. Until you.*

The corners of her lips twitched up, full, soft, warm lips that he longed to kiss again, and then her shy smile grew into a yawn.

"You should sleep now."

"No," Oona protested as another, deeper yawn overtook her. "No yet."

"You are exhausted. And as your healer I am ordering you to sleep."

"You will stay with me?" she asked him. "Until I sleep?"

"I will."

He pulled the blanket up over her shoulder and Oona burrowed into it, closing her eyes with a weary sigh.

"Sleep, Oona," Asad murmured, running his fingers back through the moonlit veil of her hair. "You are safe here with me."

"I home," she said, her voice a drowsy whisper, "with you."

CHAPTER 6

Burning

Asad was still awake when the desert sky turned from black to gray. He had not so much as closed his eyes with Oona lying next to him, but had lain there studying every line, every curve of her body, every plane and angle of her face, every pore of her alabaster skin, the arch of her flaxen brows, the fringes of her sooty lashes. It had been a strange thing to watch her sleep, so peaceful and guileless and sure of his protection, to lie there and match his breath to hers, to feel her without touching her. A strange and wonderful and torturous thing, her words, "I home with you," a constant, bittersweet echo.

The watch came in, and with a half moan, half growl Asad rolled away from Oona. He stood and ran his hands back through his hair, facing the southern steppes that meant the end of desert heat and sand. Tonight, they would camp at the base of the steppes, and tomorrow they would cross over them and onto the grassy plains of the Great Valley.

"How fares the Swan, brother?"

The Cheetah was standing behind him, speaking to him, but he was gazing down at the Dove, who slept on the bedroll next to the Swan's.

"She sleeps," Asad stated the obvious to his oblivious brother.

"That is good."

"Aye," Asad said, using the sisters' word. His brother looked up. "So, you are paying attention to something other than the Dove."

"I am paying attention enough to know there was a long conversation between kings last night, and that the Bull's company will not be turning south today," Nasim said. "Nor will the Heron's be turning north after we cross the steppes. Both will continue east with us."

"Did you find out why?" Asad asked. The Heron, King of the Marsh Lands, and the Bull, King of the Eastern Plains, were the only two kings above the Panther in age and rank in the tribes' hierarchy, and though the tribes traded and visited among each other all the time, not only at the meetings every third summer, it was strange that they had not mentioned traveling on to the Great Valley before, that they had kept it a secret from the other kings.

"No, it was a conversation among kings only."

"We will surely find out soon enough," Asad said. Their father was not a man to keep secrets for long. "In the meantime, I was about to wake the Dove so she could wake the Swan."

"Lucky dog," the Cheetah grumbled.

He was jealous because Asad had let the Dove help him settle the Swan last night, because Asad had spoken with her when the Cheetah could not, not without raising their father's ire.

Asad had found the Dove to be a good listener, quick to do as he asked, tougher and smarter than her delicate appearance suggested. She looked him in the eyes when they spoke, as the Swan did, a custom of their people no doubt, a custom Asad found he much preferred to the downcast eyes of the women of the desert tribes.

"Do not envy me over much, brother," Asad said. "The more you know her, the more you will miss when she is gone."

"This torch you carry for the Swan, it burns?"

"At both ends."

The Cheetah clapped Asad on the shoulder. "You had better douse it for now. The Panther approaches."

"Wake up, Swan."

"Ly?" Oona focused her bleary eyes on her sister's hovering face, her foggy mind trying to make sense of the strange words her sister spoke, words she understood. "Where?" Her voice cracked and her throat was parched and her mouth tasted of dirt. She tried to lift her head, but it was too heavy and started to pound. "What happened?"

"We be in desert halfway between Jackal's and Panther's," Lyrra said in the strange tongue, the desert tongue. "You have heat sickness."

Oona closed her eyes against the pounding in her head.

"I remember," she said in the same tongue. Addled as her brain was, she knew there must be a reason Lyrra spoke to her in it. "Black Mane?" she croaked as the morning's fog lifted from her mind and the night's memories became clearer.

"It was Black Mane who care for you," Lyrra said. She ran a cool, wet cloth over Oona's throbbing forehead and cracked lips and whispered in their native tongue. "There was nothing to be done for you that wasna done by his hand, Oo. He rode with you cradled in his lap like a rag doll, growling off any who dared get too close. It was he who let me wake you this morning, he who wants me to remind you not to seem too well too soon. He watches us now, as does his brother and father."

The wet cloth disappeared and Lyrra sat back on her knees. Raising a shaky hand to her forehead, Oona made a show of shading her eyes from the dawn's brightening sky.

"Water," she croaked as Lyrra helped her sit up. "I need drink."

"Here," a deep, familiar voice said as a tawny hand with long, broad fingers held out a steaming cup to her. "Drink this."

Oona breathed in the minty steam and took a sip and then another as the tea wet her throat and eased her belly.

"Thank you, Prince Black Mane."

He crouched down in front of her and she dropped her gaze from the flexed muscles of his thighs to the high arches of his sandaled feet. He reached out a corded forearm and cupped her chin with his hand and lifted her face to his, his thumb playing along the line of her jaw. Amber eyes searched hers, and Oona caught her breath at the play of light in them.

"So," the Panther's voice barked from somewhere behind his golden-eyed son. "How is my slave?"

"She lives." The Black Mane gently turned Oona's head from side to side. He took her face into both of his big cat's paws and ran his thumbs across her brows as his fingers pushed back through her sweat-plastered hair and down along the back of her neck. "The fever has left her eyes," he said. "But not her body." He pressed his fingers into the knot of pain where her neck met her shoulders and Oona winced. "She is not out of danger yet." There was real concern in his eyes as they held Oona's.

"See to her then," the Panther ordered as he strode off grumbling about pale-skinned, weak-blooded northerners.

"That was my intention," the Black Mane said with a quick smile at Oona. His hands cupped her elbows. "Can you stand, Swan?"

She grasped onto his forearms. "I try."

He stood in one sure motion, pulling her up with him, and she clung to him as her vision swam before her and her legs quaked beneath her.

"Swan?"

"I be all right," she said with a smile as shaky as her legs. "I need find my feet."

"Hold on as long as you need to." His voice was as strong and steady as his hold on her. "I am in no hurry to let go of you."

"But Panther." Oona gripped her belly muscles and slowly straightened, trying hard not to lean into the broad expanse of Asad's chest. "He watch."

"Let him. All he will see is his son the healer tending to his sickly slave, not Asad with Oona. He is blind to what he does not want to see."

"What is this?" A high-pitched shriek rent the dawn, and both Oona and Asad stiffened. "Must I witness another day of my betrothed pawing at his pale-faced pet?"

"Unfortunately, the Fox does not suffer from the same blindness," Asad said with a wry grin that made Oona giggle. He went stone still, his eyes piercing hers, and then he coughed and gave her arms a squeeze before letting go his hold of one. "Here, Dove." He turned Oona toward her sister, who stood with a sly smile on her face watching the Fox humph off. "Take the Swan over to the stand of palms and let me know if she passes water. If she does not, she will need to drink more salted water."

"No, not the gelding," Asad instructed the Crab as his man made for the packhorse Oona had fallen off the day before. "Saddle Star for the Swan."

"Star?"

"Yes, Star." Asad could trust the Crab with his plans to help the Swan and the Dove escape the Panther, but it would be better for the Crab if he did not know. Then he would not have to lie when the Panther questioned him, and he would. "Storm does not like the gelding, and I want the Swan riding beside me where I can keep an eye on her."

"Uh-huh."

"What do you mean by that?"

"I mean I am not the only one to notice how you keep your eyes on her. Be careful Black Mane, your father is no fool."

"Nor is his son."

"No," the Crab said with a shake of his balding pate. "He is not. In truth, sometimes he is too clever for his own good."

"Saddle Star."

The Panther accepted Asad's explanation for the Swan riding Star without question, and the only inclination that Oona gave of understanding what he had pulled off was the widening of her eyes as he helped her onto the mare whose bridle was lined with the hem of her tunic. If only there had been a way to get the Dove riding Wind Song, but he had not been able to come up with one, and had to settle with pointing her out to the Dove, who held her hand out to the mare in passing when they broke camp.

Asad split his time on the road watching the changing landscape as they left the desert sands for the southern steppes and observing Oona, admiring how easily her body adjusted to Star's gait, how her eyes took in everything around them, her nose twitching with the shifting wind. He thought of how her nose had wrinkled up at his threat of making her drink more salted water this morning, the closest she had come to complaining all day though he knew her head still throbbed and her body ached, unlike the Fox, whose incessant whining had plagued his ears from the time they had mounted up this morning. He could not help but compare the two, the one who had everything and was happy with nothing and the other who had nothing, yet smiled as sweet as a woman gifted with her heart's desire as a cooling breeze caressed her face.

"How do you feel, Swan?" he asked as he helped her down from Star when they stopped at noon, forcing himself to let go his hold of her slim waist as she found her feet.

"Better, my prince."

He cupped her chin with his hand and ran his thumb across a rosy cheek.

"The heat is gone from your skin," he said, and she nodded.

"The air here is no so hot, so dry." Her cool breath tickled his palm. "We gone from desert now?"

"We are," he said, his chest catching as she took a deep breath in and let it out with a happy sigh. He dropped his hand. "We have reached the southern steppes that separate the desert from the Great Valley, a place of cooling breezes and green grasses with the Great River running through it. Tomorrow night we will camp at one of the river's lesser tributaries and we will bathe in it before entering our city the next day."

Her big, green eyes widened. "We bathe?"

Asad chuckled. "Aye, Swan, we will all bathe."

The Panther was barking orders. This would be a quick break to eat and stretch only.

"Make sure you eat some flatbread and dates, Swan," he told her as his father's voice neared. "And drink plenty of water."

"Yes, my prince," she said with a dip of her head. "May I sit with Dove?"

"You may."

With her belly full for the first time in days, and her chest filling with the cooler air of the southern steppes, Oona settled into Star's easy gait with little more than a constant pull in her neck and a dull ache between her shoulders. By this time tomorrow they would be in the Great Valley, Asad's home, and Oona watched Asad's eyes grow brighter, his back straighter with each league they covered.

She should not have been watching him, not with the Panther riding in front of them and the Fox behind, but she could not seem to help it, not when she knew this would be her last day of riding beside him, her last chance of sneaking peeks at the high brow, broad nose, and square jaw of his profile. She sighed, for surely he was a man molded and carved by the hands of the gods themselves, a man whose heart was as true and strong as his form, a man she would never see nor know the likes of again.

"Swan?" Amber eyes stared into hers. Eyes she could not lie to even if she tried. "Are you well?"

"No," she said, and she was suddenly, ridiculously close to tears. She shook her head and swiped at her welling eyes. She had not cried since her mother died. Not even when she and Lyrra had walked tied and gagged past their father's bloodied body strapped to his ship's mast. She would not cry now.

"Are you in pain?"

"Aye, my prince." He leaned closer to her, and his eyes were full of worry. Oona tried to smile but failed. She glanced around. No one was watching them, not even the Cheetah, who rode on the other side of his brother. "It pain of knowing this be end of Oona and Asad."

"It is a pain I know well, my jewel," he said, his voice a caressing growl, his endearment nestling deep in the gaping hole of her chest. "And one for which I have no cure. But I promise you this is not the end of Oona and Asad. Not yet."

"What do you speak of so intimately with your sickly, pale-faced pet, Prince Black Mane?" The Fox's shrill voice stood the hairs on the back of Oona's neck on end. "Anything you care to share with your father or your betrothed?"

The horses plodded on as Oona's heart leapt and raced. She dropped her gaze to her hands and took slow, deep, calming breaths.

"The Swan was complaining of a pain in her neck and shoulders," Asad said loud enough for both the Fox and the Panther to hear. "I told her there was nothing I could do for her now, that she would have to wait until we made camp. That she should strive to be more like my lady, the Fox, who bears the hardships of the journey with queenly silence and never utters a word of complaint."

Oona dropped her head further at the Cheetah's choking sputter and the muffled coughs of the Panther's men, for the Fox had done nothing but complain in her usual manner since she had awoken this morning.

"That will be enough of that." The Panther's curt command cut short the snickering of his men. "If the Swan is well enough to complain and jest with the Black Mane, she is well enough to ride with the rest of the baggage."

Oona sucked her breath in and held it, not daring to look up.

"Be smart, brother," the Cheetah whispered through taut lips. "Give in now to win later."

"You are right," the Black Mane said loudly, as if to the Panther, though Oona was certain he answered his brother. "She belongs with her sister."

His hand flexed and took Star's rein from hers, and Oona kept her gaze fixed on the mare's mane it as he turned them around to resume her place with the servants and the baggage.

"I sorry," she said after they passed a smugly smiling Fox and her maidservants.

"It is not your fault, Swan. The Panther would have found an excuse to separate us sooner or later."

"But I make sooner."

"Perhaps, perhaps not. It is a game we play, my father and I."

Oona did not understand what game it was they played, but it was too late to ask as they came up alongside Lyrra.

"Oona?" Lyrra said, and then bit her lip. "Swan? You are well?"

"Well enough I be baggage again."

"Keep an eye on her, Dove." Asad handed Star's reins back to Oona, his hand lingering on hers, his thumb rubbing the backs of her knuckles, sending a thrill up her arm. "Make sure she drinks her water skin dry before we make camp at dusk, and if you have any problems, my man the Crab will be keeping watch."

"Yes, Prince Black Mane."

He gave Lyrra a quick smile and she smiled back and Oona's jaw dropped. Lyrra had not smiled at any man but the Cheetah since they had been captured. Asad's hand cupped her chin and gently closed her mouth, and she was grinning from ear to ear as he made a show of turning her head this way and that.

"I will check on you when we make camp." His thumb caressed her upturned lips. "And then you must eat a good meal and go to sleep." He dropped his hand and lowered his voice. "I will wake you when the camp sleeps, and we shall be Asad and Oona again."

"He didna wake me, Ly," Oona sniffed as they shuffled behind an outcropping of rock to relieve themselves. "He promised."

"I am sure he had his reasons, Oo." Lyrra lifted her tunic and squatted as Oona did the same. "He wouldna break a promise to you without good reason."

"You think so?"

"I know so." Lyrra stood and dropped her tunic to her knees. "And so do you."

Oona sighed, releasing her nagging doubts with her breath.

"What is this?" The Fox's sharp yap echoed off the rock behind Oona. "Slaves speaking in their inferior tongue behind their masters' backs?"

Oona stood and dropped her tunic as the Fox and her maidservant, a pinched-faced woman with graying hair, stopped to stand and glower at her.

"What do you speak of, Stork?" the Fox demanded.

"I speak of my sleeping the night through."

"You lie," the Fox hissed.

"No." Oona lowered her eyes, her tone. "I no lie, my lady."

"Hmph," the Fox snorted. "You may have fooled the Black Mane with your pretty promise to never lie to him, but I am not so easily fooled by the batting of your lashes and the sway of your hips, and whatever else you promised or gave him."

Oona said nothing, but she lifted her gaze to meet the Fox's.

"But then what you gave him will not seem so special after his father and any other man who wants it gets it," the Fox said with a smug smile that Oona itched to swipe off her face. "Then we will see if he believes your lies."

"How you know him so little?" Oona asked with a pitying shake of her head. "Of man he is?"

The maidservant gasped and the Fox's black eyes snapped before her hand whipped out, and as before Oona stood and took the full measure of the Fox's hand across her cheek.

"How dare you tell me what I do or do not know of my betrothed," the Fox hissed as Oona held out a hand to keep Lyrra from jumping into the fray. "Now get out of my sight, I am sick of your milky face."

Oona and the Dove emerged from behind the rocks, the Dove chattering excitedly at Oona, who held a hand to her cheek until she saw Asad watching. Dropping her hand, she grabbed her sister's arm and turned them away from him and toward the cook's fire. He turned to follow and then stopped, for the Panther watched.

The Panther had changed the guard rotation last night, placing those more loyal to him than to Asad's bribes on watch while the camp slept, making it impossible for Asad to do anything more than check on the sleeping Swan before seeking his own bedroll. He knew she must be wondering why he had not kept his promise and awakened her, but he did not think that was the reason she turned away from him. He had seen the Fox walk behind the rocks shortly after the sisters.

"Swan," he called out to her. "Come here. Let me see how you fare this morning."

He stood and shifted his weight as if impatient at her slow approach until she stood before him, her head hanging so low that all he could see was the white-blonde part of her hair.

"Look at me, Swan. I wish to see your face."

Her shoulders rose and fell with a heavy sigh as she lifted her head.

Asad saw red. "That bitch."

"How is my slave this morning?" His father's voice boomed from behind him and Oona's eyes widened. She turned so that her right cheek with the welting handprint faced away from the Panther.

"I am checking on her now," Asad said, taking both sides of Oona's face in his hands, his palms covering her cheeks. He made a show of holding her head steady and studying the whites of her eyes, careful not to get lost in the mossy green of her irises. "She looks well enough," he said casually, dropping his hands as the Panther stood to the side of her unmarked cheek. "You may go, Swan." He gave a dismissive wave of his hand. "Be sure to eat sufficient for the morning's journey."

"Yes, Prince Black Mane." She dropped a knee to Asad and then to the Panther before turning to rejoin the Dove, who still stood where Oona had left her, chewing her bottom lip.

"She will be fine," he answered his father's unspoken question. "She is a fast healer."

"Good," the Panther said. "It would be a waste to lose a slave so valuable. She will ride the gelding again."

There it was, the king's orders, the father's control, the Panther cuffing his cub. Asad pressed his lips into a thin smile.

"I will tell my man," he said, and strode off to do exactly that.

"You had best get that murderous glint from your eye," the Crab warned Asad as he saddled the gelding for the Swan. "The Panther will do worse than cuff you if he sees you glaring at him like that."

"It is not only my father. Him I am used to, him I can handle," Asad growled. "It is that sinister-handed bitch Fox. She has slapped the Swan twice now, hard enough to leave a mark on her cheek both times. I want to wring her neck with my bare hands."

"And you cannot."

Asad growled and stared up into the cloudless blue of the morning sky, grinding his teeth. He lowered his gaze to the Crab's, who waited for his answer.

"I have learned today that a man can make himself mad with wanting what he cannot have," he said. "Curse them," he spat. "Curse them both."

"Panther and Fox?" the Crab said. "Or Swan and Dove?"

"Who do you think?" Asad snarled.

"I think my first guess was correct," the Crab said with a wink and a grin that had never failed to bring a smile to the boy that Asad had been.

But Asad was no longer a boy.

"Smart man," he said to the Crab with a curt twitch of his lips.

"Smart enough to understand your frustration."

Asad gave a short, gruff laugh. "You have no—"

"There was a young woman I was to marry."

Asad snapped his gaping mouth shut. He had never heard this story of the Crab's, though the man had been with him since he was a boy of seven years. "What happened?"

"I was made your manservant, an honor that I could not refuse, no matter my personal wishes."

Asad nodded his understanding. He was not the only man trapped in this life.

"Duty and honor," he said.

"Duty and honor," the Crab echoed as he cinched the saddle.

Oona waded out into the river she had been dreaming of all day, the cold moving water sending a shiver of delight up her spine. Downstream, the Fox yelped and jumped up and down, her bare breasts bouncing and her arms waving about. Oona looked over at Lyrra and shook her head.

"I know," Lyrra said, lowering herself chin deep into the water. "I think it feels wonderful. It will be nice to be clean again."

"Aye," Oona agreed. Days on end of riding through the hot, sandy desert, topped by a layer of illness-induced sweat, had left her feeling as ripe as she smelled. "That it will."

The Great Valley was vast and green with rivers flowing down from the steppes and snaking across verdant land that stretched as far as the eye could see. The air smelled of white clouds, green grass, and moving water, nothing short of paradise after the dry, dusty desert.

Oona stretched her arms up and over her head and arched her back. She threw her arms wide and thrust her breasts to the sky, taking in one long, deep breath of fresh, invigorating air. She straightened and dropped her arms and twisted from side to side, swirling her hands in the water around her hips in half circles, and then she folded her legs up and stretched her arms over her head as she lay back in the water, her hair flowing beneath her, a light breeze teasing her nipples.

She floated along, weightless, wet, cool, and content. Water splashed her face and she grinned, thinking it was Lyrra, but when she lowered her feet and turned around it was not Lyrra's impish grin she saw, but the Fox's snide sneer. Taking a deep breath and blowing it out, Oona stood up the rest of the way and waited for the Fox to unleash her fury.

The Fox's three maidservants stood behind her like a gaggle of wet hens, poking their nosy beaks this way and that, clucking among themselves as the Fox circled the Swan.

"Why, the Swan is nothing more than a sack of white skin hanging over a pole," the Fox said with a dismissive flick of her hand. "Her breasts look more like shrunken turnips than ripe melons." She cupped her own overflowing breasts with a smug smile. "And the Black Mane, like all men, much prefers sweet melon to shriveled turnip."

Oona refused to take the bait this time. She stood, exposed and shivering, as the Fox circled and gloated.

"Huh," the Fox finally huffed. "Come, ladies," she said to her servants, who followed her back to the river's bank. "Oil my hair with the musk. It drives the Black Mane wild."

"She jealous, Swan," Lyrra spoke in the desert tongue to the Fox's departing back. "It obvious Black Mane prefer firm apples to soggy melon."

"Lyrra," Oona whispered fiercely. "We are to stay clear of trouble, not look for it."

Lyrra flicked her wrist as dismissively as the Fox had.

"She cannot hear, she too busy yapping about her melon breasts."

There was a cough and a rustling from the rushes along the opposite shore. A shadow swayed and the rushes parted to reveal the Black Mane crouched among the reeds, watching them, watching her, a lion stalking its prey.

Behind her, Lyrra squeaked and splashed, hiding her nakedness under the water, as Oona should have done, but piercing amber eyes held her in their thrall. She stood taller and leaned forward, her nipples straining toward the heat of his gaze like seedlings to the sun. Asad shifted with a burning in his eyes that singed her breath, and then he was gone, melting back into the rushes without a sound.

Asad waited until he smelled the evening meal cooking before he returned to the camp, where he ate apart from the others.

The Crab approached him as the Cheetah watched warily from a distance. "What troubles you now, Black Mane?"

"Leave me alone," Asad grumbled. "I am in no mood."

"Oh, you are in a mood all right," the Crab said. "But what I do not understand is what happened to the rational man I spoke with last, the man who agreed to duty and honor, and who now sits here growling and spitting at me like some angry beast?"

"What happened?" Asad snarled.

What happened was that after a long run to stretch his legs and cool his temper he had lain down among the rushes to catch a quick catnap, only to awaken to the sound of women's voices. He had crept up to the river's edge and found the Swan, the Dove, the Fox, and her women servants bathing in the river. He had watched Oona's alabaster torso glistening wet in the afternoon sun, her breasts round and firm, her nipples a blushing pink.

He had heard every word spoken between her and the Fox and the Dove, who had it right: he was definitely a man who preferred a firm apple to a soggy melon. Then Oona had heard him, and he had shown himself in the rushes, had let her see him watching her, and she had not dropped into the water as the Dove had, but had stood proud and fearless in his sights.

Asad had never seen such delicately hued nipples, as pink and taut as rosebuds, and he had almost succumbed to their taunting sweetness, to the pull of his swelling manhood. But then reason had won the day, and he had disappeared back into the grasses, where he had taken himself in hand and spilled his engorged seed onto the ground.

"What happened is that man overcame beast, and neither is satisfied."

"Both beast and man may have all the satisfaction they require once we have returned to the palace tomorrow where an entire household of pleasure women await your return," the Crab wisely counseled.

But not a single one of those women, with all their oiled and kohled beauty or their artisan's tricks, flamed his passions as easily or as deeply as did the mere glance of Oona's green eyes, the touch of her hand, the sweet taste of her unsure kiss, the promise of her rose-tipped breasts. None of them were her, and he was sworn to make certain she never became one of them.

"Did you love her?" he asked the Crab. "The woman you were to marry?"

His question caught the Crab by surprise, and the look on his face told Asad all he needed to know.

"What was her name?"

"Adara, the Water Lily."

"What happened to her, to Adara?"

"She is a midwife who married a trade merchant and bore him five living children."

"I am sorry, Khalil." Asad addressed the Crab by his given name for the first time in their lives together. They were master and servant, student and teacher, and more. They were friends, but until Oona, Asad had never understood what it meant to hear your name spoken as a friend. "I did not know, I never even thought to ask."

"And now you do, and I am sorry for you, and the Swan."

"Oona," Asad told him. "Her name is Oona."

"A name as beautiful as its mistress."

"Yes."

Eyes as big, round, and green as mossy river rocks danced before his, and he heard her laughter, sweet and lilting as rippling water, and Asad found his resolve. "Tell me, old friend," he asked the Crab. "How does a man learn to do without the air he breathes?"

"One painful, gasping breath at a time, my young friend, one breath at a time."

CHAPTER 7

The Great Valley

The Great Valley was one vast meadowland of rivers and streams and seas of grass that stood belly high to the horses and stretched as far as the eye could see. The air here moved across the grass like a hand through winter wheat. Oona lifted her face to the welcome breeze, smiling at the play of it on her skin. At least this cage would have air that breathed life into a person instead of sucking them dry.

At high noon they made the Great River of slow-moving, muddy water, where a company of king's guard waited to escort them across the longest and widest bridge of stone and wood that Oona had ever seen.

An earthen wall as high as three manor houses stacked one atop the other ran along the river's far shore for a league north and south each, and they rode through three separate gates with separate walls before they were inside the city, which spread out before them in a maze of earthen walls and roads, and baked brick buildings the color of sand.

They traveled down a road of smooth, hard-packed dirt wide enough for two wagons to pass each other, with tilled fields to one side and a wall of earthen bricks on the other. The wall was inlaid with colored mosaic tiles in the shapes of fish and fowl, horses and hounds, deer and lions, with flowering bushes and scented vines growing along the base that Oona could barely catch whiffs of over the earthier road.

At least two hundred people passed them on foot or in carts and wagons before they turned north onto a narrower road surrounded on both sides by smaller, plainer walls with gates and roads branching off east and west.

Everywhere there were dark-haired, sandy-skinned people who would slow or stop to stare at their king and his party, and at Oona and Lyrra. Lyrra drew her mantle closer around her face and fixed her gaze on her mare's neck, but Oona met their curious gazes with her own and heard the whispers behind their hands of the king's new slaves.

The road stopped at yet another wall with a gate of wood as thick as two men abreast and girded with hammered ore. On one side of the gate the wall had a mosaic of a blue river winding through green fields, and on the other side an ebon panther walked beside a yellow and black spotted leopard down a road paved with gold.

They did not have to slow their horses as the gate creaked open onto a road of finely crushed stone surrounded by a row of guardhouses on one side, and a field of close-cut grass with at least twenty tents of every size and color pitched across it on the other. There were cooking fires and stock lines of two to six horses at every tent, and by the look and dress of the men at the fires, they were there to trade, not soldier. Their eyes were curious in a hard, assessing way, much like the traders in the slave market, and Oona dropped her gaze and pulled her scarf over her head.

Beyond the guardhouses and fields was still another wall, where six armed guards stood watch at the gate, the metal of their swords gleaming in the sun's light. Once through the gate, Oona gasped. Where the Jackal's palace had been a compound of whitewashed, single-storied buildings, the Panther's palace stood three stories high, towering over a small city of one- and two-storied buildings, all of them the same salmon pink with decorative tiles of black and gold glinting in the afternoon sun.

"You do not look so good, brother." The Cheetah rode beside Asad as they approached the bricked courtyard outside the palace door. "Is something ailing you?"

"Aye," Asad growled, aware too late of using the Swan's word. He would need to be more careful about that. "I feel the cage closing."

"Do not worry," the Cheetah said. "We will get them free of it."

"That we will." Asad pulled at his scarf, loosening it around his neck. "It is my cage that I feel closing in on me."

His brother eyed Asad. "At least you will have your memories of her."

Asad snorted. "Bittersweet, haunting memories at best," he said as people ran from all directions to meet the Panther's company at the palace steps.

Up on the balcony of the second floor, two dark heads looked down, one shoulder high to the other, the shorter one bobbing up and down.

The Cheetah's gaze followed Asad's. "What will you tell your mother, the queen?"

"The truth, up to a point. I will tell the Snow Leopard how the Black Mane feels about the Swan, she will smell it on me anyway, but not of what Asad would do for Oona, and pray that Noor does not see it in my eyes."

A hand waved beside the bobbing head on the balcony, and Asad held his hand up to his sister and grinned. He dipped his head to his mother, who dipped hers back. Dismounting at the bottom of the palace steps, Asad handed Storm's reins over to the Ratter, his stable master, who stood hopping from one foot to the other with a big grin.

"Give Storm a rubdown and a bag of oats," he said as the Ratter eyed the stallion up and down.

"I reckon you two won again, else I'd be holding some gelding's reins instead."

"That we did." Asad slapped the Ratter on the back and nodded over toward his string of broodmares. The Ratter's eyes widened at the sight of the white dappled filly. "Her name is Cloud Dancer."

"She's a long-legged beauty sure." The Ratter beamed at his new charge. "If she's anywhere near as fast as she looks…"

"She is even faster."

The Ratter went moon-eyed and Asad laughed.

"Stable her between Star and Storm," he told him. "We will start training her after a few days' rest."

The Ratter barked orders to his stable boy about the mare and filly and then trotted off with Storm as the baggage train rode past. Asad stood with his back to the palace and met Oona's wide-eyed gaze. He flashed a quick smile, which she returned with a tremulous upturn of her mouth, her back straight and stiff as she rode past the palace for the walls of the pleasure house. Turning back, Asad glanced up to the balcony where the queen stood staring down at him.

The Crab had come to Oona late last night and asked for the rings the Black Mane had given her, assuring her that they would be returned by the Black Mane when it would be safe to do so. He had warned her that her person and all her belongings would be gone through upon her arrival at the pleasure house, and as they approached the walls, Oona's hand went to the empty space in her bodice, where the rings had been a physical reminder of Asad's promise.

A gate carved with lines curving in the hourglass shape of a woman opened to reveal the biggest, blackest man Oona had ever seen. His hair was a cap of tight curls even blacker than his skin, and his eyes were dark as pitch in a pool of white. Teeth as big and white as tusks showed as he caught her staring at him, gape-jawed. Arms as thick as oak branches flexed as they crossed his bare scarified chest.

"Boar," the Panther's man said.

"Asp," the black giant answered.

"This is the Swan." The Asp jerked his head toward Oona. "And this is the Dove. Dowry gifts from the Jackal." The Boar took their meager packs from the Asp. "Tell the Mynah they are for the second floor."

"Of course."

"The Boar," Lyrra whispered into Oona's ear in their northern tongue as the Asp turned and left. "He doesna care for the Asp."

Oona nodded dumbly, still staring at the Boar, unable to read his eyes as easily as Lyrra had his voice, so awed was she by his otherness.

"Follow me." The Boar half turned toward the three-storied pleasure house that was more pink than salmon colored, and then he stopped and eyed the sisters. "And do not let the Mynah catch you speaking in any tongue but the Panther's."

"Yes, Boar," Lyrra answered, surprising Oona, who had become used to speaking for her since their capture. "Thank you for warning."

The Boar nodded gruffly, but Oona saw that the corners of his eyes and mouth lifted briefly and she breathed a sigh of relief. Her sigh froze into a lump the size of her fist dead center in her chest as the door to the pleasure house opened and she stood face-to-face with a sharp-eyed, beak-nosed woman with hair as black as soot, but for the two streaks of snow white shooting back from her temples. She stood only chin high to Oona, and wore a one-shouldered gown of brick red worm weave embroidered with gold thread in an intricate pattern of vining flowers.

"Mistress Mynah," the Boar said with a stiff bow. "These are the Swan and the Dove, dowry gifts from the Jackal, meant for the second floor."

Dismissing the Boar with a flick of her veined hand, the Mynah looked Oona up and down, pursing her lips and poking her clawed nail into the flesh above Oona's collarbone.

"You are too skinny, Swan."

"Yes, Mistress, I be ill with heat sickness."

"We shall have to fatten you up. The Panther does not like his women too skinny. He likes them soft and pliant." She stepped up to Lyrra with a thin-lipped smile. "You, Dove, you look to be exactly what the Panther likes in his pleasure women. Play your part well and you will become one of his favorites, and there are many rewards to being such."

"Yes, Mistress," Lyrra squeaked, and Oona took her sister's shaking hand and gave it a squeeze.

"Now then, as you have heard, I am the Mynah, mistress of this house. You may call me Mistress or Mynah, and it is me you will obey here, me you will come to with any questions or complaints."

"Yes, Mistress," Oona and Lyrra said in unison.

"And if you come to me with a complaint, it had better be worth my time." Her black eyes beaded onto Oona's. "I do not like complainers."

"I no complain," Oona said. She meant to be nothing but quiet and servile during her stay here. The last thing she wanted was trouble, especially with the mistress of the house. "We obey, Mistress Mynah."

"See that you do and we will get along fine." The Mynah turned on her heels and motioned for the sisters to follow. She led the way into a large chamber with red walls, several low, ornately carved tables, and sofas covered in gem-colored linens and embroidered cushions. "This is the king's salon. This is where the Panther and his guests visit with us."

Oona gaped at the tapestries on the walls. Each and every one was of a naked woman in some form of repose, on a sofa, a bed of flowers, a garden bench, astride a horse. Hot shame rose to her cheeks, and the Mynah stared at her with her thin lips pressed into an amused grin.

"Come." They crossed the room and the Mynah pushed open a door into another smaller, plainer room of tables and sofas where half a dozen women sat and sprawled, their conversation stopping at sight of the sisters. "Now then, this is our common room. The king's salon is only used during his visits, but from this room you may come and go freely."

Oona almost laughed out loud at the word "freely" pertaining to anything in this gilded cage, and was grateful the Mynah had not noticed the uptick of her brows before Oona had caught herself. But if the Mynah had not, it seemed another had as a small, slim, doe-eyed woman with long brown hair sitting at the table closest to them, playing some sort of game with colored stones, met Oona's eyes with raised brows of her own.

"Girls." The Mynah clapped her hands once, and all eyes shifted from Oona and Lyrra to the Mynah. "These are our new sisters, the Swan and the Dove. They are dowry gifts from the Jackal."

"So, the Black Mane will wed the Fox," a low, indolent voice said. "Lucky girl."

"Lucky girl indeed," the Mynah said to a woman of perhaps thirty years with oiled black curls piled high atop her head. Her eyes were dark and heavy-lidded and her body soft and rounded, and her lazy smile was anything but friendly as her gaze flicked over Oona and settled on Lyrra with a malevolent glare that raised Oona's hackles. "Spider." The Mynah beaded in on the woman's glare. "Welcome your new sisters to our house."

"Welcome, sisters," the Spider said, and even Oona could hear the venom in her voice.

"Yes, welcome, sisters," the tiny doe-eyed woman said as she stood and smiled. "I am the Mouse."

Oona smiled back into warm brown eyes. "Thank you, Mouse."

"I am Peahl," the woman the Mouse had been playing stones with said as she stood. Her face was round and much paler than the other women's, though not so pale as Oona's and Lyrra's, and her almond eyes were as black and shining as her sooty topknot. "Welcome, sistahs."

"I am Huntress," a woman as tall as Oona and almost as black as the Boar said as she stepped forward. Her hair too was a cap of tight black ringlets, and her cheeks were scarified with five horizontal lines each, as if clawed by some wild creature. "Welcome, sisters." She squared her broad shoulders, her gaze even with Oona's.

"Thank you, Huntress." Oona squeezed Lyrra's hand. They definitely wanted this Huntress as a friend, not a foe

"Thank you, Huntress," Lyrra said, her shoulder tucked behind Oona's arm.

"I am Flute," a slender woman with the sandy skin and dark brown hair of the desert people said. "Welcome, sisters."

"And I am Butterfly," another shorter, plumper woman of the desert people said. "Welcome, sisters."

"Thank you, sisters," Oona said. "We glad of such welcome."

"The others are about," the Mynah said as she led the way out of the salon into the kitchens. "You will meet them as we go no doubt. Now then, the kitchens are open to you day and night, for the Panther likes his women well fed." She slanted a black brow at Oona, who folded her arms across her chest. "This is the Hen." The Mynah waved toward a stout, middle-aged woman who sat on a stool at a table laden with wheels of cheeses and baskets of fresh greens. "She is head cook." The Hen's small eyes darted from Oona to Lyrra to the Mynah. "Hen, this is the Swan and the Dove, dowry gifts to the Panther from the Jackal. They will be in the lavender and blue rooms."

"I will have food sent right up," the Hen said, eyeing Oona. "I see we have some fattening up to do."

Oona hugged her apparently inadequate chest tighter and followed the Mynah out of the kitchens as the Hen called out and three young women in servants' tunics came running in.

"We not be in same room?" Oona asked the Mynah as they dodged the scurrying cook's helpers and made their way down a hall.

The Mynah's black eyes snapped. "You will each have your own room, assigned by me."

"Yes, Mistress." Oona tried to keep the disappointment from her voice as Lyrra took her hand and held tight. They had slept in the same room together since Lyrra had been old enough to leave her cradle, including sharing the hold of the pirate's ship, and their room at the Jackal's.

The Mynah opened a door into a tiled chamber with a pool twice the size of the one in the Jackal's palace. "This is the bathing chamber."

"We can bathe here?" Oona said with a smile of expectant pleasure that smoothed the Mynah's ruffled feathers.

"Anytime you please, except of course during your training times, and whenever the Panther or his guests are here."

"Of course." Oona gave an obedient nod. "The Panther," she asked the Mynah. "He come here much? He come here, with guests, tonight?"

"Not likely tonight. He usually waits a night or two after he returns from a long journey." Her black eyes bore into Oona's. "I must say, Swan, you do not seem as nervous about all this as most of the new girls do." She slanted a quick gaze at Lyrra. "Or as your sister does."

Oona let herself think of what she dared not, of Asad's plan not working, of the Panther tearing into Lyrra's flesh, and her own crawled.

"If I no seem," her voice was low, shaking with that fear, "it no mean I no feel."

The Mynah nodded, satisfied, and led the way back out and up a set of stairs onto another hallway that was open to the courtyard below on one side and lined with doors on the other. She stopped before a door with a lavender tile on it.

She pushed the door open. "Swan, this is your room." She opened the next door down with a blue tile on it. "Dove, this is yours." She stared hard at the two sisters, neither of whom moved from their doorways. "These will be your private chambers from this moment on. The inside bolts are never to be shut by you, and the outside bolts will be thrown by me anytime I please."

"Yes, Mistress," Lyrra peeped as Oona stood staring into her new cage, gilded with sofas and cushions covered in linen and worm weave of every shade of purple from thistle to plum.

The Mynah shooed them each into their rooms. "Now then, I suggest you eat and rest. Your training starts tomorrow."

Asad ate little and drank even less at the supper celebrating the Panther and his guests' return. The supper where his engagement to the Fox was announced to his tribe, and his mother, the Snow Leopard, publicly welcomed the Fox to her family with queenly graciousness. He found it hard to swallow food or drink, so tight did the noose around his neck chafe, and it did not help that he kept looking for the Swan and she was not there. That at least had been some consolation to him at the Jackal's, the sight of the sway of her skirts as she walked by, the sweet scent of jasmine wafting after her, the sureness of her graceful hands as she served. Her presence had calmed him, she calmed him, and he was in need of calm.

The Fox's incessant yapping from the woman's table grated on him the entire meal. He wanted nothing more than to stuff the hem of her red gown in her mouth to shut her up. But of course he did not. He dared not. Not without starting a fight between himself and his father, a war between his tribe and the Jackal's.

Asad rubbed his jaw, which ached from gritting it against the grating sound of the Fox, and glanced over at the queen's table, where his mother sat with the Heron's queen, the Reed, and the Bee, first wife of the Bull, whose eldest son the Ox sat next to Asad. As tall as Asad and twice as thick, the Ox was larger than his father, but not as quick thinking, or as interesting. The Bull at least had entertaining tales to tell. The Ox was as dull as dirt.

Catching his mother's eyes on him, Asad forced a grin that turned into a grimace as the Fox's shrill laugh clawed its way up his spine. His mother flashed a sympathetic smile, and he took a deep breath and let it out slowly as he sat back on a cushion that felt as comfortable as an ill-worn saddle. The Snow Leopard raised her goblet to her son, who raised his in turn and took a drink of wine that tasted of vinegar.

A dutiful son to his mother, he had gone to her chambers even before he had returned to his own and told her of both the Fox and the Swan, of his distaste for the one and his fascination with the other. He told her of the Swan's marriage proposal before she heard of it from anyone else, but he did not tell her of finding the Swan shimmying out of her window and how they spent that night, or any other, together.

He told the Snow Leopard of the Swan getting the heat sickness, of the Black Mane healing her, but he did not tell Noor about Oona and Asad, nor would he. He would let the queen think her son suffered only from his impending marriage to the Fox, not from his wanting the Swan, from wishing he was marrying Oona, a slave girl in his father's pleasure house. A wish Noor might well understand, but that the Snow Leopard could never allow.

Staring into his half-empty goblet, Asad finished off his bitter brew and almost choked when his father called out to the hall at large.

"Bring me the Swan and the Dove. We will have some song and dance this night to celebrate the Black Mane's and the Fox's betrothal."

Oona and Lyrra hurried after the Asp as they made their way through the maze of the palace to the dining salon. They had been woken from their afternoon rest by the Mynah and told to dress and hasten to the palace, where they were to perform for the king and his guests. The Mynah had forced a chunk of bread and cheese down Oona's throat as two maidservants washed her with a scented cloth and combed her hair and dressed her in her green silk, which had reappeared along with the rest of her pack. At least they did not rouge her nipples and cheeks, though they did kohl her eyes.

She hated that Asad would see her painted like that, and it mortified her to think that his mother would. It was a ridiculous thing to be worried about, but she could not help but care that Asad's mother would not hate her, even if she would only ever remember her as the slave that proposed marriage to her son and escaped her husband.

Clasping Lyrra's hand, they entered a salon twice the size of the Jackal's filled with a hundred dark-haired, dark-eyed people, all of whom turned to watch them walk on shaking legs to the open circle of floor, where Nightingale sat next to a stool that was front and center to the Panther's table.

"A reel," the Panther demanded.

Oona dropped her knee to him as he sat back and folded his arms across his chest with a smile that said he knew full well what he was asking of them. Her legs at least had loosened on the quick walk to the palace, but poor Lyrra's fingers had had no such warming exercise.

"The Skipping Reel," she said to Lyrra, who bent and straightened her fingers. "Start slow."

Fixing her gaze on the Panther, Oona started to skip, her feet barely lifting from the floor. The Panther's eyes moved to her chest by the third skip and then to her thighs flashing in and out of her skirt panels. She looked to the table's right and found amber lion eyes on hers, and her heart skipped and her breath quickened. She smiled, quick and fleeting, but it was enough, the corners of Asad's mouth twitched up as Lyrra picked up the pace on Nightingale.

Bolstered by the smile in Asad's eyes, Oona looked to the queen's table and found a pair of piercing gold cat eyes on hers, eyes that Oona knew instantly, eyes that like her son's did not narrow in anger at the Swan's perusal, but held and watched and studied as Oona did the same.

The Snow Leopard sat half a head taller than the other two women with her, who Oona recognized as wives of the Heron and the Bull. Her hair was piled high atop her head and was not black like her son's or husband's, nor oiled and curled like the Fox's, but a sleek, glossy reddish-brown, and her skin was pale and smooth as almond milk. Her nose was aquiline and her mouth lushly lipped, and her fingers, which kept time to the beat of the reel on the table, were long and tapered. So regal was the tilt of her chin, the straightness of her back, that Oona would have known her as the queen even without her son's eyes staring out from her royal visage.

Oona quickened her feet to the pace of the reel and tore her gaze from the queen to glance at the Panther, whose black eyes were fixed on her kicking legs. She kicked a leg up high and around, twirling on her stable foot once, twice, three times before slamming her heel down, arms akimbo.

Applause broke out and the Panther's leering gaze left Oona's heaving breasts when the Bull gave him a hearty slap on his back. Oona dropped a knee and slowed her breathing so that when she straightened, she met the Panther's gloating grin with barely a hint of her exertion, denying him what small bit of satisfaction she could.

"A wedding song," the Panther called out, smiling smugly at his eldest son before grinning broadly toward his soon to be daughter, "in honor of my son and his betrothed."

The Fox simpered prettily as all eyes turned to her but Asad's, who sat stone faced and unmoving.

"*Rithill Aill*," Oona said to Lyrra. "We sing together."

"Your words," Lyrra said with a hint of her imp's grin, "or the song's?"

Oona raised a warning brow. "The song's."

"*Welcome, gentlemen,*" they sang. "*Welcome and here's a health to you.*"

They sang the verse in the desert tongue three times together and then Lyrra sang it again and Oona joined her two lines behind and they sang it this way another three times, Oona skipping to the harp's fast pace as a sea of dark heads bobbed and clapped along. She held up a finger behind her back and they sang the last verse together and stopped on the last note as the rhythmic clapping turned to applause.

Oona dipped her knee first to Asad whose stony glare had softened a little, and then to the Fox, whose simpering smile did not reach her eyes as they locked onto Oona's.

"A love song," a woman's voice, low and measured, said, and Oona turned to the queen. "The Reed tells me of one you sang called 'Somebody.' I would hear it."

Oona dipped her head and her knee to the Snow Leopard and the Reed, afraid to even glance at Asad. Lyrra began to strum Nightingale, and Oona began to sing.

"My heart is sore I dare not tell,
My heart is sore for somebody,
I would walk a winter's night
All for a sight of Somebody."

The queen shifted on her cushion, her head tilted, her amber cat eyes, so like her son's, holding Oona's.

"If Somebody were come again,
Then one day he must cross the main,
And everyone will get his own,
And I will see my Somebody."

The queen's gaze shifted from Oona to Asad, and Oona did the same. Asad's gaze was fixed on Oona, his amber eyes glowing embers in his handsome face. With a tremulous smile, she gathered her breath and sang the words Asad had sung to her the night he had vowed to set her and Lyrra free.

"Oh, hey, for Somebody
Oh, ooh hey, for Somebody,
I would do, would I do not
All for the sake of Somebody."

Asad's eyes burned into Oona's, and she closed hers against them else she melt from their heat and pool into a pitiable puddle there in front of his mother and father.

She closed her eyes and lifted her voice and sang out to the night sky beyond, to the stars that would guide her far away from Asad. She sang to the heavens of everything she felt for him, Asad, the Black Mane, Poet Prince of the Seven Tribes, lion four times through, and heir to the throne of the Great Valley.

"Why need I comb my tresses bright,
Oh why should coal or candlelight
Shine in my bower day or night
Since gone is my dear Somebody.

Oh, I have wept many a day
For one that's banished far away,
I cannot sing and must not say
How sore I grieve for Somebody.

Oh, hey, for Somebody,
Oh, ooh, hey, for Somebody,

I would do, would I do not
All for the sake of Somebody."

Oona's voice hung high in the salon as Nightingale's last long note faded into the night and then there was silence. Somewhere someone sniffed and coughed and Oona opened her eyes to Asad's amber embers. A gaping hole ripped open in her chest and filled with a sudden, overwhelming grief that buckled her knees.

Asad was on his feet as Oona crumpled, grasping her under the arms as her knees hit the ground. She burrowed her face into the crook of his shoulder, stifling a sob.

"Get the Owl," he roared. He scooped her up into his arms and was on his feet and moving for the door. "Send him to the queen's quarters."

"I sorry," Oona cried into Asad's neck as soon as they were out of the salon. "I sorry I do this in front of you father, you mother."

"Do not be," Asad whispered fiercely into her hair. He breathed in the sweet scent of jasmine and pressed his lips to her perfumed tresses. "They will all think you ill again from the heat sickness." He gave a ragged laugh and held her tighter. "No one will know the truth of your ailment but us."

Oona sniffed and burrowed her nose deeper into his neck and Asad pressed her closer. He slowed his pace, for as soon as they reached the queen's chambers, he would have to let go his hold and give her over to the Owl, the palace physician, and his mother, whose footsteps hurried behind him

"Set her down here." His mother swept by him and set cushions at one end of her sofa for the Swan's head. "The Owl has been sent for."

Asad laid Oona down on the sofa, his hands lingering on the bare skin of her arms, his gut twisting at her tear-stained face. It was the first time he had seen her cry, this strong, beautiful, otherworldly woman who had watched her mother die, witnessed her father's slaughter, been made a slave, survived a hellish hot hole and almost died in the desert, and she cried for him.

"Let me see her." His mother shooed Asad away and laid a hand on Oona's forehead. "What happened, Swan?"

"I- I be dizzy." Oona's voice, her entire body, shook. "Like in desert."

"She had the heat sickness," Asad said. "I told you about it."

"About how you took care of her, yes," his mother said with a knowing smile. "I remember."

Ignoring any hidden meaning behind his mother's smile, he turned to her maidservant. "Clam, go to the kitchens and bring us a pot of mint tea."

"Not salted water?" his mother said, and Oona grimaced.

"No." He shook his head as Oona sighed with relief. "She is not feverish, but overtired from the journey and the dancing. The Panther should have known better than to push her so hard so soon." He caught his mother's watching gaze and realized how angry he sounded. "But then that is why his horses never win races," he added with a disgusted snort. "He never will take the time to train them properly."

"No," his mother said with a wry smile, "he will not." She turned her smile to the Swan, who listened and watched with wide eyes. "Lucky for you, Swan, my son will."

"Yes, my lady queen." Her voice sounded steadier, stronger. "Prince Black Mane, he be good healer, he save my life."

"Yours and every other stray that crosses his path," the queen said indulgently as a knock on the door heralded the Owl's arrival.

Standing back, Asad let the Owl and the Snow Leopard examine the Swan, answering any questions directed at him about her heat sickness and how he had treated her so that they would think this spell a lingering ailment and order extra rest for her over the next few days, which was exactly the conclusion they came to.

The Clam arrived with the pot of mint tea and the Owl went to make his recommendations to the Panther as Asad and the Snow Leopard let the Swan rest and drink.

"So, Swan." The Snow Leopard handed Oona her second cup of tea. "What was it made you propose marriage to the Black Mane and the Cheetah?"

Oona choked and sputtered and her eyes grew round in her pale face.

"I...I think...better wife to prince than slave to king," she answered, holding his mother's piercing gaze a moment before dropping her own.

"I see, and in your land that is possible, a slave marrying a prince?"

"No." Oona shook her head, and then she looked up and met the queen's steady gaze. "But in my land, I, we, princess."

"But you are not in your land."

"No." Oona's green eyes were wide as she glanced around the richly furnished chambers. "We not."

CHAPTER 8

The Pleasure House

The Mynah was not at all pleased when Oona returned to the pleasure house escorted by the Owl with strict orders that the Swan should be left to rest and plied with as much mint tea as she could drink for the next three days.

"Well then, Dove," the Mynah snapped as soon the Owl left. "It looks like you will have an extra three days off as well. I am too busy to be training the two of you separately."

The next morning when Oona and Lyrra went down to break their fast they were swarmed by the entire hive of pleasure women, all of whom wanted to know about the queen, what she was like, what she wore, and how her chambers were furnished. After Oona told them of the queen's kindness at least ten times and what details she remembered of the queen's chambers ten more, all the women left but for the Mouse, the Pearl, and the Huntress.

"You really proposed marriage to the Black Mane?" the Mouse asked Oona as the kitchen servant cleared the table.

"Aye, I did."

The Mouse gave a low whistle as she looked from the Huntress to the Pearl and back to Oona.

"And what did the Black Mane answer?"

"He no answer." Oona glanced at Lyrra's raised brow before calmly meeting the Mouse's disappointed gaze. "The Panther, he say no slave marry prince."

"You are lucky that is all the Panther answered you with," the Mouse said.

"You speak of Panther's whip?" Oona said and the Mouse nodded. "You have been whip?"

"Not I." The Mouse looked to the Huntress.

"You Huntress? You have been whip?"

"I have," the Huntress said, "twice, both times trying to escape this place."

She turned her back to them and lowered the shoulder of her gown and Oona sucked her breath in. It was one thing to imagine the scars a whip left on flesh, and quite another to see it. The Huntress's entire back was covered in so many raised weals and deep gouges that Oona had to close her eyes against the raw pain that still emanated from them.

"How you live?" Oona's voice quaked as a vision of Lyrra's back, flayed bloody, came to her.

"The Owl and the Mynah nursed me."

"How far you get, when you try escape?"

The Huntress flashed a feral smile. "To the stables the first time, over the palace walls and into the city the second."

Oona nodded. There was still a remnant of defiance in the Huntress's dark eyes she understood well, and admired.

"I would not try it," the Mouse warned.

"Try what?" Oona said innocently, and unconvincingly

"They watch new comahs closely," the Pearl said. "The Huntwess is only the second woman evah to make it outside pleashah house walls." Her almond eyes narrowed on Oona's. "The other woman did not suhvive Panther's whipping."

"Where you from, Pearl?" Lyrra asked, and every woman there looked relieved to change the subject.

"I flom Fah East. I was taken by bandits flom my home when I was but ten and five."

"How many years have you now?"

"Twenty and one."

"Oo, I mean, Swan, she has twenty and one also," Lyrra said, and the Pearl gave Oona a quick smile.

"And you?" the Pearl asked Lyrra.

"I have ten and eight."

"That makes you the youngest here then," the Mouse said with knit brows.

"That no good?" Oona asked.

"Not to the Spider, who is the oldest but for the Mynah," the Mouse answered in a hushed voice. "You both would do well to stay clear of the Spider as much as you can. She is not well disposed toward younger, prettier women."

"She is a venomous bitch," the Huntress spat, not bothering to lower her voice.

Oona looked at Lyrra and then to the Mouse. "When Spider bathe?"

"In the afternoon," the Mouse told her. "Before the king visits."

"Then we bathe in morning, start this morning."

"I knew ye'd be visiting the filly this day, not three from now," the Ratter told Asad when he found him feeding Cloud Dancer one of the apples he had swiped from the kitchens. He watched the filly gently take a slice from Asad's open palm. "An' how do you find her this fine summer morn?"

"Better company than some," Asad grumbled.

"Some being yer betrothed, the Fox?"

"Aye." Asad ignored the cock of the Ratter's head at the word. "Better than the Fox by far."

"An' the Swan's?" The Ratter's button eyes shone bright with curiosity.

"The Swan? Why would you ask me of the Swan?"

"It's just that I 'eard she fainted dead away singin' last night. An' that you caught 'er before she hit ground, that you'd tended to 'er on the journey 'ere when she got the heat sickness, that she'd proposed marriage to you at the Summer's Eve feast, an' the Fox, she weren't too pleased about any of it."

"You heard all this in the one night we have been back?"

The Ratter touched a finger to his nose. "I'm not called the Ratter for nothin'."

Asad gave a short, gruff laugh.

"My mother always told me if I wanted to know what was going on in a place, ask the servants."

"Smart lady, yer mother the queen."

"Yes," Asad acknowledged. "She is smart." And suspicious after his actions last night, another reason Asad had left the palace early and not broken his fast with his family.

"So, is it true, what I 'eard of the Swan?"

Asad eyed the Ratter closely. It was one thing to have the Crab aware of his feelings for the Swan, but the Ratter, loyal as Asad knew he was, was not as circumspect.

"Yes, the Swan proposed. And yes, I tended her when she fell ill, and again last night. But she is a slave," Asad let the distaste he had for the word as it applied to Oona sour his voice, "a pleasure woman."

The Ratter's head leveled and then cocked the other way.

"Is she at least as beautiful as they say?"

"I do not know how beautiful they say she is," Asad teased. "But it is true she is at least as beautiful as this white-maned, long-legged filly I brought back."

The Ratter nodded as Asad rubbed Cloud Dancer's white velvet muzzle.

"What of Storm and Star?" Asad said, turning the conversation elsewhere. "How do you find them after their desert journey?"

"Storm's more cocky 'n ever with the new filly by him," the Ratter said with a quick grin. "An' Star, she's fine and fit, though I did find a piece of linen sewn into the underside of 'er bridle."

"I had it sewn in at the Jackal's. Star was getting anxious there, rubbing her nose on the kraals post."

"Star was anxious?" The Ratter looked over at the mare, which true to her steady nature was calmly munching away at her bucket of oats.

"I figured it was because of the Falcon's men sneaking around the kraals at night, trying to get to Storm and drug him."

Asad hid his smile as the Ratter erupted. "They was trying to what?"

"Drug Storm, so that we would lose the race."

"Why those—"

"Settle down, Ratter. I caught the Falcon's man red-handed before he got to Storm."

"Did ye beat him to a bloody pulp at least?" the Ratter asked with a murderous glare.

"No, he was only doing his master's bidding."

"An' what of his master, the Falcon?"

"Oh, he paid for it," Asad assured him. "Through the nose." The Ratter's ropey body relaxed. "One thing," Asad added. "No one is to know of this."

"What?" The Ratter's body clenched and his fists balled up again. "Why?"

"We would not want the Fox's family besmirched, now would we?" Asad asked with a sardonic smile that was not missed by the sharp-eyed Ratter.

Oona woke to the bell ringing three times, the signal that the Panther was in the pleasure house and that all pleasure women were to gather in the king's salon. Splashing water from the washbasin over her face, she combed her hair and donned her green silk. By the dusky sky outside her window, she had slept the afternoon through, and she vainly hoped the rest had done some good for her shadowed eyes and hollowed cheeks, for the Mouse had told her that if the Panther came, so most likely would his sons.

Rinsing her mouth with a swallow of cooled mint tea, Oona smoothed her skirt and opened the door to her chambers, joining Lyrra as they followed the line of women filing down the stairs.

"I know the Mouse is the Black Mane's favorite, and that he always picks her when other men visit," an excited voice said somewhere in front of Oona. "But I hope he picks me tonight."

Lyrra's fingers squeezed Oona's as a chorus of voices seconded the hope.

"I hope the Ox does not pick me," another voice said over the chorus. "He is as dull and slow in bed as out."

"I do not mind slow," still another said, "as long as the man knows what he is doing and where he is going."

They laughed a hard, knowing laughter that Oona had heard the older, married women of her clan laugh when talking amongst themselves. Oona clasped Lyrra's hand tighter.

The king's salon was lit with candles at every table and smelled of smoke and perfume and spiced wine. Oona and Lyrra stood inside the door and watched as half the women went straight for the tables where the men were seated and the others spread out among the empty tables and sofas. The Mouse waved them over to her table where the Pearl and the Huntress also sat, and Oona and Lyrra made their way with grateful smiles.

Oona's smile grew grim and the hairs on the back of her neck bristled as they passed the table where Asad sat with the Cheetah, surrounded by four women, one of them draping her arms around Asad's shoulders and whispering into his ear.

At the Panther's table the Spider sat on the king's lap, her fingers playing with the oiled curls of his beard. The Panther was smiling as the Spider's hand trailed down from his beard to the curls of his chest hairs, and then he said something to the Bull, whose laughter bellowed out. The Heron, who sat across from them, crooked his finger at a slim, dark-haired, dark-eyed woman who looked like a younger version of his wife, the Reed, and the woman stood and went to sit on his lap.

"Who is that woman," Oona asked the Huntress, "the one with the Heron?"

"That is the Eel. She and the Spider are thick as thieves."

"I see," Oona said. And she did. Inexperienced as she was with men on a carnal level, she knew enough about the power a woman connected with a man wielded to see exactly what it was the Spider and the Eel were doing, claiming their power, their lap thrones. She glanced at the prince's table, expecting to see the woman who had been hanging all over Asad sitting on his lap, but his lap was empty and his eyes were on hers.

He stood and Oona's cheeks flushed hot as he strolled in her direction. She glanced at the king's table, where the Panther sat watching his son, his smile gone.

"He is coming," the Mouse said in a loud whisper. "The Black Mane is coming to our table."

Every woman there, including Lyrra, smoothed their skirts and sat up straight with pretty smiles on their faces. Every woman but Oona, who dropped her gaze to the floor only to find it filled with his sandaled feet.

"Swan?" His voice, deep and resonant, burrowed into her spine and straightened it. "How are you feeling?" She lifted her gaze and amber eyes held hers. "Any more fainting spells?"

Oona shook her head. "No, Prince Black Mane," she said, the smile in his eyes melting the vision of the woman wrapped around his shoulders from hers. "I no more faint."

"Good." The corners of his mouth turned up. "I am glad to hear it."

Oona smiled at their old game and his grin widened. Hands clapped loudly behind them, Oona jumped up a foot at least from her cushion, and the Black Mane grimaced and squared his shoulders.

"Mynah," the Panther roared with a thump of his chest. "I wish for the Swan's and the Dove's training to start tonight. Have two wash basins, soaps, and oils brought out, teach the sisters to wash and oil my sons' feet in a manner proper for the men of the Seven Tribes. They will be serving many soon enough, better they learn now."

Asad considered reminding his father about the Owl's recommendation that the Swan rest for three days, but the Panther had not forgotten. He was choosing to impose his rule over his slaves and his sons publicly, where the Heron and the Bull could witness it, and where his wife and palace physician could do nothing. Asad could though. He could speak up and walk away, but then the Swan and the Dove would suffer the Panther's wrath, and he and his father would come to blows, or worse.

So he said nothing as the kitchen servants brought out the foot basins and trays filled with soaps, oils, and towels, and set them down beside him and the Cheetah.

"Now listen and do as I say," the Mynah told the sisters. "First you must kneel in front of the man."

Asad nodded to the Dove, indicating that she should tend to him. The last thing he wanted was to have Oona touching him in front of his father. But before the Dove could bend a knee, the Panther called out.

"No, Dove, you will bathe the Cheetah's feet, and the Swan the Black Mane's."

Asad silently cursed his father as Oona knelt down before him, her eyes cast down and her hands folded in her lap.

"First, remove his sandals," the Mynah instructed, and Oona untied the straps to Asad's sandals and slipped them off and set them to the side. "Now lift the man's robes to his knees, there," the Mynah said approvingly as Oona gathered the hems of Asad's robe and rolled them up onto his knees, her fingers never touching his skin. "Now set a towel down for the man's feet and ask him to pick a bar of soap."

Oona smoothed a towel out and Asad set his feet down on it. She picked up the tray with the soaps and held it up to him, her big green eyes meeting his.

"Which soap would you recommend, Swan?" he said as the sweet scent of jasmine swirled around his head.

"The, ah, the rosemary smell good, my prince. Is said to revive."

Asad grit his jaw and nodded. He needed calming, not reviving, but he would not let anyone watching see it, especially not the Panther.

"Now wet his feet with a cup of water," the Mynah instructed, "using half a cup for each foot."

Oona scooped and poured and Asad eased his jaw.

"Now soap up your hands and rub it in with your fingers to lather it up, starting at his ankle and working your way down to his toes."

Oona lathered her hands and Asad tensed and his calf twitched as she picked up his scarred left foot and placed it forward on the towel. Her long fingers rubbed tender, tensile circles around his ankle and into the meat of his heel, and he began to relax as she rubbed the top of his foot and then the arch. She slid her fingers under the ball of his foot and pressed her thumbs down, squeezing gently. Asad groaned and Oona jerked her hands away.

"I sorry, Prince Black Mane," she said, meeting his gaze for one brief moment before dropping hers. "I no mean hurt you."

"It is a pain newly formed, Swan," he said, his voice low, husky. "Yet one I will never wish undone."

Her head dropped lower, and Asad fought the urge to cup her chin and lift her gaze to his. To see his pain reflected in her beautiful green eyes.

"Continue, Swan," the Mynah snapped. "You must wash his entire foot."

Asad steeled himself as Oona rubbed and pulled gently on each toe, one by one, the scent of jasmine and rosemary mingling and teasing his senses.

"Now rinse and dry with the clean towel," the Mynah's voice snapped Asad back.

Oona poured another cup of water over Asad's foot and then wrapped the drying towel around it and set it down on her thigh as the Mynah instructed so that he would not have to hold his foot up as she patted it dry. He moved his foot up her thigh a bit, kneading her taut flesh beneath the towel with his toes, and her cheeks flushed and reddened.

"Now the other foot."

Oona licked her lips in concentration and Asad's cock tightened. He shifted on the stool and laid his hands over his lap to hide his growing desire as Oona took his right foot in her hands, staring over her head and trying to relax and enjoy the soothing feel of her hands soaping his foot. It was hardly the first time he had had his feet bathed by a woman, and all of them trained in the art of pleasing a man, but it was the first time Oona had bathed his feet, or touched him for such a prolonged period of time in front of others, and his hold on his desire and his sanity was wearing thin.

"Good, Swan, good, Dove," the Mynah said when they had finished drying. "Now have them pick their oil and pour a small amount onto your palms and rub them together like so, to warm the oil."

Oona touched a tub of myrrh and looked at Asad, who nodded, pleased but not surprised that she knew his preferred scent. He would know hers anywhere. He breathed in the perfume of sweet jasmine and green grass, of misting rain and brisk breezes, of her, and closed his eyes as the scent of his own earthier sweat and musky myrrh melded with hers. He half purred, half groaned as she began to oil his feet, and pressed his hands down harder over his swelling cock.

"Now, wipe the excess oil from their feet and your hands with the towels," the Mynah said, "and then strap their sandals back on."

Asad held his breath, his delicious torture almost at an end. Oona wrapped the sandal straps around his ankles and her fingertips lingered on his coursing pulse a moment before she tied the straps.

She sat back on her heels and wiped a fine sheen of sweat from her cheeks, keeping her gaze on Asad's feet.

"Now take the basins to the kitchens," the Mynah instructed the sisters.

Oona collected the towels into the basin, and Asad blew his breath out in a slow, steady stream. Their eyes met as she stood, and hers were lit with the same fire that burned in his. She bowed low and he dipped his head and forced his gaze to remain fixed ahead and not follow the gentle sway of her skirts as she made her way to the kitchens.

When it was safe to do so, he stood and strode over to the table the Mouse sat at, his father's black gaze on him the entire way.

Oona could not sleep. She could not get the image of Asad leaving the salon with the Mouse out of her head: his arm wrapped around her shoulders as they took the stairs to the Mouse's bedchambers. Oona kept envisioning him holding the Mouse in his arms, his hands running up and down her back, his lips kissing hers as they had kissed Oona's.

She tried sitting at the open window, but the memory of another open window, of Asad waiting for her, taking her hand and leading her off to the Jackal's kraals, of the words he spoke to her there, telling her they were fire and air, that fire could not live without air, made her want to howl at the horned moon. She paced, she straightened her few belongings, she combed her hair until it shone in the reflection of the obsidian, and then she paced some more.

Cracking her door open, she peered out into the dark, empty hall and considered trying to find her way down to the baths. The Mynah had told her that they had free use of the baths, and though Oona was fairly certain that did not mean the middle of the night, she could always plead ignorance if she was found out. She pulled the door open enough to slide out into the hall when a scraping sound came from outside her window. Standing with her hand on the door handle, ready to slam it shut or fling it open as need be, she watched a large, tawny hand grasp onto the windowsill from outside, followed by a corded forearm and a mane of black hair.

"Asad."

She pulled the door shut as he hoisted himself up and over the windowsill. "Why you here? I see you go with Mouse into her chambers."

He grinned, and his voice was low and steady, unlike Oona's racing heartbeat, as he went to the door and threw the inside bolt shut.

"You did see the Black Mane go with the Mouse into her bedchambers," he said, "you, and the Panther, and everyone else, exactly as I wanted them to." He closed the distance between them on silent cat paws and stopped a hand's breadth from her, his eyes holding hers. "But what no one else will see, not even the Mouse, who lies sleeping and dreaming, is that I, Asad, chose her because her chamber is next to yours, and even if she does wake to find me gone, she will not tell a soul."

"She will not?" Oona's breath was slowing, but her heart was still hammering. "Why she will not?"

"We have a bargain, the Mouse and I."

"Oh." Oona did not ask him what bargain he and the Mouse, his favorite, had between them. She did not think she could bear to know.

"Oona?" His hand cupped her chin and tilted it up so that she was forced to meet his gaze. "What is troubling you so that you will not look me in the eyes?"

Clenching her welling eyes shut, Oona shook her head.

"Remember your vow to me." The pad of his thumb brushed her lips. "To always tell me the truth."

Oona took a deep, shaky breath and opened her eyes to piercing gold orbs. "It...it...you have lay with Mouse." Her words came out in a rush, and his thumb stilled along her jaw. "You have lay with all women here. I know. I hear them speak of you. I hear them say they hope you pick them for night."

He smiled and Oona pushed her hand up between them and off his chest as she stepped back, glaring at him.

"Is funny, what I say?"

"No." He shook his head, his magnificent head that had lain on other women's pillows. "It is, well, truth be told, it makes me smile to know you are jealous of any other woman." He stepped closer and ran his fingers back through her hair, caressing her cheek with the pad of his thumb. "For while it is true I have lain with many of the women here, you, my jewel, are the only woman I have ever truly wanted."

What Asad told Oona was the truth. He had lain with almost every woman in his father's pleasure house, but never because he had truly wanted them. He had wanted their bodies, their carnal skills, the physical release they provided him, but not them. He wrapped his hand around Oona's neck and pulled the one woman he yearned for, body, mind, and soul, into his embrace.

"I, Asad, choose you, Oona," he whispered fiercely into her hair. "Know this, believe this, no matter whose chamber you see me enter."

She sniffed into his neck. "I will." She lifted her face to his, her heart in her beautiful green eyes. "I do."

"Good." His breath was as ragged as her gaze. "I am glad."

He lowered his mouth to hers, hot, hard, and demanding. He held her tight and kissed her so that she would never again doubt the desire he felt for her, and her body melted into his, as pliant and giving as her lips.

"You are mine, my jewel," he growled and nipped. "As I am yours."

She answered him with a sighing kiss, opening her mouth to his tongue as he tasted and explored, tempted and teased. The tip of her tongue met his, tentatively at first, then growing bolder, thicker, wetter, thrusting and parrying with his.

Rumbling his pleasure, Asad ran his fingers under the one-shouldered sleeve of her gown and slowly pushed it down her arm until the bodice fell away, exposing her firm, round breasts with their tips of rose pink.

He filled his hand with the soft weight of Oona's breast and she gasped. Smiling into her lips, he began to rub his thumb over the rosy bud. She moaned into his mouth and her nipple pebbled under his touch. Asad deepened his slaking kiss, far from sated. He kissed and nibbled his way down her chin, the column of her neck, pressing his lips to her hot pulse. He lowered his head and laved and suckled her straining bud, a starving man granted the sweetest of succor, and his cock grew hard as she twined her hands through his hair and arched her back with a low, soughing moan.

Kissing his way to her other breast, he rubbed his thumb where his mouth had left a warm, wet heat circling her nipple. Oona sucked her breath in and let it out in a ragged sigh as he slowly moved his other hand down her back and splayed it across her backside, reveling in the sleek tautness of her dancer's body. Asad growled low and deep. He slanted his mouth across hers and drank of her hot sweetness, his thirst for her as deep as the sea.

Cupping her tight, round backside with both hands, Asad pressed her closer, grinding his rigid, throbbing cock against her pelvis through the layers of his robe and her gown. She did not startle or shy away, and Asad reached for her hand to place it over his straining bulge and then stopped.

She moaned and pressed closer, and Asad tore his mouth from hers with a groan. Her lips, slick and red from their kiss, lifted to his, and he knew if he reached up under her skirts that her woman's lips would be equally as slick and swollen with desire. He stepped back and held her at arm's length, fighting to slow his breath and cool his heat while staring into green pools of desire.

"Oona." He dragged in a ragged breath. "I want to be an honorable man for you, my jewel." He pressed her hand to his chest, his heart hammering beneath it, and took in another, deeper breath. "But it is a struggle between Black Mane and Asad, man and beast, and your beauty, your willingness..." He lowered their hands and let go his hold of her.

"I sorry I make it so hard on you."

Asad's laugh came fast and harsh. "The only thing you make hard on me, my beautiful temptress, is my manhood." He grinned wickedly as her gaze dipped to the bulge beneath his robe and her cheeks flushed bright pink, though but a moment ago she had been grinding against it.

She was an innocent temptress, and Asad almost wished he had not claimed to be such an honorable man where she was concerned. But if he gave in to his baser desires and took her here, he'd wager coin on the Mynah and his father sniffing them out. And if the Panther found her no longer a virginal maid, he would kill her. And then Asad would kill him.

"Come, my jewel." He took her by the hand and sat down on the sofa beside her. "My intentions were not to ravish you," he said with a wolfish grin that left her cheeks burning, "but to tell you of the Cheetah and my plans for your and the Dove's escape from here."

Oona woke to the Panther and the Mynah staring down at her.

"King Panther?" She sat up, clutching her bed linens to her chest. "Mistress Mynah?"

"Get up, Swan," the Panther ordered.

Oona dropped the bed linens and swung her legs over the side of the bed and stood, her cheeks blazing as the Panther raked over her flimsy nightshift with his black eyes.

He jerked his head. "Mynah, check the bed."

The Mynah pulled back the bed linens and ran her veined hands up and down the sheet before she bent down and sniffed at them. She straightened and shook her head at the Panther.

"Check the Swan," he said.

Oona glanced from him to the Mynah, not at all sure what the Mynah was to check her for when the Mynah lifted up Oona's shift and stuffed her hand into her woman's parts. Oona gasped and jumped back and the Mynah lifted her fingers to her nose and sniffed. Again, she shook her head at the Panther.

"No man has left his scent on her," the Mynah said, and Oona's cheeks blazed even hotter as she tried to imagine what the Mynah would have smelled had Asad not been the honorable man he was.

Oona had wanted his kiss to go on forever. She had wanted to melt into his eyes, his hard, warm body, him. She would not have held back anything, any part of herself from him, and he had known it. The Mynah stepped over to Oona's washbasin and picked up the cloth. "Her washcloth is dry and her basin water unused."

The Panther grunted and grabbed a hank of Oona's hair and pulled her out the door with him.

"Where is my eldest son," he yelled out into the hallway. "Black Mane, show yourself."

They stood in the hall as door after door opened and sleepy-eyed women and men in various states of undress stepped out of them.

"What in blazes are you yelling about, Panther?" the Bull grumbled as he tied the sash of his loose robe around his bulging belly.

"Black Mane," the Panther roared, ignoring the Bull and yanking hard on Oona's hair. "Come forward, now."

The Mouse's door burst open and a snarling Black Mane strode out to face his father in nothing more than his loincloth.

"This had better be important." He glared at the Panther, his jaw setting as his gaze took in the Panther's hold of Oona's hair. "I was in the middle of something."

Oona could not take her eyes off the ridged muscles of Asad's flat belly, the dark furring that led from his belly to the bulge of his manhood, which his loincloth did little to hide, and which she had felt the hard, hot length of pressing against her through their clothes last night.

The unbidden image of him pressing his roused manhood against the Mouse, of him kissing the Mouse as he had Oona, whispering huskily in her ear, tore open a gaping hole in Oona's chest. Asad had told Oona her wanted her, and only her, and Oona wanted to believe him, but the certainty that he had lain with the Mouse, and most, if not all of the other women here, made it next to impossible.

"What ails you now, Swan?" the Panther demanded. "Your face is as green as your eyes. You are not going to faint again, are you?"

"No, my king Panther." Oona shook her head and swallowed a great gulp of air and refused to look Asad's way even as he turned to look sharply at her.

"Good." The Panther yanked her forward and Oona had to hop and skip to keep from stumbling as he pulled her through the door into the Mouse's chambers. "I have had enough of sickly slaves."

The Mouse sat up in her disheveled bed, her hair tousled, her cheeks flushed and the nipples of her bare breasts taut. "My king, is something amiss?"

"No," the Panther said with a leer. "Apparently not." He pulled Oona back out of the room, past Asad, whose earnest gaze was searching Oona's face. "As you were, my son."

Oona blinked back hot tears of shame and anger and shook her head at Asad as he stepped toward her, his head cocked first one way and then the other.

"By the gods," he muttered loudly as he yanked open the door to the Mouse's chambers. "What was that all about?"

The Panther let go his hold of Oona's hair as the Mouse's door slammed shut, and her bile rose at his chilling grin.

"You and your sister will play and sing tonight at the Feast of Knives," he told her. "Wear your white worm weave and your sister her gray. And no fainting."

CHAPTER 9

Knives

Asad was in no mood for a feast, but he was in a great mood for a fight. Glad as he was that he had managed to stay out of the Swan's bed, and that his decision had proven to be the right one, it did little to alleviate his lack of release. For despite his show for the Panther and every other person in the hall, he had not lain with the Mouse, nor taken matters into his own hands as he had by the river. He wanted Oona. He wanted to feel her raw, instinctual response to him, to hear her breath catch and feel her passion unfold beneath his caresses, not the practiced moans and thrusts of a pleasure woman. He wanted Oona as fire wanted air, to light, to flame, to burn, and if he could not have her, then he would take his pent-up energy and use it against his opponents tonight.

They would draw knives to see who fought whom, victor fighting victor until there was only one man left standing, and Asad intended to be that man this night. The Bull and the Ox he was not worried about. He watched them during the meal and they both ate and drank as they normally would, not as men about to compete in a knife fight.

Perhaps they thought their size and strength would prevail, which it might if it was hand-to-hand fighting, but knife fighting, that was a matter of speed and skill and cunning, and the Bull and the Ox were neither fast moving or fast thinking. The Cheetah and the Grebe, the Heron's son, had the speed and the skill, but both were too good-natured to be cunning. The Panther, though he was slowing with age, he still had enough skill and more than enough cunning to be the victor of every knife fight he had ever been in, until tonight.

Feeling the Panther's eyes on him for about the hundredth time that evening, Asad lifted his cup to his lips and made the motion of swallowing, though he did not drink a drop of the spiced wine. The Panther smiled and Asad pretended to take another swallow before setting his cup down.

"Ahh, here they are," the Panther called out as heads turned toward the entrance to the salon. "The Swan and the Dove come to entertain us."

Asad refused to turn and look, keeping his gaze on his cup until a pale, slender foot followed by a long, lean leg and a veil of white worm weave floated by. Oona the Swan stood in the clearing in the center of the salon that was to be her stage, chin up and back straight, her eyes as big and green and round as the first night she had stood before him over a moon ago.

Like that night, her eyes were lined black with kohl and her cheeks and nipples stained pomegranate pink, but unlike that night there was no fear in her eyes as she gazed upon the Panther, but a fierceness Asad was heartened to see, though it would surely goad the Panther should he notice it.

Her gaze softened as it met Asad's, but did not linger, and Asad lifted his cup to his lips and smiled as her gaze panned over the gathering before settling meekly at her feet.

"'The Song of Gilgamesh,'" the Panther roared, and the Swan dipped her knee.

Oona stood next to Lyrra and Nightingale, her gaze fixed above the gathering's heads as she concentrated on the words to the song of the desert hero Gilgamesh. She sang and Lyrra played, prompting Oona when she forgot a word, stringing out a certain note when Oona struggled with a certain phrase. Only when they had finally made it through the song did Oona lower her gaze to the faces of the crowd, smiling slightly and dipping her knee to the applause.

"A reel," the Panther called out, and Oona pressed her lips together and dipped her other knee.

Lyrra began to pluck the "Cat's Cradle" and Oona moved her feet. Asad was frowning and she gave him a quick smile and started skipping faster, reassuring him as best she could that she was up to a reel, and was relieved to see his frown smooth out. Beside him the Cheetah watched Lyrra play, his eyes never leaving her even as Oona's legs flashed in and out of her skirt panels.

Next to the Cheetah sat a boy of no more than ten years who looked as the Cheetah must have at that age, and beside him another boy of perhaps eight, who had the Panther's stocky build and curly black hair and who grinned from ear to ear as she kicked and twirled and skipped and hopped. She flashed him a smile and his eyes widened and he dug his elbow into the side of the younger version of the Cheetah.

A large, tawny, corded hand with blunt-tipped fingers that had played Oona's body last night as deftly as Lyrra played Nightingale now reached over and gently closed the boy's mouth.

Asad grinned as he ruffled the boy's curls, and he said something that made both boys nod and grin, and then he sat back and lifted his cup to her before putting it to his lips. Her cheeks flushing as much from the smile in his eyes as the exertion of the dance, Oona glanced at the Panther. His eyes were still fixed on her high kicking legs, as were the Heron's and the Bull's. Kicking and turning one last time, Oona slammed her heel down and stood still, arms akimbo and chest heaving as applause broke out.

Taking her bow, Oona straightened and looked from the king's table to the queen's. The Snow Leopard's inscrutable gaze was fixed on Oona, her lips pressed tight. Oona bent a shaky knee to the queen, whose piercing gaze never wavered as she dipped her chin in acknowledgment.

"'The Sailor's Tale,'" a man's voice, neither soft nor loud, yet commanding all the same called out. It was the Heron, the only man whom Oona had ever seen the Panther act in any way subservient to.

She had learned enough of the Seven Tribes' ways, and the Panther's, to know that it was because the Heron was senior in the tribe's hierarchy, and not because the Panther perceived any personal superiority of the Heron's. From what Oona had seen and heard of the Heron, he was a man who watched everything, giving nothing of his intentions away, and striking with precision after much deliberation, unlike the brash Panther or the plodding Bull.

The Heron was a king who had earned the loyalty and respect of his tribe, and whose first wife, the Reed, truly loved him, as he loved her. He had not stepped out of another woman's room this morning. He had left the pleasure house last night when the other men had retired with their chosen pleasure women, presumably returning to his wife's bed.

"'The Sailor's Tale,'" Oona said and dipped a knee to the Heron.

Oona imagined her own journey to come as she sang of the flight north across the great valley, of a port city where she and Lyrra would walk freely, buying their passage on a ship with the horses and jewels Asad would provide them.

She felt the rolling of a ship beneath her feet once more, the salty sea spray on her face, and her voice swelled. She sang of the sailor's glad homecoming while dreaming of her own, of her grandmother's sweet smile and her grandfather's warm embrace. Her voice faltered as she realized anew that even if she and Lyrra made it home, they would never see their mother or father again, and she found Asad's steady gaze on hers as she sang her last sad note.

"'A Wedding Song,'" the Fox yipped.

"*Rithill Aile,*" Oona said to Lyrra. "My words."

"Tonight she will be kind to him,
The prince is my darling."

The prince is my darling. Oona's words swam round and round Asad's head as the Panther called for one last reel and the Fox simpered and preened, holding court at her table as if she were already queen. Taking an actual sip of his wine, Asad sat back and admired the pure physicality of Oona's dancing. With her grace and strength and quickness of body and mind, she would make a good knife fighter. He imagined her taking it to the Fox in a fight and found himself smiling like a drunken fool, a smile the Panther watched and tipped his cup to. Asad tipped his back and pretended to take a long, deep draught.

The reel ended with one last pluck of the Dove's harp and a flash of the Swan's leg and then the Dove stood and took her bow beside her sister. They straightened and stood, waiting to be dismissed, their eyes on the Panther, their hands clasped tight.

"Take a seat, Swan, Dove," the Panther said, raising every brow in the salon, including the Swan's and the Dove's. "I wish for you to watch the fights, see how we men of the Great Valley wield our blades."

"My King." Oona gave a dip of her knee. She glanced around the salon and wisely did not seek Asad's gaze. "Where we sit?"

The Panther made a show of thinking on her question, as if he had not planned it out already. But Asad knew his sire too well. The Panther was a schemer, unless he was angered, and then the only thing he thought of was tearing whatever or whoever had made him angry apart.

"Sit there, with the maidservants." The Feast of Knives was one of the few feasts that palace servants were allowed to attend, and the Panther waved his hand toward a table on the back edge of the stage, the table the queen's maidservant the Clam sat at.

The Crab sat at the table next to the maidservants, his worried gaze on Asad, who had told the Crab of his determination to be winner of the knife fights tonight, to beat his father, an outcome the Crab had warned against. Asad had downplayed the Crab's worries then, but now the Crab's worries seemed well founded, for surely the Panther intended to show the Swan and the Dove, and everyone else here, that he was still king, that he still ruled his city and his sons.

The Panther stood. "Fighters, let us prepare ourselves."

"Will you beat our father tonight?" Azzam, the Panther's son by his fourth wife, asked Asad as he stood.

"We will see, Little Leopard." Asad ruffled the boy's curls. "We will see."

From the talk and the wagers among the women of the pleasure house, Oona knew that the Panther had not lost a match since becoming king, and that the Mouse and the Huntress had wagered against him for the first time tonight, placing their bets on the Black Mane.

"How fighters win?" Oona asked the Clam as the combatants returned to the hall, having changed from their robes to belted short tunics. The Black Mane's hair was tied back with a strip of leather as it had been their night in the cedar tree, and Oona tried hard not to stare at the line of his jaw, the breadth of his shoulders, his trim waist and well-muscled legs as the Clam explained a point system for specific touches, slashes, and jabs.

"They fight until one man has accumulated seven points or makes a kill," the Clam said.

Oona snapped her head around. "Kill?"

The Clam explained. "A kill is a stab to the heart or a slash of the neck or hamstring.'

"They not fight with real knife?"

"No, they use wooden knives. See, they bring them now."

A burly manservant carried in a basket and set it in the middle of the stage. Each fighter reached in and pulled out a knife sheathed in plain brown leather.

"They will know who they fight first by the color of their blade," the Clam explained as the fighters pulled the knives from the sheaths, each wooden blade dyed either red or green or yellow.

The men paired off, their backs to the servant's tables, the Panther and the Bull, the Black Mane and the Ox, and the Cheetah and the Heron's son, who was called the Grebe, and who looked to be of the same age as the Cheetah, with his father's slim build and alert eyes.

"Do they all fight one another?" Oona asked as the Panther and the Bull took center stage.

"No." The Clam's eyes never strayed from the fighters. "Only the winner of each fight then fights the other winners until there is only one."

Oona quit asking questions as the Heron raised a knife with an ivory hilt and metal blade high above his head. He slashed the blade down through the air and the Panther and the Bull started to circle one another, each grasping their wooden knife in one hand, holding the other out for space and balance. They lunged and jabbed, thrust and parried, the hall erupting into yells and shouts as their fighter either scored points or took hits. The Clam kept count out loud, so Oona knew the Panther led the Bull by five points to three when Asad turned around, his eyes serious beneath furrowed brows as they sought and held hers. She smiled, meaning to encourage him, but her smile only seemed to disconcert him more as he glanced from her to the Crab, who slowly shook his head at Asad. Running a hand through his beard, Asad turned back around to watch the Panther finish off the Bull.

The Crab was watching Oona now, his brows furrowed as deeply as Asad's had been.

"The Panther," she asked the Clam, although she already knew the answer. "He always win fights?"

"He does, and has, for the past ten and four years straight."

"He good fighter," Oona said, stating the obvious.

"He is, as is his son, the Black Mane. It has come down to the two of them the past four fights."

"Ah." That was why the Panther had bid her stay. He meant to beat Asad in front of her, and by Asad's straight back and stiff shoulders, he meant to beat the Panther.

Next up was the Cheetah and the Grebe. The Grebe moved deliberately and struck with a pointed precision, but he was no match for the Cheetah's longer reach and sure-footed quickness. The Cheetah beat the Grebe seven points to five.

Asad rolled and set his shoulders as he walked into the fighter's circle and faced the Ox. The Heron lifted his knife and slashed it back down and Asad charged straight at the Ox with a roar that froze the Ox where he stood. Asad struck with one mighty killing blow straight to the Ox's heart and the Ox stood, dumbfounded, his knife dangling unused and useless in his hand.

The hall was silent for a full breath, and then a sibilant hissing from the Ox's side mixed with thunderous applause from the Black Mane's as he strode out of the circle. His back to the royal audience, he met Oona's wide-eyed gaze and winked. The Clam sat back and stared at Oona as she pretended to study a speck of nothing in the air above her head until the next fight was called.

The match between the Black Mane and the Cheetah was more like a well-practiced dance than a fight. They were each of them grinning from ear to ear as the Heron's knife lifted, and when it dropped the Cheetah leapt forward, only to be swatted away by the lion's knifeless paw. The Cheetah circled and so did Asad, shifting their balance from foot to foot, tossing their knives from hand to hand, and then Asad struck, and the Cheetah jumped back and to the side, Asad's knife just grazing his ribs.

"One point, Black Mane," the Clam resumed her scorekeeping.

Lyrra's eyes followed the Cheetah's every move, and she clapped as he tagged Asad's thigh for a point.

"One, one, two, one," the Clam said as Asad countered with a blow to the Cheetah's shoulder, and he gave Asad a quick jab to his gut. "Two, two."

They broke and circled again, and Oona admired the sure swiftness of their footwork, the play of their thigh muscles tensing and releasing, their bellies gripping and twisting, their corded arms arcing and cutting as they traded point for point.

"Six, six," the Clam said as the Cheetah feinted to one side and landed a quick jab to Asad's forearm.

The Cheetah squared his feet and made to jab again when Asad leapt around him with his back to the Cheetah's in a half circle that had the Cheetah twisting to meet him as he landed, but Asad's knife touched the side of the Cheetah's neck before his feet hit ground.

"Seven, six, kill point," the Clam said. "The Black Mane has the bloodlust tonight."

"What you mean?" Oona tore her eyes from Asad's heaving chest as he caught his breath and bowed his head to his brother.

"The Black Mane always beats the Cheetah, but always before by points, never by a kill."

"Oh." Oona tried not to read too much into the Clam's words, or the curious rise of her brows. "Now Black Mane fight Panther?"

"Yes, after the Black Mane has rested a bit."

When the Black Mane and the Panther took the stage and faced each other, the hall went dead silent. The Heron slashed his blade through the air and lion and panther crouched, the muscles of their thighs and corded arms flexing as they circled one another, their wooden blades clasped tight and ready to strike.

The Panther struck first, lunging straight at Asad, who leapt back and to the Panther's side, landing a jab to the Panther's ribs and eliciting a snarl from the king.

"One, zero, Black Mane," the Clam whispered as lion and panther resumed their crouched circling.

Asad feinted and parried the Panther's blow with his bare arm, taking a hit as he slashed his blade across the Panther's belly.

"One, one, two, one, Black Mane. Why did the Black Mane cut and not stab for a kill?" The Clam looked to Oona as if for an answer. Oona shrugged.

The Panther regrouped and sprang with a roar at Asad, who took a glancing blow across his upper arm as he twisted and turned and slashed the Panther across the back, followed by a stab to his side.

"Three, two, four, two, Black Mane." The Clam glanced at the queen, whose gaze never left the combatants.

From across the room came the Fox's high-pitched twitter, and Oona swore Asad winced as he and the Panther resumed their circling. The Panther jabbed his blade into the air once, twice, three times before lunging at Asad and nicking him on his arm as Asad set his feet and slashed the Panther's forearm before he could jump back.

"Five, three, Black Mane." The Clam's voice had a worried hush to it.

Whispers rushed through the hall like wildfire through dry grass as heads bent together and last-moment wagers were laid. The Crab was eyeing Oona again and pulling on his beard. The excited hiss of the crowd turned her attention back to the fighters in time to see Asad leap toward the Panther, deftly twisting in midair and avoiding the slashing arc of the Panther's blade as his hit the Panther's shoulder.

"Six, three," the Clam said, sucking air between her teeth.

The Crab shook his head and lowered it into his hands. Oona looked back at Asad, who met her gaze a moment before pivoting as the Panther charged. He had easily side-stepped the Panther's charges before, but this time he stepped straight back and took the full weight of the Panther barreling into him. The Panther raised his blade high and plunged it into his son's belly and then his chest. Asad let out a grunt of pain and lay prone on the floor as the Panther stood and raised his blade in victory.

"Kill point, the Panther," the Clam's voice rushed out in relief.

"So, you are going to play sore loser now, my son?" The Panther pushed back his stool and grinned over the rim of his cup at Asad.

His father calling him son told Asad he had made the right choice in throwing the fight, but still it rankled. He promised himself that next fight, once the Swan and the Dove were safely away, he would beat the Panther, and soundly.

"That is exactly what I am playing," he said, lifting his tunic to show the welt on his belly, which would be a bruise by the morrow. The Panther gave a low whistle, pleased with his victor's mark. "You have unmanned me, Father," Asad added for good measure. "I am too sore to enjoy the company of any woman tonight." Asad let his tunic drop and took a long draught of wine. He lifted his cup to the Panther, the Cheetah, the Bull, the Ox, and the Grebe. "I will retreat to my lair to tend my wounds and my pride."

"Do not feel too badly, Black Mane." The Panther slapped Asad on the back. "You put up a good fight tonight."

Asad nodded and said nothing. He drained his cup and left the men's table for the women's.

"I am abed, my Lady Queen," he told his mother.

"So early, my son?" Her voice, her demeanor, gave away nothing, but her eyes watched his intently. "Are you injured?"

"Only my pride."

Fine black brows arched high over piercing keen eyes as she stood and laid a hand on his forearm.

"It was an interesting fight between you and your father."

"One whose point I still feel sorely," he said with a wry grin that raised her brows even higher. "And so, my Lady Queen, I bid you good night." He dipped his head to the table, pointedly refusing to meet the Fox's expectant gaze. "Ladies." He winked at his sister, the Gazelle, who grinned back.

"Swan, Dove," the Panther called out. "You will attend to me, now." The Panther stood, and the Swan and the Dove stepped quickly to stand before him, heads down. "Come." He grabbed Oona by the shoulder and yanked her to him, and Asad's hand balled into a fist. "Accompany me back to the pleasure house."

Asad started toward them when he felt a hand on his shoulder, its touch soft but tenacious.

"I am feeling rather tired myself," his mother said. "Walk with me to my chambers, my son, before you seek your own."

He was ready to shake his mother's hand off and go after the Panther and the sisters when the Cheetah stood and shook his head at Asad before joining their father and several other men as they left the salon. He would watch over the sisters tonight.

The queen did not say a word to Asad until they were in the hall leading to the family's private chambers with the Clam and the Crab walking a discreet distance behind them.

"That would have been rather foolhardy of you, Black Mane," she scolded, "going after the Panther like that."

Asad said nothing.

"You almost beat the Panther in a fight that you then gave to him, and smartly done." Her eyes bored into the side of his head. "And yet a moment later you are ready to lose all the goodwill your dive gave you over some girl? What is going on under that black mane of yours?"

"She is not some girl."

"What?"

"She is not some girl." He stopped and stood and stared his mother and queen in the eye. "She is Oona, the Swan, daughter of Aaron, granddaughter of Olwain, and Princess of the Clan Macleod. And if he hurts her, we will fight again, and not with wooden blades."

Bowing stiffly to his mother, he headed for his chambers, alone.

Oona lay floating on her back in the bathing pool, staring up at the ceiling tiles laid out in the images of seven women in various states of undress lounging and bathing in a river's pool with rainbow-hued fish swimming below broad-leafed lily pads with brightly plumed birds flitting atop the cat-tailed reeds. Lyrra floated beside her, her eyes closed, a tired smile on her face. The Cheetah had come to the pleasure house with the Panther after the knife fights last night along with the Heron and the Grebe, the Bull and the Ox, and he had paid Lyrra more attention than he should have, catching the eye of the Panther and the Spider, who had spent most of the evening fawning over the Panther and whispering in his ear.

They had all gone to their beds late, and Oona had been awakened in the pitch of night by the Panther and the Mynah bursting in and searching her and her chambers as they had the dawn before. And when she and Lyrra made their way down to the bathing pool later that morning, Lyrra told Oona that the Panther and the Mynah had searched her chambers and her body last night as well.

Embarrassed as Lyrra had been by the search of her person, she grinned every time she spoke of the cause, of the Cheetah's attentions to her, and Oona was too pleased to see her sister smile to make much of it while they enjoyed the peace and calm of the bathing pool. There would be time later to remind Lyrra that it would be better if she and the Cheetah ignored each other in the Panther's presence, a trick she and Asad had managed with varying success.

"Look what we have here floating in our pool, ladies," a voice echoed loudly in the tiled chambers. Oona lifted her head. The Spider and the Eel and a wide-hipped, raw-boned desert woman whose name Oona could not recall stood at the steps into the pool. Oona lowered her feet and planted them on the solid bottom of the pool as Lyrra did the same. "A Swan as pale and thin as watered goat's milk, and a Dove who thinks her puny goods enticement enough for the Cheetah."

"Look what we have here, sister," Lyrra said in their highland tongue, "a spider who spews venom."

Oona glanced sideways at her sister, who stood straight and stiff-backed beside her, her hands fisted below the waist deep water.

"What did you say, Dove?" the Spider hissed. She took two menacing steps into the water and stood with her arms akimbo, glaring at Lyrra. "Tell me what you said, you lily-faced bitch."

Oona's jaw dropped, but Lyrra's chin lifted.

"Insulting me will no make me tell you, Spider," Lyrra said with much of her old spirit.

Glad as Oona was to see it, she wished Lyrra had chosen another time to get it back as the Spider strode through the water toward Lyrra, her face contorted into a mask of pure malice.

"What did you say to me?" She stood nose to nose with Lyrra as the other two women entered the pool and stood to each side of the Spider. "I will have it out of you, Dove, one way or the other."

"Remember, sister," Oona spoke to Lyrra in their northern tongue, figuring it would be better to be punished for speaking their forbidden language than for getting into a fight. "We are to avoid trouble."

"Now what did you say, Swan?" the Spider demanded.

Oona held her hands palm up to the Spider as the robed figures of three more women entered the chamber. Their heads were covered with their mantles and Oona could not see their faces, but they would at least be witnesses that she had tried to stop the fight that was threatening.

"I say, Spider," Oona spoke in as calm and steady a voice as she could manage, "that we new here. We no want fight you." Oona spread her hands out to include the Eel and the raw-boned woman. "Our new sisters."

"That is smart of you, Swan," the Spider said, her black eyes bright, her smile dripping poison. "But unless your sister tells me what she said, it will not matter what you want."

Oona looked to Lyrra, her eyes pleading with her sister to back down.

"I will tell you what I say," Lyrra told the Spider, who smiled smugly, "when you tell Swan you sorry for insult her."

The Spider's indolent eyes widened and she burst into cackles.

"Why would I ever apologize to the Swan?"

"Why would I ever tell you what I say?"

"Because I will beat you bloody here and now if you do not."

Lyrra shrugged. "You will try beat me no matter what."

The Spider's grin was chilling. "You are so right," she said.

Her arm shot out and she grabbed Lyrra by the hair and yanked her head down into the water. Oona sprang for the Spider and the Eel tried to block her, but Oona threw an elbow to the Eel's jaw that sent her reeling back into the water. Oona pushed the Spider's outstretched hand away and grabbed her by the hair. The raw-boned woman lunged for Oona, and met Oona's foot in her belly, flying back with arms flailing and landing in the water with a loud grunt and a splash.

"Let her go," Oona told the Spider, who hissed and spit but did not let go her hold of Lyrra. "Let her go," Oona growled into the Spider's ear before pushing her head face down into the water. Still the Spider held on, and Oona pushed her head farther down.

Oona had seen Lyrra's gulp of air before her face hit water, and she knew how long her sister could hold her singer's breath, longer, she was wagering, than the soft-fleshed, sluggish Spider.

"Enough." Oona's head snapped up and around to the side of the pool where the robed women stood.

"Let her go, Swan," the tallest of the women said in a voice to be obeyed, a voice Oona recognized.

Oona let go her hold of the Spider, who came up spitting and sputtering as Lyrra surfaced, pushing her hair back from her face and sucking in a deep breath. The robed woman dropped her headscarf and Oona dropped a knee.

"My Lady Queen."

"I spoke with the Swan this morning," the Queen told Asad as he took a seat at her table. "And the Dove."

"Did you?" Asad accepted the honey wine she poured him. "Well, that explains why you summoned me to your chambers." He looked around. Not a maidservant was in sight or hearing distance. "Alone."

His mother, the queen, lifted her cup to him.

"And how did you find them?" he asked, taking a drink of his wine.

"In the bathing pool with the Swan holding the Spider's head underwater."

Asad choked and sputtered.

"They are not as delicate as they look, your Swan and Dove."

"No," Asad agreed, dragging in a full breath. "They are not."

"We had a lovely talk, the Swan, the Dove, and I." His mother sipped her wine while watching him over the cup's rim. "They told me of sailing with their father, of the pirates, the slave market, and the Jackal buying them as a dowry gift for his daughter and my son."

Asad growled into his drink and the queen took another sip of hers.

"I asked them of Summer's Eve, of the night they first performed for the Panther, the night the Swan proposed their marriages to his sons." The queen's eyes pierced Asad's. "I asked the Swan if she had ever asked you what your answer would have been. And she answered in that charming way of hers, what it matter, it will no be." His mother smiled, slow and deliberate. "She is a terrible liar, much worse than you."

"So she is." Asad chose to ignore the broader implications of her words. It was one thing to lie bald-faced to his father, he had done so most of his life as a matter of survival, but to his mother he had never lied outright, and he would not now. "She is a terrible liar, much worse than me, and she told you the truth. She has never asked me what my answer would have been, nor does it matter now. She is a pleasure woman in the Panther's palace, and I will marry the Fox."

"So she is." His mother reached out across the table and laid her hand on his. "And so you will."

Asad pulled his hand away and raised his cup.

"To my first marriage," he said, not even attempting to hide the anger he felt, anger his mother would understand only too well.

His mother raised her cup.

"To your first marriage," she said in her best queenly voice. "May it bring everything it should to the Seven Tribes."

Asad took a long draught of his sweet honey wine, which soured on his tongue.

"May I ask you something else?" his mother said with a patient smile that Asad mirrored. "Was it because of her, because of the Swan, that you threw the fight last night?"

"Partly," he said. "The fact that the Panther commanded the Swan and the Dove to stay and watch told me he intended to show he was still king, and though I knew Asad could beat Ka'azir, I also knew the Black Mane should not beat the Panther, not in front of the Heron and the Bull, or the Swan and the Dove would likely pay with the skin from their backs."

His mother winced and Asad was sorry for it, but she had asked.

"Then well done, my son, indeed, quite princely of you."

"I thought so." He gave his mother a wry grin. "And you despaired I would never learn to be prince first."

"Well, I would not say I despaired," she said with a teasing grin of her own. But then her eyes grew serious, and she laid her hand over his. "Truly, Asad, I have a mother's pride in you for the man you have become, and a queen's for the prince you are, the king you will be."

"Thank you, Mother. It is good to know my marrying where I should instead of where I would is worth something to somebody."

CHAPTER 10

Falling

By noon, every woman in the pleasure house had asked Oona and Lyrra about the queen's visit. The Snow Leopard had only crossed the threshold of the pleasure house three times before. Twice with the Owl as a healer, and once as a jealous young wife, when she had sought out the Spider, the Panther's favorite at the time. That she had sought out the Swan and the Dove their third day there was a matter of great speculation.

They told the story they had been asked to tell by the queen, that she had been intrigued by their strange looks and wished to learn of their faraway land and their journey from there to here. A story that was true enough, but omitted the crux of the matter, which was that the queen wanted to know about the Swan and her son.

Oona had answered her with the same manner of truth, telling her that she greatly admired the Black Mane for saving her life in the desert, that she thought him the best of men, a true prince, and that she had never asked him what his answer would have been to her proposal. She did not tell the queen that she dreamed daily of what he would have answered given his choice, of what it would mean to be Asad's woman, the Black Mane's wife. She only told her that she understood he was a prince, meant to be a king, and she was a slave, meant to be a pleasure woman. She did not say that the prince had vowed to set the slave free.

The Mynah, who had been one of the hooded women with the queen and the Clam at the bathing pool, told the story of Oona and Lyrra's fight with the Spider and the Eel and the raw-boned woman, who was called the Goat, to the others with much glee. Apparently, she and the Spider were not on the best of terms, and the incident did much to bring Oona and Lyrra up a few notches in the Mynah's estimation.

Oona and Lyrra were in the common room, still surrounded by women asking question after question, when voices could be heard in the king's salon. The Mynah was directing the Boar to set Nightingale down in the center of the salon, and Lyrra danced into the room and ran her hands up and down the harp's carved frame, a happy smile on her face.

"The Panther requests a private audience tonight," the Mynah told them. "Only you, Dove, and you, Swan, will attend him. And him only."

Lyrra's smile froze, as did Oona's blood.

"Private audience," the Spider seethed. "First the queen and now the king. What is so special about these two milk-faced sisters?"

"Talent." Lyrra plucked a single, lingering note. "Something you no have, Spider, outside of bed."

Oona was not the only woman to gasp aloud.

"Out," the Mynah commanded with a sharp clap of her hands. "Everybody out, back to your meal."

"May I stay, Mistress Mynah," Lyrra asked. "To practice for king's audience tonight?"

"Yes, of course," the Mynah said, eyeing the Spider as she filed out, grumbling into the Eel's ear. "You may stay and practice, and I will come for you when it is time to prepare yourselves." She looked to Oona. "Will you stay as well, Swan?"

Oona shook her head. She had not been able to eat much of her noon meal while answering so many questions, and now that she was recovered from her heat sickness, her appetite had seemed to triple. If she was going to sing and dance for the Panther tonight and not collapse from nerves, she needed sustenance.

She filled a bowl with juicy red and orange melon and resumed her seat in the common room, the Mouse sitting on one side of her and the Huntress the other, flanking her and glaring off any other woman who dared approach, assuring Oona of some small peace in which to finish her meal. Why the Mouse had befriended her so quickly, and did not seem the least bit jealous that the Black Mane had shown interest in her, baffled Oona. She liked the Mouse, she truly did, but her eyes were not the only thing green about her whenever she thought of the Black Mane and the Mouse together, of the Mouse ever being his favorite.

The lively notes of the "Cat's Cradle" from the salon had Oona tapping a foot along, but then she thought of dancing for the Panther alone, and her foot missed a beat. Lyrra would be there too, of course, but she could bury her face into Nightingale and avoid the Panther's eyes. Oona would not be so lucky. She would have to sing and dance in front of him, and only him, unable to ignore his black gaze. There would be no amber lion eyes offering her safe haven.

A few of the other women were tapping their feet or bobbing their heads too. Lyrra's harp truly could speak to people. Hopefully it would speak to the Panther tonight, give him some pleasure and ease his anger toward the sisters, his suspicions. Asad had said that the Panther would not expect physical favors from them until their training had been complete, but that did not mean he would not strip their backs with his whip if angered enough.

The "Cat's Cradle" ended and the first melancholy strains of "Deep Peace" filled the air. The Pearl's face took on a faraway look as the Spider and the Eel got up and left the salon. Across the room the Mynah sat with her eyes closed, a sad smile playing across her thin lips, and Oona was reminded that she and Lyrra were not the only women here against their wills.

Asad finished brushing Storm and made way for the Ratter carrying the stallion's bucket of oats. The Ratter eyed Asad's sweat-stained tunic as he sat the bucket down in front of Storm.

"Run some of the steam off ye, did ye?"

"Some," Asad said, "but not near enough." He could have run Storm a hundred leagues and barely cooled the well of anger that simmered deep inside him, threatening to boil over every time he thought of the night to come. The Panther had made a point of letting him and the Cheetah know of his plans for a private audience with the Swan and the Dove, and that they were to perform for him in their silks, oiled and kohled and painted to his liking.

Asad clamped his jaw and clenched his fists at the fear and embarrassment the sisters would be forced to endure, yet he did not dare visit the pleasure house to reassure them. The Panther's spies were everywhere. All he could do was keep out of the Panther's way and pray that Oona would be able to maintain her grace and calm whilst she and her sister were being ogled and degraded by Asad's father.

He had ridden Storm long and hard dwelling on such thoughts, wearing them both out as much as possible without running the stallion into the ground or making himself late for the evening meal, which would cause his mother concern and anger his father, who no doubt looked forward to rubbing the coming evening into his son's face.

"Ye'll be wantin to wash up here." The Ratter set down a bucket of clean water.

"Thank you, Ratter." Asad pulled his tunic off and dipped his hands into the bucket, splashing cooling water over his face and chest and arms.

"What's it about this time?" the Ratter asked as he handed a drying towel to Asad.

"What is what about?" Asad dried his face.

"Tearin' out of the stables early an' returnin' late for supper all in a lather, the both of ye."

Asad threw the towel at the Ratter's head, but the old stable master was quicker than he looked and caught it easily.

"Well?" The Ratter's hands sat on hips as bowed as his legs.

"Go ask the Crab," Asad growled, "since you two enjoy discussing me so much."

"It's the woman then, the Swan," the Ratter said with a slow nod of his head. "The Crab said ye'd been gitten moodier 'n broodier about 'er."

"Did he now?" Asad fixed the Ratter with a scowl as he pulled a clean tunic from the cupboard. He had been late to supper after riding enough times to keep one at the ready.

"'At he did."

"What else did he say?"

"'At the Panther was lucky to win the fight last night."

Asad shrugged into his tunic. "What does that have to do with the Swan?"

"Accordin' to the Crab it had everthin' to do with 'er."

"How so?"

"Accordin' to the Crab, the Panther's luck woulda been much diffrint if'n the Swan weren't there watchin'." The Ratter rubbed the side of his nose. "An' accordin' to the Crab, if'n the Panther keeps pushin 'is luck, 'e's goin ta feel the Black Mane's blade twixt his ribs sooner rather 'n later."

Asad pinned the Ratter with his haughtiest princely stare.

"Tell the Crab he talks too much."

Oona stood gazing out her window as the sun set below the palace walls, turning the cloudless sky from blue to yellow to orange. She was supposed to have been resting before her audience with the king tonight, but she was unable to sleep, or even sit or lie down, and had gone back and forth from pacing the length of her room to staring out the window, for as soon as dusk turned to dark, the palace would sup and the maidservants would come to paint and dress her.

She kept telling herself not to fear, the Panther would not touch them sexually. All they had to do was play his game, be meek and subservient and not displease him. Smile prettily and sing and dance reel after reel if he wished. She told herself this over and over again, but still a niggling fear gripped her belly and would not let go its hold.

"There is nothing to fear," she whispered to the reddening sky, trying to replace the image of the Panther's hard, black glare with the Black Mane's warm amber gaze in her mind's eye. "We will be gone from here soon enough. Asad has promised. Asad—"

A startled cry whipped Oona's head to Lyrra's window. She opened her mouth, but her scream was soundless, caught in her throat as she watched Lyrra fall, face down, arms outstretched and hair streaming out behind her, her skirts flapping around her legs. She hit the ground with a sickening thud where she lay sprawled in an unnatural, unmoving silence.

"LLYYRRAA," Oona screamed loud enough for the entire city to hear as she ran from her room into the hallway, where the Spider and the Eel came running toward her from beyond Lyrra's open door.

"What is it, Swan?" the Spider said as Oona flew past them.

"Dove," she yelled as she ran down the stairs two at time. "She fall."

The Mynah was at the foot of the stairs, reaching out to slow Oona down, but Oona tore through her grasp. She ran straight out the door into the courtyard, the Mouse and the Huntress on her heels. The Boar was bending over Lyrra's still body.

"She breathes," he said as Oona knelt beside her sister. "But she does not hear us, and she bleeds from her nose and mouth."

"Pick her up," Oona said, and the Boar scooped Lyrra's limp form into his massive arms. He started for the pleasure house. "No." Oona grabbed his arm. "Take her to palace, to Black Mane and Snow Leopard. They will know what to do."

"You must not," the Mynah cried, wringing her hands together. "We must send for the Owl to come here."

Lyrra's head hung slack and her eyes were unseeing, her skin ashen but for the bright red blood dripping from her nose and mouth.

"No." Oona shook her head at the Mynah and fixed the Boar with a pleading gaze. "There be no time. We need get her to Black Mane. Now. He not be angry with us. I swear it."

"The Black Mane may not, but the Panther will be," the Mynah insisted.

The Boar hesitated and then turned for the gate, half walking, half running as Oona led the way, the Mouse and the Huntress on each side of him, shooing off the others who had come to see what all the fuss was about. They stopped at the gate and Oona pushed it open.

"You enter the palace at your own risk," the Mynah screeched as Oona slammed the gate behind her and the Boar. "Do not say I did not warn you."

"Which way?" The Boar glanced wildly around the grounds between the pleasure house and the palace. He had likely never been beyond the gate since the day he had been brought here.

"There." Oona pointed to the door that she and Lyrra had been led through last night as people stopped to stand and stare at them. "That is door to kitchens."

Asad entered the salon as the Panther took his seat beside the Hyacinth, his seventh wife, dutifully pregnant with her second child. The supper and the seating being informal, Asad took a seat between his mother and his sister at a table where the Cheetah and his mother, the Caracal, also sat.

"You made it," his sister said with a grin.

"Just," his mother, the queen, said with one finely arched brow.

"I was riding Storm," Asad explained, "and lost track of the time."

"Oh?" His mother's other brow rose. "Was the sun hidden by clouds?"

"No." Asad shook his head. "But my mind was."

"Why, brother?" the Gazelle asked as all the adults at the table exchanged knowing glances.

Asad opened his mouth to give his sister some inane explanation when the door to the kitchens burst open and the Swan flew into the salon followed by the Boar carrying the Dove.

"Dove fall," she cried as Asad stood. "She fall from chamber window."

The Cheetah was two steps ahead of Asad as they dodged tables to reach the Swan and the Dove. Asad laid his fingers on the Dove's neck and felt a faint pulse.

"She lives," Asad said.

The Cheetah let out a shaky sigh.

"You will heal her?" Oona's eyes were wild with fear.

"I will do my best." Asad wished he could give her better. But he would not lie, not to her. The Dove was in a bad way.

"Take her to my chambers," the queen said from behind Asad. He turned and met the concern in her eyes with his own.

"Fetch the Owl," he told the Cheetah. "Tell him what happened. He will need his potions."

The Cheetah gave the Dove one long worried look and then he turned for the door.

"Follow me," Asad told the Boar.

"Halt," the Panther's bellow filled the salon. "I said halt," he yelled again as the Cheetah hesitated at the door and looked to Asad. "Do not look to your brother, boy, I am king here, and nobody moves until I say so."

"But the Dove could die," the Cheetah said, the closest to challenging the Panther he had ever come in his life, and enraging him further.

"If she dies, she dies." The Panther gave a callous wave of his arm. "She is mine to let live or die, as the Swan is mine to flay the skin from her back for daring to bring the Dove here and interrupting my supper."

"No," Asad said. He took Oona's hand in his and faced his father. "She is not."

The Panther stood to his full height, chest out and eyes narrowed.

"She is not what? Not mine to do with as I will?"

"Not anymore," Asad said, Oona's heart hammering against his arm.

"Pray tell," the Panther said with a sneer at their intertwined hands. "Why she is not."

"Because the Swan is mine," Asad declared as a collective gasp filled the salon. "I am claiming her, and her sister, the Dove."

"You would challenge me, boy," the Panther raged, "over a woman?"

"No, old man," Asad snarled. "Not over a woman, over this woman."

"Why you insolent, upstart cub." The Panther charged, red faced and spitting mad. "I will flay the skin from her back and yours."

"No," Asad roared with all the pent-up fury and frustration of the last ten and four years. He let go of Oona's hand and met the Panther's charge chest to chest, pushing the Panther back a step as Oona jumped to the side. "You will not."

He stood nose to nose with his huffing father, his challenge given. The last time his father had threatened to whip him, Asad had been a boy of ten. This time he was a man fully grown, protecting what was most dear to him in all this world, and he would not back down. When the Panther still said nothing but continued to billow hot air, Asad turned to Oona, whose face was almost as white as the Dove's. "Go," he told her. "Go with my mother, take the Dove and tend her. I will be with you shortly."

"No, Asad." Oona shook her head, her eyes wide and wild and pleading. "Do not do this, not for me. I take Panther's whipping."

"You are damned right you will," the Panther spat.

Asad grabbed the Panther by the throat with one hand and the Panther's knife hand with his other.

"I promised myself many years ago that no woman I cared for would ever feel the bite of your whip again," he told his purple-faced sire, "and I intend to keep my promise." He knew he only had a short time before the shock of his actions would wear off and the Panther would start to fight back. He inclined his head to his mother. "Take them, now, every moment counts." He tightened his hold on the Panther's throat, his pulse pounding beneath Asad's fingers. "Now, Father," he said, his voice low and his meaning clear, "do you want to continue this discussion in front of all these people, or shall we go someplace more private?"

"So, it is Oona and Asad, is it," the queen muttered as Oona hurried behind her, the Boar following with Lyrra in his arms. The queen glanced over her shoulder at Oona and shook her head. "And promises made to be kept, and the Panther to be challenged, and not over a woman, over this woman."

As much as Oona wanted to apologize to the queen for putting her into this situation, she thought it best to remain silent until the queen asked for a response, for she was still a servant here, at least until the challenge was settled between the Black Mane and the Panther. And though she had every faith in Asad, and prayed that it would not come to blows between father and son, king and prince, she truly had no idea how the whole of the situation would turn out. For now, she needed to concentrate on Lyrra, and that meant keeping quiet and doing everything she was told to by the queen.

Blood still seeped from Lyrra's nose, and her face had gone from pale to ashen. Oona looked up at the Boar, who met her worried gaze with one of fear and wonderment. She wanted to tell him not to worry, that the Black Mane would do everything in his power to protect him from the Panther's wrath as well, but all she could do was lay her hand on his arm and give him a quick smile of forced bravado, one that she needed to believe as badly as he.

"Here." The queen pushed open the door to her chambers and led the way through the sitting room Asad had carried Oona into what felt like an age ago and into a room with the biggest bed Oona had ever seen sitting grandly in the middle of it.

Panels of pale gold worm weave draped down from a frame of intricately carved bedposts, and a cover of the same pale gold, embroidered with green vines and red flowers, lay over the bed. "Lay her here," the queen instructed the Boar as she pulled down the bed's linens.

Oona's eyes welled as the Boar lay Lyrra down onto the soft mattress. She had known the queen to be kind, letting Asad tend to Oona on her sofa, visiting them in the pleasure house, but to put Lyrra in her own bed. All Oona could do was meet the queen's gaze over the prone body of her sister and hope she saw the humbling gratitude Oona felt.

Footsteps and voices filled the outer chambers, and then the Clam entered, followed by a stooped man with long, flowing gray hair and a beard down to his belly.

"The Cheetah said the girl fell," the Owl said as the Cheetah stepped into the room, his eyes instantly on Lyrra, his face blanching almost as pale as hers.

The queen nodded to Oona. "Her sister, the Swan, saw her fall."

"She fall from her room," Oona said, the vision of Lyrra falling, of her skirts flapping and her hair streaming out behind her, landing with a sickening thud and lying crumpled and still, buckling her knees. She grabbed onto the side of the bed and hung her head until the vision stopped swimming before her eyes. When she looked up again, the Queen was feeling Lyrra's pulse while the Owl gingerly moved her neck and head.

"Her neck is not broken," the Owl said, and the Cheetah released his breath in a loud rush. The Owl's fingers made their way down Lyrra's arm while the queen felt the other from shoulder to fingertips. "Her collarbone is dislocated," the Owl said, "but I am certain I can realign it. It should heal with time and a sling."

Oona sighed with relief, for Lyrra would not have been Lyrra if she could no longer play her beloved harp.

The Owl gently poked and prodded Lyrra's belly and nodded to the queen. "No swelling of her abdomen," he said, and then frowned as his fingers moved to her left knee and Lyrra moaned. He took both hands to her knee and pushed and kneaded the reddened, swollen flesh. "Her knee is dislocated as well," he said, "but I do not think any bones are broken or any sinew torn. It will have to be realigned as well, and then splinted."

A flushing heat rose from Oona's belly to her face, and the room began to swim around her as she shivered and her skin rippled with goose flesh.

"Come, Swan," a voice said in her ear as a hand took her by the elbow. She turned to see the Cheetah's face close to hers, his voice soft and calming. "Sit before you fall." He lowered her onto a stool that materialized beneath her as the Owl's and the queen's voices floated beyond her. "The Dove is in the best of hands. It is good she feels pain in her leg, it means she is not paralyzed."

"But the pain not wake her," Oona managed a hoarse whisper. "Should not pain wake her?"

The Cheetah said nothing and Oona focused on his face until she saw her answer in his worried eyes, and her heart hammered in her ears so loudly she could hear nothing else. The Cheetah's head turned and Oona followed his gaze to where Asad was walking toward her, his arms opening as their eyes met. She flew into his embrace and buried her face into his neck as his strong arms held her tight.

Asad pressed his lips to Oona's forehead, holding her close as she burrowed deeper into his chest.

"You and Lyrra are under my protection now," he told her. "No further harm will come to you."

Emerald eyes welling with tears lifted to his.

"Truly?" she said with a tremulous smile that wrenched his gut.

"Truly."

"How?"

Asad looked up from her probing eyes. Every person in the room was waiting to hear his answer.

"I told the Panther he did not want to fight me over this, that I would not take a fall this fight." He gave them all a purposely cocky grin.

"And?" his mother said.

"And we agreed that the Swan and the Dove are free women from this moment on and will be let to leave for their home when the Dove is able."

"And?" she repeated.

"And I will marry the Fox without further complaint and sire a fine eldest son with her."

Oona stiffened in his arms.

"What else did it cost you?" his mother said.

"Two brood mares and studding Storm out to the Panther's mares until one conceives a colt."

"That is all?"

"Yes, Mother, that is all." If any man could consider the bedding of a woman he despised as all. He looked down at Lyrra, who lay still and unconscious as the Owl washed the blood from her face. "How fares the Dove?"

"Her collarbone and knee are displaced," the queen said. "But she is young and both injuries should heal with time and rest."

"And her head injury?"

Oona went still.

"We are unsure. The Owl and I have been discussing whether to give her Dream Flower, to deepen her sleep that she may rest and heal, or wait and see if she..." Oona's head snapped up and the queen's concerned gaze held hers a moment before she continued. "Or whether we should wait and let her wake on her own first."

Oona woke to the low glow of candlelight with her head craned sideways, her arm outstretched and her hand clasping Lyrra's, which was cold and clammy despite the warmth of the night. Straightening on her stool and stretching her stiff neck and shoulders, she peered closer at Lyrra's ashen face. Her sister still slept the sleep of one half in this world and half in the next.

After much discussion by the queen, the Owl, and Asad, it had been decided to give Lyrra enough Dream Flower to keep her from pain while they realigned her shoulder and knee, and then to wait and let her wake on her own, *if* she woke on her own.

They had tried to downplay the danger Lyrra was in of not waking ever for Oona's sake, and the Cheetah's, who slept on a sofa across the room, as did the queen. But Oona understood enough to know that the longer Lyrra slept this unnatural sleep, the greater the chances she would never wake, or that when she did her mind might never be the same.

Asad lay sleeping on a sofa beside a table laden with the Owl's mendicants, his handsome face at peace after a day that had changed so much for him, for her, and Lyrra: for all of them.

He had gone against his father, the king, for her. He had saved her from the Panther's whip when she would have gladly paid for Lyrra's life with her flesh. He had saved them from slavery and given them their freedom, at a cost to his own. For now he would not only have to wed the Fox, but bed her as well.

Fighting an overwhelming urge to crawl onto the sofa beside him and burrow deep into the safe warmth of his chest, Oona let her breath out in an unsteady sigh. Taking her sister's right hand in both of hers, careful not to disturb her left arm in its sling, Oona lifted it to her cheek and let the tears she had kept dammed until now spill freely.

"Oh LyLy," she cried softly, trying not to wake anybody. "I am sorry, so sorry, for all that happen, all because I would not stay and marry where I should have, and now here we be, where we should not be. And I cause Asad to fight with father, for us. Oh LyLy, he is man of such honor: man I honor above all others. Man I must leave for his sake and ours, and I...I cannot bear it, not without you. So please, sister, please come back to this world, to me, and I...I will leave this man, my lion, my somebody, and I will get you home. This I swear to you."

"Do you realize you were speaking in the desert tongue?" The low, resonant timber of Asad's voice filled Oona's head, her heart.

"You hear?" she said.

"Every word." His eyes gleamed amber in the candle's low light. "Did you mean what you said?"

Oona smiled through her tears. "Every word," she said, and then his arms were open and she was in them, her nose burrowed into the safe, familiar warmth of his neck as his arms closed around her and held her tight.

"I sorry, Asad," she whispered fiercely into his neck. "I sorry I cause you to fight you father."

"Do not be, my jewel," he said, stroking her hair. "It was bound to happen sooner or later. In truth you did me a favor. I have lived with the knowledge of who and what my father is, like it or not, my whole life. Now it is his turn to learn to live with me, Asad, as I am. Not as he wishes me to be."

Oona lifted her head and met Asad's gaze straight on.

"Then he will be proud of his eldest son, lion four times through," she vowed. "For true Asad is man any father be proud of."

"Yes, well, that remains to be seen." He glanced over her head and gave a wry smile. "My father, the Panther, has never appreciated my desire to protect the women I care for from his wrath."

"Women?" Oona said. It was the second time this day he had said this. The horrible vision of the Huntress's scarred back came to Oona, and then another of the Huntress, naked, in Asad's arms. Oona stiffened and then dropped her head. The Huntress was her friend. She had risked her back again helping Oona get Lyrra to the palace. If the Huntress and Asad had a fondness for each other, Oona should be glad, though she felt anything but pleased at the thought of him turning to the Huntress or the Mouse after she was gone.

"Women," the queen said from behind Oona.

Oona turned in Asad's arms as the queen rose from her sofa and walked to them. Oona made to pull out of Asad's embrace, but his arms held her tight.

"No, my jewel," he said softly. "There is no need to be anything but Oona and Asad here in these chambers. Besides, I am fairly certain my mother has suspected my true feelings for you from the day we returned from the Jackal's."

"I had suspected, yes," the queen acknowledged. "But as of tonight, I would say it is perfectly clear to all the regard you have for each other." She smiled, not unkindly, and Oona felt the heat rush to her cheeks as the queen's eyes settled on hers. "You ask of the women my son speaks of." She turned her back to them and dropped the shoulder of her gown to reveal three scars snaking across the middle of her back. "There are only two, Swan," the queen said over her shoulder, "you and I."

"The Panther," Oona gasped as the terrible truth sunk in. "He whip you? His wife?"

"The summer of Asad's tenth year." The queen pulled her gown up and turned to face them. "My husband thought me unfaithful to my marriage vows and took his whip to me. Asad heard me cry out and came running into my chambers."

Her eyes took on a faraway look and the line of her mouth was grim. "My son tried to protect his mother from his father, but he was only a boy and his father rewarded him with the back of his hand, leaving him with a blackened eye." She gave her son a sad, fleeting smile that made Oona's heart clench. "He swore to me then, my young cub, that no woman he cared for would ever feel the bite of the Panther's whip again."

"And Asad, the Black Mane, Prince of Great Valley, lion four times through," Oona said. "He always keep his word."

CHAPTER 11

Lines in the Sand

Asad shifted on the sofa and pushed a wayward strand of fine white blonde hair back from Oona's cheek as she stirred in his arms, his wrist brushing the tip of her nose as her heavy lashes fluttered and eyes green and faceted as cut emeralds stared up into his.

"Asad," she breathed, her lips upturned in a sleepy half smile.

"Oona."

Her half smile widened into a full smile that reached her eyes for one brief moment and then it was gone as she turned her gaze to the bed, where her sister lay unconscious.

"Lyrra?" she said, pushing herself up.

"Lyrra still sleeps," the Cheetah said from the other side of the bed where he stood watch over her.

"The effects of the Dream Flower will be wearing off soon," Asad told Oona. "The Owl checked her a short time ago and was not overly concerned she had not woken yet."

She released her breath in a long, shaky sigh, and Asad wrapped his arm around her shoulders and held her to him, whispering into the jasmine-sweet veil of her hair.

"Try not to worry too much, my jewel, the Dove is not as frail as she seems to others, this I have seen for myself." He smiled into Oona's hair, remembering the night he had watched them shimmy out of their chamber window from his perch in the cedar tree, the long, well-muscled line of the Swan's leg as it stretched out over the drugged guard, the swift, agile ease with which the Dove had swung out of the window and landed soft and sure on her own two feet. "Oona, there is something that has been bothering me about how this happened."

Oona lifted her questioning gaze to his.

"I have seen the Dove move," he said. "I have seen her climb out a window, seen her ride, and my mother told me of her actions in the bathing pool with the Spider and the Eel, of how she stood up to the Spider. Lyrra is almost as strong and graceful as you, so what I do not understand is how she came to fall out of her window. Was she feeling ill?"

"No," Oona said with a slow shake of her head.

"Would she have jumped, for fear of the Panther, of the night to come?

He hated asking it, hated to think it could be true, that fear of his father, of their upcoming audience with him, had driven the Dove to leap from her window to certain injury and possible death.

"No," Oona said with a sureness that eased his fears. "She believe what you say about Panther not touch us yet. She believe you and Cheetah will help us escape." Her eyes grew round and she sat up straight. "She no fall, or jump. She would no leave me here alone."

"Someone pushed her?" It was the Cheetah who voiced the horrible thought, who stood with both hands balled into fists. "Who," he demanded, "who would wish to harm the Dove?"

Oona turned her wide eyes to Asad. "It was Spider and Eel. I see them in hall when I run to Lyrra's room."

"Are you certain?" Asad knew even as he asked that the Spider and the Eel were both capable of such malevolence.

"Aye," Oona said with a slow nod and a hard glint in her eyes. "They the only others there, they not far from Lyrra's open door. They hear me scream her name, they turn from run away to act like they run to her room."

"Those bitches," the Cheetah spat. He glanced down at the Dove's ashen face. "They will pay."

"Brother?" Asad asked as the Cheetah began to pace in circles, not unaware of the irony that it was him attempting to calm his brother down instead of the other way around. "What is it you intend to do? Go to the Panther? You know we cannot prove anything. It will be the Swan's word against the Spider's and the Eel's."

"The Panther," Oona said. "He not believe me over them."

"No," Asad agreed. "He will not."

"What about when the Dove wakes up?" the Cheetah said. "When she remembers?"

"Memory can be tricky after a head injury," Asad reminded him. "And even if the Dove does remember, the Panther will choose not to believe her over two of his favorites." *Who are both lying bitches.* Asad smiled grimly. Two could play at that game. "The Spider and the Eel," he said, "they do not know the Dove has not yet woken, or that she has not named them her attempted murderers."

Oona smoothed the fine linen weave of the one-shouldered marigold yellow gown the queen had given her to wear as the Boar announced their presence at the pleasure house, a curious half smile on his face as he held the door open for them. The Cheetah had given the Boar three gold pieces and a handclasp of thanks for his help in carrying the Dove to the palace, and Asad had promised him protection from any repercussions. From the look in the giant's black eyes and the way he stood at Oona's side as the Mynah approached, his loyalty was theirs.

"Bring the Spider and the Eel to me in the king's salon," Asad ordered the Mynah, his tone brooking neither question nor argument.

"Of course, Prince Black Mane," the Mynah said with a dip of her knee, her sharp eyes taking in Oona's gown as she left to do his bidding.

They sat at the king's table, Oona on a stool between Asad and the Cheetah, the Boar standing guard behind them as the Mynah walked in, followed by the Spider and the Eel.

"Stay, Mistress Mynah," Asad said as she made to leave. "I want you to hear this."

"As you wish, Prince Black Mane." She stood off to the side, glancing over at the closed door to the salon, where, no doubt, all the other women of the house stood with their ears pressed close.

"Do you know why we are here?" Asad asked the two women standing before them in a stern voice.

"No, Prince Black Mane," the Spider answered in her usual indolent manner.

"No, Prince Black Mane," the Eel echoed, her eyes darting back and forth between the brothers and Oona.

"No?" Asad cocked his head at the Eel. "Is there nothing more you would like to tell me of what happened yesterday concerning the Dove?"

"No, Prince Black Mane," the Spider answered quickly as the Eel stood dumbly, her hands working worriedly in the lap of her gown. "There is no more to tell."

"Is that so?"

"Yes, Prince Black Mane."

"Are you sure?"

"Of course, Prince Black Mane," the Spider said as the Eel's chin trembled.

"Tell me again," Asad said, "that I may hear it with my own ears."

The Spider let her breath out with a sly half smile. "We, the Eel and I, were coming up the stairs when we heard a scream. The Swan came running out of her room and into the Dove's. We followed and saw the Dove on the ground outside her window, the Boar standing over her."

Asad eyed the Spider and then the Eel. "What is it you think happened to the Dove?"

"She must have fallen," the Spider said, all wide-eyed innocence, "or jumped. Everybody here knew how afraid she was of the Panther."

The Cheetah tensed and Oona laid her hand over his as Asad pinned the squirming Eel with a predatory gaze.

"Is that what happened, Eel? Now is your chance to tell me the truth of it."

The Eel looked to the Spider, and the Spider's eyes narrowed.

"Y-yes, P-Prince Black Mane," the Eel stammered. "Tha-that is the t-truth of it."

Asad stood to his full height, as did the Cheetah, who offered his hand to Oona as she rose to stand between them.

"You will be pleased to hear that the Dove has awakened from her injuries," Asad said. The Spider paled and the Eel's forehead and cheeks shone with beads of sweat. "She has told us she remembers looking out her window and the feel of hands pushing her from behind, and the Swan, who saw her fall, saw you two running away from the Dove's room before turning to run toward it."

"The Swan lies," the Spider spat.

"No," Asad said. "She does not. Not to me."

Oona stood straighter and lifted her chin higher as a warm rush of pride coursed through her veins.

"Where is the Panther?" the Spider demanded. "He will believe me over this lying bitch Swan."

"I would be careful of my next words if I were you, Spider," Asad growled. He stepped around the table to stand no more than a pace from the posturing Spider and the cowering Eel. "The Swan is mine now, as is the Dove. Lie to me again, and I will wring the truth out of you."

He took another step forward and the Spider stepped back as the Eel crumpled to the floor, her hands grasping at the hem of his tunic.

"Have mercy on me, Prince Black Mane," she cried. "I only kept a look out."

"Shut up, Eel," the Spider hissed.

"Who pushed the Dove?" Asad's voice was calm and his manner kind as he helped the Eel stand. "Tell me now, Eel, and it will go better for you. Who pushed the Dove out of her window?"

"It was the Spider." The Eel dissolved into tears. "It was the Spider who pushed the Dove."

"Liar," the Spider screamed. "You are all liars."

She turned to run, to where Oona did not know, nor, she guessed, did the Spider, but it did not matter as she got no more than four paces before the Cheetah and the Boar closed in on her.

"Hold her," the Cheetah said as the Boar's arms clamped around the spitting, clawing Spider. "This is for the Dove."

Grabbing the Spider by the hank of her hair, the Cheetah pulled his blade out and sawed through her hair, the Spider cursing and thrashing in the Boar's hold until the Cheetah stood holding the glossy black length of her pride in his fist. The Spider gave one piercing scream and then fell to the floor as the Boar let go his hold of her. The door to the salon burst open and twelve women rushed into the salon to stare wide-eyed and gape-jawed at the Spider, who kneeled with her face in her hands.

"We found out the truth of the matter," Asad told the Panther. "I would think you would be glad to know what really happened to the Dove."

The Panther glared at his two eldest sons in the privacy of his council chambers.

"I would have been gladder of two obedient sons who let me, the king, deal with such matters."

"You mean you would have been gladder to have two sons who did nothing to right a wrong?" Asad asked. "To remain ignorant of the truth, despite their misgivings, to let the Spider and the Eel go unpunished for their misdeeds?"

"The Spider and the Eel are mine to punish or not," the Panther said. "They are no concern of yours."

"They tried to kill the Dove." The Cheetah stood glaring at the Panther, his hands in fists at his sides, all signs of the peacemaker gone from him. "And she is my concern."

"Enough." The Panther slammed his hands down on the table. He straightened and stood with his shoulders back and chest out, trying to intimidate them as he had when they were boys. "Is it not enough that my eldest son turned on me for a slave woman, and now you too?"

"We suffer from the same affliction, my elder brother and I," the Cheetah said. "And we have the same desire, to see the Dove and the Swan safely away to their homeland."

The Panther gave a dismissive snort. "You suffer from being your mother's sons, not mine."

"Why thank you, Father," Asad said with a tight smile. "We will take that as the compliment I am sure you meant it to be."

"Do not push me, boy," the Panther snarled.

"Do not call me boy, old man," Asad snarled back. "I am a man, full grown, and so is Nasim." Their father's eyebrows shot up at the Cheetah's given name. "And we will be treated as such by you."

"Then act it," the Panther spat. "Act as men, as princes of the tribes."

"We are," Asad roared. "And we have been. We have acted as princes first and men second despite our personal wishes as we have been taught by our father and our mothers. If we had not, then the Swan would already be my wife and the Dove, Nasim's."

The Panther opened his mouth and then snapped it shut, speechless for the first time in Asad's memory. That he had expected his sons to back down was obvious, that they had not had obviously thrown him.

"So, Father." Asad took advantage of his father's momentary confusion. "What do you intend to do to the Spider and the Eel for their attempt on the Dove's life?"

"Humph, well," the Panther huffed. "I have not considered it fully yet."

"Consider this, my king," Asad said. "If it were the Dove who had pushed the Spider, her back would be flayed and bleeding by now."

The Panther eyed Asad. "You are advocating the whipping of the Spider?"

"I am."

"You, who stood against me for one slave, now want me to whip another?"

"The Swan you would have whipped for attempting to save her sister's life. The Spider you should whip for attempting to take the Dove's life."

"I will do it if you do not wish to," the Cheetah offered when the Panther did not answer.

"You have done plenty enough already." The Panther pulled on his beard as he looked from one son to another. "Now leave me, both of you, I have more important matters to consider than slave women fighting among themselves."

"Talk to her, Swan," the queen said as she dribbled broth into Lyrra's mouth. "Sing to her. Give her something to come back to."

"She can hear me? She will know what I say?"

"I do not know for certain that she can, and I do not know that she cannot. But I do believe somewhere in her mind she will know your voice, even if she does not know your words."

Oona thought about what she would say, what she could say in front of the queen. "I may talk to Dove in our own tongue?"

"Yes, of course you may, Oona. It will likely do the Dove good to hear a voice of her homeland."

"You call me Oona." Tears sprang to her eyes.

"Yes," the queen said with a bemused smile. "So I did. It must be from hearing my son call you so. He tells me it is the custom in your land."

"Aye, I mean, yes, my queen, it is."

"Then it will be the custom here, in the lands that are my private chambers. Here we can be Noor and Oona, but only here."

"Oh, thank you, my queen." Oona stood and threw her arms around the queen's shoulders. "Thank you, Noor, for everything." She gave her a quick hug and then dropped her arms and stepped back, suddenly shy and unsure.

The queen eyed Oona for a long moment, and then took Oona's hands in hers.

"It is I who should thank you, Oona."

"Thank I? For what?"

"For caring for my son. For honoring him for the man he is, not for being the Black Mane, Prince of the Great Valley. For giving him that at least, even if he may not keep it."

"But he may keep." Oona's voice was a choked whisper. "It be his, always."

The queen nodded and her smile was sad and bittersweet as she gave Oona's hands a gentle squeeze before letting go her hold.

"You and I," she said with a slow shake of her head. "We have much in common."

"You speak of Oryx father, of man you love, but not allow to marry."

The queen said nothing for a long moment, her face impassive, but her eyes, so like her son's, spoke of emotions Oona knew well.

"My son told you that?"

"Yes."

"What else has he told you?"

"That Panther, he no believe Gazelle his daughter."

The queen's brows rose and she smoothed her skirt.

"It is true," she said. "That is why he whipped me ten and four years ago. I had told him I was with child, his child, and he would not believe me. He knew of my love for the Ram, the man I would have married given my choice, and he had found us talking together alone in the gardens three moons earlier."

"He think Ram is Gazelle father?"

"To this day."

"And you and Ram?"

"Never spoke again."

Asad recognized the "Sailor's Tale" as soon as he and the Cheetah walked into the queen's chambers, though Oona was singing it in her northern tongue.

"How fares the Dove?" he asked. He could see for himself that she still did not swallow as his mother dribbled a few drops of broth into her mouth.

"A little better," she said, setting the cup and dipping rag down. "Her skin is warmer to the touch, and her pulse, though weak, is steady."

Asad gave Oona a quick, reassuring smile, hating that it was all he could do for her.

"What did the Panther say about the Spider and the Eel?" the queen asked.

"He said he will take it all under advisement."

"It is in the king's hands now." She wiped her hands on her apron. "You have done what you can. You have won the Swan and the Dove their freedom. Now you must let it go."

Asad nodded to his mother's wisdom. "The Panther has requested my presence at a meeting he holds today with the Heron and the Bull and their war counselors."

"War counselors?"

"My guess is the Panther means to make a move against the Oryx," Asad told her, as Oona listened intently. "He has been making noise about it since we left the meeting of the tribes."

"And the Heron and the Bull?" the Queen asked. "Where do they stand on warring against one of the Seven?"

Asad shrugged. "I will let you know after the meeting."

"And you, my son? Where do you stand on this?"

"Trade is always better than war," Asad said. "And I, for one, do not hold a father's wrongs, whether real or imagined, against his sons."

"I am glad to hear it."

"You will not be glad to hear this," he said, and two pairs of eyes, one gold and one green, were on his. "The Panther has requested the Swan's presence at supper tonight."

The queen's eyes closed for a moment and she took a deep breath before fixing them on Oona.

"You no worry," Oona said with a quick shake of her head. "I no go. I stay here with Lyrra."

"It is not a request you can refuse," Asad explained. "And you can be sure he has his reasons for wanting you there, as you can be sure it is not for your company or my pleasure."

Oona bit her lip as she looked from Asad to the queen, who laid a kindly hand on her arm.

"It will not be a formal supper tonight," she told her. "So you may sit at my table."

"The Fox," Oona said. "She will no like."

"Good," Asad said with such force that both Oona's and his mother's heads jerked up. He reached into his pocket and held his hand out to Oona, the abalone ring in his palm. "I asked you before to wear this ring for me, once you were safely away and none could see. Now I ask if you will wear this ring for me, Oona, from this moment on, for all to see."

"Even Panther?" she squeaked. "And Fox?"

"Especially Panther and Fox," he said with a wicked grin that made her pale cheeks blush instantly pink.

"I will." She smiled through welling tears as he held the ring over her marriage finger, and then slipped it onto her middle finger, knowing he did not have that right, that he was sworn to make sure some man of her clan would. "I will wear for you, Asad, always."

His mother graciously said nothing, though her tight-lipped smile and worried eyes told Asad all he needed to know of her opinion of the matter.

"Oona, the Swan, this is my daughter, the Gazelle."

The queen nodded at the girl already sitting at the table, a younger version of her mother with thick, russet brown hair and copper eyes flecked with gold.

"Is honor to meet you, Gazelle," Oona said. "You brother, Black Mane, tell me much of you."

"He has?" she said with an impish grin that brought a young Lyrra to mind, and a pang to Oona's chest. "He has told me nothing of you." She patted the stool beside her. "You must sit here next to me, Swan, so that I may find out all about you for myself."

The queen tsked at her daughter, who remained unabashed as she and Oona took their seats, but before the Gazelle could begin her questioning, a slim woman with shining brown hair and eyes took the last seat at the table.

"So," she said, "this is the Swan who causes the Black Mane to challenge the Panther, and the Cheetah to cut the hair of the Spider."

"Caracal," the queen said with a regal dip of her head. "This is Oona, the Swan. Swan, this is the Caracal, the Panther's second wife and mother of the Cheetah."

Oona waited for the Caracal to acknowledge her with a nod of her head before speaking.

"My lady Caracal, is honor to meet you."

The Caracal studied Oona with eyes as quick and warm as her son's.

"My son has told me of you and your sister," she said at last, smiling kindly. "I do hope the Dove is improving."

"Queen Snow Leopard say she is little better," Oona said, fighting sudden tears at this unexpected concern. The Jackal's wives had never done anything but look down their noses at Oona and Lyrra. In his household only the Sparrow had shown them any kindness. Yet here, in the Panther's palace, the two women of highest rank sat with her and spoke with her and treated her with kindness. She knew much of it was due to their sons, as she knew that their sons had learned this kindness from their mothers.

The queen reached out and patted Oona's hand, which only made more tears threaten.

"Try not to worry, Swan," she said. "The Owl will take good care of the Dove."

"Thank you, my Queen," Oona sniffed as she fought to stifle her tears and her fears, lifting her hand to wipe away the one and only tear to escape.

"What a beautiful ring you wear, Swan," the Caracal said.

Oona quickly hid her hand in her lap and looked up through lowered lashes at the queen, who sighed and shook her head.

"The Black Mane gave it to her," she told the Caracal, whose finely arched brows rose and knitted.

The Gazelle's brows rose clear to her hairline.

"Our husband will not like this," the Caracal said, the hint of a smile in her eyes.

"No," the queen agreed. "He will not, which is, no doubt, one of the reasons his son did it."

The Gazelle grinned from ear to ear.

The Caracal glanced across the salon. "The Fox."

"Will like it even less," the queen said as the Caracal lifted her chin to where she gazed.

"What," the Fox's shrill voice rang out in the salon, "is that milk-faced slave doing here?"

"The Swan is my son's guest," the Panther roared out from his seat. "One he honors above father and betrothed, duty and tradition."

"My father, the king, requested her presence," Asad said from his table, his voice calm and steady and loud enough for all to hear in the suddenly quiet salon. "I asked my mother, the queen, to show her the hospitality of our palace and sup with her."

The Fox sneered. "As you have shared the hospitality of your bed with the whore."

Oona's cheeks blazed.

Asad stood, slowly, deliberately. "Be careful what you say of and to the Swan, Fox. She is my friend, my guest. I will not have her slandered."

"Even by your betrothed?" The Fox looked from Asad to the Panther, who watched it all with his jaw set and his thick arms crossed tightly across his chest.

"Especially by you." Asad's gaze impaled the Fox as she stared at him gape-mouthed.

"Well," the Fox huffed. "Your mother may do your bidding, but I refuse to sup in the same room with your...friend."

"Then I suggest you leave through the kitchens and ask that a tray be sent to your chambers from tonight until the time the Dove is able to travel," Asad said with a tight smile.

His gaze swept over the Fox and the scowling Panther to find Oona's and hold it, his tight grin softening at the smile of thanks in her eyes. Dipping his head to her, he started to sit, then straightened back up as the Fox made her way not toward the kitchens but for the queen's table, where she stood, arms akimbo, glaring down at Oona.

"You may have fooled the Black Mane and the Snow Leopard, Swan," she hissed. "But you have not fooled me. You are still nothing but a—"

"Be careful of what you say next, Fox." The queen's voice was soft but stern, as was her expression.

"You would choose her," the Fox whined, "a slave, a strumpet, over me, your son's wife, his queen?"

"I would choose for you to learn to keep your temper and your tongue in check," the queen told her, and Oona quickly hid the smile that came to her unbidden. "For when you are wife and queen, you will need to be able to do both quite often."

"As you say, I am not wife or queen yet." The Fox sneered down at Oona as she pulled her arm back and up, but where before Oona had taken the Fox's blows, both physical and verbal, she would do so no more. Oona stood as the Fox swung and grabbed her hand in midair.

"What do you think you are doing, slave?" the Fox shrieked, her wrist writhing in Oona's tight grip.

"I no slave no more," Oona grit out between clenched teeth. "And you no hit me no more. You try hit me again, I hit back."

The Fox stood staring dumbly at her wrist in Oona's hand for a long moment as the salon went silent, and then her jaw dropped and her eyes lit with a hatred Oona knew too well.

"Where did you get that ring?" the Fox demanded. "You stole that ring from my father's house. She stole this ring from my father's house," she said loud enough for all to hear as she raised her wrist and Oona's hand high enough for all to see. "The whore is a thief as well."

"Enough," the Black Mane's roar reverberated through the watching silence. Oona dropped the Fox's hand and her own as Asad strode across the salon to stand beside her. "I gave the Swan this ring," he told the Fox before lifting Oona's hand in his and holding it high. "I gave the Swan this ring," he announced to the salon at large. "I bought it from one of the Jackal's pleasure women and gifted the Swan with it." He lowered their hands and twined his fingers through Oona's, lowering his gaze and his voice to the Fox. "Which begs the question, Princess, how do you recognize the ring of a pleasure woman?"

"I uh…uh," the Fox sputtered and stammered, "my uh…father, must have shown it to me, before gifting it to the Sh…his uh…woman."

"I see," Asad said with a smile that told the Fox and every person there that he did indeed see. "Well, now it is the Swan's, my gift to her, as is a certain ruby ring once worn by the Falcon."

"My brother's ring?" the Fox gasped. "He said he lost it in a wager."

"He did. He lost it to me in a reckless wager."

"And you gave it to her?"

"I did."

"But why?" the Fox asked with such a pathetic wail that Oona almost felt sorry for her. Almost.

"Because what my father said is true. I honor her above all others."

The Fox's gaping mouth slowly closed into a sneer. "Give your slave all the trinkets she covets, it matters not to me." She puffed her considerable chest out. "I will be queen one day, whilst she will still be nothing but a whore."

Asad started forward and the Fox jumped back. Oona laid her hand on Asad's forearm.

"It no matter what she say," Oona told him as his gaze met hers and his arm flexed beneath her fingers. "You and I know truth of us."

The muscles of his arm relaxed, but his glare followed the Fox as she stomped off, and then his head cocked as the Ox stood and offered the Fox a seat at his table, which Oona was fairly certain went against the tradition of the tribes. And against that same tradition, the Fox flopped onto the proffered stool with a flounce of her skirts and a pouty smile plastered on her face.

Oona squeezed Asad's arm. "I sit back down now," she said.

Asad hesitated.

"You mother and sister, Caracal, they make me welcome."

Asad blew out his breath and nodded to the table of watching women, then handed Oona down to her cushion as if she were some precious, breakable treasure.

"Ladies." He bowed and strode back to his table, where the Cheetah and the two younger boys Oona had seen before sat. He ruffled the curls of the older boy and said something to make the younger grin, and then he looked over to the queen's table to find three women and one gape-jawed girl staring at him.

The Panther stopped Asad with a hand on his shoulder as they made their way out of the dining salon. "That was quite a show you and your Swan put on, Black Mane."

"Was that not what you wanted?" Asad shrugged his father's hand off. "Was that not what you expected when you commanded the Swan's presence at supper?"

"I expected you both to act with more decorum."

"Though you knew the Fox would not," Asad scoffed. "And as you knew I would come to the Swan's defense. Did you know that the Ox would go against tradition and seat the Fox at his table?" Asad eyed his father, who chewed on his beard and gave no answer. "To what purpose did you set this up?"

"To see what kind of man my eldest son has become." The Panther's black gaze measured Asad's.

"I am as I was raised to be," Asad told him. "Prince first, Asad second. This I have always been. This is the man you willingly see, the man who will wed that bitch Fox for the sake of the tribes. I am also a man who cares for the Swan, a woman a prince of the Seven Tribes may not marry. A brave and beautiful and honorable woman who I will not stand to see slandered and abused. This is the man you will not see. But he is here." Asad thumped his chest with his fist, "One with the other, whether you wish it or not."

"And the man who argued with his king against going to war with the Oryx in front of the council this day, which man was he?"

"He is one and the same, and he will continue to argue for trade and against war with the Oryx for as long as he has breath."

The Panther's black eyes snapped. "The Oryx is a young, weak upstart of a king. We should remove him and place an older, wiser, stronger king in his stead."

"One of your choosing."

"Yes."

"One who is not eldest son and rightful heir of the Ram," Asad argued, using the traditions his father loved so well. "One who is not a direct descendant of a line of the Seven Kings?"

"It has been done before," the Panther huffed, "when a king's line has been found lacking. He did not even take an eldest daughter as first wife and queen. He married a third daughter and it took her a year to get with child."

"He married a princess of the tribes for love," Asad said, "with the blessing of the Heron and the other kings. And from what I saw and heard at the meeting of the tribes, the City of Hills has done well under the rule of the Oryx and his queen, young and inexperienced though they may be."

"What would you know of it? You have been too busy mooning over that northern whore of yours to pay any attention to the tribes' business."

Asad clamped his jaw and grit his teeth. The fact that the Panther had just called Oona a whore right after Asad had declared he would not have her slandered, that he had brought her into this argument that had nothing to do with her, told Asad that the Panther was beyond rational argument. And if the Panther was willing to go after the Oryx for his own petty, personal reasons, then Asad had little doubt he would go back on his word concerning the Swan and the Dove if angered enough.

"What," he asked the Panther, his voice, his own anger, under tight control, "is it you want of me?"

"I want to know if you, my eldest son and heir, will stand by his father and king when I go to war against my enemies."

Asad squared his shoulders and held his father's gaze.

"I will always stand by my father's side against his true enemies."

The Panther held Asad's unwavering gaze for a long moment, the unspoken question of the Oryx hanging between them. He opened his mouth as if to speak and then gave Asad a gruff nod and stalked off toward his personal chambers. Asad turned in the opposite direction, heading to the queen's chambers, to where his mother and Oona had returned sometime earlier. As he passed by the main salon's open door, the Fox's high-pitched giggle mingled with the lower monotone of the Ox.

It wasn't that Asad cared about the Fox turning to the Ox for friendship or comfort, or whatever it was the two found with each other, for despite what he had promised his father, he would never lay with the Fox. Once Oona and, hopefully, Lyrra were safely away, the Panther would have nothing to hold over Asad that could possibly entice him to bed the Fox.

Any offspring of hers would not be from his seed, and his pride was not such that it would stop him from revealing her adulterous nature. It was the irony of having spent the better part of the day defending the Oryx against his father and the Bull because of his mother's perceived infidelity with the Oryx's father that had him grinding his teeth and shaking his head.

He stepped through the door to his mother's rooms to the sound of excited voices. Entering her inner chambers, he had barely enough time to open his arms as Oona flew into them.

"Lyrra swallow," she cried through smiling tears. "Lyrra swallow."

CHAPTER 12

Brawn

Lyrra progressed overnight from swallowing to moving her fingers and toes to moaning with pain when the Owl checked her splint and sling the next morning. Yet as much as it hurt Oona to hear her sister's pain, she knew it was good that Lyrra felt it. By noon, Lyrra's eyes fluttered open for a brief moment, and by eventide they stayed open long enough to focus on her sister's face.

"Oo?"

"Aye, Lyly."

"Wha?"

"You fell," Oona said in their native tongue, not wanting to be rude to the others, but unsure if Lyrra's mind would be able to understand the desert tongue. "You hurt your leg and shoulder."

Lyrra shifted and winced as she glanced at her sling. She tried to lift her head and look down at her leg, but she dropped it back onto the soft pillow with a grimace.

"My head hurts," she said.

"You have been sleeping betwixt this world and the next for two nights and a day," Oona told her. Gently, she brushed the hair back from her sister's forehead, which felt warm and dry. "The Queen, the Black Mane, and the Owl have been tending you, and the Cheetah has barely left your bedside."

"He is here now?"

"He is." Oona glanced to the other side of the bed, where the Cheetah stood shifting from foot to foot. "He waits to speak to you."

"He does?"

"Oh aye, sister, he does. Shall I tell him he may speak with you now?"

Lyrra started to nod her head and let out a groan. Behind them the Owl and the queen were discussing a dose of Dream Flower. The Cheetah sat on a stool and leaned over Lyrra so that she would not have to turn her head to see him.

"I am glad you are come back to me, to us," the Cheetah said, and Oona let go of her sister's hand and moved to where Asad stood watching his brother and her sister, welcoming Oona with open arms as she nestled into his hold.

"Will you walk with me tonight, Oona?" Asad murmured in her ear, sending shivers down her spine.

Oona nodded into his neck, breathing in the musky spice of his scent. They had not been alone together since he had climbed through the window of her chambers in the pleasure house, the night he had kissed her with such heat that the memory of it stoked a simmering ache deep in her belly. A kiss she longed to experience again.

"I will," she said, her voice deep with a newly familiar yearning.

"Good, I am glad." He hugged her closer, and Oona melted into him. "I will come to the balcony after my mother has gone to sleep. Dress to move, there is someone I want you to meet."

The horned moon had risen over the city's eastern wall when the queen's chambers finally went dark, and Asad climbed up the vined trellis onto her balcony. The Dove had not been moved to the healing house, or even to another, more private, room yet, allowing the queen to keep a close eye on her, as well as on Oona and Asad.

He had not waited long when the door slowly opened and Oona stepped out, still wearing a flimsy night shift. Seeing Asad, she smiled and carefully closed the door, and then she reached under the cushions on the balcony's sofa and pulled out a rolled-up bundle of clothes.

"Turn around." She motioned with her hand at Asad, but he shook his head.

"Not for all the gold in all the seven kingdoms, my jewel."

He sensed more than saw the flush in her cheeks in the waning moon's dim light, and then she turned her back to him and pushed down the sleeveless shoulders of her shift, exposing exquisitely carved shoulder blades. Asad sucked a slow, cooling breath in as she dropped the shift to puddle at her sandaled feet. Her back was long, straight, and leanly muscled, her hips lusciously curved, and her backside rounded and taut as two perfectly shaped pears. She stepped out of the puddled shift and bent over to pick up the bundle of clothes and Asad let his breath out in a heated rush.

Oona stood straight and still, and Asad dragged his hungry gaze up from her ripe backside to see that she was watching him over her shoulder. She stood naked in the moonlight not more than three paces from him, and his heart was thumping and his cock was throbbing. What he wanted to do was lay her back onto the sofa and sate his gnawing hunger, but his mother, her sister, and at least two maidservants slept on the other side of the door from them.

"Hurry," he rasped, the confines of his loincloth growing tighter. "I beg of you."

She pulled on her short brown work tunic and covered her pale hair with a dark scarf before turning to face him.

"Where we go?"

"It is a surprise," he said, stepping to the balcony's wall, away from her, from temptation. "A surprise I think you will like."

He climbed over the wall and down the trellis and stood watching her climb down after him. He told himself it was to be ready to catch her if she were to fall, and it was, but the sight of her long legs stretching down and out from her short tunic, the flashing glimpses of her taut backside, still so clear in his mind's eye from mere moments ago, had his loincloth straining at its seams.

Oona's feet touched ground and Asad picked up the knotted climbing rope he had hidden in the bushes and slung it over his neck and shoulder.

"Come," he said, reaching for her hand, grinning as she took it and twined her fingers through his, a perfect fit.

Asad led her through the garden and over the palace wall, keeping to the night's shadows and trying not to think of how other body parts of theirs would fit. When they made the pleasure house, he cupped his hand and boosted her up and over the wall into a side yard where three liquidambar trees stood sentinel alongside the main house, their top most branches stretching out over the flat roof. Uncoiling the rope, Asad took the rock tied into a net at one end and threw it up and over the lowest hanging branch of the tallest tree, letting the rope out and lowering the rock back down. Tying a loose cinching knot, he tightened the rope around the branch where a groove had been worn into it and tugged hard.

"You first," he said to Oona, whose wide eyes blinked.

"How high we climb?"

"To the roof."

She glanced up to the branch a good ten feet above them and blew her breath out. Gathering her strength, she grabbed the rope and jumped up to the first knotted foothold, climbing hand over hand, knot by knot, shimmying her way up the rope as Asad stood below admiring her game spirit and her lithe strength. When she reached the branch, she swung her leg up and over it and pulled herself onto her belly.

"You turn," she whispered loudly, and he swore she laughed.

Asad had climbed up this tree with this rope a hundred times over the last three years, but he had never been so eager, or climbed so quickly before. Of course, he had never been chasing the flash of long-limbed legs before. Oona was grinning from ear to ear as Asad untied the rope and coiled it around his neck and shoulder, and then she followed him as they climbed the upper branches, stopping on a sturdy limb overhanging the roof. Asad started to tell her they would have to jump down when she turned and leapt, arms spread and toes pointed, soaring through the night and landing on the roof light as a feather. Asad crouched and dropped down onto the roof and caught her arm and pulled her into his embrace.

"Fly to me, my Swan," he whispered fiercely into her hair, "only to me."

His heart beat against her chest and his belly sucked in and out in time with hers. Her scarf had fallen off her head, and Asad ran his hand through the moonlit veil of her hair and lowered his mouth to where her blood coursed through her neck. Her pulse was quick and strong, and her gasp, when he nipped and suckled, sent his pulse pounding.

He took her mouth with his, wanting, needing, claiming, and she gave him all, matching him kiss for kiss, nip for nip, her lithe body pressing into his, the soft heat of her belly couching his straining cock.

"Black Mane?"

Oona gasped and stiffened and Asad silently cursed at the head poking up out of the roof's trapdoor, a door Asad had not heard open over the thrumming of his own blood in his ears, and elsewhere. He turned Oona so that she faced the door, and kept his front side hidden with her backside.

"Oona the Swan," he said through clenched teeth, "meet Brawn, the man who will escort you and the Dove back to your home."

Oona stepped down the ladder into the candlelit attic of the pleasure house, glancing around at the undisturbed cobwebs in the timbers and corners of the ceiling, and at the tapestries and rugs piled along one wall. Several dust-covered chests, and a table and jumble of stools were stacked against another wall. In the middle of the room were two sofas covered in worn blankets and holey linens. The Mouse sat on one of the sofas, grinning like a cat that had eaten her namesake with the man called Brawn standing next to her.

Of medium height and build with short, cropped, earthen brown hair and beard, he had light brown eyes that swept Oona from head to toe. His nose sat askew on a not-unhandsome face with a jagged scar across his left cheek, and another that ran from the middle of his forehead to his right ear. He wore a leather overtunic of the same light brown hue as his skin, with a thick leather belt from which hung not one but three hand blades in plain leather sheaths. Both forearms were covered in lacquered leather cuffs, and he wore boots, not sandals.

He whistled, long and low. "My sister did not exaggerate," he said with a wink at the Mouse. And then to Asad, "If her sister looks anything like her, I am going to need more men."

Oona bristled, Brawn grinned, and Asad growled. "First rule for any man hired, hands off."

Brawn grinned wider. "As I said, my sister did not exaggerate, about either of you."

Asad laid a possessive hand on Oona's shoulder. "The Mouse most likely understated my side of it," he said, and Brawn gave a short, quick laugh.

Oona looked from Brawn to the Mouse and back, seeing the resemblance now in their coloring, their wide grins and bright eyes. "Mouse is you sister?"

"She is my twin sister," Brawn said.

"Twin?" Oona did not understand.

"We shared the same womb," the Mouse said, pulling her brother down to sit beside her. "We were born at the same time, Ferret and Mouse."

"Ferret?" Oona shook her head as Asad sat them down on the other sofa.

"Ferret was the name given me by my parents as a child," Brawn explained. "And Brawn is the name I gave myself as a man."

Oona looked askance at the man, who was neither large nor especially brawny, though well-muscled and without any excess flesh.

"It keeps people guessing," he said. "Keeps them wary of my physical abilities, when what they really should be worrying about is my brain."

"What they truly should worry about is the Ferret's ability to sneak in and out of a place," Asad said. "It is how I met the blackguard, sneaking through the halls of this place in the middle of the night, seeking to either free his sister or kill the Panther."

"Actually, I was hoping to accomplish both." Brawn flashed a feral grin. "But the Black Mane stopped me and made me a bargain I could not refuse."

Oona glanced from one grinning man to another. "What was bargain?"

"I could not let him kill my father," Asad said. "So, his choice was to fight me then and there, to go through me to get to my father."

"Which I wisely chose not to do."

"After which I convinced him not to try to free the Mouse, for the Panther would hunt them to the ends of the earth and kill them in an all too public manner."

"And in return for not killing the Panther," Brawn said, "the Black Mane promised to protect my sister, to claim her and keep her from other men, though he could not keep her from the Panther after her corruption of a husband sold her to the king for being barren."

"And the Black Mane has kept his promise." The Mouse's big brown eyes shone with something akin to idolatry. "After the first few moons, the Panther lost interest in me."

"And you become Black Mane's favorite," Oona said, her voice as dull and heavy as her heart.

"Oona." Asad rubbed the pad of his thumb over her clenched knuckles. "I have never lain with the Mouse."

Oona's heart stopped.

"It would be like lying with my sister."

"No," Brawn said, touching the hilt of one of his sheathed blades. "It would be like lying with my sister."

Asad quirked a brow at Brawn as Oona's heart resumed beating, triple time.

"When I go to the Mouse's chambers," Asad said, lifting Oona's hand and gently blowing his warm breath over her clenched fingers, "I sleep, that is all."

"That is not completely true," the Mouse said with a teasing grin that had Oona gripping Asad's hand even tighter. "One night last week you snuck out of my room and into another's for most of the night." The Mouse wiggled a finger at Asad and Oona. "You thought you were being so clever, but I knew, I knew the first time I saw you two together in the king's salon that you were mad for each other."

"Oh, Mouse." Oona's breath rushed out with her words. "I be so glad. I want be you friend, but I, I be so jealous, and, and why you not tell me?"

The Mouse spread her hands out to her brother and Asad. "It was not my secret alone to keep," she said, "or to tell."

Asad and Brawn agreed on hiring four more men to help escort the Swan and the Dove to the northern seaport, from where only Brawn and two others would sail with the sisters to their home in the Green Isles. When Brawn returned to the Great Valley, Asad would reward him with enough gold to buy the Mouse from the Panther. As the

Mouse said, she had never been one of the Panther's favorites, and if Asad made sure to single her out after the Swan left, he was almost certain the Panther would sell her to her brother out of spite to get back at his son. As long as the Panther stayed ignorant of the fact that it was her brother who Asad had hired to get the Swan and Dove home safely.

After Brawn left through the attic's trap door and the Mouse went back down to her room, Asad turned to Oona, who had been catching up on pleasure house gossip with the Mouse while he and Brawn made their plans.

"Alone at last, my jewel." Asad reached out to pull Oona to him. He had been waiting all day and night for this moment, but she stepped back, away from his outstretched hand, her back stiff and chin raised. "Oona?" No woman had ever refused him before. Not even her. "Why do you step away from me?"

"Why you not tell me?"

"About the Mouse and me?"

Her chin jutted out and Asad grinned. Oona the Swan had a stubborn streak, and a jealous one by the narrowed glint of her eyes. Asad grinned wider. No woman had ever been jealous over him. Oh, there had been petty jealousies amongst the pleasure women over whom he would pick for a night, but their jealousy had been as fleeting as the night's pleasure. And then there were the princesses of the tribes, whose jealousies were about the Black Mane, prince and heir to the throne, and how marriage to him would make them queen. Not one of those women truly cared about Asad. The only one who did was standing him off, green eyes blazing.

"Oona." He stepped forward and her spine lengthened. "I did tell you, tonight."

"Why you not tell me before? You think is funny, I be jealous?"

"No." He shook his head. He shrugged. "Well, yes." Her green eyes shot daggers at him. "I do not think it funny, but it does make me glad." He squared his shoulders and met her heated glare head on. "It makes me, Asad, glad that you, Oona, care enough about me to be jealous of any other woman, because I am jealous of every other man who so much as looks at you."

"You are?"

"I am. And I am especially jealous of whatever *clansman* will be lucky enough to make you his bride once you return to your homeland." He stepped forward, and this time she did not back away, but put her hands in his when he reached out. He rubbed the pad of his thumb over the abalone of her ring, the ring he had given her to remember him by. "And now we had better leave this room before I give in to my jealousy and ruin you for that man."

"But there be no *clansman* for me, Asad. There be no other man for me but you, ever."

Everything Oona knew about Asad, everything she felt for him, yearned for, craved down to her bones, was in her eyes. She held nothing back.

"Are you sure, Oona?" His voice was a low growl, and his amber eyes reflected the longing in hers.

"I be sure, Asad."

Before he could argue further against it, before her courage failed her, Oona kissed Asad, tentative at first, her lips feather light on his, then growing bolder as he kissed her back and folded her into his embrace. Running her fingers through the short curls of his beard, she smiled into his low moan and curled her fingers into the hair at the nape of his neck. With a sigh of complete surrender, she opened her mouth to his tongue, tasting the salty wetness as she explored his mouth with hers, his groan resonating down to the throbbing between her legs.

She clasped him tighter, pressing her body closer, melding into his, their mouths taking and giving, their breaths mixing.

"Ahh, Oona," he whispered into her lips, "my beautiful, enticing, otherworldly jewel. I want to make love to you, to make you my bride in deed as well as heart, but I dare not."

"Why you dare not?" Oona pulled her lips from his far enough to meet his gaze. "If you do not, no man ever will."

"If my seed were to take inside you, my father would never let you bring it to fruition."

"How he would know?"

"Your maidservant, she will know if your moon flow came or not, and she will tell the Panther, she would have to, or be whipped herself."

Oona chewed on her lower lip. Her moon flow was already a fortnight late, and she had done nothing. They had done nothing to plant his seed in her. If they did, and she did become pregnant, the Panther would find out sooner rather than later. Oddly, the thought of carrying Asad's bastard babe did not worry her, but losing the babe did.

"How Panther keep babe from being?" she asked.

"The Mynah, she has the knowing of teas and tisanes to uproot a growing babe from a woman's womb."

"That is why pleasure women no have children?"

"It is one of the ways," he said. He pushed a lock of her hair back behind her ear, a gesture as sad and tender as his smile. "If you were with my child and we somehow managed to keep it from the Panther, either you would have to stay or I would have to leave with you. I could not bear to lose you and our child, and I will not send you off on such a long and dangerous journey carrying our child without me."

"Then come with me," Oona said without thinking, though she had thought of it a thousand times since he first told her he would help her and Lyrra escape. "Come with us."

For a moment, a fleeting moment, Oona saw the same flash of yes in his eyes that she had seen the night she had proposed marriage to him, and then the moment, the light in his eyes, was gone.

"I cannot," he said. "I am to be king. My father would come after us, and he would not stop until you were dead, or I killed him."

Oona nodded. She knew what Asad said was true, and right, but knowing it and feeling it were two extremely different things.

"But," he said, cupping his hands over her backside and pressing his pelvis to hers, "there are ways to give each other pleasure without consummation."

"There are?" Oona squeaked as he slowly rubbed his pelvis against hers.

He grinned and bent his mouth to hers as he splayed one big, warm, lion's paw across her backside, pressing her even closer and rubbing his thumb over a peaked nipple with the other.

"There are," he whispered huskily. "There are many ways hands and mouths can give pleasure."

Oona stared into amber embers burning with a heat she yearned to feel, to melt into and be consumed by.

"Teach me?" she breathed.

Asad took Oona's breath with his kiss, hot and urgent and demanding, his body hungry for the sweet succor of hers, his soul a guttering fire starving for life-giving air, for her. She kissed him back, her lips, her mouth, her tongue warm, wet, and slaking, her breath sweet, hot, and stirring, her soft mewls and breathless moans melding into a passionate melody with his whispered endearments and feverish groans.

He trailed a blaze of hot kisses down the jasmine-scented hollow of her throat and slipped the sleeves of her tunic off her shoulders, baring her perfectly round, rose-tipped breasts. Cupping the soft white flesh of one in his hand, he smiled at how perfectly it fit into his palm. Teasing the eager nipple with his thumb, he flicked the other with the tip of his tongue, his smile growing along with his cock at her gasp. He took the pebbled bud full into his mouth and suckled, groaning as Oona gasped again, her hands in his hair. She moaned and gripped his head as he lifted it from her breast, and then sighed as he lowered his mouth to her other breast and laved its rosy peak.

Returning his lips to hers, he pushed her tunic down over the swell of her hips to pool at her feet and stood back to gaze upon her. Asad had held her in his arms many times now. He knew the feel of her long, leanly muscled contours, the full softness of her breasts, the taut roundness of her backside. He had seen her naked from her waist up in the river, and had admired the lithe length of her backside earlier on the balcony, but he had never before seen her in all her natural glory.

"Upon my oath, Oona," he rasped huskily. "You truly are the most beautiful woman I have ever seen. The gods themselves must have created you of alabaster and moonbeams."

She flushed from head to toe, her cheeks and nipples turning a rosy pink as she stepped out of the rumpled tunic at her feet.

"Now I see you," she said with a shy smile and bold eyes that nearly had him bursting at his seams.

He shucked his tunic and loincloth and watched her eyes grow wide. He swelled with pride and her eyes grew even larger.

"Have you never seen a naked man before?" he asked, his voice surprisingly steady despite the rapid pace of his heart.

She shook her head, her gaze locked on the iron-hard erection at full attention between his legs.

"Do you trust me, Oona?"

She licked her lips, his cock jumped, and she nodded. "I do."

He stepped closer, so close he could feel her without actually touching her, their chests rising and falling in time, their bellies sucking in and out in rhythm, and then he closed the chasm between them and held her so that they touched, skin to skin, from chests to thighs. She shivered, though it was warm as day and he was burning from the inside out. He kissed her, softly, tenderly, murmuring sweet endearments into her mouth, her ears, her hair, lightly running his hands up and down her arms until she stopped shaking. Slowly, patiently, ready to stop if she grew fearful while praying fervently that she would not. He eased his hand down the taut smoothness of her belly to the triangle of curly hair a shade darker than pale. Deepening his kiss, he gently pushed a finger through her golden weave, breathing in her shallow sighs and deep moans as he slowly and deliberately ran his fingertip over her woman's flesh, lightly at first, barely skimming her cleft, the tip of her clit, then stroking a little harder, a little deeper into her hidden folds, until he slid his finger deep into her molten core.

Oona gasped and arched and threw her head back as Asad rubbed his finger back and forth, in and out and around, spreading her wet heat as she pressed herself into his palm. She began to move on his hand, and he moved with her, pressing and rocking, rubbing and circling, concentrating on her stiffening nubbin of pleasure until she went rigid, his mouth capturing her cry of rapture.

His hand slick with her release, he spread it over his throbbing cock and then took her hand and gently wrapped her long, sinuous fingers around his passion-forged rod.

"Rub your hand up and down, like this," he whispered into her panting mouth, and then he was panting as she moved her hand over him, slow and tenuous at first, gripping lightly, then gripping tighter and moving faster and harder as he thrust into her hold.

He clamped his jaw to keep from spilling his seed like some untried boy into her hand, but then she kissed him, hard, with tongue, their breathing as steep and ragged as the peak he was fast reaching. He came in hot, undulating waves of tortuous release, his cry echoing in her mouth, his head, in his very marrow.

For the second time in her life, Oona's legs gave out, and as before, Asad was there to catch her. Scooping her up in his arms, he lowered her onto a sofa and then leaned over her, his amber eyes dark with concern.

"Did I hurt you, Oona?"

"No, I not hurt, I..." Oona sucked in a great breath of air and tried to think of how to describe how she felt, boneless, weightless, spent, as if every nerve in her body had been strung taut and then let to fly. "I, I no have words for how I feel."

Asad smiled, sad and bittersweet. "Nor do I, my jewel."

He lay down beside her and Oona ran her fingers through the patch of curly black hair on his rock-hard chest. A vision of Beorne grunting and rutting away at Igrid flashed through her mind's eye. Beorne's lovemaking had not looked at all pleasurable, and his one kiss with Oona had been coarse and sloppy in blazing contrast to Asad's kiss: his lovemaking had been achingly tender and sensuous. Oona's body, sated and content, warmed at the memory of their play.

"Is always like this," she said, "between you and woman?"

"No." Asad pushed a lock of hair from her cheek behind her ear. "It is not," he said, his voice deep and languid. "In truth, it has never been like this between me and any other woman." He cupped her cheek in his palm and Oona could smell the scent of their love play on his fingers. She burrowed her nose into his palm and breathed it in. "I have never felt like this with or about any other woman."

"Even with Mouse?"

He turned her face to his, his eyes serious. "I told you I have never lain with the Mouse."

Oona grinned. "I know," she said with a giggle. "I get back at you for not tell me sooner."

"A sore loser and a poor winner," he said, tweaking her nose. "Who would have thought?"

"My sister, my father, mother, grandmother," Oona said. "Only my grandfather never admit it."

"You were his favorite."

Oona smiled. "And he be mine. I be much like him, as Lyrra be much like our grandmother."

"You will be glad to be home with them again?"

"I will. We will, though it be hard with no mother, no father."

Tears welled hot and fast in Oona's eyes and a fist-size stone stuck square in the middle of her chest.

Her parents were gone, her mother passed over six moons ago and her father either dead or a slave on some pirate ship. Except in her dreams, she would never again see her father standing on the deck of his ship, strong legs braced and white-blond hair blowing in the wind, his face covered in salt spray and his grin as wide as the sea. And except in her memories, she would never again hear her mother's gay laughter or her sweet lullaby

She buried her face in Asad's shoulder and breathed in the musky, male scent of him. She tasted the salty tang of his skin, pressed her ear to his chest and soothed herself with the steady beat of his heart, the gentle caress of his hand in her hair. Soon, too soon, all this, everything that was Asad, would be nothing but dreams and memories as well.

"I will miss you, Asad," she whispered. *She already did.*

"Ahh, Oona, my jewel." He hugged her tight. "I would rather you could stay here with me, but the Panther would never let you live." He kissed her forehead. "Brawn will get you home safe."

Oona lifted her gaze to meet Asad's. "You trust Brawn?"

"He may be a sell sword and a thief, but once he has given his loyalty, it is given for life."

Asad shifted onto his back and drew Oona in so that she lay with her head on his shoulder, his arm wrapped protectively around hers. "He is quick thinking, swift acting, and sure-footed, and the cagiest fighter I have ever known. I would trust him with my life." He kissed her forehead. "I have entrusted him with what is dearest to me in all the world: your life."

They lay without speaking for a while, their smiles tender and lazy and their fingers trailing lightly over each other's shoulders, chests, and bellies. Oona's belly tightened as Asad's fingers trailed lower and their touch turned more deliberate.

"Asad?"

"Oona?"

"I have hear women here speak of pleasuring with mouths. You will teach me, now?"

Asad flipped her onto her back in one swift, sure move. He brushed the straining peaks of her nipples with his chest and lightly rubbed the soft head of his growing manhood along the inside of her thigh.

He grinned, and his eyes burned. "It will be my pleasure, my jewel, and yours."

CHAPTER 13

Treachery

Oona woke with the warm flush of the night's memories and the bloody rush of her moon flow. Her maidservant, a taciturn woman with the first streaks of gray in her hair called the Palm, studied her chamber pot's contents before covering it and carrying it out to empty. When the Palm returned a short time later, she handed Oona three thick absorbent bleeding cloths. Oona considered asking the Palm how the Panther had received the news of her moon flow, but decided against it. It was not the Palm's fault she had to report to the Panther, and Oona would not take it out on the poor woman, who had likely never known any other life than that of a servant emptying chamber pots.

Lyrra still slept so Oona drank a cup of mint tea and went back to bed. She would not be expected, or even allowed, to partake of palace life until her moon flow ceased, and though it meant she would not be able to spend time with Asad, it also meant she would not have to face his family and try to hide her feelings for and about him, and what they had done in the attic last night.

Her nostrils flared as she recalled the earthy musk of Asad's skin, and she licked her lips and tasted again the salty sweetness of his kiss. Melting warmth heated her core and her skin tingled everywhere his big, strong hands had touched and kneaded and teased, and she grew as hot and wet between her legs as his mouth had been suckling her nipples, and other, even more sensitive parts of her body that she still blushed to think on. Rolling onto her belly, Oona stuffed her face into her pillow with a stifled groan.

Now that she had known the pleasure of a man, and not just any man, but Asad, the Black Mane, lion in name, power, and fierce, masculine grace, she could never accept, much less welcome, Beorne's kisses, his touch. Not when she would be yearning for Asad, comparing him or any other man to Asad, against whom every other man paled.

Although Oona's maidenhead had not been breached and she was, she supposed, still a virgin, she could lie and say that she had been raped by the pirates, or the Panther. Beorne was meant to be chieftain. His pride and his clan's honor would not allow him to marry her, and Lyrra would never expose her lie.

Oona shook her head and blew out a short, harsh breath. She could not, would not, deny her love for Asad, nor would she cheapen it with lies. She would tell the truth, that she had given herself willingly to the man she loved, the only man she would ever willingly have. Grandfather would forgive her, eventually, and she could live out her spinster's life at Silver Water Keep, a woman in love with the memory of a man to her dying day.

Punching her pillow, Oona rolled onto her back with a determined set to her jaw. If she was going to be without a man the rest of her life, then she was going to make as many memories with Asad as possible, once she was able. The trick would be getting through the next several days of her confinement without going mad for want of him.

She was diverted from her delicious memories and torturous yearnings when the queen entered the antechamber of her rooms that Oona and Lyrra now occupied, looking as serene and unruffled as always. No doubt the Palm had informed the queen of Oona's bodily functions.

"Good day, Swan, Dove," she said as Lyrra stirred and rubbed her eyes open, "and good news. The Dove is healed enough that you two may move into your own chambers today."

"Thank you, my queen," Oona said, sitting up and swinging her legs off the bed. She felt the queen's eyes on her nipples, perpetually aroused since her and Asad's love play and poking through her gauze-thin night shift. "You be much kind and generous to have us in you chambers so many days and nights. We be no more trouble to you."

"You have been no trouble to me, either of you," she said as Oona stood and went to the washbasin. "And your new bedchamber is only three doors down from mine, so that the Owl and I may still keep a close eye on the Dove."

Asad tapped on the balcony door and smiled when it creaked open and Oona slipped out into the dark of night in her thin night shift and into his embrace.

"Ahh, Oona, my jewel." He buried his nose into her nape and breathed in the perfume of sweet jasmine and fresh air, of green grass and earthy woman, of her. "I have missed you today." He nibbled the lobe of her ear and she shivered. "I have been trapped in a room with loud, chest-thumping men all day, arguing about whether to war against the Oryx, and trying to act like I was paying attention when all I could think about was you and your soft moans and tender flesh."

She laughed, soft, low, and knowing. A woman's laugh, and knowing it was he who had brought out the woman in her nearly burst Asad's seams.

"What they would say if they know you be here with me now, an unclean woman?"

He nuzzled her ear. "They would say that you have tempted and corrupted me," he whispered huskily, "when in truth it is I who have corrupted you."

"How you corrupt me?" She tilted her head and held his gaze.

"Though we have not consummated our love, any other man would say I ruined you for marriage last night."

"You ruin me for any other man first time ever our eyes meet."

Asad stared into eyes as big, round, and shimmering wet as river rocks, eyes that would haunt him until his dying breath, and likely beyond.

"I would have said yes," he said, answering the question she had never asked him. But then she had never needed to: she knew. She had seen it in his eyes then, as she saw it now. But he wanted to tell her. He wanted to say the words. "You are the bride of my heart, Oona. I love you."

Her eyes smiled into his. "You my lion, my somebody. I love you, Asad."

He curled his fingers around hers and they stood side by side under the stars, holding hands and watching the silver sliver of a crescent moon rising in the eastern sky, saying nothing. *For what more was there to say?*

"Oona?" It was the Dove's voice calling out for her sister. "Oona, where are you?"

"I be right in," Oona called back over her shoulder.

"Tomorrow, a dressmaker will come to measure you and Lyrra for new clothes," Asad told her. "I have given her orders for two traveling tunics with leggings and mantles as well as a gown for each of you for the feast celebrating my birthday." *And betrothal.* "A shoemaker will come as well. You will need a good pair of boots."

"When is you birthday?"

He chuckled. Any other woman would have been asking about the new clothes. "It is the first and twentieth day of the lion's moon. There will be a procession through the city that day, and I am to ride with my father on one side of me and the Fox on the other." Oona frowned. "After the procession there will be a feast, and I would have you and Lyrra play and sing for me, if you wish to, and Lyrra is up to it."

"I may sing 'Somebody'?"

"I would be disappointed if you did not."

Dressed in her new traveling tunic and leggings of mint green linen, Oona practically skipped alongside Asad as they made their way to the stables, reveling in the light summer breeze on her skin. During her five days of confinement much had happened. The war council had agreed to wait until spring before any final decision on warring against the Oryx, much to the Panther's displeasure. After the decision, the Heron and his people had departed the city for their own.

The Ox and the Fox were seen in each other's company daily, causing tongues to wag and the queen to caution her future daughter, only to be ignored in the Fox's usual snippy fashion. All this Oona knew because each night Asad had knocked on her balcony door and they had snuck out to the gardens to stroll and talk, hold hands and kiss, undisturbed but for the simmering passions they dared not give in to again, not yet. Not until tonight.

Asad had promised they would go to the attic room tonight, and Oona blew her breath out long and slow, trying to calm her heart and cool the heat between her legs as she anticipated the night and the play of Asad's hands and mouth. The man was a master musician, and Oona's body an eager instrument.

They entered the stables, where a slightly built, middle-aged man with bowed legs, wispy gray hair, and bright, black eyes came around the corner carrying a bucket of oats. At the sight of them, the man dropped his lower jaw and the bucket, barely missing his sandaled feet.

"Oona the Swan," Asad said, "meet the Ratter, my stable master."

"Is honor to meet you, Ratter," Oona said as the man closed his gaping mouth. "Black Mane tell me much of you, how good you be with horses."

"Yer even more beautiful 'an they say, mistress Swan," the Ratter said, rubbing his jaw. "No wonder the Black Mane's so far gone as 'e is."

Oona blushed at the compliment and Asad huffed.

"We are here to introduce the Swan to Blaze and Brick," he said. "Blaze will be her saddle horse and Brick her pack horse on her journey home."

The Ratter nodded. "They're in the kraal, long with Storm 'n at other long-legged filly you brought back with you," he said with a wink at Oona. "There's carrots in 'at bucket over yonder." He nodded at a wall where six buckets were lined up, filled with carrots, apples, and oats. "Blaze, 'e's a glutton fer 'em."

Asad set the bucket of carrots down at the kraal gate and whistled sharply three times. A thundering of hooves sounded, followed by a herd of about ten horses running toward them from the far field. Storm was in the lead, his black mane and tail flying, and Cloud Dancer was right behind him, her long legs seeming to skim over the ground.

"Cloud Dancer be fast," Oona said, admiring the filly. "I think you will win wager with Panther."

Asad grinned and nodded as the horses neared. "I believe I will," he said. He winked at Oona. "But then I seldom lose a wager, and never over a horse."

The herd gathered at the gate, snorting and pawing at the ground beyond the bucket full of carrots. Oona recognized Star and reached out to pat her neck. She ran her fingers under the nose strap of the mare's bridle.

"Star still have my skirt hem on her bridle," she said.

"Aye," Asad said with a sheepish grin, "so she does."

He handed out carrots to the horses, which pushed and jostled for position around Storm, who held his ground as leader of the herd. Cloud Dancer took a carrot from Oona with a happy nicker, her whiskered lips soft and gentle.

"She likes you," Asad said. He cocked his head and sighed. "I do not think I will ever be able to look at her and not think of you, my two white-maned, long-legged, dancing beauties."

Oona blushed and Cloud Dancer pranced away as a horse with a chestnut red coat and white leggings pushed its way up to the fence.

"That is Blaze," Asad told Oona as she held a carrot out to the gelding. "He takes direction well and has a comfortable seat. He has the speed and endurance of a desert horse, and the toughness of a northern steppes horse. He does not shy easily and has an even, easy temper. I believe you two will get along well."

"Hello, Blaze," Oona crooned, and the gelding flicked his ears forward. "You and I be good friends soon I think." She offered him another carrot and he snorted softly into her hand, tickling Oona's palm. Oona laughed lightly, and Blaze whinnied and nodded his head, the carrot's green tops waving in the air. "See," Oona said. "We already be."

A thicker horse with a darker chestnut coat and black leggings grabbed the swinging carrot top and tried to pull it out of Blaze's mouth, but Blaze held on tight. Oona laughed as the two tugged and pulled until the greens tore and the black-legged horse ate them while Blaze munched the carrot.

"That," Asad nodded at the darker horse, "is Brick, Blaze's younger sibling by two years."

Oona held a carrot out to Brick, who quickly took her offering and walked away to eat it as Blaze nickered for another.

"Brick is not so fast or comfortable a ride as Blaze," Asad said. "But he too is even-tempered and sturdy, and he will follow his brother anywhere. If you like, you can ride Blaze tomorrow while I start training Cloud Dancer."

"Oh yes," Oona said as she reached into the bucket for the last carrot. "I would very much like."

She started to straighten and stopped. The Ox and the Fox stood outside the stable doors, watching her and Asad. Behind her, Asad cursed under his breath and took her arm as she stood tall and squared her shoulders. He picked the bucket up with his other hand.

"Come on," he said, swinging the bucket with purpose and heading for the stables. "Let us see what those two are up to."

They had taken no more than five steps when the Ox and the Fox turned and walked away so quickly that they were almost running back toward the palace.

Asad bathed after supping and was trying to rest up for his night later with Oona, who had supped in her chambers with the Dove and was, he assumed, resting up for the night ahead as well. The light in her emerald eyes this afternoon had told him she looked forward to it as much as he. She was an eager and passionate lover, her pleasure neither taught nor forced, and as much as he had enjoyed their midnight walks in the gardens, he had missed making love with her. He got up from his bed and paced his chambers, jumpy as a cat on hot coals.

He tried to think of anything but Oona's soft skin, her low moans and throaty laugh. He concentrated on his plans for the sisters' trip home—a sobering exercise—on Brawn and the sell swords he would hire, on getting Blaze and Brick sound for the journey, and of the Ox and the Fox watching them at the kraal this afternoon. It was not that he cared one way or the other that they had become friends, perhaps even lovers. In truth, he hoped they were lovers, and since neither one of them were particularly smart or circumspect, they would be found out sooner or later. He hoped it would be in time to save him from marrying the Fox. Once Oona and Lyrra were safely away, he would make it his priority to expose them. What bothered Asad about their newfound alliance was that he did not trust either one of them separately: together they were worrisome.

There was a knock at the door, the Crab's knock. Asad quickly flopped onto his bed.

"Enter."

"Early night?" the Crab asked as he spied Asad sprawled out on his bed in his night tunic.

Asad feigned a yawn. "As you see."

"Well, the Panther has other plans for you. He has called a meeting and he commands your presence."

Asad did not have to feign his irritation. The war council had already come to an agreement three days ago. He had been looking forward to this night with Oona for days.

"When am I expected?"

"They wait for you as we speak."

Asad rose from the bed and the Crab started to open the chest that held Asad's clothing.

"I will get myself dressed," he said. "I need you to take a message to the Swan, to tell her that I do not know when I will be done with this meeting, but that I will come to her after."

"Of course, my prince," the Crab said with a low bow and raised brows.

Oona tried to pay attention to the game of colored stones she and Lyrra played in their new chambers, but her mind kept straying to other games she wanted to be playing with Asad in the privacy of the pleasure house attic.

"Concentrate, Oo," Lyrra scolded.

"Huh?"

"That is the third time you have tossed a stone into the wrong cup." Lyrra waved her hand over her growing pile of stones. "Not that I dunna like winning, but at least try to make it a wee more challenging."

"Oh." Oona peered down at the board with the carved niches for the stones. "Where were we?"

"I am here in this room, sister," Lyrra said. "I've no idea where you are."

Oona blushed. Her mind had been up in the attic with Asad, doing things she blushed even harder over, things she could not tell Lyrra about. There was a knock at the door and she jumped up and practically ran to open it.

"Mistress Swan." The Palm stood on the other side, shifting from foot to foot. "I have a message for you, from, about Prince Black Mane."

"A message?" Asad had only ever had the Crab deliver messages between them. Earlier this evening, the Crab had told her the Black Mane would be detained and that he would call on her afterward, but perhaps the Crab had been detained as well.

"You are to meet him where you were this afternoon, with the carrots."

Oona grinned. She did not care who delivered the message, as long as it meant she could be with Asad tonight.

"Thank you, Palm."

Oona shut the door and ran to her chest, where she pulled out her new boots and put them on. If she was going to meet Asad at the kraals in the dark of night, she didn't want to be stepping into horse droppings wearing sandals, though she did wonder why they were meeting at the kraals and not the attic. She hoped there was not anything wrong with one of the horses.

Asad was not at the kraal when Oona got there, but there was a bucket of carrots next to the gate, so she whistled and shook the bucket. Soon she heard the thunder of hooves and then she saw the dark shapes of horses running toward her under the dim light of the waxing moon. Storm arrived first, followed as before by Cloud Dancer, and then Blaze and the others. She laughed softly as they jostled for position, whinnying and nickering as Oona handed the carrots out.

"Where you master be?" she asked Storm. "He rule your heart as he do mine?" The stallion snorted and stepped back, rolling his eyes, and Oona laughed at herself. "Now I be jealous of horse."

A rough hand covered Oona's mouth and another grabbed her around the waist, holding her tight against a man's chest wider and softer than Asad's. Hot breath blew into the side of her face, smelling of stale spirits.

"Your master is nowhere he can help you now, you northern whore."

Oona bit the hand over her mouth at the same time she stomped on a foot. The hand dropped from her mouth, but before Oona could break free, the man circled his arm around her neck and pulled tight. Sucking in what air she could, Oona swung the bucket up and hit him alongside his head. He bellowed and let go his hold of her waist and grabbed the bucket, wresting it from her grip with such violence that Oona's wrist snapped. Oona opened her mouth to scream for help, but he squeezed her neck so tightly she did not have enough air to cry out. She did have enough to gouge his arm with her fingernails and stomp his foot again.

"Stop your damnable dancing," he puffed into her ear, and Oona doubled her efforts, though it cost her air she could not spare.

The man tightened his grip around her belly and jerked her up off the ground. He hauled her to the gate and fumbled to get it open as Oona fought his hold, twisting and thrashing and flailing, but she could not breathe and she was losing strength. The man dragged her into the kraal and slammed the gate behind them, his breath fouling what little air Oona managed to suck into her screaming lungs.

"Here we are," the man said as he squeezed even tighter. Oona fought to remain calm as the pounding in her ears grew louder. In front of her the hazy outline of a horse wavered. "Now be a good slave and go to sleep, and you won't feel a thing. I am going to make it look like you were trampled by the Black Mane's own horses, after I have my way with you of course." He laughed low and coarse. "The Fox will be avenged and I will be well rewarded, and the Black Mane will be nothing but a sorry cuckold."

Oona gave one last, futile heave against the man's unyielding hold, and a lion roared.

Asad was up and over the fence in one leap, landing next to the Ox and smashing his fist into the brute's face with the next. The Ox let go his hold of Oona and stumbled back as Oona fell to her hands and knees, gasping for breath.

"Oona?" She held a hand up and sucked in air.

Asad blew out a relieved breath and then rounded on the Ox.

"You broke my nose," the Ox blubbered through blood and spittle.

"I will rip your throat out, you craven piece of offal." Grabbing the Bull by the neck with one hand, Asad pulled his waist blade with the other.

"Asad, no," Oona rasped, still on her hands and knees. "You must not." She stood and staggered over to him, placing her shaking hand on his arm. "Asad, please," she begged. "Do not kill him."

"He would have killed you, and worse." Asad glared into the Ox's bulging eyes and pressed the blade into his thick neck enough to raise a weal of blood.

"Aye," Oona wheezed, "he would have, but you can no kill him. Think of you family, you tribe. It will start war with Bull's tribe."

Asad shook his head and growled. "Not if they never find his body. I could kill him and dump his weighted body into the river. No one would ever know what happened to the pollution of a man." Asad grinned at the idea and then stepped back as the Ox pissed himself. "He does not deserve to live."

"No," Oona agreed, her voice ragged, "he does not, for he is lowest of men. But Fox, surely she know he be here, maybe others know or see. You can no chance it, Black Mane, consequences be too many."

Oona's calling him Black Mane reminded him of whom and what he was, and gave Asad pause.

"Please, my lion," she said. "I will lie for you if need be, but I vow never lie to you, and truth be you must let Ox go, let him live with shame of man he be."

Asad relaxed his arm under Oona's hand as he blew his breath out and nodded to her. He snarled into the bloody, spittle-smeared lump that was the Ox's face and gave his throat a vicious squeeze.

"I would kick you in the testicles to make certain you never attack another woman," Asad said with a sneer as he glanced down the Ox's urine-soaked tunic. "But I do not want to stain my sandals with your coward's piss."

"My father—"

"Your father will never hear of this," Asad growled and the Ox cowered. "Nobody will ever hear of this." He moved his blade with slow purpose up the Ox's throat and over his chin and held it to his bulbous, pulpy nose. "If they do, I will hunt you down and geld you properly." Pressing the point of his blade to the side of the Ox's face, Asad sliced a neat arc from his ear to his chin. "So you will remember the Swan's mercy and my promise." He tapped the tip of his blade on the Ox's quivering chin. "Touch her again and I will slit your throat from ear to ear, and no one, not your father, not mine, not all the kings of the seven tribes, will stop me." He pushed the Ox's chin up, forcing the cowering bastard to meet his murderous glare. "Do we have an understanding?"

"Ye...yes."

Asad let go his hold of the Ox so suddenly that the Ox dropped to his knees. "See you and that bitch Fox hold to it," Asad snarled, then kicked the piece of offal upside the head.

The Ox crumpled to the ground, senseless. Asad grabbed him by the tunic and Oona held the gate open and followed as Asad dragged him over to a mound of horse dung and left him lying face down in it. Taking Oona by the hand, he led her back to the stables, surprising the sleeping Ratter.

"Put two guards on the kraal," he ordered. "Day and night until the Bull and his company leave."

The Ratter swung his bowed legs over the side of his cot and rubbed the sleep from his eyes, taking in Asad and Oona from head to toe.

"What 'appened?" he asked.

"The Ox," Asad spat the name, "went after the Swan." Beside him, Oona shook and Asad pulled her in tight. "If I had not arrived when I did..." Oona buried her face into his shoulder and shuddered. Asad clenched and unclenched his fist and his jaw. "You will find the Ox beside the kraal, unconscious in a pile of dung," he told the Ratter. "Feel free to give him a kick or ten if he stirs, but make sure he returns to the palace before dawn. Remind the ass not to mention myself or the Swan when he tells whatever story it is he comes up with to explain his injuries." Asad eyed the Ratter. "I expect you to keep our names out of it as well."

Asad led Oona to the Ratter's bed and sat her down on it, growling and grumbling as he took a clean rag from the cupboard and dipped it into the wash basin of cool, clean water and then gently wiped the blood from Oona's swelling lip, his anger burning hotter with every swipe of the cloth.

The Ox had meant to rape and then to kill Oona. That much Asad had heard. And he would have too, the spineless cur, if Asad had not gone to Oona's chambers after the meeting, and Lyrra had not remembered the exact wording of the Palm's message, a message that Asad had never given to the Palm.

"I will kill the whoreson yet," he swore. "When I think of what he would have done to you."

"No, Asad," Oona said, her voice as weak and pale as her face. "You did right, as you must, for you tribe."

Right or wrong, what Asad wanted to do was to go back and finish the cowardly corruption of a man off. But Oona was right. If others knew or saw, then there could be a war between the tribes over it. Swallowing his ire, Asad tasted the bitterness of his own gall.

"What did he say to you, Oona?"

"He say he will kill me, make it look like horses trample me after he...he take my body." She closed her eyes and took in a shaky breath as Asad's gall threatened to rise again. "He say it be poetic payback, and you be left a sorry cuckold." She opened her eyes, and Asad could see the broken veins of red in the whites of them. "What is cuckold?"

Asad dipped the wash linen again, as much to cool the rag as his own fury. "A cuckold is a husband whose wife is unfaithful," he said, wiping the dirt from her cheeks. "Which means the Fox was in on it with the Ox. He is still angry about the knife fight, and too much the coward to go after me, so they went after what I treasure most in this world." Asad brushed a strand of hair from Oona's cheek and tucked it behind her ear. "Their revenge would have taken the very heart from me, my jewel, if he had managed to carry it out."

"But he did not," she said, her eyes shining into his as he rubbed his thumb over her petal-soft cheek. "They did not. You stop him. You save me, again."

Oona woke to the low glow of candlelight, cradled in warmth. Her throat was on fire and her head pounded behind her eyes, which refused to focus. For a moment her addled mind took her back to the desert and the heat sickness, but then she remembered the kraal, the Ox, and she shuddered.

Arms as strong as iron and as gentle as a lover's caress held her close and safe.

"Asad?"

"Oona."

"What time is?"

He shifted his hold and pushed a strand of hair back from her cheek and peered into her eyes. The pounding behind them intensified as Oona tilted her head back to meet his gaze, but at least her eyes were focused enough to see the concern in his.

"It is after midnight," he said. "Time to get you back to your chambers and your sister."

"No." Oona shook her head and pressed her nose to the crook of his neck, breathing in the warm, musky male scent of him. "I no go back yet. I stay here with you longer."

She felt his cheeks rise. "We can stay for a while longer," he whispered into her hair, "but not too long. You must be back in your rooms before the palace wakens."

Oona nodded. "What we do about Ox and Fox?" she asked. "And Palm?"

"I will speak to the Palm first thing in the morning, before the Ox or the Fox have a chance to get to her. I will get the truth of the matter from her." He kissed Oona's hair, about the only place on her body that did not ache. "As for the Ox and the Fox," he growled low and deep, "they are another matter entirely."

He shifted on the Ratter's hard, straw-ticked bed, his arms holding her tight. "If they were smart, they would stay away from you and me, and each other, but I do not give either of them much credit there. The trick will be to give them enough rope to hang themselves whilst making sure they do you no more harm, for if they did, I would have to kill them both, consequences be damned."

"You think they will try?"

"I think they are both too spoilt and foolish not to."

Oona licked her swollen lips and nodded. "I may ask a thing of you, my lion?"

"Anything."

"May Crab teach me to knife fight?"

"No."

"But..."

"I will, once you are healed."

CHAPTER 14

Lessons

Asad rode Storm north along the river road until the stallion's sides were heaving and Asad's fury and frustration had lessened, though he still clamped his jaw and clenched his fists every time he envisioned Oona's bruised neck and bloodshot eyes.

When he had questioned the Palm this morning, she admitted that it was the Ox who had told her to give the Swan the message to meet Asad at the kraals. She swore she did not know it to be a lie and a trap, and Asad had no reason not to believe her, especially after the stricken look on the woman's face when they entered the Swan's chambers together and the Palm saw Oona's injuries. The poor woman fell to her knees and begged her mistress's forgiveness, which Oona kindly gave, earning the Palm's vow to serve only the Swan and the Black Mane, and to tell them of any and all gossip she heard from the other servants about them, the Ox, and the Fox, a task Asad had set the Crab to as well.

After breaking his fast in the dining salon and noting the absence of both Ox and Fox, Asad had headed for the stables, intending to start Cloud Dancer's training. But his anger still seethed and seemed to seep from his every pore, which the filly would surely sense, so he saddled Storm and headed north, torturing himself with riding the same road Oona would be taking on her journey home and away from him, as soon as the Dove was able.

The Dove, like her sister, was a quick healer. The splint was off her leg and she was already walking with the aid of a crutch, and the Owl predicted her arm would be out of the sling in a matter of days.

Returning from his ride in time for the evening meal, Asad sat with the Cheetah at the table next to the king's, eating more meat and drinking more wine than was his usual in an attempt to sate his bloodlust. The Fox sat quietly at her table, picking at her food and shooting darting glances Asad's way. By the last course of honeyed dates there had still been no mention of the Ox's absence, and the wine had done little to dull the sharp edge of Asad's anger.

"Where is the Ox tonight?" he asked the Bull, who coughed and sputtered. "I did not see him this morning either."

The Bull wiped droplets of wine from his mouth and beard. "My eldest son was called to the stables late last night to see to one of our stallions," he said loudly enough for the closest tables to hear. "This stallion can be ill-tempered and our stable master was unable to calm him, so he sent for the Ox, who has a way with dumb beasts."

Aye, because he is one.

If the Bull heard Asad's disgusted snort, he took no visible notice, but the Cheetah and the Panther did.

"The stallion was crazed," the Bull continued, "and pinned the Ox against the wall and trampled my son before he was able to get out of the stall."

A collective gasp sucked in air.

"The Ox lives," the Bull said, and relieved breaths rushed out. "But he is severely injured. The Owl says he has a broken nose, and two, if not three broken ribs, a dislocated jaw, a cut to his face from the horse's hoof, and too many scrapes and bruises to count." He met and held the Panther's disconcerted gaze. "We must avail ourselves of your hospitality for a while longer, my friend, until the Ox is able to ride again."

"My house is yours," the Panther said, and raised his cup. His black eyes narrowed on Asad for a brief moment before he dipped his head to the Bull. "To your son's recovery, may it be quick and complete."

Asad raised his cup and drank deeply, glad he had not kicked the Ox in the testicles after all, or the coward's departure would have been delayed even longer.

"Where is your milk-faced pet, my Prince Black Mane?"

Asad glared at the Fox, who sat at the queen's table.

"The Swan is abed with a severe headache," he said. "She has had them before, and will require the dark and quiet of her chambers for a few days until they pass."

The Fox puckered her lips and shook her head. "What you see in such a pale-faced, weak-blooded creature, I will never know."

"No," Asad agreed. "Of that I am certain."

By the second day of her confinement, Oona could swallow without pain and the constant throbbing behind her eyes had dimmed to a dull ache. Her voice still rasped and her neck and shoulders still cricked, but according to Lyrra, who knew the truth of Oona's injuries, the whites of her eyes actually had some white in them again.

The Palm was most solicitous in her attentions, and dutifully guarded her mistress from any and all would-be visitors, including the queen, explaining that the Swan was sleeping and that even opening her eyes or trying to speak caused her great distress. The only person she would let pass was the Black Mane, who came to check on Oona several times a day and evening, treating her as if she were some fragile little songbird who could withstand no more than feather-light touches and pecking kisses.

By the fourth day Oona was pacing the confines of her cage. Even Lyrra had been able to hobble outside and enjoy fresh air and blue sky daily on her walks in the garden with the Cheetah, whilst Oona was forced to hide indoors, and she was heartily sick of closed shutters and solid walls.

On the fifth morning, Oona met Asad at the door to her chambers, dressed in her new traveling tunic and leggings.

"Today you teach me knife fight," she said.

He shook his head. "You are not fully healed yet."

"I be Swan, not titmouse. And Lyrra say my eyes no more red and my neck no more bruise. And if I no get out of chambers this day, I go mad."

Asad cocked his head, eyeing her from head to toe.

"What matter?" she challenged him. "You be afraid Swan beat Lion?"

Asad laughed. "You really are a poor loser."

Oona sashayed past him out into the hall, into freedom. "You coming?" she said over her shoulder, smiling as he covered the distance between them in two long strides.

He took her hand and Oona twined her fingers through his, thrilling at the familiar heat between them.

She gave him a sidelong grin. "Maybe after, tonight, we go to attic room?"

"Are you sure?"

Oona stopped and pulled him to her in the empty hall. She wrapped her arms around his waist and pressed her pelvis to his, smiling into his warm lips as he groaned.

"Do this feel sure?" she whispered fiercely, and then his mouth was on hers, and his kiss was hard and demanding, and his arms were iron bands.

"Kill point, Swan," Asad said as Oona swiped her wooden blade across the back of his leg, a move that would have hamstrung him had it been a metal knife. He dropped to his knee on the lawn of the courtyard and then threw his wooden blade at her, its point hitting her padded chest dead center. "Kill point, Black Mane."

"But…"

"In a real fight, Swan, never trust that your opponent is dead. Make certain."

She jumped at him and jabbed, holding her blade's point to his jugular. Asad grinned as the crowd they had attracted in the main courtyard applauded. He wrapped his arms around her shoulders and pulled her down and rolled her under him. The crowd hooted.

"You really are a sore loser," he teased before giving her a smacking kiss, and then standing before giving her a hand up.

Oona brushed her tunic off, her long, lean dancer's legs flexing beneath the tight leggings, and Asad growled at the gape-jawed, moon-eyed men watching. Apparently oblivious to the stares, Oona tossed her blade from hand to hand and crouched. "Again," she said.

Asad roared, but Oona did not even flinch. He gave a feral grin and shifted from side to side, but Oona held steady, watching his feet, not his hips or his head, as he had taught her. He stepped to his right and she leaned to her left, he stepped back and she stepped forward, he pretended to stumble, and she lunged forward, but he was ready for her and side-stepped her lunge. He struck out with his blade where her shoulder had been and found only air as she dropped to her knees and slid by him, her blade slashing first his thigh and then the back of his knee.

"Kill point, Swan," she said, scrambling to a crouch with a gleam in her eye and a fine sheen of sweat on her skin.

"Well done, Swan." Asad circled her with a predatory gaze. It had been ten days since their night in the attic, and he was beyond hungry to taste her again. In truth, he could have devoured her whole right here in front of the twenty or so gawking men and women watching them, and by the look in her eyes, she would relish the feast. He circled closer, his nose twitching at the warm perfume of her skin. The night could not come soon enough.

The crowd stirred and their buzzing grew louder and more strident. Asad tore his gaze from Oona's and followed the stares up to a second-story balcony, where the Ox leaned over the waist-high wall, watching. A low hiss emanated from Oona, and Asad thinned his lips into a sneer. He held the tip of his wooden blade to his neck and made a slow cutting motion from one ear to the next, his eyes never leaving the Ox, who stumbled back from the balcony wall and disappeared into his room.

"That is enough for today, Swan," Asad said to Oona, who opened her mouth to argue. He stepped in close and whispered low as he took her wooden knife, "Save your energy for tonight, my jewel."

Asad heard the soft grunt Oona made when she started her ascent up the rope ladder, and he noticed how she climbed slower this time, how she dropped to the roof instead of leaping. He had been right in stopping the knife-fighting lesson when he had, despite her protests. Whether she would admit it or not, her body had taken a beating at the hands of the Ox, and four days of resting and healing, or as Oona referred to it, forced confinement, had barely been enough. A better, less selfish man would not have had her climbing trees in the middle of the night in order to make love to her. A better man would have insisted she rest up, his head overruling his heart and his baser desires. But where Oona was concerned, Asad's heart, and hers, ruled, at least for tonight.

The attic door was open, the low glow of candlelight shining from below. Asad motioned for Oona to stand back as he pulled his waist blade, and then he crouched down onto his hands and knees and leaned over the doorway as a pair of dark eyes blinked up at him.

"Black Mane."

"Brawn?" Asad sat back on his heels.

"I was not expecting you here tonight."

"Nor I, you."

"I am visiting with my sister while I can, since it will be many moons before we meet again once I leave with the Swan." Brawn poked his head out and glanced past Asad to Oona. "I see the Swan is with you." He grinned and waved his hand. "Come in, come in. My sister will be glad to see you. She has been worried since the Swan took to her sick bed."

He disappeared down the ladder and Oona looked to Asad, who shook his head and shrugged.

"It is the infernal gossip of palace servants," he said. "It is near impossible to keep anything from them for long."

The Mouse had Oona in a tight hug almost as soon as Oona's feet hit the attic floor.

"Oh Swan, I am so glad to see you." She stepped back and held Oona at arm's length, studying her face. "Is all right with you? And the Dove? She heals from her injuries as well?"

Asad cocked his head at the Mouse's "as well", and Brawn studied him as intently as the Mouse studied Oona.

"Dove heal well," Oona told her. "She walk with crutch and be out of sling soon. She will be glad to play harp again." Oona smiled shyly at Asad. "Maybe we play and sing for Black Mane birthday feast?"

"That would be a wonderful birthday gift," Asad said, and Oona beamed. He took her hand and sat her down beside him on one sofa as the Mouse and Brawn sat on the other, exchanging a quick glance between them. "What?" Asad said.

Brother and sister exchanged another quick glance before Brawn answered. "There has been talk as to the timing of the Swan and the Ox both taking to their chambers on the same morn," he said, "neither of them to be seen for the next four days, as well as the cause of the Ox's injuries, since the Bull's stable master was bragging about how there wasn't a mean bone in any of his horses a few days before the Ox's accident."

"There has, has there?"

"As well as of how the cut on the Ox's face looks more like a knife's blade than a horse's hoof, and how, if it was a horse's hoof, the bruising should be on that side of his face, not the other."

Oona was gripping Asad's hand, and he gave hers a gentle squeeze. Let the palace servants talk all they wanted. None of them had any proof as long as the Ox and Fox kept their mouths shut. And the Ratter and the Palm would not tell. Nor, Asad knew, would Brawn or the Mouse. They had too much to lose.

"The Ox is as poor a storyteller as he is a fighter," was all Asad said, but it was enough to spring the Mouse from her sofa onto her knees before Oona.

"Did he hurt you badly, Swan?"

"He try," she said, answering much as Asad had. "Black Mane stop him."

"And this goes no further than this room," Asad said. "I want your oaths on it."

"You have them," Brawn vowed, and the Mouse nodded. "There is one more bit of news you may be interested in," he said. "It seems the entire city has heard the story of the Black Mane challenging the Panther over the Swan and the Dove, and they have given the Swan a new name."

"What name?"

Brawn shifted uncomfortably.

"What name?"

"The Ivory Queen."

A chill took hold of Asad, settling in his bones and leaving Oona's hand in his the only touch of warmth in his entire body. He had been ready to hear that Oona was being called his mistress or whore, but not queen. Queen would be so much worse when the

Panther heard of it, and he would, if he had not already. Queen could enrage his father to break his bargain and have Oona killed by someone more adept at assassination than the dimwitted Ox.

Oona nestled into Asad's shoulder after Brawn and the Mouse left the attic, breathing in the musky scent of male and myrrh, and fighting back tears. It had been decided that she and Lyrra would leave the Great Valley, escorted by Brawn and his handpicked sell swords, the day after Asad's birthday feast.

"I know is for our safety that we must leave so soon," she sniffed. "But I no want leave you, Asad."

Asad tucked her in closer and kissed her forehead. "Nor do I want you to leave me, my jewel. But if Brawn has heard you called the Ivory Queen, it will not be long before the Panther hears of it, and he will not be pleased. I fear he will use it as a reason to go back on our bargain."

"He would try kill me and Lyrra?"

"He would try."

"And you would kill him."

Asad's sigh rumbled into a low growl. "I should challenge him and take the throne outright. Then you truly would be my Ivory Queen, my one and only."

Oona swallowed her tears and her heart. "I can no be reason you kill you father, my lion, and other kings, they would no let me be you only queen. They would name you weak and try make war on you as Panther try make war on Oryx."

Asad cupped her chin and lifted it, his amber eyes burning into hers. "How is it you understand so much of my world, are willing to sacrifice so much for it when the Fox, born and bred to be queen, is unable to see past her own selfish wants?"

Oona's decision to flee rather than marry Beorne had likely cost her father his life and nearly Lyrra's as well. She would not be so selfish again, but her reasons were not as selfless as Asad gave her praise for. "Is not you world I care about Asad, is you."

215

He tilted her chin up and lowered his lips to hers, and soon all Oona cared about, all Oona knew, was the urgent give and take of his kisses. She had waited the past ten days, no, her entire life, to make love with this man, and if she only had another ten days and nights with him, she was going to make the most of them.

As if reading her thoughts, Asad pulled her tunic up over her head and tossed it to the floor, his own following an instant later. His mouth claimed hers and she gave herself over to his probing kisses, the intimate touch of his hands, the warm friction of his skin against hers. She explored his body with her mouth and hands, learning how his male nipples would harden and peak as she kissed and suckled, how the light furring of his chest hairs tickled her nose, how her breath could make the muscles of his belly twitch and tighten, and the feather-light touch of her fingers could make his staff grow hard and pulsing hot.

Oona straddled Asad and he groaned. He grasped her hips in his big warm paws and moved her back and forth over the thick, hot ridge of his erection, and Oona's body vibrated with ripples of molten heat and melting sensation. She poised her woman's lips over the soft, straining head of his manhood and smiled in delicious anticipation, but as she started to lower herself down onto him, as her eager flesh kissed his, Asad pulled her hips up and rolled her onto her back.

"As much as I wish otherwise, my jewel," he rasped, "we dare not fully consummate our love."

Oona opened her mouth to ask why, though she knew full well why. Asad had explained it all to her before, the danger of his father discovering she was no longer a virgin, the chance of her becoming pregnant, Asad's refusal to let her journey home carrying his babe. She knew it all, understood it all. "But is not there a way to consummate without spilling seed, planting babe inside me?"

Asad's lion eyes narrowed on hers. "Who told you that?"

"Mouse." Oona wrapped her hand around his shaft of skin-clad iron and he moaned. "Is true?"

"It is."

She squeezed and he groaned.

"Why you not tell me this?"

He moved in her hand, growing even larger, even harder.

"I do not trust myself with you," he growled.

"I do. I trust you," Oona whispered fiercely. Holding his heated gaze, she smiled invitingly as she clasped both hands on his broad shoulders and spread her legs beneath him. He buried his face into the crook of her neck and held his body above hers. She lifted her pelvis until his manhood nestled in her woman's weave and her blood thrummed.

"Oona."

Asad's voice was a low, warning rumble, but Oona was beyond heed. Lowering her hands to his tensed buttocks, she splayed her fingers and pushed down as she raised her pelvis even higher, sighing as the soft head of his shaft pressed against her aching flesh.

"Asad." His name was a caress, a plea: a demand. She wanted him, all of him, now. "Make me you bride, my lion. Be my husband tonight."

He answered her with a kiss that drew her breath, her very soul from her. "I will," he growled as he took himself in hand and slowly, surely, slid the probing head of his manhood into Oona's yearning flesh, a little deeper each gentle push, each breath. "I will make you mine." He took her mouth in his and thrust once, fast and hard and deep, his kiss swallowing Oona's little cry of surprise. He stilled and lifted his head, his amber eyes burning into hers. "You are mine, Oona the Swan, my jewel, bride of my heart."

Oona's body relaxed and molded itself around him, enveloping him, welcoming him, reveling in the fullness of him pulsing deep inside her. "And you be mine, Asad the Black Mane, my lion, my somebody."

She ran her hands back through his magnificent black mane and lifted her mouth to his, taking his breath with hers, suffusing hers with his, gasping with pleasure as he began to move inside her, slowly at first, gently. He smiled against her lips as she rocked in rhythm with him, their bodies moving together in a dance of their own, their pace growing more rapid, Asad's thrusts deeper. Oona grasped his broad shoulders with both hands and wrapped her legs around his waist, holding tight and breathing hard as a mounting tension built deep inside her. Asad set his hands to either side of her shoulders, and then placed one around the base of his staff, his thumb pressing her nubbin of flesh to his and rubbing it in delicious, torturous circles.

"Let go, my jewel," he rasped low in her ear, his breath as ragged as his voice. "I cannot hold my release much longer."

Oona braced her feet wide, opening her body, her soul to Asad, unabashed and unashamed, basking in the heat of his amber gaze as he plunged deeply, again and again, and wave after cresting wave of bone-melting contractions washed over and through her.

Her body was still humming when Asad pulled out and spilled his wet, warm seed on her belly. He took the corner of the sofa linen and gently wiped the milky liquid from her belly, then lay along the length of her.

"Ahh, Oona," he crooned, tucking her backside into his front. "You are mine as I am yours. We share a bond that no king or land, time or distance will ever sever."

Asad stood beside the Cheetah, watching Oona and the Dove ride Blaze and Wind Song around the safe confines and soft dirt of the training kraal. The Owl had removed the Dove's arm sling yesterday, and though she still walked with the aid of a cane and had needed assistance mounting Wind Song, which the Cheetah had readily given, she rode with an easy and confident seat.

Oona caught Asad's eye and gave him a knowing smile that brought an instant throb to his ever-eager cock. It had been three days and nights since they had consummated their love in the attic, and they had made the most of them, climbing up the tree as soon as the dark of night arrived, and not climbing down again until the first gray streaks of dawn. Asad had known his share of pleasure women, but he had never known such pleasure with a woman before. Oona's passion flowed in her veins, simmering below her pale, cool skin, and flaming bright and hot at his touch, inflaming his own until they burned together, their bodies melded, their souls scorched and rising reborn.

He met her knowing smile with a leering grin, eager for the night yet to come, his grin growing wider as her chest rose and fell and her cheeks flushed the same rose petal pink of her nipples. A low growl rumbled from his groin to his throat and caused the Cheetah to eye him sidelong.

"Brother?" The Cheetah glanced around, but there were none but the sisters riding and chatting happily. "What ails you now?"

Like Asad, the Cheetah had lain with pleasure women since he was ten and four, but unlike Asad, the Cheetah's relationship with the northern sister he adored was still one of chaste friendship. And Oona had only told the Dove of her and Asad kissing. She said she would tell Lyrra all after they returned home and Lyrra was a married woman. Then she had stroked Asad's manhood and his pride, saying that she only prayed her sister found a man who satisfied her as Asad did Oona.

"The same thing that has ailed me since the night of Summer's Eve," Asad answered his brother. "My trap continues to close around me, and I have only seven days and six nights before I spring it shut by my own hand."

"At least you will have your memories of her." His brother spoke to Asad, but he was looking at the Dove.

Asad said nothing. How could he explain to his brother the bittersweet torture of loving and losing Oona, when the thought of her riding away from him was like a fist to his belly? He watched her knee Blaze into an easy gallop, her pale hair flying out behind her, the lilt of her laughter floating on the wind, and the fist in his belly twisted and turned. *All I will have left of her is memories.*

She pulled Blaze up at the fence where Asad and the Cheetah stood, her grin thinning and her head tilting as she caught Asad's eye, and then her gaze shot over his shoulder and narrowed. Asad turned as the Crab approached.

"The Panther has requested the Swan's and the Dove's presence in the salon for the evening's meal," he told Asad. "There is to be an announcement."

The supper was formal so Asad sat in his robes at the elder son's table with the Cheetah and the Ox, who wisely took the seat farthest from Asad. His face was no longer swollen and misshapen, but he still chewed slowly and the skin around his right eye was a mottled black and blue and yellow. The cut along his left cheek a red weal of scarring skin. He was also prone to fits of coughing that left him holding his ribs and sweating profusely.

Asad refused to speak one word to the pollution of a man, and the Cheetah, who knew of the Ox's attack on Oona, would only answer a direct question of the Ox's with cold civility. Eventually the Ox stopped speaking entirely, which was just as well, for it took all of Asad's princely training and considerable will to keep from finishing what he had started at the kraals.

He did catch the Ox glancing across the room at the Fox several times, but she was too busy glaring daggers at Oona, who sat across the table from her, the Dove and the Gazelle between them, to take notice. The Panther, who had demanded the women sit at the same table, watched their uncomfortable silence with narrowed eyes and a thin smile throughout the meal. At last the honeyed dates were served. Asad pushed the bowl over to the Cheetah.

Damn you, Panther, get on with it.

The Panther stood and the salon went quiet. He lifted his cup and pushed out his chest. "Friends, family, honored guests." His gaze fanned across the room, lingering a moment on Oona's table and stopping as he met Asad's impatient glare. He smiled, cold, calculating. "It is my pleasure to announce the agreement of the betrothal of my daughter, the Gazelle, to the Bull's son, the Ox."

There it was, the Panther's punishment, his retaliation for the Ivory Queen, for Asad defending Oona against the Ox. He would willingly sacrifice his daughter and Asad's beloved sister to become third wife to a man he knew to be a dullard and a defiler of women, all to teach his son and heir a lesson. But what lesson? That a man's character did not matter, only his position? That tradition must be kept at all costs? That his father, while a strong king, was a hardheaded, black-hearted, selfish man? Asad glanced at the Gazelle, whose face had gone more pale even than Oona's. He swallowed the roar ripping its way up his throat.

Do not give the Panther the satisfaction. Think like a tribesman, not a brother, act like a prince, not a man. The Gazelle will not be of age to marry for another two years, time enough to deal with this. For now, keep the Swan and the Dove safe.

Asad stood amid the grassfire of congratulations and well wishes sweeping the salon. He met his mother's gaze, her eyes bright and her lips pinched in a queenly mask of composure. He turned to the Ox and held his own cup high as the salon quieted. "May you endeavor to deserve such a precious treasure as my father has gifted you," he toasted loudly, his voice surprisingly calm and steady for the blood boiling in his veins. He turned to his sister's table and lifted his cup to her. Beside her, the Fox looked about to cry. "May you find every happiness in your future marriage, my sister."

Which would not be to the Ox.

Asad would make certain of that.

"You father know what Ox try do to me, what manner of man he be," Oona said as they sat on the sofa in the attic later that night, "and still he give Gazelle to him in marriage?"

Asad nodded. "That is why he has done it," he ground out, the muscle in the side of his jaw ticking, "to get his revenge on me."

"For me. Because of what you do for me."

Asad stood and began to pace the small confines of the attic, his hands clenching and unclenching. Oona reached out to touch his hand with tentative fingers, smiling as he stopped his pacing and twined his fingers through hers. She stood so they were chest to chest and she looked him straight in the eye.

"You will help Gazelle escape marriage the same as you help us escape life as slaves."

"How did you—"

"I know you, Asad. I know you never let you sister suffer that man."

She ran a hand through his beard and felt the hard line of his jaw relax. He ran his fingers down the length of her arm and pushed a lock of hair behind her ear.

"I may toss the piece of offal into the river yet," he growled.

"I sorry I stop you before."

"No." He shook his head. "You were right. When I deal with him next, it will be after much consideration and planning." He grinned, dark, wild, and dangerous, a hunter with his prey in sight. Oona's breath caught and her insides stirred. He was a lion four times through, her lion, and she was drawn to the wild ferocity lurking beneath his veneer of princely civilization, air to fire. "But first, I must be sure you and your sister are far and safely away."

"First you must make love to me," Oona purred.

Slowly, deliberately, he trailed the tips of his strong, tactile fingers down the length of her neck and along the ridge of her shoulder, his gaze predatory as he pushed the sleeve of her tunic down, exposing the fleshy mound of her breast. His fingertips lightly brushed her budding nipple, and Oona sighed and licked her lips, lips he claimed with a fierce, demanding kiss. A kiss Oona returned with demands of her own.

She was his and he was hers. For now, for tonight, nothing and no one else mattered.

Much later, as they lay entwined in a languid afterglow, Asad reached over Oona into the bundle of his discarded clothing on the attic floor and pulled out a beaded leather sheath wrapped in a leather belt and handed it to Oona.

"A gift for you, my knife-fighting dancer."

Oona unwound the belt exposing the boned hilt of a double-edged dagger, its top carved into the head of a lion atop the arched neck of a swan whose open wings formed the crossbar.

"Oh, Asad, is beautiful," she said, pulling the blade out and turning it this way and that, admiring the glinting sharp edges. She sheathed the knife. "You give me too much," she chided gently. "And I give you nothing."

"That is not true," he said. "You have given me you, your heart, your body, and your love. Have you not?"

"I have. I will. I do. I give to you freely and for always."

He smiled and Oona's heart cracked.

"Then you have given me everything."

The Palm carried a covered platter in to the sisters' sitting salon as Oona was strapping her new dagger around her waist.

"I bring you a noon repast, Mistress Swan," she said, setting the platter down on the table. "You slept in and did not break your fast this morning." She lifted the linen cover to display a loaf of fresh baked flatbread, a wedge of herbed goat cheese, a bowl each of sweet melon and bitter greens, and a cup of beer. "You must eat, Mistress, to build up your strength for the journey to come."

"Thank you, Palm, is kind of you, but Dove and I are to visit pleasure house today, to say our farewells, and we be promised a feast of Hen's best cooking." The Palm looked crestfallen, especially as she eyed the beer. "How you get beer, Palm?" It was a drink reserved for special feasts only.

"I told the cook that the Black Mane ordered a cup for you." The Palm grinned and shrugged. "Even if he did not, he would not begrudge you it, and it is said to be a tonic for building up strength."

Oona herself did not care for the bitter, yeasty drink, which Asad knew. It occurred to Oona that it had been brewed in preparation for his birthday celebration, and that the Palm had likely never so much as tasted a sip in her entire servant's life.

"You eat, you drink, Palm," she said. "You sit and savor this feast you have brought me while Dove and I be gone."

"Oh, Mistress, I could not."

"Yes, you could. No one ever know. It be my gift to you for take such good care of me and Dove."

The Palm eyed the cup of beer and licked her lips and Oona laughed. Lyrra came out of her bed chambers, dressed and ready to go, and Oona gathered up the bundle of her green worm weave gown and Lyrra's blue, gifts meant for the Huntress and the Pearl. In Oona's pocket was the Falcon's ruby ring, her gift to the Mouse. She had considered leaving her white worm weave to one of the women, but in the end she could not part with it, for it was what she had worn the night of Summer's Eve, the first time she had ever lain eyes on the Black Mane.

"Enjoy, Palm," she said over her shoulder. "We be back in time for supper."

The Crab waited outside the door to escort them to the pleasure house, where he turned them over to the Boar with the Black Mane's instructions that he was to remain by their sides until he handed them back over to the Crab for their return to the palace. Asad and the Cheetah were busy preparing the horses and packing supplies for the sisters' journey. Normally, Oona would have chafed at Asad's overprotectiveness, but the stench of the Ox's foul breath and even fouler intentions still clung to her.

It was the first time the women of the pleasure house had seen Lyrra since her fall, and it would be the last, for the Black Mane's birthday celebration was in two days and the sisters would be leaving the morning after. Oona was content to step back as Lyrra was swarmed by every woman in the sitting salon but for the Spider and the Eel, who were nowhere to be seen. The Mouse hung back with Oona.

"Brawn will be here tonight," she told Oona. "I went up to put clean linens on the sofas, but found only one needed to be changed. The other already had fresh, fine linens over it."

Oona blushed and the Mouse grinned.

"You know the Black Mane has not set foot in the lower floors of this place since you left it," she said. "The other women are not so pleased about this as am I. They have wagers on when he shall resume his visits once you are gone from the city. The Butterfly says the same night, but she is wagering on what she wishes and not on what is obvious for all to see."

Oona said nothing, the thought of Asad returning to lay with any other woman, ever, turning her heart as green as her eyes.

"The Mynah wagered the longest time of three moons," the Mouse said, and Oona smiled fondly at the mistress of the house. "I wagered seven days."

Her words closed Oona's throat and sat like stones in her belly, but the Mouse grinned and leaned in closer.

"What I did not explain about my wager was that I expect he will show and pick me and that he and I will sit up all night talking of his love and my brother, and wondering where they are on their journey."

"Oh, Mouse," Oona whispered fiercely, "I want go home, but I no want leave. Yet I must, for sake of so many: for Lyrra, for Gazelle, for Asad, his family, his throne, and his city. I must leave him to stay alive, but it will kill me here." She laid her hand on her chest over her bleeding heart. "How am I to leave him?"

"With your back straight and your eyes forward," the Mouse said. "Because you have no choice." Her eyes welled with tears. "Because we, none of us, have a choice in this."

Asad and the Cheetah met the sisters and the Crab outside the palace door. By their bleary eyes and red noses, the sisters' farewells had been teary. Asad released the Crab from guard duty and tucked Oona into his shoulder and kissed the top of her head, breathing in the achingly sweet perfume of night jasmine and summer breezes…of her.

"The horses are in good form," he told her, his voice husky with the knowledge that soon her perfume would only be a memory, that every time he caught a whiff of jasmine in the night air his belly would grip and his chest gape. "The supplies are packed and under the Ratter's guard. No one will be able to get within ten paces of them without his hay fork in their backsides."

Oona nodded, laughed, and sniffed into his shoulder, and Asad hugged her closer. *By the gods, how am I ever going to let her go and not go mad for want of her?*

"Huntress and Pearl like their gowns of worm weave," she told him as the four of them made their way down the hall to the sisters' chamber. "Mouse's eyes grow big as ruby in Falcon's ring. I tell her if word get back to Fox that Swan gift Mouse ring, I not be upset, unless Mouse get in trouble for it."

She was grinning through her tears and Asad ruffled her hair. "The Fox can do nothing to her. The ring was yours to gift. The Mouse will be smart enough not to flaunt it before the Panther." He pushed open the door to her chambers and stepped in and stopped in his tracks. "Stay back," he said, his nose twitching at the sour, acrid stench of the room. He pulled his waist blade and motioned for the Cheetah to stay with the sisters, and then he crept into the room, following his nose to where the Palm slumped stiff and unseeing on the sofa, her tunic soaked in urine and feces, white froth on her blue lips and an empty cup in her cold hand.

CHAPTER 15

Farewells

Oona stood staring down at the Palm and then dropped to her knees and touched the backs of her fingers to the Palm's cold cheek.

"Poison was meant for me," she whispered.

"What?"

"Food, beer, all was meant for me." Eyes as big and round and wet as mossy river rocks held Asad's. "Palm have prepared for me, tell cook you order beer for me. She, she worry I not strong enough for journey, and I, I tell her, you eat food, Palm, you drink beer, my, my gift to you."

"But the Swan and the Dove are leaving in three days," the Cheetah said. He clasped the Dove's hand in his. "Why poison her now?"

"Why indeed?" Asad growled. If it was the Ox and the Fox again, it was out of petty hatred and jealousy, but if the Panther was behind it? He stood and pulled Oona up with him. "Go," he told the Cheetah, "bring the king, the queen, and the Owl. And brother, tell no one else for now."

The Owl inspected the icy white of the Palm's fingertips and toes, the froth on her lips, and then he pulled the empty cup from her hand and sniffed the rim.

"It was Insane Root," he said.

Asad glared at the Panther.

"You think I had her poisoned?" the Panther huffed. "Why would I poison a servant?"

"The beer was meant for the Swan," Asad said, wondering if, in truth, he did not already know. "The Palm drank the poison meant for the Swan."

The Panther huffed. "And why would I poison the Swan when she is to leave in three days? Why would I martyr the bitch and have my son grieving over her death and blaming me for it?"

The Panther spoke sense.

"Then it was the Ox and the Fox, again," Asad said.

"Again?" The queen glanced from Asad to the Panther and back to Asad. "So, the rumor is true? The Ox attacked the Swan? And you beat the Ox?"

"I would have killed the murderous piece of offal with my bare hands if the Swan had not stopped me."

The Panther humphed and Asad clenched his fists.

"The Swan stopped me from killing the Ox for the sake of the tribes," he told his father. "Something neither the Ox nor the Fox took into consideration either time."

The Panther humphed louder.

"And you knew this?" the queen said to her husband, her voice as hard as her eyes. "You knew this about the Ox and still you promised our daughter to such a beast?"

"I promised your daughter to a prince and heir to a throne," the Panther spat. "It is a good match, a better match than she rightfully deserves, bastard daughter of a queen, to become third wife to a future king."

Asad unclenched his fist and laid his hand on his mother's rigid shoulder and squeezed gently. The Gazelle would never be given over to the Ox, not while Asad had breath in his body. He glanced at Oona, who stood quiet and wide-eyed beside the Dove.

"What do you intend to do to the Ox and the Fox?" he asked the Panther.

"Nothing."

"Nothing?" Asad clamped down on the white-hot rage threatening to erupt from his chest.

"I will not punish a prince and princess of the Seven Tribes for attempting revenge on a slave who means nothing to the tribes, no matter how enthralled my son is with her. If she lives long enough to leave this place, fine. If not, it is nothing to me. She is nothing to me. She is no Ivory Queen."

Asad grit his jaw even tighter, willing himself not to throttle his father then and there. He felt a hand on his forearm, soft, cool, and calming. He met Oona's gaze and his rage congealed into a cold lump in his chest.

"We leave tomorrow morn," she told him, her voice a cracked whisper. She took in a deep breath and squared her shoulders and faced the Panther. "Swan and Dove will leave tomorrow morn."

It was decided that the Palm's death would be kept a secret until after Oona and Lyrra left on the morrow, so they packed their belongings and moved back into the queen's chambers for their last night in the City of the Great Valley, their old chambers now the Palm's temporary tomb. The Panther also decided that the sisters would perform one last time for his household and guests after the evening meal, and though neither Oona nor Lyrra had the heart for it, they knew better than to refuse.

Asad rode into the city to find Brawn while Oona and Lyrra took their last baths for what would likely be many moons, with the queen herself as escort, and the Crab standing guard outside. They ate what supper they could stomach in the privacy of the queen's chambers and then dressed for their last command performance, the specter of the Palm's dull, unseeing eyes haunting Oona's every step, the looming shadow of the morrow's parting shading her every thought.

They entered the dining salon, Oona in her gown of white worm weave and Lyrra in her gray, to a grassfire of whispers that swept from table to table as they made their way to the cleared patch of floor that was to be their stage. The meal was not a formal one, and Asad and the Cheetah sat with both of their mothers and the Gazelle while the Panther sat with the Bull and the Ox, whose jaw dropped at the sisters' entrance. Closing his mouth as slowly as he recovered his wits, the dullard swung his great blob of a head at the queen's table, where he met Asad's heated glare and gulped so loud and hard Oona thought he might have actually swallowed his own tongue.

As she passed the table where the Fox sat with three young wives of the Panther, Oona lengthened her spine and stared down her nose at the out-foxed vixen and then gave the bitch her back, smiling at the hiss of breath following her. She took Lyrra's hand and stood, chin high, in the middle of the salon as servants set Nightingale and a stool down beside them.

The Panther clapped once and the salon went quiet. "The Swan and the Dove will entertain us tonight to celebrate the promise of betrothal between the Ox and the Gazelle."

Oona flicked her gaze over the Panther's gloating grin to Asad's tight jaw, his amber lion's eyes as alert and wary as the night of Summer's Eve. She took in a deep breath and blew it out, as much to steady her voice as her courage. Tomorrow she would be gone from here, and Asad would be free to deal with his father without worrying about her safety, he would be able to assure his sister that she would never be at the mercy of the Ox, and perhaps he could even find a way to avoid marrying the Fox. But for tonight she, Oona the Swan, would sing to Asad, the Black Mane.

"'The Sailor's Tale,'" she said, and closing her eyes, she began to sway to Nightingale's sweeping melody. But where before she had felt the surge of the sea carrying her off to adventure, tonight all she felt was the inexorable tide pulling her away from Asad. When she sang of the sailor's homecoming, she felt neither joy nor peace, but only a small measure of satisfaction. She had kept her promise to Lyrra. She had kept her from becoming a pleasure woman to the Panther and had ensured they would be allowed to make their journey home. And her leaving would, for now, keep Asad and his father from coming to blows, and would keep his tribe and his city intact, but it would rip the heart from her.

"'A Wedding Song,'" the Panther called out before Oona had even straightened from her bow.

Oona dipped her knee to the Panther and then glanced at the pale-faced Gazelle. She met Asad's somber gaze and dragged air past the stone in her throat. She held a finger up behind her back to Lyrra, the signal that she would sing alone. She dipped her knee to the Ox, who squirmed on his seat as she refused to drop her narrowed gaze.

"Welcome gentlemen," she sang to him in her highland tongue.
"Welcome and here's my oath to you.
Tomorrow there will be no wedding,
Tomorrow she will remain a maid,
My prince will make it so."

Asad had no idea what words Oona sang to the Ox, but the tone of her voice and the look in her eyes told him all he needed to know. He took the Gazelle's trembling hand in his and squeezed. The Ox would never have her. Asad would make certain of it, but he could not tell her that, not yet. His sister was no actress and he needed the Panther to witness her fear until after the Swan and the Dove were safely away.

Oona skipped in place, singing the wedding song in the desert tongue the next verse, and then she smiled at Asad, a woman's smile, warm and seductive.

"Welcome, gentlemen," she sang.
"Welcome and here's health to you.
Tonight there will be a wedding,
Tonight she will be a wife,
The prince will be a husband."

The heat building in Asad's groin spread to his grin, and Oona's eyes lit and her cheeks flushed as she dipped a knee to the applause. Asad glanced sideways at the Panther, who was scowling, as if sure that something had gotten by him, but unsure of what exactly it was. Asad glanced back at Oona, whose gaze flicked over the Panther.

"We play and dance reel," she said, "in honor of King Panther."

She bowed her head to the Panther, whose scowl relaxed, and then Oona straightened and took in a deep breath and blew it out as the Dove plucked her harps strings.

The gathering clapped their hands to the rhythm of the Swan's flying feet, and the Panther began to clap along as well. The Swan and the Dove took but a beat before moving into another, even faster, reel, and the Panther roared his approval.

Asad met Oona's spinning gaze for one brief moment and nodded his acknowledgment of what she had pulled off, and she flashed him a dazzling grin. She was as quick of mind as she was fleet of foot.

As much as Asad would miss her, he would never regret having known and loved her.

He clapped loudly as Oona slammed her heel down, arms akimbo and chest heaving, and the Cheetah even whistled as the Dove stood and took a bow beside her sister. When the applause died down, Oona whispered into the Dove's ear. The Dove resumed her seat and bent her forehead into her harp's carved frame, and Oona sucked in and blew out a long, slow breath, her eyes locked onto Asad's.

"'Somebody,'" she said. "I will sing 'Somebody.'"

The Dove plucked her harp and the melancholy notes plucked at Asad's heartstrings. His throat constricted and closed as Oona sang.

"My heart is sore, I dare not tell,
My heart is sore for Somebody,
I would walk a winter's night
All for a sight of Somebody."

He squeezed a breath past the fist-size stone in his throat and swallowed. He felt more than saw a hundred pair of eyes on him, but he had eyes only for Oona, losing himself in their mossy green depths as the honeyed smoke of her voice permeated his soul.

"Why need I comb my tresses bright,
Oh, why should fire or candlelight
Shine in my bower day or night
Since gone is my dear Somebody."

Oh, I have wept many a day
For one that is banished far away,
I cannot sing and must not say
How sore I grieve for Somebody."

Asad closed his eyes against the sorrow engulfing him, the pain reflected in the emerald facets of Oona's bright eyes.

"Oh, oh, for Somebody.
Oh hey, for Somebody."

He opened his eyes to hers and mouthed the words, his vow to her, as she sang the last lingering notes.

"Oh, I would do, what I would not
All for the sake of Somebody."

Oona walked hand in hand with Asad down the hall, keeping her eyes on the queen's straight back, striving for the same outer fortitude. Inside, Oona was a step away from shrieking and pulling her hair out as she ran down the hall and threw herself out the window, for as soon as they made the queen's chambers, she and Asad would have to part until the morning, when she and Lyrra would ride away from the City of the Great Valley, and she and Asad would part forever.

She tried telling herself that it would be better this way, a clean break, no night of maudlin lovemaking and teary farewells. But she knew that was a lie. She would give her soul to make love with Asad one last time, to spend her grief and anger in fiery passion, to lay one more night in the strength of his arms, the peace of his embrace, to be with him.

They reached the door to the queen's chamber and Oona braced herself for a chaste kiss on the cheek from Asad as Lyrra said a shy good night to the Cheetah and followed the queen into the salon. But Asad neither kissed Oona's proffered cheek nor loosened his grip on her hand.

"Do you trust me, Oona?" he whispered in her ear.

"I do."

"Will you come with me, Oona the Swan? Will you stay with me until the dawn?"

"I will."

"Good." He grinned, fierce and predatory. "I am glad."

He shut the door to his mother's chambers and Oona turned to go back the way they had come, the way to the pleasure house, but Asad stood fast.

"We will not spend our last night together hiding away in a dusty attic," he said. He twined his fingers through hers and turned for the hall leading to the men's quarters. "We will spend this night together in my bed, making sweet love and tender memories."

"Is usual," Oona asked as he whisked her down the empty hall, "for prince to take woman to his bed?" She had understood that the men always went to the woman's bed here, as at the Jackal's.

"No," Asad told her. "It is not. In truth, you will be the first woman ever to lie in my bed, and the last."

"I glad," Oona said with more emphasis than she had intended. But she did not regret it, especially when Asad stopped and kissed her at his chamber door, hard, and with such heat that they were both panting when they finally broke the kiss.

Asad's salon was furnished sparsely compared to the queen's. There was only one tapestry on the wall, of a black-maned lion lying atop a rocky cliff surveying the fertile valley below, a sleek, tawny-pelted lioness watching alertly beside him. There were also two red sofas scattered with a few pillows each and a table with three stools, its top covered in parchments, several hollowed reeds with tapered writing edges, and a tub of stain so purple it was almost black. The top parchment was covered in the cuneiform symbols of his desert language, and the one beneath it was a map showing the road north and west to a port on the Mid Earth Sea, with cities and water holes marked along the way, the same angular woman's face portraying the north star as on the map Asad had given Oona at the Jackal's.

"These are for your journey," Asad said, shuffling the parchments. "A missive of safe passage through the desert kingdoms and a map." He took his wrist cuff off and placed it on Oona's upper arm. "I want you to wear this. It will be proof of my protection for those who cannot read."

Oona flexed her arm and the cuff's lion roared in the candlelight. She rested her hand bearing the abalone ring on the boned hilt of her blade, which she had not taken off since Asad had gifted it, except to bathe, sleep, or make love.

"You give me too much, my lion. And I, I give you nothing but trouble with you family."

"There you are wrong, my jewel." He ran his hand up and down her arm, and Oona shivered though it was still warm as day. "You have given me, Asad, your love, and you have let me love you, Oona." He cupped her chin and tilted it up, his amber eyes piercing her heart. "And as for the trouble with my family, you are not the cause. There has been trouble between us, amongst us, since the Seven Tribes first joined together three hundred years ago. And I would wager there will still be trouble three hundred years from now." He huffed. "My father and I, our disagreements are more extreme than most."

"And when I be gone, you be able to settle them, to save Gazelle from Ox, keep Panther from war on Oryx. You become king, good king." Oona knew this was what he meant to do. What he was meant to be. And by leaving she would help to make sure he fulfilled his destiny. "But tonight," she said, "you be mine."

"As you will be mine."

Asad pushed the door to his bedchambers open and Oona stepped inside and caught her breath. Asad's bed was as big as the queen's, the posts topped with carved lion heads and the drapes of worm weave a dark wine. On the wall beside the bed hung a tapestry of two horses, a stallion as black as pitch and a mare as white as milk galloping across a green meadow, manes and tails flying against a blue sky.

Asad followed Oona's rapt gaze to the tapestry.

"Is Storm Chaser and Cloud Dancer?" she asked.

"No. My mother gifted me with that tapestry the summer I turned twenty and one, after the last meeting of the tribes, when it became obvious that the Jackal was holding the Fox close, intending her to become my first wife and queen. She told me not to despair, that there would be someone in this world for me, someone I would love who would love me in return."

"She no think it be slave woman."

Asad ran a hand down the veil of Oona's hair. "And yet she was not surprised when it did turn out to be you," he said. He glanced at the tapestry he had lain staring up at the past three years, dreading his impending marriage to the Fox and dreaming of that someone. "Perhaps she knew how I am drawn to long-legged fillies with manes the color of moonlight." He ran a fingertip along the winged edge of her collarbone and under the shoulder strap of her gown.

"Perhaps she knew that I would fall in love with an otherworldly dancer whose voice of smoked honey would cast a spell over me, and whose ivory skin and emerald eyes would enthrall me on sight." He pushed the strap down and exposed her breast.

"Did you know that I wanted to undress you the moment I saw you walk out of the night's shadows in this gown of gossamer worm weave?" He nipped her jawline, her throat, the nape of her neck, and she shivered.

"That I longed to taste your pale, enticing flesh?" He kissed her shoulder, her collarbone, her rose-pink nipple, and she moaned.

"That I burned to claim you?" He lowered the gown over the curve of her hips, his mouth following, and kissed her golden curls.

"To brand you as mine?" He flicked the tip of his tongue over her sweet, tender woman's flesh and she groaned. "Did you know that I would have said—"

"Yes." Her breath rushed out in a sigh. She ran both of her hands back through his hair and lifted his gaze to her, smiling down at him, her lids heavy with desire. "I did," she said. "I do."

Asad stood and Oona stepped out of her sandals, out of the puddle of her gown, and untied his waist belt. "Did you know your eyes warm me from inside out first time ever you look at me?" she whispered huskily.

He sucked his breath in as she ran her hands up his chest and under the sleeves of his robe. She stepped closer, the rosy tips of her breasts teasing his as she shucked off his robe.

"That I could feel you heat, here," she pressed her pelvis against his. "You strength beneath you robes by looking at you."

She ran a finger inside the strap of his loincloth, her fingertip gently rubbing the swollen head of his straining cock. "Did you know I truly want be you wife that night, and every night since?"

"Yes," Asad growled, untying his loincloth and freeing his staff to stand at full attention. He closed the space between them, pressing his throbbing cock to the soft, giving heat of her belly. "I did. I do."

"Then make me you bride tonight, Asad. Stay with me, inside me, until all passion is spent and seed is spilled. Make me you wife."

"I will."

He lowered Oona onto his bed, a bed he had slept alone in before her. A bed he would sleep alone in again after her. He ran his hands down the length of her arms, her back, her legs, his fingertips memorizing every lithe muscle and soft curve. Her skin was as smooth as worm weave and as cool as morning dew, and he smiled against the plush pillows of her lips as her skin warmed beneath his touch.

She moaned, low and throaty, as he teased her nipple with the pad of his thumb, and then he laved the rose-pink tip with his tongue, and she arched her back, her nipple pebbling in his mouth, its twin rock-hard with need as he rubbed its peak. He glided his hand down her taut belly and she groaned as he pushed a finger through the golden curls of her woman's weave. She was slick with need already, and ready for him.

Oona clutched the bed linens as Asad slowly, deliberately, kissed his way down her belly, stoking the fire between her legs with his warm lips and tensile tongue. Flames of pleasure licked up and down her spine, then turned molten at her core. She spread her legs wide, surrendering to his tactile onslaught, her blood pounding, her senses thrumming, and then his kisses stopped.

He rose over her, teasing her with the soft, probing tip of his manhood, and Oona wrapped her legs around his waist, desperate with need of him, for him.

"What is it you want, Oona?"

"You, Asad, only you, all of you."

His eyes never left hers as he entered her with slow purpose, sliding in and then out, in and then out, a little deeper each time, until Oona was panting and gripping his backside, and then he sank his shaft inside her up to his hilt, filling her completely. Oona sighed as her intimate muscles gave and contracted around him, holding his thick, throbbing heat, tight.

She smiled into amber embers and clenched her muscles around his iron brand.

"What you want, my lion?"

"This," he growled, moving inside her. "Only this, only you, always."

Oona reached up and ran her fingers through his beard and pulled his mouth down to hers.

"I am yours, my prince," she whispered fiercely into his lips. "Only yours, forever."

His mouth moved over hers, claiming hers, and his body moved with hers in a fevered dance of give and take, of want and white-hot need. Their passion burning bright as the desert sun, melding them together and splintering into a thousand shards of blinding light.

Asad lay in the languid afterglow of their lovemaking as the sky outside turned from night's ebon pitch to dawn's emerging gray with Oona's backside tucked into him, her long, lithe legs intertwined with his, light skin against dark. They were two people with different skin, from different lands, of different tribes, and yet they had known each other, had understood each other, had burned for each other on sight.

He ran his hand down the length of her arm and twined his fingers through hers. A perfect fit. He nuzzled the nape of her neck, tasted the sweet saltiness of her cooling sweat, breathed in the tantalizing perfume of green grass and earthy woman, of warm summer breezes and night-blooming jasmine, of her.

He wondered how long the bed linens would hold her scent, the musk of their lovemaking, how long his senses would be able to recall her fragrance at will. He buried his face in her hair and squeezed his eyes tight.

He would not ruin their last moments together by turning mawkish. They had both determined to be brave and resolute with what they must do. They had both knowingly sacrificed too much for the sake of others—her sister, his family, his tribe—for Asad to shame himself or her by weeping like a child now.

"Oona, my jewel," he whispered in her ear. "The sun rises and so must we."

"No." Oona shook her head and buried her face deeper into the pillow, pulling Asad's hand to her chest and curling into a tight ball.

Asad curled himself around her, pressing his half-hard cock against her firm buttocks. He nibbled her ear and rubbed the goose bumps of flesh that rose instantly on her arms.

"Come now, wife," he said, trailing his fingers down her waist, her hips, between her legs, smiling into her hair as she moaned softly.

"Aye, husband," she murmured, moving against the pressure of his fingers. "I will come soon enough." She rolled over to face him and ran her fingertip up and down the growing length of his erection. "As will you."

She hitched a leg over his hip and fit herself to him, her breath releasing in a long sigh as he slid into her warm, welcoming sheath. Asad ran a hand back through her hair and watched her sleepy eyes focus on his. He began to move inside her, slow and deliberate, his gaze locked on hers, branding her mossy green eyes, the blacks of her pupils wide with passion, into his memory. This was the last time they would make love together, and he was in no hurry to end it, no matter how high the sun rose.

It occurred to Asad that they had never made love in daylight before, that this would be their first time, their last, and only, that it would be the last time he spilled his seed into her, and he prayed to every god of his and the few he knew of hers that his seed would not take root. For he had kept his word to Oona last night, he had made her his wife in word as well as deed, and she had made him her husband, holding him tight as he shattered inside her and became whole again.

And then they had made love again, and again, their bodies melding, their souls rising and flaming together in a bone-melting release. And now they found that release one last time, their bodies sated, their souls seared, their love, ashes scattered to the four winds.

After breaking their fast and saying their teary farewells to the queen, the Caracal, and the Gazelle in the privacy of the queen's chambers, Oona and Lyrra walked through the halls of the Panther's palace alongside Asad and the Cheetah one last time. Oona's throat constricted and her chest ached as they walked out of the palace doors toward the stables. She would truly miss the women of Asad's family, especially his mother, who understood all too well Oona's love for her son.

The Ratter sniffed and snuffled as he led Storm, Blaze, and Brick out to them.

"Take care of him, Ratter," she whispered, and kissed his wet cheek.

"I will, Swan," he said, standing back and swiping at his nose. "You have me word on it."

The Crab joined them as they met Lyrra and the Cheetah outside the stables, already on their horses, and clasped Oona's hand.

"It has been an honor to know you, Oona the Swan," he said, bowing low over her hand. "An honor I shall never forget."

"Thank you, Kahlil," Oona said, "for everything."

He nodded, sniffed, and then squeezed her hand before dropping it and standing square-shouldered and stone-faced as Asad cupped his hand for Oona's booted foot, lifting her up onto Blaze's saddle of wood and felt made to fit Oona. Her last gift from him.

Asad swung up onto Storm's saddle in one swift, cat-like move, and Oona flushed with pride. By the gods, he truly was a king among men, a lion four times through, and he had been hers for two moons, two horrible, wonderful, breathtaking, heartbreaking moons.

Asad edged Storm up alongside Blaze and held his hand out. Oona twined her fingers through his.

"A perfect fit," he said with a grin that melted her insides.

They rode for the palace walls side by side, hand in hand, and Oona would have given her soul to be able to go through the rest of her life hand in hand with this man. But this world would never let it be so. This world, his world, had made him prince and her slave, and yet they had crossed the chasm between them with one look. They had known each other on sight, had loved each other fully and completely, a love that would have to last Oona the rest of her life.

The Panther had forbidden his sons to ride any farther with the sisters than outside the palace walls. He had them by the short hairs, and he and they knew it. If they went against him, he could still go after the Swan and the Dove. Asad would not feel at ease until the sisters were on a ship halfway across the Mid Earth Sea, and the way his chest squeezed, he would likely never draw a full breath again. Oona the Swan had become the air he breathed, and he was about to send her away from him forever.

The north gate closed behind them with the scrape of wood, the clang of metal, and the thud of Asad's heart. King's guards stood in the gate's tower, watching, no doubt, with orders to report back to the Panther on the men that the sisters left with, and to make sure that his sons stayed. But Asad had expected this. Brawn and the others waited at the border of the open field beyond the wall, close enough to be seen but far enough to be unrecognizable.

Oona edged Blaze up beside Storm once more and held her hand out, and Asad's throat constricted as he took it in his. He glanced back at the Cheetah and the Dove, and his throat closed as they too joined hands for their last ride together. He checked Storm as the stallion champed at the bit, ready to bolt the moment his reins slackened. Asad glared back over his shoulder at the gate tower and pulled at the neck of his tunic, his own reins tightening with each step closer to the waiting men.

"Brawn." Asad begrudgingly let go of Oona's hand and dismounted, sizing up the four men standing beside Brawn, all fit and in their prime, and sell swords all. Behind them was a line of five saddle horses and a small wagon hitched to a mule, and tied off to the wagon was another mule.

"Black Mane," Brawn said, "Cheetah." He indicated the men. "This is the Hound, the Blade, the Scorpion, and the Hawk."

The Hound was as tall as Asad, with an even broader build and ham fists to wield the battle-axe slung across his back. The Blade was shorter and slimmer, with sharp eyes, a quick smile, and an impressive assortment of fighting and throwing blades tucked into his belt and leather over-tunic. The Scorpion was tall and lean with hooded eyes, a bow and quiver of arrows strapped to his back and another bow and two more quivers on his horse. And the Hawk, eagle-eyed and beak-nosed, had a gray-winged falcon dancing on his fist, jessed but un-hooded.

Asad nodded to each man in turn.

"This is Oona the Swan," he said, "and her sister, Lyrra the Dove."

Each of the men looked up and down at the still-mounted sisters, their eyes alit with interest and male appreciation, but none of their gazes lingered or leered. No doubt Brawn had stressed Asad's first rule regarding the sisters, which was hands off. He trusted Brawn's choice of men, but they were men, and Oona and Lyrra were women: beautiful, tempting, defenseless women. The Blade's eyes lit on Oona's bone-hilted knife. Well, Asad amended, not completely defenseless. He had a few bruises from Oona's wooden blade to attest to her agility and ability with a knife.

"This is a document of safe passage." Asad handed the scroll to Brawn, who glanced at the wax seal with the image of a lion's roaring head impressed into it before tucking it into the pocket of his over-tunic. "Now remember, ride during the cooler times and make sure the Swan rests in the shade during the heat of the day."

"I remember."

"There is no hurry. Her safety comes first."

"And last," Brawn said with an amused grin. "I know. I will see her and her sister safely through their grandfather's door. We have all given our sworn oaths to protect the Swan and the Dove, with our lives if it comes to that."

Asad nodded. He turned to Oona, who sat pale and quiet as she met his gaze, her hair a veil of moonlight in the morning sun.

"Keep your scarf over your head, my jewel," he said inanely. "It will protect you from the glare of the sun and the stares of men."

"I will, my lion."

"And be sure to drink salted water if you become overheated. And tell Brawn if you feel the least bit ill. Do not attempt to brave it out."

"Yes, my prince."

He took her hand in his, the first part of her he had ever touched, and now the last. He lifted her hand and pressed his lips to the backs of her fingers. "Promise you will sing to me, Oona the Swan, my jewel, bride of my heart. Sing to me as you cross the wide sea to your Green Isles. Sing to me as you skip across the fields of your highlands, as you sit before your hearth fire." He lowered his voice to a hoarse whisper. "Sing to me as you lie awake in your bed at night, as you sang to me in my bed last night."

She turned her hand in his and ran her long, graceful fingers through his beard.

"I will sing to you, Asad the Black Mane," she said, and her voice was smoked honey. "I will sing to you as I have never and will never sing to another man. You, my prince, my lion, my somebody. I will sing to you until all breath leave my body, and then I will sing to you from next life. This I vow."

"And I will hear you, my love, and I will find you, and we will be together again. This I vow."

CHAPTER 16

Betrayal

Her head craned over her shoulder, Oona rode away from Asad, watching him grow smaller and smaller as the gaping hole in her chest grew deeper and wider. With each interminable, inexorable step of her mount she watched his amber eyes fade into pinpricks, his full mouth thin into a pale line. And when she could no longer distinguish the handsome planes of his beloved face from his magnificent black mane, she raised her arm in farewell and turned away.

The roar that filled the air rent her soul.

Lyrra wept openly, but Oona's eyes were dry. She stared ahead unseeing and uncaring, and where her heart should have been, she felt nothing but emptiness, an emptiness so vast and dark and complete that not even the heat of the desert sun could penetrate the chill that possessed her, wracking her body so that she shook as if taken by a deadly ague.

"My lady Swan?"

Oona met Brawn's concerned eyes, so like his sister's, and her throat constricted. She forced the corners of her lips up into what she hoped resembled a smile and shook her head as hot tears threatened. Brawn nodded wordlessly and turned his gaze back to the road ahead as Oona sucked a deep breath of air in and past the lump in her throat, and then let it out. *I will not*, breathe in, *cry*, breathe out. *I will not*, breathe in, *cry*, breathe out. Slowly, surely, with each breath in and out, her throat loosened and her breath eased.

She concentrated on the sights around her as they followed the road north along the river, passing wagons overflowing with the first cutting of green hay and jangling tinkers' carts full of the wares of their trade. Small, round, hidebound boats laden with the morning's catch of silvery fish bobbed south toward the City of the Great Valley, the city of thousands that she, Oona the Swan, was leaving so that Asad the Black Mane could be king someday.

Rubbing her fingertip over the swirl of abalone on her ring, Oona glanced at Lyrra, who no longer wept, but only sniffed and sniffled. Oona squared her shoulders and lengthened her spine. She had kept her promise to her sister. Lyrra had remained unsullied and untouched and they were on their way home, protected by the Black Mane's decree of safe passage for those to whom it mattered, and by five sell swords for those to whom it did not.

The Hawk rode ahead of them, out of sight, his falcon soaring in circles high above, and the Hound rode rear guard. Brawn and the Blade rode alongside Oona and Lyrra, and the Scorpion drove the wagon. None but Brawn even spoke to the sisters, and he said little, only pointing out certain landmarks and not seeming to expect any answers, which was just as well, for though Oona was able to drag air down around the stone in her throat, she was unsure if she could push any words up past it.

They rode by open fields of sunflowers, their bright yellow faces following the arc of the late morning sun, their petals perfuming the warming air, and then past groves of almond trees, where field workers were busy shaking branches so that the nuts would fall onto coarsely woven blankets spread beneath the trees. They stopped at the outer border of the last grove as the sun hit its noon zenith, taking advantage of the trees' shade.

Oona sat beside Lyrra, glancing up and expecting to see the Crab's balding pate and searching eyes wander by, but saw only the Blade's knives glinting in the sun. She accepted a piece of flatbread and a slice of melon from Brawn, and remembering Asad's admonitions, took a bite of bread and chewed the dry, tasteless morsel, forcing it down with a long draught of water. The melon at least was juicy and easier to swallow, and by the end of the repast the lump in her throat had dropped and settled in her belly.

After finishing their meals, the men looked to the horses, checking their hooves and gear, and Oona stood, pulling Lyrra up along with her.

"We be ready to go," she said.

Brawn eyed her up and down. "But the Black Mane insisted we rest during the heat of day."

"I know what Black Mane say, and why." He had worried about Oona getting the heat sickness again, but the sickness she had now was so much worse, the urge to turn her horse around and ride back to Asad so strong, that she wanted only to get as far away as possible, as quickly as possible, from the City of the Great Valley. "I be fine to ride."

Brawn furrowed his brow. "You will tell me if you are not?"

Oona nodded. Lyrra was not home safe yet, and Oona had not come this far to die in this cursed land.

Asad clicked his tongue and gave a gentle shake of Cloud Dancer's lead rope, pleased as the filly picked up her pace, her long, lean legs dancing as she circled the training kraal. He tried to concentrate on the white dappled beauty prancing before him rather than the three king's guards watching him from various distances, none of them even attempting to be discreet about it, which proved his decision to stay visible on the palace grounds was a correct one rather than jump on Storm and ride off into the western grasslands to the river camp where he had watched Oona bathe a moon ago. Still, it rankled that his father thought he had to be watched over like some petulant child. Asad had given the Panther his word, and he would keep it.

When Cloud Dancer had a fine sheen of sweat built up under the afternoon sun, Asad walked her back to the cool of the stables, where he rubbed her down and treated her and Storm each to a bucket of oats.

"You are a rare beauty, my dancer," he crooned into Cloud's mane, as white as Oona's but neither as fine textured nor as sweet smelling. "Just like your namesake." He ran a hand along the proud arch of the filly's neck and down her back, dreaming of Oona's leanly muscled body, and he laughed, short and gruff. "So, this is what I am come to, fondling a horse."

He glanced at the stable's open door, at the shadow of the guard standing outside of it, fighting the urge to charge over and tear the guard apart, to hunt down the other two, and any others the Panther had set on his trail, and beat them all to a bloody pulp, even though he knew they were doing their king's bidding. Yet still he stood with his hands fisted and his jaw clenched, wanting to rip into something, to vent his rage at his father, at the traditions of the Seven Tribes, at the world, his world, without Oona.

Tearing his dirty tunic off and splashing water over his face and arms, Asad yanked on a clean tunic and strode from the stables to the palace for the evening meal, his three hound dogs trailing behind him.

Upon his entrance, the Panther called out for him to sit at his table, where the Bull and the Ox also sat. The Fox flounced down at the queen's table, sitting right next to the Gazelle. His authority established for all to see, the Panther settled into a conversation with the Bull about the Ox and the Gazelle and the further uniting of their two tribes. A lifetime of princely training had taught Asad to hide his true feelings, and so he was able to sit mute as a statue, only opening his mouth to chew his meat or take a long draught of his wine, refusing to take his father's bait. Not here, not yet. Not until Oona and Lyrra were at least seven days gone, time enough to have made the seaport and found passage on a ship. Seven days, and then the Ox and the Fox were fair game for the lion.

When the meal was finished, Asad stood and without a word, picked up a filled pitcher of wine and strode out of the salon, his three shadows reappearing as he made his way to his chambers, where he slammed the door shut.

His intention was to drink himself blind, but the wine tasted of vinegar, and a pale ghost in white worm weave haunted his chambers. Everywhere he looked he saw Oona's smiling face, heard her lilting laughter, felt her feather-light touch on his skin. And his bed still held the scent of sweet jasmine and earthy lovemaking. He threw open the door to the balcony and paced its confines. He imagined the campsite where Oona and the others should be spending the night, one he knew well from his many journeys to and from the City of Hills, which should be a three-day journey at the easy pace he had instructed Brawn to take. He stopped his pacing and gazed at the full face of the moon, wondering if Oona was doing the same, if she was thinking of him at this moment, missing him as he missed her, as fire missed life-giving air.

There was movement in the courtyard, one of the king's guards settling into his position for the night on a bench with an open view of Asad's balcony. Asad knew without checking that the other two would be positioned outside his door and at the hallway's entrance. The Panther was taking no chances, which meant he did not trust Asad to keep his word. *Because the Panther did not intend to keep his.*

A growl ripped its way up Asad's throat, and he purposely staggered back into his chambers, leaving the balcony door open. Taking a long draught of wine, he let some dribble down his chin onto his tunic and then threw open the door to the hallway, almost hitting the guard who sat on a bedroll beside it. He huffed at the guard, his breath hot and smelling of spirits. He placed his hands on either side of the door's frame and leaned out into the hall.

"Crab? Crab." He swung his head back and forth and let his jaw hang slack for a moment before bellowing at the guard. "Get me my manservant. I want another pitcher of wine, and a plate of bread and cheese. Now," he barked before slamming the door shut.

The Crab entered Asad's chamber a short time later carrying a tray laden with not only bread and cheese, but with dates and figs as well, and a full pitcher of wine. Asad was already dressed in a black tunic and leather leggings with a black scarf thrown around his neck, and was strapping his belt with his waist blade on.

"You are going after her," the Crab said, setting the tray down on the table.

"I am."

"But your father—"

"Will not keep his word."

"You have proof of this?"

Asad shook his head and squared his shoulders.

"Why else would he set three men to watch my every move?

"Because he suspects you will do exactly this."

Asad stuffed the bread and cheese and fruit into a sack.

"What if you are wrong, Black Mane?"

Asad had already considered this, over and over and over again.

"If I am wrong, then the Swan will continue on her journey and I will return and prostrate myself before the Panther and marry the Fox without complaint." He poured the wine into a skin. "But if I am right..." He tied the wineskin to the bag with a vicious jerk. "I cannot, I will not let any harm come to her, not if I am able to prevent it."

The Crab rubbed his balding pate. "How can I help?"

Oona opened her eyes to dry dirt and scrub brush. She rolled onto her back with a stifled groan and stared up into a sky as dull and gray as her soul.

"Oo?"

Lyrra's voice called as she put her hand on her sister's shoulder. Choking back a sob, Oona rolled onto her side and met Lyrra's questioning gaze.

"I leave him, Ly," she whispered past the stone in her throat. "I leave him, and he, he let me go."

Hot tears welled and threatened to spill, and Oona pressed her hands to her eyes to stem the flow.

"You had no choice, Oo," Lyrra insisted in their highland tongue. "And he didna either. Not if we were to survive. The Panther or the Ox, or that bitch Fox would ha' tried to kill you again. And they wouldna stopped trying 'til you were dead."

"Or you were." Oona dropped her hands and held her sister's serious gaze. "Or Asad would ha' killed them, which could ha' started a war between tribes." She sucked in a deep breath and blew it out. "I know you are right, that us leaving is right for everyone...else."

"But not for you and him."

"No." Oona sighed. "Not for Oona and Asad."

The sounds of footfall and blankets being shaken out carried over the low tone of men's voices, and Oona pushed up and stood and stretched her arms over her head. She bent down and touched her toes and then she straightened and twisted side to side, welcoming the gentle pops of her spine and hips. She would never take a soft bed for granted again. *She would never lie in a big soft bed cradled in Asad's arms again.*

The thought hollowed her.

"Oona?"

Oona tried to focus on Lyrra's face, but all she saw was a pair of amber eyes burning into hers. A low, keening moan started somewhere in her chest and clawed its way up and out her throat.

"You must sit, Swan." A man's voice, but not Asad's. "Before you fall." Hands held her arms and gently pushed her down onto her bedroll, but they were too small, too cool, the hands of a ferret, not a lion. "Are you ill, Swan?"

Oona shook her head and curled into herself as the first sob tore loose. Even smaller, softer hands gently ran up and down her back.

"She need let it out," Lyrra said over Oona's swelling sobs. "We need let her."

Hot, angry tears fell from Oona's eyes as her belly gripped and her chest gaped, tears for the Swan and the Black Mane, creatures from two different worlds, destined to spend their lives apart for the sake of those worlds.

Tears for Lyrra and the Cheetah, for their newly blooming love, nipped in the bud by the same uncaring worlds, tears for the Palm, who had lived a life of servitude, only to die horribly and alone for her loyalty to Swan and Black Mane.

Oona sobbed, hoarse and wordless for her father, lashed to the mast of what had been his ship, his escape from the grief of losing his wife, her mother, the sweetest, gentlest soul in this or any world, who had been taken from it, from her family, too young, too soon.

She shed tears of raw grief and a fathomless sorrow for Asad and Oona, who would never be again, and she wept with a futile, teeth-gnashing rage that left her body as spent as her soul.

The rising sun slowly warmed the empty hull of her body, and Oona sniffed and wiped her face with her sleeve. Weary to the bone, she gave Lyrra a tremulous smile and stood on shaky legs and walked over to Brawn, who sat by the camp's snuffed fire studying the map Asad had drawn. The other men glanced with sheepish grins at her puffy, tear-streaked face, and turned quickly away again as they saddled the horses.

"I be sorry," she told Brawn. "Sorry I cry, embarrass men."

"Do not be," Brawn said, folding the map and standing. "There is not a man here who would not give his left, er, ah, eyetooth, to have a woman such as you weep over them so."

Heat suffused Oona's cheeks, and she was perilously close to tears again. Taking a cooling breath in and blowing it out, she straightened her spine and squared her shoulders and met Brawn's even gaze.

"Tell me what to do," she said. "How to pack and saddle horses, break camp."

"Are you sure, my lady? It is no trouble for us."

"I am Swan, or Oona, no lady. I no be frail princess to be coddled. I need learn how to take care of myself and horses on journey."

Brawn grinned, the Hawk hooted, and the Hound muttered into his mount's mane loud enough for all to hear. "The Black Mane has as good an eye for women as he does horses."

Asad and the Cheetah walked the edges of the site where Brawn should have camped overnight, twice.

"There are no signs they spent the night here," Asad said, glancing up at the noon sun, "though they did pass through." He jutted his chin toward the road, where the fresher hoof prints of at least ten horses carrying the heavier weight of armed men overlaid the older prints of horses carrying lighter riders and a cart. "As did those following."

"We do not know to what purpose they follow," the Cheetah said. "Or even if they are following the sisters' company."

Ever the peacemaker, the Cheetah still held out hope that their father had not gone back on his word. But Asad knew better. It was why he had sent the Crab to fetch the Cheetah and his manservant, the Crow, to Asad's chambers last night, along with several pitchers of beer and wine. And admit it or not, it was why his brother, Nasim, had come. They had put on a show for the Panther's guards, banging around in Asad's chambers and singing bawdy love songs off key, all the while packing for their journey and making their plans. The Crab and the Crow then doubled their banging and their singing, changing pitch and positions around the chambers as Asad and Nasim crept down the dark side of the balcony onto the courtyard and made their way under the cover of night to the stables.

Bearing no crests, their heads cloaked and their lacquered chest plates and weapons hidden beneath plain robes, Asad and Nasim had ridden out of the city gate in the dark before the dawn, when the Crab was to leave Asad's chambers and wake the queen with the news of the brothers' departure, along with Asad's instructions to hide the Gazelle somewhere safe from the Panther and the Ox until his return. If Asad did not return within seven days, the Crab and the Ratter were to take the Gazelle and his stable of horses and ride as hard and fast as possible for the City of Marshes. The Heron was the one king Asad trusted to give them sanctuary, and the only king the Panther would not seek vengeance against.

They had fit Star with the Gazelle's saddle to make the Panther think Asad had taken her with him, and it had been the Ratter's idea to dress up in a maid's robes and cover his head and ride out with the brothers to complete the ruse. Once out of the watchtower's sight, the Ratter had discarded his feminine clothing and made his way back into the city and the stables before the Panther discovered his sons were gone.

With any luck, and the Crab's and Crow's continued coming and going from Asad's chambers, the Panther would think his sons sleeping off their night of spirits and would not send any men after them until the morrow at earliest.

Swinging back up onto Storm's back, Asad glared down at the heavier prints of the war horses, even more certain now that the Panther had sent men after the sisters. Were they why Brawn traveled at such a fast pace? Did he know they were being followed, and by whom?

Oona shaded her eyes and glanced up at the noon sun. Exactly twenty and five years ago, Asad, the Black Mane, had been born. Today he would be riding in the procession celebrating his birth, and the Fox would be riding beside him as his future queen. And tonight, if they continued to make good time, Oona would be in the City of Hills.

"The city is in the next valley beyond those hills," Brawn announced as they remounted after a short break to rest and water the horses and eat a quick meal of jerky and flatbread. He grinned at Oona. "At the pace we have been traveling, we should be inside the walls by dusk."

They had gained almost an entire day by taking short breaks and riding into the night under the light of the waning gibbous moon, and Oona and Lyrra had gained the sell swords' respect with what Brawn called their sand.

Oona checked the lead rope tying Brick to Blaze and climbed up onto her saddle, one of her many gifts from Asad. Her breath caught and her belly dropped as his smiling eyes came to her unbidden, and she clamped her eyes tight against the prick of tears behind her lids. Clucking her tongue, she turned Blaze's head toward the road as Brawn started to turn his horse, and then stopped, gazing at the road south and holding his hand high.

A cloud of dust soon turned into the Hound, who had been riding rear guard, coming in at a full gallop.

"Ten and two riders," he yelled as he pulled his lathered horse to a stop and pointed behind him. "Two leagues back, all armed and riding hard. I cannot swear to it, but I think they wear the Panther's colors."

Brawn swore under his breath. "If the Panther shows his colors, then he means to have us all killed, leave no witnesses." He glanced at the hills ahead. "And they mean to do it before we reach those hills."

"How far ahead is the Hawk?" the Hound said.

The Blade shaded his eyes and peered up into the sky. The Hawk's falcon already soared over the hills' southern slopes. "Too far to be sent for and brought back in time to help fight."

Brawn turned full circle, scanning the dry brush surrounding them. "There is enough dried grass and kindling to start a fire, but nothing large enough to send the Hawk a signal." He glanced back down the road they had traveled, where the riders could barely be seen, like ants with the sun glinting on their lacquered armor. "Nor would he reach us in time, unless we managed to hold them off for a good while."

"Or kill them outright," the Hound said, slapping his war axe against one palm with a gleam in his eyes.

"Ten and two against four." The Blade spat onto the ground and tightened the belt around his over tunic. "Not the best of odds."

"We have had worse," Brawn said with a shrug. But Oona could see the worry in his eyes.

The Scorpion pulled his extra bow and quivers from his pack. "I figure that hillock up there will give me the best cover."

"Here, burn this," Lyrra said, stopping every man there as she pulled Nightingale from her packhorse. "Burn my harp. She will send message to Hawk."

"Lyrra, no," Oona gasped. "You can no burn Nightingale."

"I can no play her if I be dead."

"There will be no need to burn the harp," Brawn said. "Swan, you and the Dove empty the cart, then gather what dry grass and twigs you can find, any dried horse or goat droppings too." He tossed Oona the flint from his saddlebag. "Start a fire while the Hound breaks up the cart. Blade, stake the horses behind that hillock over there, we don't want them running off. We will need them."

If we survive.

Though he did not say the words, his and every person's face there spoke the thought.

Her fingers numb and clumsy with fear, Oona struck the flint one, two, three times before she finally managed a spark. With Lyrra's help, they coaxed the spark into an ember and then into a flame. The Hound tossed the planks of broken cart into a pile next to them and they fed the eager flame carefully, layering the wood for the longest burn and most smoke. The sound of hoof beat and men's shouting drew their attention to the approaching storm of dust and riders. Oona wiped her hands on her leather leggings and gave silent thanks to Asad. The leggings would give her freedom of movement as well as some protection in the fight to come. She pulled her bone-hilted knife from its sheath and grabbed Lyrra by the hand.

"Blade," she called out. "You have extra knife for Dove?"

He eyed the Dove for a moment and then pulled a small-handled knife from his vest and tossed it so that it stuck blade first into the ground at Lyrra's feet.

Oona held up her empty left hand. "You have second for me?"

He grinned and tossed another small knife at her feet. "Do not charge the men," he said. "Keep beyond their reach and use your smaller size and fleetness to jab and slice, like so." He made a slashing movement at the back of his knee, his hamstring, his underarm. "And if a man grabs hold of you, stab and twist, here," he pointed to his lower back, "or here." He made a jabbing motion below and up under his rib cage.

Oona nodded and watched with a mouth as dry as the desert as the riders closed in, all of them armed and wearing the Panther's colors under lacquered breastplates. She swallowed, hard, and gave Lyrra her best impression of a brave grin. The riders were no more than a hundred paces from them when a rider fell off his horse, the Scorpion's arrow sticking out of his neck. Another rider peeled off from the group toward the hillock the Scorpion took cover behind, and he too fell to the ground, shot through the head. Oona gave a feral snarl as the other riders charged straight for them, one of them with an arrow stuck in his arm and another with an arrow in his leg, but still they came.

Planting her feet wide, Oona gripped her blades. "Farewell, Asad, Prince Black Mane, my husband, my somebody," she whispered to the sky. "I will wait for you in next world."

Beyond the riders a lion roared, fierce and fearsome.

"AASSAADD."

Oona's scream ripped the heart from Asad's chest, and replaced it with white-hot fury.

"OOOONNAA."

Asad pulled his sword and cut Star loose. He pressed his knees to Storm's sides and the stallion surged forward, Nasim on River beside them. Asad's war cry had slowed the Panther's men, and now four of them peeled away from the other six and rode for Asad and Nasim, spreading out to circle around them.

Asad recognized every man. They were palace guards, good soldiers all, and loyal to the Panther. They would follow their orders. The question was, had they been ordered to subdue the Black Mane and the Cheetah if they encountered them, or to kill them? At a nod from Asad, Nasim split left as Asad split right. The guard to the far right notched an arrow and aimed at Asad. He let it fly as Asad twisted sideways in his saddle and the arrow glanced off his breastplate. If he had been facing forward, the arrow would have pierced his heart.

Asad had his answer.

Lying low along Storm's neck, Asad rode straight at the shooter, who notched another arrow to his bow. The shooter lifted the bow and arrow to aim, but Storm was thundering down on him and he shot too soon and too short. The arrow sank into the ground moments before Storm galloped over it and into his horse, broadside. The guard grappled for his stumbling mount's reins and fought to stay seated, and Asad swung his sword high and slashed it down, slicing into the man's neck.

The coppery scent of fresh blood assailed Asad's nostrils as he pulled his blade free. Storm snorted and went walleyed, and Asad wheeled the stallion around in time to block the strike of another guard's sword.

Metal rang on metal as they thrust and sliced, blocked and parried. Between the blood on his sword and the sweat on his hand, Asad was losing his grip. Edging Storm right up against the other horse, Asad lifted his sword high and the guard raised his in defense. Dropping his sword, Asad grabbed the man's sword arm by the wrist with one hand and pulled his waist blade with the other, slicing the crook of the man's elbow down to the bone. The man screamed, blood spurted, and his sword hand went limp. Asad gave a great heave and shoved the guard off his horse and onto the ground. Well trained, the warhorse stood stock-still. Asad slapped him hard on the rump and the horse bolted. Asad pulled back on Storm's reins and the stallion reared up. He slackened the reins and Storm came crashing down onto the man's chest with his front hooves, splitting the guard's breastplate into pieces and crushing his chest.

"Nasim?" Asad glanced about wildly. To his left his brother fought on foot with one guard, the other slumped motionless over his mount's back.

"Go," Nasim yelled, "go."

The clanging of metal and screams and shouts of men were all Asad could make out as he rode past one man sprawled out on the road, an arrow sticking out of his neck, and then another with an arrow in his eye. He searched for Oona and his heart stopped, though his blood still pounded in his ears. She and the Dove were fighting a palace guard, a trained killer with a long sword, who swung and slashed and stabbed at them as they danced around him, nipping and jabbing at his legs with their puny blades.

Asad urged Storm forward, his eyes never leaving Oona. His heart beat triple time when she tripped over another man lying in a pool of blood and fell onto her backside. Somersaulting back over the body, she landed on her feet, but she had dropped her knives, and the Dove was limping on her injured leg, too slow to be of any help as the guard they fought closed in on Oona.

"Brawn," Asad yelled, but Brawn was already fighting off two men. The Hound and the Blade were fighting one on one, and Asad was too far away to do anything but watch helplessly as Oona turned to run.

The guard raised his sword as Oona slipped and fell forward. She held her arm up to block the sword as it came slashing down, and Asad saw red.

"OOONNNAAAAAA."

Asad charged Storm straight into the mass of men and swords, scattering them every which way. Storm knocked the man who had struck Oona down onto his knees, and Asad leapt from the stallion and grabbed the man by his hair, pulling his head back and cutting his throat with one slice. Tossing the gurgling man aside, Asad bent down over Oona, who lay unmoving in the dirt.

"Black Mane," the Dove's warning came in time for Asad to duck another guard's sword as it swung for his head.

Rolling away, Asad pulled his waist blade and leapt to his feet as the man stiffened and then fell forward, a knife sticking out of his back, Brawn standing behind him, panting and grinning. Saluting Brawn with his blade, Asad picked up his sword and looked for his next opponent, but the only men left standing were his, but for the Scorpion, who lay dead and unseeing with a knife in his back.

Asad dropped to his knees and cradled Oona, his heart in his throat.

"Oona?"

Her eyes fluttered open, and he took in her big, round, beautiful green eyes.

"Asad." She breathed his name. "You come for me."

He pushed a stray lock of bloodied hair from her dirt-streaked face. He had never been so glad to see anyone in his life. "I should never have let you go." He held her tight and she flinched and sucked in air. "You are hurt?"

She lifted her left arm with a grimace, and Asad cursed at the slice that ran from the top edge of his gold wrist cuff on her upper arm and across her shoulder. "You wrist cuff save me from lose arm."

Gingerly, Asad touched the edges of her wound with his fingers. "It will need washing and binding," he said, "and stitches when we get to the City of Hills."

Oona nodded and glanced around at the bloodied sell swords and the dead guards. She began to shake and her teeth to chatter as Asad had seen many a soldier do after a close battle.

"A blanket," he yelled, "and a skin of wine." Scooping Oona up in his arms, he carried her over to what was left of the cart and sat her down on it. Nasim helped the limping Dove over to the cart and sat her down beside Oona as Asad wrapped the proffered blanket around their shoulders. A skin of wine was thrust into his hand, and he gave it to Oona. "Drink some, both of you. It will warm your blood and settle your nerves."

He turned to tend to the business of the dead men, but Oona grasped the hem of his tunic. "Do not leave me, Asad," she whispered through white lips.

Asad knelt down and kissed her, softly, tenderly, until her lips warmed beneath his. "I am not leaving you, Oona. You and Lyrra are safe now."

She sighed, her breath mingling with his, and grasped his tunic tighter. He kissed her again, harder, hungrier, the victor claiming his prize.

"Ahem."

Asad opened one eye to see Brawn and the other sell swords standing and watching them.

"I hate to interrupt you, Black Mane," Brawn said, the grin on his blood and sweat-streaked face belying his words. "But there are the dead to be dealt with, and a city to make before the sun sets."

CHAPTER 17

City of Hills

Oona rode cradled against Asad's chest as they entered the City of Hills. Though she had assured Asad she was able to ride Blaze, he'd insisted she ride with him on Storm, and the breadth and warmth of his solid chest against her back had been a constant reminder that he was real, that she had not fallen into some sort of delirium and dreamed him up. The throbbing of her injured arm was real enough too, but it was nothing compared to the joy of being with Asad again.

After the fight, Asad had washed and bound Oona's arm, and then done the same for the Hound, who had a deep gash on his right thigh. Brawn and the Blade both had minor cuts and scrapes, as did Asad and the Cheetah, and the Hawk had ridden up as the tending of wounds had finished.

The men told him of the skirmish as they gathered up their provisions and spread them among their saddle packs since the cart was nothing more than two wheels and a floorboard. They had set about the gruesome task of stripping the dead of their armor and clothing and packing it on the mules: proof against the Panther. What was left of the cart they placed over the smoldering fire, and then laid the Scorpion and the dead guards on it, feeding the fire until its flames lit the cart.

Then they rode north, away from the stench of burning flesh and the Panther's bitter betrayal, the embers of which smoldered deep in Asad's eyes.

The sun was setting over the western hills as they rode up a winding road through the city and up to the palace, which sat shining silver and white as a pearl atop the highest hill. Palm trees lined the entrance to the palace, swaying in the cooling breeze as dusk turned to night, and the Oryx himself met them at the palace steps, lit with servants holding oil lamps.

"Black Mane, Cheetah." He dipped his head to the princes. "My watchmen sent word that you were to come." He took in Oona seated before Asad, and Lyrra on her mount, and each sell sword in turn, and then his gaze settled on the pile of guards' gear on the two mules, the Panther's black and red visible in the light of the lamps. "Come," he held out his hand, "and welcome. Once you are cleaned and fed, I will be interested to hear the tale of your journey here."

Asad refused to leave Oona's side until the palace physician had sewn the last stitch and bound her arm with fresh strips of linen. Oona flexed her arm. The bandage was neither too tight nor too loose, and though the sewing of her wound had not been pleasant, the numbing balm the physician had smeared on it had helped lessen the pain.

"I may bathe still?" Oona asked the physician, who was called Bones, and who resembled the Owl in looks and mannerisms.

"Yes, Mistress Swan, you may bathe. Though, try not to get your bandage wet, or I will need to bandage it again."

"Then you give me clean strips to bandage after," Lyrra told him. "Swan can no get near water without get wet."

Bones looked askance at Lyrra, unsure.

"The Dove is quite good at tending wounds and applying bandages," Asad assured him.

Lyrra preened.

"Would you care for a draught of Dream Flower for any pain, Swan?" Bones asked.

Oona shook her head. "No, is not so bad." She had seen what the oil of the Dream Flower did to a person, and Lyrra had told her of the vivid strange dreams she'd had while dosed with it. Oona wanted to be awake and aware. She did not want to miss a single moment with Asad, for she was unsure how many or how few they would have.

The physician moved on to the Hound's leg, and Asad led Oona out of the surgery. A maidservant was waiting for them as they came out.

"Swan, this is the Pear," he introduced her to the portly, middle-aged desert woman, who dipped a knee to Oona. "She will take you and the Dove to your chambers, where a meal awaits you, and then to the baths. I must meet with the Oryx."

"I will see you again, tonight?" Oona hated the whine of her voice, but she could not help it. She had been parted from him for two of the most miserable days and nights of her life, and she could not bear to be away from him now.

Asad lifted her hand to his lips, his eyes holding hers, his amber depths lit with promise.

"We will see each other again before the night is through."

After they bathed, Lyrra rewrapped Oona's arm in the salon of their chambers, a richly furnished room with two sofas covered in soft yellow linens and pillows of orange and umber worm weave. There were two separate bedchambers, one on each side of the salon, and a balcony overlooking the royal courtyard. These were no servant's chambers.

"Who these rooms belong to?" Oona asked the Pear.

"They are for the king's second wife, Mistress Swan, whoever she may be. The Oryx will choose next meeting of the tribes."

Oona knew the Oryx had met and married his first wife, the Willow, after the previous meeting of the tribes, and that she had not traveled with him to this past meeting because she was heavy with her first child.

"The Oryx and Willow, their marriage be happy?" Asad had told her that a palace's servants knew everything. One only had to ask.

"It is," the Pear said.

"And they be good king and queen to serve?"

"They are, Mistress. The City of Hills will thrive under their rule, as it did under the Ram."

Oona was glad, for she knew Asad truly liked the Oryx. He would be a good ally to the Black Mane once he was king. *But what and where would Oona be?*

"Thank you, Pear," she said. She yawned, as much for effect as from the toll of the past days and nights. "We have all we need. You may find you own bed and rest."

Oona's body was weary to the bone, but her mind was spinning with a hundred unanswered questions. She could, at least, answer one before she attempted to sleep.

"Lyrra?" She sat on the sofa beside her sister and took her hand. "I promised to keep you safe from the Panther and get you home again to Silver Water Keep, and I will, but…"

"You dunna want to leave the Black Mane."

"No."

Lyrra squeezed Oona's hand. "And I willna leave you, sister. Our mother is gone, and our father dead, or slave on some pirate's ship. What is there to go home to?"

"Grandfather."

"We can send him word."

"It will break his heart, his only grandchildren and heirs never returning to his hearth, his clan."

"He let you sail away from the clan so you wouldna have to marry a man you didna love. He will understand your staying to marry a man you do."

Oona loved Asad, body and soul, and she wanted nothing more than to be with him, but there were so many obstacles between them still: the Panther, the Fox, and the traditions of the tribes.

"What if marriage isna possible?" Oona spoke what she feared to still be true.

"Would it matter?"

"I didna think it would, I truly didna, but now…" Oona shrugged. "I canna abide the idea of sharing him with other women, whether as a wife or a mistress. Nor would I be content to witness him siring children with others, especially as mistress, knowing any child of ours would be bastards with no claim to their father." She laughed short and harsh. "It seems I am more clanswoman than I thought."

"Does the Black Mane know how you feel?"

Oona shook her head. "How could he? Even I didna not until this verra moment."

When Asad and Nasim left the Oryx's council chambers, where the Heron had joined them, the hour was late, past midnight. He and the Reed and their company had headed east, as if returning to their city after leaving the Panther's, and then had turned north and west for the City of Hills, where the Heron warned the Oryx of the Panther and the Bull making noise about attempting to replace him. The Reed also wished to be with the Willow, her niece, through the birth of her first child.

The Ram had known he was dying and that his son would become king, and though tradition dictated the Oryx should marry an eldest daughter, the Ram had allowed him to marry for love. The Willow was third daughter of the Oak, king of the Northern Woodlands, and his second wife, the Kestrel, sister to both the Reed and the Caracal. Their marriage had gone against the tradition of the tribes, and was another strike against the Oryx as far as the Panther, the Bull, and the Jackal were concerned, along with his age and inexperience. But other kings, along with the Heron and the Oak, were willing to give him a chance to prove himself capable of ruling a kingdom of the Seven Tribes. A son and heir would go far in providing such proof.

Oryx and the Willow's marriage gave Asad hope for himself and Oona.

"I still cannot believe our father went against his given word as he did," Nasim said as they made their way down the hall to their chambers.

"I wish I could say the same."

The Panther was a hard man and a demanding king, a staunch traditionalist who had always presented himself as a man of his word. He had lied. And Asad had been wrong to believe him. He had been wrong too at how far his father's betrayal would go, and at how deep the cut of knowing his father had ordered his sons' deaths festered. How could a father have his own sons killed? *How would a son kill his father, if it came to that?*

They were questions he would have answers to soon enough, but not tonight. Tonight, all he wanted to know was the feel of Oona in his arms, warm, whole, and safe.

After saying goodnight to Nasim at his chamber door, Asad turned and loped through the empty hall for the women's quarters. He stood at the door to the sisters' chambers and pressed his ear close, hearing nothing. He pushed on the door and grinned, the inside bolt had not been thrown and the door swung open into a salon dimly lit by a guttering candle. There were two doors leading to two different bedchambers, but only one was ajar.

Padding quietly to the open door, he peered in and was struck by the vision of Oona sleeping on top of the covers, her lithe limbs sprawling languidly across the dark linens, the white veil of her hair fanned around her face, as serene and familiar and mysterious as the moon's.

He dropped his waist belt and stripped off his tunic and slowly slid in alongside her, curling his body around hers as she sighed and tucked her backside into him. Careful of her bandaged arm, he wrapped his around her waist and buried his nose into the nape of her neck, warm and damp with sleep. He breathed in the sweet scent of jasmine and summer breezes, and he let his breath out in a ragged sigh.

"Asad." Warm breath tickled his ear. "Asad, my lion, time to wake." He roused to a voice of smoked honey and spread his paw over a firm buttock, pressing Oona close to his waking manhood. She moaned, sweet and soft, and then scooted back. "We cannot," she whispered huskily. "There be company about."

A low murmuring of voices came from the salon beyond the closed bedroom door, and Asad grumbled and gave her a pat on her rump and a quick, smacking kiss on the lips before he threw back the bed linens and stood to get dressed. He did not miss the approving glow in Oona's gaze as she watched him, and damned if his cock did not stand up and crow.

Last night he had been so worn out, all he had needed was the sweet succor of Oona in his embrace, but now, after a good night's sleep... He glanced at the bolted door and then gazed down at Oona, at the way her smile changed from admiring to desiring, and he leaned over her, bracing his hands to either side of her shoulders, running the tip of his manhood over the soft skin of her belly. He lowered his head and kissed her, his cock jumping at her quick inhale and pressing into her slow exhale.

A knock at the door had them both holding their breath.

"Mistress Swan?"

Asad held a finger to his lips.

"Mistress Swan?" The door rattled. "Mistress Swan?" The servant's voice was louder, insistent. "Are you well?"

Oona's eyes crinkled up at the corners, as did her luscious lips, still slick from his kiss. Her belly shook with quiet laughter, jostling his eager cock. "I am well, Pear," she called out, deflating Asad's expectations. "I be out soon."

Asad stepped out of Oona's bedroom clad in his tunic and a scowl. The tray of cheese and fruit and flatbread the Pear held clattered so that Oona took it from the servant and set it on the table. The Pear managed a shaky knee dip and Asad acknowledged her with a nod.

He took Oona by the hand and drew her aside. "You realize that every servant in the palace will know of this, of us, before the noon repast."

Oona blushed and shrugged and then her eyes grew wide. "Will Queen Willow still wish meet me?"

"The Willow is much like her aunts, the Caracal and the Reed. I would wager my best brood mare that she will want to know every intimate detail of how we came to be here. She has been confined to the palace these last moons of her pregnancy. You will be a welcome distraction for her."

Oona chewed on her bottom lip. "What I should tell her?"

"The truth. We need not hide anything from anyone anymore, my jewel. The Willow is no prudish traditionalist, I am sure she will understand how it is between us."

Oona's bottom lip pushed out. "I wish I did."

It was as close to petulant as he had ever seen her, and he bit back a grin. "Do you trust me, my jewel?"

"I do."

He ran the callus of his thumb over her bottom lip. "Today I must be Black Mane. The Cheetah and I are to meet with the Heron and the Oryx to come up with a plan for dealing with the Panther, whilst you, Swan, will entertain queens." He cupped Oona's chin and placed a not-so-chaste kiss on her lips. "Tonight, we will be Asad and Oona again, I promise."

The Reed opened the door to the Willow's chambers, her face a mask of queenly calm while Oona's belly was dancing a reel. It was important that the Reed and the Willow accept her and Lyrra, but as mistresses or future wives or mere diversions, even Oona was not certain, for Asad had promised her nothing past tonight. She was dead certain that the Panther would not accept her as anything but a corpse, and any ally she could claim against him would be more than welcome.

She and Lyrra followed the Reed into a salon with walls of umber covered in rich tapestries of woodland nymphs and lush gardens, where an exceptionally pregnant woman sat on a mossy green sofa, propped up by cushions covered in embroidered worm weaves all the colors of autumn leaves.

Pushing up with her hands and leading with her belly, she stood to greet Oona and Lyrra. Of average height, with long lustrous hair the color of burnished bark, she was still slim, even in her last moon of pregnancy, and had smiling brown eyes and a grin that Oona returned without hesitation.

"Welcome, Swan." She dipped her head to Oona and then to Lyrra. "Welcome, Dove. I am the Willow."

Oona and Lyrra dipped their heads and a knee each. "Queen Willow," they spoke in unison, and the Willow's grin widened.

"My husband and my aunt have told me much about you two, and I can see for myself that they have neither of them exaggerated your beauty, nor your effect on the Black Mane and the Cheetah."

"Thank you, Queen Willow," Oona said, and her cheeks flushed as hot as Lyrra's were pink.

"Please." The Willow took Oona by the hand and pulled her down on the sofa to sit beside her. "We need not be so formal here amongst ourselves, call me Willow. My aunt Reed tells me you call the Black Mane by his birth name, and that he calls you by yours."

"Aye, I mean yes, is tradition in our land."

"But not here, in our land," she said as the Reed and Lyrra sat on the sofa across from them.

"No," Oona agreed. "Is not tradition here. Is one of many reasons I..." After six moons in this land of the Seven Tribes, she had learned to keep many secrets, to lie even, but Asad had assured her that she need not hide her true self anymore. She searched the Willow's open, eager gaze, and the Reed's, which, though more circumspect, held no judgment. "Is one of many reasons I love Black Mane."

There, she said it out loud to someone other than Asad or Lyrra, in truth, to two queens of the tribes, either of whom could have her thrown out or into chains for her impudence. Yet they neither recoiled nor chastised, but only smiled knowingly, two women who loved their husbands.

"The Black Mane and the Cheetah must care for the two of you very much," the Willow said, "to go against their father as they did." A shadow passed over her eyes and she laid a protective hand over her belly, swollen with child. "The Panther is not a king to have as an enemy. And he is joined by the Bull and the Jackal against my Oryx."

Oona laid a hand over the Willow's on the sofa. "Is true," she said, "Panther be bad enemy to have, but you have good friends in Heron and Reed, Black Mane and Cheetah, Swan and Dove." She patted the Willow's hand and drew upon her faith in Asad. He had not let her down yet. He would not let the Oryx and the Willow down. Not without a fight. "Together we all find way to deal with Panther, Bull, and Jackal."

The Willow turned her hand in Oona's and squeezed. "And to celebrate our new friends," she said, "we shall have a feast tonight in your honor." She glanced at her aunt. "I am told you two sing and play and dance. Would you honor us by doing so tonight?"

Oona looked to Lyrra, who flexed her fingers and nodded.

"It be our pleasure," Oona said.

"And ours, I am sure," the Reed spoke for the first time. "I have told my niece how affecting your music is."

"Perhaps," the Willow said with her infectious grin, "it will affect another marriage proposal?"

It was a generous sentiment, well intentioned, but Oona would not propose to Asad again, certainly not publicly, or even privately.

A proposal of marriage would have to come from him, for he would be sacrificing the most by marrying her, and the biggest obstacles preventing it still remained.

He had told Oona she was the bride of his heart, and she believed him, but that was in their own special world, only the two of them. In the real world, love was not always enough. This much Oona had learned to be true.

Something was wrong with Oona. She did not meet Asad's gaze as she and the Dove walked into the courtyard dressed in their gowns of white and gray worm weave, and her smile, when she finally glanced Asad's way, was strained and fleeting and did not reach her eyes. Her back was stiff and her shoulders squared as she and Lyrra took their seats at the queen's table beside the Reed and the Willow, who were all smiles and friendly welcomes.

Asad had not seen or spoken to Oona since the morning, but he did not think her sulking over his absence. She knew he had been meeting with the Heron and the Oryx, and sulking was unlike her. But something was definitely wrong, for she would not look his way again, though he sat at the next table, his eyes boring holes into the side of her head.

He had been told by the Oryx that the meeting with the Willow had gone well, and that the Willow had declared herself and the sisters to be fast friends, so what had occurred between this morning and now?

Had she heard of the plan Asad and Nasim and the kings had decided on? That Asad and Nasim would leave tomorrow for the City of the Great Valley, while Oona and Lyrra remained safely in the City of Hills?

Asad and Nasim would ride undisguised, while the others, the Heron, the Oryx, Brawn, and the sell swords, along with six of the Oryx's and Heron's men-at-arms, would be dressed in the cloaks of the Panther's dead guards. They would enter the palace and confront the Panther with his lies and deceit and negotiate a solution to this enmity between the Panther and the Oryx, whose only true offense was that he was the son of the Ram.

When that was done, Asad and the Panther would come to an agreement over the Swan, one way or another. Asad hoped it would not come to a fight, but he knew his father well enough to expect it. The gods knew Asad was angry enough at the Panther to see any threat through, even usurpation by hand-to-hand combat, which Oona had sought to avoid at all costs.

Asad half stood at least ten times during the meal, determined one moment to ask her what ailed her, and then sitting right back down the next, minding his manners as a guest in the Oryx's palace. He ate almost as little as she, pushing his food around and drinking more beer than was his usual, making feeble attempts to keep up his end of any conversation while keeping a watchful eye on Oona, his ears alert to the sound of her subdued voice and the lack of her melodious laughter.

As a prince, Asad had not been raised to consider a woman's feelings. Women were meant to see to his needs, not the other way around, and truth be told, he had not really cared about any women but his mother and sister, other than what momentary pleasure they could afford him. But as a man, he cared about Oona's feelings, even more than his own, and it was driving him mad seeing her so upset and not being able to fix whatever it was that disconcerted her, at least not until after the feast. After the feast she would have to tell him, for she would not lie. Not to him.

The meal finished and the torches lit, Oona and Lyrra excused themselves and then returned a short while later to the makeshift stage in the middle of the courtyard. Lyrra sat on a stool and ran her fingers up and down her harp's strings while Oona stood looking at anyone and everyone but Asad, who sat no more than five paces from her.

"We sing 'Sailor's Tale,'" she announced with a dip of her knee to the Oryx.

She sang with neither the fear of the night of Summer's Eve, nor with the later conviction of her and the Dove's escape, but with a melancholy acceptance that had Asad on the edge of his seat. When she sang of the sailor's happy homecoming, she finally met his gaze, and Asad dropped off the edge into an abyss. He had seen that same hollowed look in her eyes many times over the past moon. She was saying good-bye to him.

As the sisters performed the "Tale of the Spring Maid," Asad racked his mind trying to figure out why. Why was she saying good-bye to him now? Now that they were together again, safely away from the Panther and under the protection of the Oryx, where they need not hide their feelings for each other?

Had the Dove insisted on continuing their journey home and Oona agreed? Asad glanced from the Dove's happy smile to the Cheetah's adoring grin. They did not look like two young lovers about to be separated. And the kings and queens present were clapping with open approval as the sisters took their bows, not a frown of disapproval among them. What had happened between yesterday, when she had begged him not to leave her, and tonight?

"'Somebody,'" Asad said as the clapping started to quiet down. "I would have you, Swan, sing 'Somebody.'"

And then he would know.

Oona swallowed hard past the constricting lump in her throat and nodded her head.

"My prince."

She clasped her shaking hands together and closed her eyes against the hot tears welling behind her lids, took a deep, calming breath in and let it out. When she opened her eyes, her knees almost buckled from the heat in Asad's. She took another deeper breath in and blew it out slowly as she twisted and turned the abalone ring on her finger round and round, stopping when she realized Asad was watching. She swiped at her threatening tears as Lyrra plucked the opening notes to "Somebody."

"My heart is sore, I dare not tell,
My heart is sore for Somebody."

Oona sang to Asad and only Asad, her voice full of the pride and the pain of loving him, of having been loved by him. She may well mourn him for the rest of her life, but she would never regret having loved him. She sang their song as if for the last time, and Asad listened to every word as if it were the first time, his amber lion eyes never leaving hers.

"Oh, oh, for Somebody,
Oh, hey, for Somebody
I would do, would I do not
All for the sake of Somebody."

The last, long, melancholy note lingered and Oona bowed low as the courtyard sat in stunned silence before bursting into applause. Oona straightened and met Asad's burning gaze with a tremulous smile.

Asad stood and the courtyard went quiet. His lion's gaze held Oona's, keen, intent, a hunter who has sighted his prey, and Oona could no more turn and run than she could breathe.

"I, Asad, the Black Mane, Prince of the Great Valley, propose marriage to you, Oona the Swan, daughter of Aaron, granddaughter of Olwain, Chieftain of the clan Macleod. Eldest to eldest, soul to soul, heart to heart."

Oona's heart stopped, and then beat triple time.

"You would marry me?" Her words flew out on fluttering wings of hope.

"I would. Here. Now."

Her heart leapt into her eyes and Asad's shone hot and bright as molten gold.

"But…" As much as Oona wanted to throw herself into Asad's arms and say yes she would marry him, she would marry him and love him and be his faithful wife until the day she died, she had learned that love was not all that mattered, not in his world, not in hers, not in any world. "What about Panther?"

Asad's eyes narrowed and his jaw ticked. "The Panther has abdicated any rights as father or king to me."

"You family?"

"Anyone in my family whose opinion I care about will understand."

"You kingdom?"

"The City of the Great Valley will stand, whether it is ruled by the Panther, or his eldest son, or his second," he said, glancing at the Cheetah, who jerked his head up and then back and forth, "or the seventh son of his seventh son."

"Traditions of tribes?"

Asad huffed. "The Oryx was able to marry for love, against tradition. I am claiming that right for myself." He turned to the Heron. "Perhaps it is time for some traditions to change."

The Heron dipped his head in acknowledgment but said nothing, and Asad turned back to Oona.

Oona shook as if she had the ague, but she managed to lift her chin and hold Asad's steady gaze.

"If we marry, I claim right of *clanswoman* to be only wife."

"I accept," he said, not even glancing at the Heron or the Oryx.

But Oona did. The Heron, as usual, gave nothing away. The Oryx dropped his jaw to his chest and then snapped it shut. She looked to the Reed, who sat as still and composed as her husband, and at the Willow, whose eyes were as big as her belly. Oona looked to the Cheetah, who was looking at her, not Lyrra, grinning from ear to ear.

"You would do to this?" she asked Asad, dead serious. "You would go against you father, you tribe, you traditions, to marry me?"

Asad's grin was lethal.

"I would do, what I would not," he sang in a low growl, "all for the sake of somebody."

CHAPTER 18

Choices

"Husband."

Oona sank down onto the bed's soft mattress and lifted her arms up to Asad dressed in nothing more than an inviting smile that he eagerly accepted, easing himself onto the bed and settling his legs between Oona's. He braced his elbows and grinned into eyes shining green and faceted as cut emeralds, his chest swelling with love, his manhood with pride.

"Wife."

The Heron had presided over their marriage ceremony in the courtyard under the waning gibbous moon, where Asad and Oona had spoken the words and pledged their oaths, with Nasim and the Oryx standing for Asad, and the Dove and the Willow for Oona.

Asad had known his entire life that he would marry someday, but he had fully expected it to be somebody like the Fox, a princess chosen for him by his father to further the tribe's interests. Never had he expected to marry for love, or to love his wife with every fiber of his being.

He lowered his mouth to claim Oona's, but she pushed her hands up against his chest.

"I want go with you to Panther's."

"What?"

"I want be with you when you tell Panther we married."

"Why?"

"I want see his face, and Fox's."

"No." Asad shook his head. "It would not be safe for you. I am your husband, Oona. It is my duty to keep you safe."

Oona grasped his shoulders, surprising Asad not for the first time with her physical strength.

"I not marry you to be safe, Asad. I be clanswoman. Clanswomen stand with their men, fight beside them against enemies. I not hide who or what I be no more. I proud to be you wife."

Even as a slave, Oona the Swan had never been subservient. There had always been that flicker of defiance in her. One of the many things that had drawn Asad to her, but no husband wanted to be fighting with his new bride on their wedding night.

"I have heard of wives withholding themselves from their husbands to get their way," he said. He nipped her fingers on his shoulder and nestled the head of his manhood deeper into her nest until his throbbing head kissed her fleshy woman's lips.

He did not truly think Oona would withhold sex from him, it was not in her nature to be so controlling, and her warm, slickening flesh told him she was as eager as he to consummate their marriage. "Do all clanswomen use sex to win arguments with their husbands?"

"I not know," she said, her voice of smoked honey low and husky. She rocked her hips up, shooting a bolt of desire from Asad's cock to his addled brain. "Is working?"

Asad groaned and grit his teeth. It had been three days and nights since they had last made love, and he had been anticipating this night all day, all his life. "I could not say," he ground out. "I cannot think about anything but how much I want to bury myself deep into your molten sheath, to claim you as my true bride at last."

She pulled back enough so that their intimate flesh no longer touched. Asad growled and Oona grinned like a cat with a fat, juicy mouse in its sights.

"You really are a poor loser," he grumbled.

"And you still not answer me."

Asad pushed himself up and sat back on his knees, his staff standing at full attention, straining to close the chasm between itself and Oona's enticing heat. He raked both hands back through his hair.

A traditional husband would tell her no and be done with it. But Asad was not a traditional husband. He had promised Oona that she would be his only wife and that he would never lie with another woman as long as she lived. It had been no hardship to promise her fidelity. In truth, Asad had no desire for any other woman. Oona had told him once that she felt safe with him, that he was home to her, and she had become his home, his safe haven, where he could be Asad, only Asad, and still be loved. The thought of losing her ever again lowered his staff to half-mast.

"I cannot assure your safety, Oona."

"I know."

"I do not wish to mourn my wife so soon after our wedding."

"Nor I my husband."

Asad cocked his head and stared down into Oona's serious eyes. "You know I can beat the Panther?"

"Aye, my lion." She reached up and ran a hand through Asad's beard. "In fair fight."

Asad laid his hand over hers. "The Heron and the Oryx and the Cheetah will all be there to make certain it remains a fair fight, if it comes to that."

Oona ran the pad of her thumb over Asad's lower lip. "Do not make me stay here and worry, Asad. I want be with you, no matter what happen."

She really did not fight fair. "If you do come with me, with us…" Her eyes lit up and the corners of her luscious mouth lifted. "You must promise to stay by Brawn's side, no matter what."

"I promise." She wrapped her hand around the back of his neck and drew his head down to hers and kissed him, soft and inviting.

Asad propped himself on his arms and gave her his best beastly leer. "Is my lady wife as generous a winner as she is a poor loser?"

She ran her long, elegant fingers down his spine and cupped his backside, opening her legs and pressing his growing staff along her warm, welcoming flesh.

"Aye, my husband," she hummed. "She will be most generous."

When they approached the same back gate into the City of the Great Valley that Oona and Lyrra had ridden out of only seven days ago, the time was past midnight. So much had changed in those seven days Oona's head was still spinning. She was Asad's wife, a princess, returning to the palace where she was meant to be a pleasure woman under cover of night and in disguise to confront the Panther. How it would all play out, she truly did not know, but she and Lyrra were no longer slaves, they were free women, free to make their own decisions, and Oona's was to be with Asad, no matter what happened.

Only the Black Mane and the Cheetah showed themselves to the gate guards. Oona and Lyrra, the kings and their guards, and the sell swords all rode disguised in the tunics and colors of the Panther's dead guards, pulling their head scarves close as they rode into the sleeping city.

The streets were empty of all but a few drunkards stumbling home, or street curs scrambling away as they passed. Oona shivered in the eerie quiet though the late summer night was almost as warm as day. She glanced over at Asad, unsure for a moment if he was real, or if she had indeed been given the oil of the Dream Flower after her injury and everything since had been a wishful dream. She reached up and touched the stitches in her still-tender upper arm. They were real enough, and so was the palace gate they were fast approaching.

Asad and the Cheetah hailed the guards, who opened the gates without question. Oona let out the breath she had been holding. Position definitely had its advantages.

Avoiding the palace, they took the long way around to the stables, where the Ratter was already awake and rousing the stable hands, warning them to be quick and quiet with the horses.

All of the travelers but Asad and the Cheetah maintained their disguises, but the Ratter still gave Oona a wink as she walked past him and out into the courtyard.

Moving swift and silent among the night's shadows, they made their way to the palace, entering through the kitchens, which were empty of servants. Crossing the dining salon, Oona thought of all that had occurred here. Her fainting and being carried to the queen's chambers by Asad, the knife fights, and how Asad had thrown the victory match, the night Lyrra had fallen, and Asad had claimed the sisters, had bought their freedom with his own.

She reached out and took Asad's hand, smiling as his fingers twined through hers. She held on tight as Asad led the way through long, echoing halls to the Panther's council chambers, and there she and the others waited while Asad and Nasim searched out their menservants.

The Panther, the Snow Leopard and the Gazelle, the Bull, the Ox, and the Fox, all were to be brought to the council chambers.

The Heron lit several candles and oil lamps and then he and the Oryx both took seats at the main table as their guards took up positions beside them and at each entrance. The sell swords circled around Oona and Lyrra, their sharp eyes taking in the weapons displayed on the walls, the tabletops covered in tablets and scrolls, one of which the Oryx studied intently.

Oona stood inside her circle of sell swords on legs as sturdy as wet sea grass, clamping her jaw to keep her teeth from chattering and clasping Lyrra's hand. Brawn whistled low and wagged his brows at Oona, and she stifled a nervous giggle.

The queen arrived first, a robe over her night shift, her hair loose and hanging in thick waves down to the middle of her back. The room's shadows hollowed her cheekbones and cast dark circles of worry under her eyes. She glanced at Oona before dipping a knee to the kings.

"Welcome, King Heron, King Oryx."

"Thank you, Queen Snow Leopard," the Heron said.

The Oryx said nothing, but the smile that passed between him and the Snow Leopard was genuine.

The queen turned to Oona, whose throat went instantly dry. Brawn and the Hound stepped aside as she approached. Oona dropped Lyrra's hand and her own knee to the queen. She straightened slowly, peering up at the queen beneath lowered lashes. Did she know? It was one thing to be a slave who loved her son, and quite another to be his wife.

"Welcome, daughter," the queen said. She took Oona's hands in hers and placed a kiss on Oona's cheek. "Truly," she whispered, kissing Oona's other cheek.

The door burst open, and the queen and Oona jumped back from each other as the Panther strode in, followed by the Bull and the Cheetah.

The Panther's black eyes fixed on Oona for a long moment before they took in the others in his chambers, skimming over the sell swords and guards, and stopping abruptly at sight of the Heron and the Oryx sitting together at his table.

The Panther should have acknowledged the Heron, as was his due, but he jutted his chin out and narrowed his eyes on the Oryx as he claimed the seat to the Heron's other side. The Bull sat beside him.

The Crab entered the chambers as the kings settled themselves, accompanied by the Gazelle, who took one look at the kings sitting stiff and silent at the table and quickly went to stand between her mother and half-brother.

"Where is the Black Mane?" the Panther asked, his demanding voice breaking the waiting silence.

"He has gone to bring the Ox and the Fox to this meeting," the Cheetah answered. "He will be here as soon as possible. It seems he is having difficulty finding the Ox, who was not in his bed chambers."

"At this time of night?" the Bull said, yawning. "Has he tried the pleasure house?"

"I had better luck in the Fox's bed chambers."

Asad stood in the doorway as every person in the room swung their heads in his direction. He stepped aside and motioned with his fisted blade at the Ox, who shuffled in, head hanging, pulling the tie of his gaping robe tighter around his bare, bulging belly. Asad motioned at the Fox, whose robe of sheer worm weave did nothing to hide her nakedness underneath, but the Fox stood rooted. He grabbed her by the arm and pulled her through the door.

"I bring you the Ox and the Fox," he said to the room at large. "A cowardly corruption of a cur and his cuckholding vixen."

The Bull bellowed loud enough to wake the entire palace. "How dare you speak of a prince and princess of the tribes so?"

"How dare I speak the truth?" Asad was beyond princely manners, beyond couching his words. He was done with lies. "Would you rather I finish what I started at the kraals when your son tried to rape and murder the Swan in collusion with the Fox? What I would have finished had the Swan not stopped me?"

"What do you mean by that?" the Bull blustered.

Asad huffed. "Come now, Bull," he said, omitting the proper address of king. "The Ox attacking the Swan and my beating him, for it is one of the worst-kept secrets in this palace."

"As is the fact that the Fox is breeding," the queen said.

Every jaw there dropped, including Asad's. But then the Fox snapped hers shut and she jabbed a pointed finger at Asad. "I carry the Black Mane's child," she cried, wringing her hands. "He forced himself on me. I, I only went to the Ox after, in shame and fear, seeking consolation."

Asad laughed short and harsh. "Why would I force myself on you, a woman I detest," he said, "when I have the love of the woman I adore?" He smiled at Oona, cocooned in the circle of sell swords, their sharp blades reflecting the lamps lights, drawn and at the ready. "My wife."

"Your what?" The Panther shot up from his seat.

"My wife. We were married by the Heron, in the palace of the Oryx, four days ago."

The Panther stood at his full height and breadth and slammed his fist onto the table. "You married the northern whore?"

Asad cleared the table in two leaps, pinning the Panther's back against the wall, his blade at the Panther's throat as the other kings scrambled up from their seats.

"I told you before, Panther, I will not have her slandered." A lifetime of lies and deceit, of being used and manipulated by the father he once worshipped and had learned to despise, burned white-hot and deep.

Asad pressed the blade edge closer, drawing a thin weal of blood. The Panther did not move. He did not even blink. "You did not listen then," Asad growled, low and guttural, "but you will now. Oona, the Swan, is the woman I love, and I sent her away because of you, for you," Asad swallowed his gall, "you lying sack. You tried to have her killed, to have me killed, and Nasim."

The Panther started to open his mouth.

"Do not speak." Asad rolled his blade so that the tip pricked the soft underside of the Panther's jaw, a kill point. He took a deep breath in and blew it out, slowly. He had to control his anger, not let it control him, or he would be no better than the Panther. "Do not say a word. I will speak and you will listen for once."

The Panther blinked.

"Think well on what I say before you answer," Asad said. "For your answer will determine your future." Asad removed the blade from the Panther's throat but kept his grip tight and his gaze even with his father's. "Will you accept the Swan as my rightful wife? Will you claim her as your daughter and future queen of this city?"

The Panther wiped the weal of blood from his throat and bared his teeth. "Never."

Asad squared his shoulders and narrowed his gaze. It was not as if he had expected any other answer from the Panther.

"Then I give you one of two choices," he said "Either I challenge you and kill you right here and now and take the throne, or you agree to let me and the Swan and any of my household who wish to follow us leave this city to live in peace." Asad leaned in and growled low. "And if you go against your word again and try to harm the Swan in any way, I will come back and kill you."

"You think you can beat me, boy?" the Panther snarled.

Asad smiled, slow and deliberate. "I know I can, and so do you and every other person in this room who watched me throw that knife fight. The only reason you are still standing here breathing is because my wife begged me not to kill you outright."

The Panther snorted, and Asad leaned back.

"There are two more conditions by which you must abide if you choose to live and remain king," he said. "Firstly, you, the Bull, and the Jackal will stop trying to start a war with the Oryx. He is rightful heir to the throne and a good man. He will be a good king, given the chance, certainly better than the Ox, should the lummox manage to live long enough to become king."

The Bull started to sputter, but the Heron raised his hand.

"If you two choose to wage war against the Oryx," the Heron said, "you will have to go against not only the Oryx, but myself and the other northern kings as well. We will outnumber you four armies to three, if not five to two, for the Jackal, while not the most honorable of kings, is practical. He will not likely fight against his best interests." He glanced meaningfully at the Bull and the Panther. "I suggest you agree to keep the peace among the tribes. It would be much more profitable for all than your ill-conceived war."

"And secondly?" the Panther asked Asad through gritted teeth.

"The Gazelle will not marry the Ox. The Gazelle will never be made to marry such a pollution of a man."

"Who is she to marry then?" the Panther asked. "Who will take her, bastard daughter of a dead king?"

"I will." The Oryx stood and dipped his head to the Gazelle. "I will take her as my honored second wife, if she will have me."

The Panther hissed at Asad. "You would marry your half-sister to her own half- brother?"

"The Gazelle is no sister to the Oryx," Asad hissed right back. "She is your daughter, as I am your son. And she loves you equally as little. You have made sure of it."

"I raised you to be strong, to be a king, not some moonstruck, calf-eyed—"

"You," Asad roared, "did not raise me." He lowered his voice to a low growl. "You tried to control me, to mold me into your twisted version of a prince. The only thing you taught me was to lie and manipulate, to rule with an iron fist, without consideration for anybody or anything else. My mother raised me and taught me to have a care for anybody but myself. It was the Crab who taught me to govern, to always consider my duty to others before my own pleasure."

"And how is choosing your northern whore over your family putting duty before pleasure?"

Asad stood nose to nose with the Panther. "I would have chosen my family and the Swan together, for she has become the heart and breath of me, Asad, the man, but you would not have it, you chose tradition, you stubborn, hide-bound ass."

"Tradition is what keeps our tribes strong, our bloodlines pure."

"Tradition is what keeps our tribes stagnant, our bloodlines full of idiots like the Ox and the Fox. You may be a strong king, but you are a miserable man, and I choose to be a good man who loves his wife, whose children will love and respect him. I choose to be a man first and a king second, for how else can a king hope to understand the people of his tribe?"

The Panther blew out an exasperated breath. "The people do not need to be understood. They need to be ruled, and to follow the rules. They find comfort in tradition."

"In some traditions, surely," Asad said. "But do you truly believe a slave finds comfort in knowing his children will be born into slavery with no chance to better their position? That a prince finds comfort in knowing his life is set out before him, step by step by step, according to tradition?"

"Yes. It is the way it is. The way it has always been."

"Not for me," Asad said. "Not for the Oryx or the Cheetah. Nor for the Heron, who has enough sense to know that things change, and we must change as well, we must open ourselves up to the world, not wall ourselves off from it, or our tribes will dwindle and grow weak."

"What concern is it of yours?" the Panther snarled. "When you are so determined to leave it all for the sake of your milk-faced pet?"

Asad huffed. Had his father even listened to a word he had said? Had he truly expected him to? He glanced around the room, at all those watching and waiting to see how this game between Panther and Black Mane would play out, for it would affect each and every one of them. He held Oona's wide-eyed trusting gaze for a long moment and then he turned to face the Panther.

"Make your choice, now," he said. He was done talking.

The Panther gave a snort of disgust and looked to the Cheetah.

"Will you stay and inherit the throne from your king and father?" he asked.

The Cheetah stepped over to the Dove and took her hand in his.

"No, Father," he replied. "For if you will not accept the Black Mane's choice of wife, you will not accept mine."

"Go then, the lot of you. Take your faithless whores and plotting kings and leave. Leave my palace, my city. I do not need you. I have five more sons to succeed me."

"But what of me?" the Fox whined. "I have been cheated of a husband. I am meant to be queen."

"This is what you would have me marry?" Asad asked the Panther. "This is who you would have become queen? This spoiled she-dog who can think of nothing and no one but herself when the fates of kingdoms are hanging in the balance? Who would not shed a single tear if I slew you right here and now, as long as she could still be queen? When the Swan, whom you have exiled and tried to kill, begged me to spare your miserable life?" Asad glared at the Fox. "Marry the Ox, if he will have you," he told her. "I care not. You are no longer any concern of mine."

"Apparently none of us are," the Panther grumbled.

"I gave you a choice, Father," Asad said. "Now you must live with it." He turned his back to the Panther and met Oona's gaze. Eyes as big, round, and green as mossy river rocks, eyes that had known him, Asad, at first sight.

"As I will live with mine."

EPILOGUE

Summer's Eve had a horned moon setting in the western sky, a night of joy and celebration that swelled Asad's chest so with pride and joy he thought his tunic would split right open. He glanced out over the city square, filled with hundreds of revelers, people from all walks of life who had come to start a new life in a new land, enjoying the first feast of their new city's bounty. One year to the night when Asad had first laid eyes on Oona, one year of a strange, winding, and wonderful journey that had brought him here, with her.

"What ails you, brother?" Nasim asked, settling onto the cushion beside him as their wives took the stage in the center of the square. "You have not stopped grinning all night, except to fawn over your wife and exhort her to eat more roasted goat and sweet melon."

Asad grinned even wider. "Oona is with child," he replied. "She told me this evening as we dressed for the feast." When Asad had admired her breasts, which felt heavier in his hands, and felt rosy nipples that were even more sensitive than usual to his play.

"Congratulations, my brother and king." Nasim gave Asad's back a hearty thump. "When is the princeling due to arrive?"

"Late winter or early spring. I will send a messenger to my mother tomorrow. She made me swear to let her know as soon as possible so that she could be here for the birth of her first grandchild." He smiled. "The Crab's wife, Adara, will take good care of Oona until our mother arrives, but I will feel better having two experienced midwives to watch over Oona and the babe."

"If the Panther allows her to leave."

"Even the Panther knows what he owes his queen. He will not naysay her."

Asad had begged his mother to leave the Panther and come with them, but she would not leave her king and her city without a queen.

The Oryx and the Heron had left for the City of Hills the morning after Asad's and the Panther's final confrontation, for the Oryx was anxious to get back to his pregnant wife, the Willow.

It had taken Asad and Nasim another five days to make their arrangements and prepare for the long journey ahead. They had both given their servants the gift of freedom, and the offer of joining them to find and settle a new land. Kahlil, the Crab, had immediately gone into the city and offered marriage to his old love, Adara, the Water Lily, and she had accepted, bringing along her two youngest sons. The Ratter declared he would go wherever his beloved horses went, and Asad had given him Star as his own, and the promise of breeding her with Storm.

Brawn had convinced the Panther that he was secretly buying the Mouse for the Black Mane, so that the Swan would think her husband's favorite belonged to another man, and the Panther had sold the Mouse to him for a pittance. Oona, in on the plan, had played the part of suspicious wife well for the Panther, who could not look at her without a scowl, and refused to speak a word to her or Lyrra unless it was to curse them.

The Gazelle had accepted the Oryx's proposal, much to the queen's relief, for the Panther still denied she was his and would, no doubt, have found a man as loathsome as the Ox to marry her off to.

Brawn and the other sell swords, the Blade, the Hound, and the Hawk, had all decided to take their chances with the Black Mane now that the Panther knew who they were, and they had sworn their blades and loyalty to Asad and Oona. Asad was glad to have them, as was Oona.

When they left the city, at least a hundred people were gathered outside the gates, ready to join their company. Farmers with wagons full of roots and seed, and shepherds with small flocks of goats and sheep, bricklayers with bent backs that straightened with every league, and stone masons with their picks and axes, tailors with bolts of cloth, and tinkers with their carts full of various and sundry wares, all eager for a new life in a new land, where the Black Mane had vowed to govern fairly, and all people would be free.

They'd stayed in the City of Hills long enough for Nasim and Lyrra to be married by the Heron, and a day later to celebrate the birth of the Oryx's and Willow's son. The Gazelle, having witnessed the love between the new parents, asked to be released from her betrothal to the Oryx, who had happily obliged, and talked at length with Asad about the idea of having only one wife, for now he was king, no one could force him to marry other women.

Following the Great River north, they had collected people from every city they traveled through until their company numbered three hundred when they settled in a delta between two lesser rivers along the southern coast of the Inland Sea.

The valley had rich, verdant pasturelands, and the black, loamy soil proved fertile for farming. The sea provided fish and salt, and within the first three moons of their arrival, ships laden with goods had anchored in the bay, eager for new trading partners.

There were vast woodlands to the east, which they felled for lumber to build and trade with, and Oona and Lyrra had taught the desert people about pitched roofs and indoor hearth fires in preparation for the colder, wetter winters. The houses and outbuildings they built were a mix of wood, stone, and brick, and the main city was set on the high ground overlooking the floodplain, with the places of trade and inns for travelers built along the newly built docks below.

Asad caught Oona's eye as she stood ready to sing and dance and his grin split his face in two. She was still a wonder to him, growing daily in beauty, grace, and wisdom. Her courage in taking this journey with him, her lack of complaint as they rode for days and weeks on end, as they lived in tents for another moon before their first house, little more than a room with four walls, was built, had impressed not only him, but every other man and woman who looked to her as their queen. Her kindness and understanding, her willingness to share whatever she had or knew with others, had quickly endeared her to the people, and even more to Asad, a thing he had not thought possible. He respected her opinions and asked her advice on matters large and small. And true to her word, she always told him the truth.

She was air to his fire, his life's breath, and soon she would bring a new life, born of their love, into this new world.

With Oona, Asad had become the man he always wanted to be.

Oona stood in the middle of the stage, surrounded by torchlight and basking in the heat of her husband's amber eyes. Her husband, Asad, the Black Mane, Prince of the City of the Great Valley, King of the City on the Inland Sea, lion four times through, father of her unborn child, her somebody.

She blinked back tears of pure joy and breathed in the cool, salty, summer breeze. She stood tall and gazed out over the sea of brown heads, so like and yet so different from those she had stood in front of, head bowed and knees shaking, one year ago.

Then she had been a slave, chattel for barter, commanded to perform for the amusement of her masters, dressed in a gown meant to show more than it hid. She wore the same gown of white worm weave tonight, but with a linen under-bodice that covered her tender breasts. And tonight, she was a queen, her worth her own, and she would sing freely, rejoicing for the people who were her family, her friends, and her tribe.

Placing a hand over the softening roundness of her womb, she met Asad's amber gaze and caught her breath. She let it out slowly, her belly warming at the fire in his eyes, and hers lit with anticipation, for they would have their own celebration in the privacy of their bedchambers later.

She smiled a woman's smile, knowing and full of promise, and Asad's burning gaze scorched her to the marrow, branding her. She was his as he was hers, and had been from the first moment their eyes had met one year ago.

Lyrra began to strum the first notes of "The Sailor's Tale" on Nightingale, bringing Oona back to the solid footing of the stage. She took in a breath and opened her mouth to sing when the sea of people parted and a head of white-blond hair surged toward the stage. Asad leapt up, blade drawn, blocking the man's way as Brawn and Nasim circled him, and the Hawk and the Hound were instantly at Oona's and Lyrra's sides.

"*Athair*," Oona cried. "Father."

Oona and Lyrra rushed to their father, throwing themselves into his open arms as Asad and Nasim stepped aside.

"Oh, *Athair*," Oona cried in her highland tongue. "We thought you dead."

"It would take more than a wee knock to the head to kill me, my *nighean*." He kissed her forehead and then Lyrra's and hugged them close.

"Ah, my sweet lasses, I never thought to see you or hold you again, though I ne'er gave up hope. I knew my girls were survivors." He tousled their hair as he had when they were still in side braids. "You have too much of your *mathair's* heart and my stubbornness to do otherwise."

His tears fell freely, unashamedly, and Oona pressed her wet cheek to his, covered in a beard that was bushier and grayer than she remembered. Somebody coughed politely and she looked up and met Asad's curious gaze.

"*Athair*, Father," she said, switching back to the desert tongue. "This is my husband, Asad."

"It is an honor to meet you, Aaron of the clan Macleod," Asad said.

He held out his hand as was the highland custom and Oona smiled as her father took it and shook it, holding it for a moment longer than was customary, both of them opening and closing their fingers after letting go and nodding to each other.

"You are Black Mane?" her father said in a stilted desert tongue.

"I am. And this is my brother, Nasim, the Cheetah, husband of Lyrra."

Nasim stepped forward and shook their father's hand. "It is an honor to meet you at last."

Their father took in the four of them, his grin as warm and bright as the noon sun on a calm sea, and Oona's heart swelled. How she had missed that grin.

"I hear of Black Mane and Ivory Queen at port on southern coast," he said. "Of two sisters from far north, slaves, who marry princes and build city on the Great Inland Sea. I think, who else can be but my girls, and I jump ship and come to find my daughters, my *nigheans*. And here you be."

"Aye, here we be." Oona said.

She glanced at Lyrra's open, happy smile. She found Asad's hand and twined her fingers through his, his grip strong and true.

"Home."

ABOUT THE AUTHOR

Michele James lives in a southern California beach town with her understanding husband, two lazy house cats, and two crazy cattle dogs. She is the proud mother of two fully functional adults, and is Oma to the world's most adorable grandson.

A mostly retired veterinarian technician, she enjoys reading everything from cereal boxes to serious tomes, watching movies without commercials, cooking, gardening, walks on the beach (especially in winter), and practicing yoga.

CONNECT WITH MICHELE:
website: michelejamesauthor.com
instagram: @michelejamesauthor
facebook: facebook.com/michelejamesauthor

www.BOROUGHSPUBLISHINGGROUP.com

If you enjoyed this book, please write a review. Our authors appreciate the feedback, and it helps future readers find books they love. We welcome your comments and invite you to send them to info@boroughspublishinggroup.com. Follow us on Facebook, Twitter and Instagram, and be sure to sign up for our newsletter for surprises and new releases from your favorite authors.

Are you an aspiring writer? Check out www.boroughspublishinggroup.com/submit and see if we can help you make your dreams come true.